A Big Life
In a Small Town

D1736315

Diane Greenwood Muir

Cover Design Photography: Maxim M. Muir

Don't miss the first book in
Diane Greenwood Muir's

Bellingwood Series

All Roads Lead Home

CONTENTS

ACKNOWLEDGMENTS

I rarely read through acknowledgments. I don't know those people, but I'm always glad the author does. When it came to writing my own, though, I discovered that I wanted everyone to know the people I know. It occurred to me over and over throughout the writing process that I couldn't have done this without them.

Thank you to my family and friends who understand my need for solitude. Distractions are the bane of my creativity and I will choose those over work every day. Not only do they understand me, but the encouragement I get keeps me motivated to continue writing.

Rebecca Bauman. She reads the rough chapters every day, then tells me they're wonderful. When my confidence is low, some days I need to hear that just to get started again. Her artistic creativity also helps me turn Max's photography into book covers. It's good to have wildly creative friends.

I have an amazing team of editor / proofreaders. They question me, correct me, and push me to do better. If there are errors, it's on me, though. I'm a stubborn sort of a girl. Thank you to Tracy Kesterson Simpson, Linda Watson, Carol Greenwood, Alice Stewart, and Edna Fleming. It's very difficult for me to bare my unpolished soul to the world, but I trust them to treat it with a little respect and a whole lot of passion for excellence. I'd like you to meet and get to know each of them, because as individuals they are so uniquely qualified to do this for me. I presume upon their time and they offer me their talent.

Getting the first book published gave me a little credibility when asking questions about the second book. Fortunately, I know a lot of people who know about a lot of things.

Thank you to the brilliant Bernie Doerr who responded when I needed a push in the right direction regarding a doctoral thesis in mathematics. She gave me the idea, I made it up from there, so if it is insane, it's my fault.

Thank you to Rob Marsh, my paramedic cousin. He told me things I might not have wanted to know about the human body and how it reacts to trauma, but at least Polly stayed out of the hospital with his help.

I'm not sure what I was thinking when I decided to add horses to Polly's world. I loved them as a child, but if it weren't for Alice Stewart, I would never have spent much time around them. She let me hang out with her and Cherokee in high school and when I realized Polly was going to do this, I knew who to ask for help. She's given me some of the most incredibly detailed information I could ever hope for and her veterinarian husband, Jay, will also help keep Polly's animals healthy. Both Alice and Jay have a huge passion for horses and it's great fun to reconnect with a high school friend at this level.

CHAPTER ONE

"Elise Myers is one week away from beginning her ..." Jeff Lindsay walked into the office, chewing a bagel and watching to make sure he didn't spill the cup of coffee he was carrying. Looking up, he realized Henry and Polly were peering intently at a laptop on the far side of the conference table.

"I'm sorry," he said. "I didn't mean to interrupt."

"No, that's fine, Jeff," Polly replied. "We're looking at plans for a barn. What were you saying about Miss Myers?"

"A barn?" he asked. "You're building a barn now?"

Henry shrugged and shook his head. "I'm afraid Polly has caught the construction bug. We aren't finished working on this place yet," Henry gestured to encompass the expanse of Sycamore House, "and she's already planning the next project."

Polly caught the two of them smirking and said, "I have plans for this place and laughing at me isn't helpful."

"Who's laughing?" Jeff asked, sitting down beside Henry. "There's no laughing here. So ... where are you putting this barn?"

She cocked her head at the back wall and said, "The concrete pad where the old gymnasium used to stand. We'll put a white post and rail fence up around the property and it will be absolutely gorgeous. Look at the gambrel roof over this beautiful red barn. White trim, white roof, white fence. It's perfect!"

"Perfect for what, though?" he pressed.

"Perfect for horses. Think of the fun we can have," she responded.

"You don't have enough animals in your life with two cats and a dog?" Jeff shook his head and sat down on the other side of Henry. "I have a bad feeling this menagerie is only in its infancy."

Henry chuckled in agreement.

Jeff set his bagel and coffee on the table and leaned in to look at the plans. "So. A barn."

"Glad you're on board, buddy," Henry laughed as he clapped Jeff on the back. "The next thing you know, she'll want you to take guests out on trail rides!"

"Well, that's never gonna happen. I don't ride horses," Jeff said, his upper lip turning into a bit of a snarl. "I gave it up when I was in high school. 'He's gentle,' she said. 'He loves people,' she said. The damned horse put his head between his front legs and tried to toss me off before we left the barn. I don't know why he didn't like me, but he and I agreed it was mutual. That was the last time I was on a horse. And I don't intend to start up again, thank you very much."

Polly was laughing as he spoke. "That's a fabulous story. You're pure entertainment, Jeff."

"I'm a city boy. Just because you have me working in rural Iowa doesn't mean I'm giving up my city ways. I still believe in the goodness of cities littered with burger joints and coffee shops. There's no room for horses in my happy little world."

Henry said, "Wait until the weather gets nicer. The Brennans ride their horses into town to do business and get groceries. People love taking pictures of the horses standing in front of the grocery store and some of the best photographs are when Dr. Lisle's Mercedes is parked on one side and a motorcycle is parked on the other. There are more than a few of those pictures hiding in scrapbooks in Bellingwood. I think Dr. Lisle does it on purpose."

2

"I'm starting to learn that the unexpected is to be expected," Jeff said. "Let me know when you expect me to milk cows and pluck chickens. I'll help you hire my replacement."

Polly laughed, "Don't worry. If there are cows and chickens anywhere around my house, they'll be neatly cleaned, packaged and in the freezer."

This time it was Henry's turn to laugh out loud. "Now, I have a story," he said. "My junior year in college, several of my buddies and I moved into a house off campus. One of the guys, Roy Dunston, was from the south side of Chicago. Dad had purchased a side of beef that summer, so I took some back to school with me. Of course the packages weren't labeled, they scrawled words in grease pencil on the front telling me what the cut was. When Roy asked me about it, I explained what I had and he wouldn't believe me! Meat didn't come from cows on farms, it came from grocery stores. Let me tell you, he was completely shocked when I explained where milk came from. He didn't eat cereal for the next three months. I brought him home for Christmas that year. He'd never seen anything like the life we have here in Bellingwood, but he must have come to appreciate it. Even though he's a lawyer in Chicago, he schedules a week every year to bring kids from his old neighborhood to Iowa to spend time on a farm. I'll have to tell you more about him another day. There are a lot of kids who have a bigger and better life because one man went to school at Drake and was exposed to a bunch of hicks from the Midwest."

Polly creased her forehead, "He really didn't know where meat and milk come from?"

"He wasn't the only one. He talked to some of his fraternity brothers later on and they were all shocked by the revelation. It's startling to realize that people grow up never seeing livestock or open fields." Henry shook his head. "I guess we probably don't understand what it means to live on top of each other in an inner city neighborhood, though."

"Well, you two can go on and on about how wonderful it is living out here in the country, as long as I don't have to play with your pigs," Jeff smirked. "That would really mess up my shoes."

He waggled his foot, showing off a pair of elegant leather loafers. "These babies will never encounter horse crap as long as I can help it."

"Uh huh," Polly sneered. "Never say never."

"Alright then," he said, "How about if I say I hope they never encounter horse crap. Will that get the never say never jinx off my back?"

"If you're lucky. But don't count on it," Polly said. "You didn't finish telling me about Elise Myers."

"She was in the kitchen getting coffee a few minutes ago and said she was within a week of starting to write her thesis. Her research is finished and data has finally been returned, she's nearly finished gathering references, so it is time to begin writing. She asked me to let you know she would probably flip-flop her schedule. I guess she does her best writing in the middle of the night. Can you imagine?" Jeff laughed. "I don't know where people come up with these things."

"Whatever works," Polly said. "But, I can't stop construction and noise during the day for her."

"We talked about that. She says she'll be fine. She's used to it and wears ear plugs when she sleeps. I guess she did this all through college and surely, that had to have been worse than this!"

"Then, I'm fine with it," Polly responded. "Tell her to let me know how she wants me to handle her linens and what she'd like to do about food during those midnight hours. I will make sure she's well taken care of."

Henry and Polly went back to browsing through barn plans when all of a sudden Jeff threw his arms up in the air and shouted, "Eureka!"

Both looked at him in shock. He laughed. "I've always wanted to do that. But, I've got a great idea! We're going to have a barn raising!"

Henry settled back into his chair and thought for a moment. He turned to Polly and said, "It's not a bad idea. We could pay for some skilled labor and we could certainly use a lot of extra help to get the walls raised and the roof up. What do you think?"

What came out of Polly's mouth was, "eh ... eh ... eh."

Jeff pressed forward, "We could start early on a Saturday morning, work all day, then have a hoe-down in the evening. We'll hire a band," he slipped into a terrible drawl, "get the women-folk to cook us up some grub for lunch and a real wild west meal for supper ..."

"Do I get to see you in overalls?" Polly chuckled.

"No. I'll be in styling boot cut jeans, with a fancy western cut plaid shirt, Dearie. I might even buy a pair of cowboy boots," he chuckled. "But, I suppose we could make it a ... no, we don't need to make it a theme day. We only need to feed 'em and entertain 'em. What do you think?"

"I think it sounds great." Polly said. "What about you, Henry, can you make it work?"

"Yes," he replied. "I can. I've never done anything like this before, but it could be good. It should probably go up while the ground is still hard and before the spring rains start. I'd like not to worry about everyone out there freezing to death, but so far the winter hasn't been too bad. It should be fine."

Jeff jumped up from his seat, grabbing his coffee and bagel. "I'm going to get started. I've got another party to plan!"

He walked into his office and pushed the door shut. Henry laughed, "I think you did well when you hired that one!"

"He never sits still! Do you know we already have five wedding receptions scheduled for spring and summer and he's working with two groups who want to have their class reunions here? That Christmas party was a great idea. He'll probably book the rest of the year after the barn raising," she said.

Henry pointed back at the barn on the computer screen. "This has room for six stalls, a tack room and one other room. Are you planning on having that many horses?"

"I don't know, but we have the space for it and I'm not about to short change my future by not building enough at the outset," she said.

"Then, these are the plans we're using! I'll get things moving."

Henry started to stand up, then sat back down.

"The glass company will be in this afternoon to measure for the doors to cover the bookshelves in the auditorium. Creating displays in there for all those items from the crates you found in the basement is a great idea. I'll bet people show up simply to wander around and look at the displays," he said.

"I'm going to ask Andy to organize and arrange the pieces. When do you think they'll be ready for her?" Polly asked.

"She can work as they go, so any time."

"Polly! Where are you?" Sylvie's voice rang out as she came in the door.

Polly stood up and walked out into the hallway.

"I'm right here, what's up?"

"There was an opening for the Culinary Institute!" Sylvie shouted. "I start classes this semester! I can't believe it!"

"That's awesome, Sylvie!"

"You're the one who did this for me," Sylvie said.

"What do you mean, I did this for you?" Polly asked. "You got into the program all on your own."

"You gave me confidence when you asked me to do the Christmas party. I talked to Lydia and she told me to go for it. I didn't want to tell you until they accepted me, but I talked to them this morning and I'm in!"

Sylvie's excitement practically had her vibrating in her shoes.

"Girl, I'm so proud of you," Polly said.

"Have you told your boys yet that their mom is going back to school?" Henry asked, as he came out of the office and stood beside Polly.

"No, I didn't tell them, because it wasn't supposed to happen until next fall. Oh no, I haven't made any plans for them!" she exclaimed. "What will they do after school if I'm not home yet?"

"They'll come here," Polly declared. "Then you can pick them up when you get back into town. I have plenty of space for them to do their homework and they can help with my animals."

"That's terrific!" Sylvie responded. "I start next week!" she continued, "Can you believe it?"

Then she stopped. "I need to think about my job. I thought I had time to think about this before I started. I'm sure they'll let me work on weekends, but I don't want to lose that job. I'm going to need it when I'm not taking classes."

"Come on into my office," Polly said. "You need to sit down and talk this out." She turned to Henry, "I'll see you later. Thanks!"

Polly pulled Sylvie behind her into her office and pointed to a chair, "Sit." Sylvie sat.

"I can't presume to know what your finances look like, but we're going to help you make this work. Has Jeff talked to you about some of the events we have coming up?"

Sylvie nodded. "Yes, but those don't kick off until late spring and summer. I have some savings and that should help. I need to think through how to make this work. I just got so excited!" She smiled at Polly. "It feels good to finally have a plan for my life. I was beginning to wonder if I would be working at the grocery store until I died. It isn't a bad job, but it never felt like it was enough. I want Jason and Andrew to see me living a bigger life, too," she continued. "They're both so bright and I don't want them to think the only thing their mom can do is this. I want them to see that I have dreams and can make them come true."

"You will be great, Sylvie!" Polly exclaimed. "And your boys are going to be as proud of you as I am!"

"Now if I can just keep them fed and in a home, I'll be fine."

"Let's just take it one step at a time, alright?" Polly said. "And there's another big party coming up."

"What are you doing this time?" Sylvie asked, her eyes brightening.

"We're going to have a barn raising," Polly said. "You're going to have to cook breakfast and lunch for the workers and that evening we're going to have a dinner and dance after the sun sets. Do you want to try to manage it?"

"A barn raising? I've never seen one of those. In fact, I don't think anyone around here has ever seen one. Do you think people will get involved?" Sylvie asked.

"Jeff and Henry are putting it together, so I think it will be crazy successful," Polly said. "Do you want to take care of the food for the day?"

"Of course I do! Thank you." She paused, "Do you think your friend Bruce's wife would come over and help me again? We seemed to get along well and she's pretty good in the kitchen."

Polly picked up her phone and punched some numbers into it, then smiled as Sylvie's phone buzzed. "There's her number. Give her a call and ask. You know that's your kitchen now, don't you?"

"That kind of overwhelms me," Sylvie said quietly. "I can't believe you have this much faith in me."

"Just say you won't leave me when you get your certification," Polly laughed. "I'm going to need you for a long time."

"I won't leave you when I get my certification," Sylvie teased, "unless I get chosen to host a show on the Food Network. How's that?"

"It's great!" Polly laughed. "Have you told Lydia yet?"

"No, I had to tell you first!" Sylvie exclaimed. "But, I should tell her, shouldn't I? I have to get ready for work! I've got to run!"

Sylvie picked up her purse and leaped out of the seat. "I'll talk to you later!" she said as she left the building. Polly waved at her through the window of her office. One more thing had dropped into place. She was going to have a certified chef on staff at Sycamore House. Unbelievable.

Henry and his crew were working in the final area they needed to complete inside the building, and it had become a big deal. The room was being split into four separate spaces. His temporary shop had resided here and it was finally time to make decisions about how it should be finished. That had been the original intention for the morning meeting, but they'd gotten sidetracked by a barn.

Framing for the four rooms was in place and Doug and Billy were there to start the electrical work. Henry looked up from his workbench when Polly entered.

"Have you finally decided what you want in here yet?" he asked. "The time is now."

"Stop it," she chided. "You've got the plans in front of you. I'm not going to change anything today."

"Well, you've been changing your mind since the day we started. Every other room in the place made sense to you, why did this one take so long?"

"I don't know. I wanted it to be a little bit of everything, I guess. I think we've got a good plan in place now." Polly pointed to the back corner of the building. "A classroom with tables," then she pointed at the room just behind Henry, "a room with a dozen or so chairs for book clubs, bible studies, meetings, whatever," then she pointed at another room, "a computer room with study carrels, and this open space will just be a lounge. That all makes sense, doesn't it?"

"Good enough," he replied. "Windows into these two rooms, right? But nothing into the classroom."

"Right," she said. "See, I told you. You know what's going on."

"I know what's going on here, but what I don't know is when I'm going to get you to go out with me again?"

The sudden turn of conversation had Polly blushing. Their first date had happened several weeks ago and with the excitement of the holidays, they hadn't found another opportunity. It had been a dream of a first date; Henry had gone all out. When she expressed a desire to go slowly, he respected her wishes. The only problem was her friends. They already considered the two of them a couple and she was worried Lydia and Beryl would have her married to him by the end of the year. Polly gave a slight shake of the head as she thought about that possibility. It wasn't what she wanted at all. There was too much happening in her life to settle down into marriage.

Henry interrupted her reverie, "The question wasn't that serious, Polly. Is there a reason it is taking so long for you to answer me?"

"Oh!" she laughed, "I'm sorry! Uh, well, uh. My mind wandered," she said as her voice trailed off. This time she blushed from embarrassment.

"Me asking you if you will go out with me again caused your mind to wander?" Henry looked down at the workbench and shook his head. He braced his hands on the edge, then looked up again. "That doesn't give a man much confidence, you know."

"Okay," she said. "I apologize. Here's the deal. Lydia and Beryl already have us married with children. I'm not ready for that."

"What!" Henry's laugh carried an edge of panic. "I'm not ready for that either. I only wanted to go out for dinner and a movie."

Polly snorted back a laugh. "You're right. I'm letting them get to me. So, let me take you out, then."

"Am I supposed to be a twenty-first century man and tell you that's a great idea?" he asked.

"If you aren't courting me for marriage," Polly paused and looked at him through her eyelashes, "then I believe we can forego standard dating traditions and be comfortable with either of us making plans and paying for the evening. Don't you?" The look on her face dared him to disagree.

"Fine," he huffed. "You can take me out. I'm not a cheap date though. I want a nice dinner and you have to buy me popcorn at the movie. We aren't splitting a small one either. I want my own."

"It's a deal," she said. "Friday night?"

"Friday night," he replied, "It's a date."

"She hasn't taken us out for our date yet," came a voice from behind her. Polly turned around to see Doug Randall and Billy Endicott standing there with silly grins on their faces.

Doug continued, "She promised us steak. Have you had steak yet, Billy?"

"Nope. No steak," Billy sighed. "I think she was just teasing us."

"Every man in my life wants something from me! Dates, steaks, and what do you want from me?" she whirled on Jeff as he joined the group.

"Ack! What?" he said. "I'm almost afraid to ask!"

"If it's a date for Friday night, she's already busy," Doug said. "With him," and he pointed to Henry.

"She's not my type," laughed Jeff. "And she's my boss. No dating allowed, you know."

"What did you need, Jeff?" Polly giggled. She was continually surprised at how much fun life was since she'd moved back to

Iowa and started building a life here.

"Whoops, I guess I do want a date. Can I set the date for the barn raising?" he asked.

"Don't be surprised if you do and we have a blizzard that day. Iowa is mean that way," Henry said.

Polly put her hand up to stop Henry's words. "Don't listen to him. Iowa loves me. Set the date."

She walked out into the hall with Jeff and smiled at Jerry Allen, her electrician, as he walked past her.

"I spoke with Sylvie about cooking. She agreed and is calling Hannah McKenzie to assist her."

"I'll coordinate with her." Jeff shook his head, then said, "I forgot to tell you. There's another guest coming in two weeks. You're going to want to get those other two rooms finished."

Polly stopped walking, took a deep breath and said, "Well, that did it. Now, I'm feeling overwhelmed. Is there anything else I need to know about?"

"Polly, it's only ..." he looked at the clock on his phone, "Nine o'clock in the morning. There's going to be a lot more you need to know about today."

She punched him lightly in the arm. "Thanks for all your support. I'm going upstairs to get the laundry, clean the bathrooms and spend some time divining how to decorate those other two rooms."

Polly was on the fourth step when the front door opened and Lydia Merritt walked in. She was the first person to welcome Polly to Bellingwood, and had quickly become one of Polly's closest friends. She was quick-witted and as Polly soon discovered, a passionate mama bear when it came to her friends, her family and random small children. She and her husband, Aaron, the Sheriff, had raised five of their own kids to adulthood. Her love for people extended in triple measure to any child she came in contact with.

She saw Polly on the steps and said, "Isn't Sylvie's news great?"

"It is! I'm so glad you encouraged her. Come on upstairs. I need your advice on decorating these last two rooms."

CHAPTER TWO

Polly woke up the next morning as she had every morning since Brad and Lee Geise gave her two kittens ... warm. Her German Shepherd Labrador mix, Obiwan, continued to get bigger and bigger, and was sprawled out next to her on the bed. For some reason, Luke crawled under the blankets and slept at her feet, while Leia chose to find a warm spot between Polly and the dog. She had discovered that turning the thermostat down two more degrees at night meant she slept much better. The kittens had also introduced Polly to very early morning hours, begging her to feed them.

She wasn't looking forward to this morning's run. It was only eight degrees outside and she heard the wind whistling around the building. Polly snuggled deeper into the blankets, hoping the cats wouldn't wake up, but apparently they already sensed her wakefulness and began meowing in her face from both sides of her head.

"All right! I'll get up, but I'm not going to like it," she announced to the room and looked at the clock. "You're fifteen minutes early this morning, the heat hasn't even come up yet." She picked Luke up and held him over her head. "You're gonna be lonely for a day, buddy. Little girl has surgery this morning. Do you think you can live without her for a while?" Polly brought him down and nuzzled his face, then set him on her chest while doing the same exercise with Leia. "You're not going to like today either, but it has to be done."

Then, she said conspiratorially, "and Dr. Ogden is a hottie. So, you be good while I flirt with him." Obiwan lifted his head, harrumphed and dropped back down on the pillow beside her.

"Now, don't give me that attitude," she said to him as she put Leia back down between them. "I am not in a relationship with Henry and I reserve the right to look at gorgeous men and appreciate their finer attributes." Obiwan grunted in acknowledgment.

"Exactly," she said. "Don't be giving me any sass. I'm not about to become anyone's wife for a very long time." Her dog shut his eyes and began to snore.

Polly pulled the blankets back and shivered. "You guys keep my bed warm, but getting up before the rest of the place heats up is painful!" she complained.

The cats stood beside each other and watched as she pulled her robe on over her pajamas. She picked them both up and walked through the living room to the kitchen where she put them on the floor. Luke began weaving through her ankles, rubbing his face on her toes and flopping his body on the floor in front of her as she reached into the cupboard for the container of cat food. Leia walked over to the dish and sat down beside it, cleaning herself.

"Darn." Polly said, pulling her hand back from the cupboard, "I'm sorry guys. I can't put food down for you until after I get Leia to the doctor." She walked out of the kitchen with both cats following her.

"Luke, you're lucky the Giese's neutered you before bringing you to me. It's all a distant memory." Little boy kittens needed to be neutered early so they didn't become tom cats. Luke recognized immediately that he wasn't getting fed and started loudly meowing.

"I know, I know ... it's hell," Polly agreed. "But, I'm pretty sure you'll live." She bent over and scooped him up as she walked back into the bedroom. "Alright, big guy," she said to Obiwan. "It's time to get your lazy butt out of bed. I'm going to pull on enough clothes to make me look like Nanook and you're going to make sure you hurry. Got it?"

Polly put layers of clothes on, ending with a jacket, gloves, hat and scarf. She caught a whiff of perfume as she wrapped the scarf around her neck. It was a Christmas gift from Andy and smelled just like her. Obiwan watched from the entryway of her apartment as she finished getting dressed. When she picked up the leash, he stood on his back legs, looking for a place to land his front paws on her chest. Polly backed up and said, "No. Down," and pointed at the floor.

He dropped to the floor and looked up at her, his tongue hanging out to one side. Polly snapped the leash on his collar, opened the door and the two trotted down the steps and out the front door. Her automatic front lights and the street lights were all that were shining since it was so early and Polly pulled out the flashlight she kept in her jacket pocket as she guided Obiwan to the side of the building. There had been a few light snowfalls and her dog was much happier playing in the cold and snow than she was. After ten minutes of walking and stopping, Polly was ready to turn around. Obiwan looked at her, his big soulful eyes pleading for more.

"I'm sorry, buddy. It's cold out here and that wind is killing me!" She turned around to head back home. Obiwan followed, but not with the same excitement he'd begun the morning's excursion. They got back to the apartment and he went into the kitchen, expecting her to follow.

"Not until after I drop little girl off, buddy." Polly said. "I don't want her trying to eat your food." Obiwan sat down beside his dish and when she didn't follow him, began pushing it with his nose across the floor.

"I know, I know," she said, "Patience isn't something you're used to exercising this early in the morning. But, I promise. It won't be too long. I'll come right back and get both of my boys taken care of."

He cocked his head to one side as if he was listening to her, but he continued to nose his dish at her. "Well, this is new!" she exclaimed, "and kind of cute, but it won't do any good." Polly up picked the dish and set it on the counter.

"I'm taking a shower," she announced. "Will you guys be good while I'm gone?"

Polly peeked around the corner into the living room when she came out of the shower. Sure enough, she had made her animals angry. The cats were both on the kitchen counters and Obiwan had managed to knock his food dish off the counter onto the floor. He had tipped it upside down and pushed it into the water dish, spreading water across the floor. She couldn't see any other destruction, but let out a loud "Hey!"

Two cats jumped to the floor and ran over to her, refusing to admit they'd been involved in any wrongdoing and the dog pushed the food dish out of the water dish, creating more of a mess.

"Obiwan. Come," Polly said in the sternest voice she could muster. He looked sideways at her, considered ignoring the command, but found he couldn't. He walked across the living room, his wet feet leaving marks on the hard wood floor.

"That's a good boy," she affirmed when he got to her. "Now all of you. In the bedroom while I get dressed." Polly took hold of Obiwan's collar and guided him into the bedroom, while scooting the kittens along with her feet. She closed the door behind her and looked at her audience.

"I'm sorry to disrupt your morning schedule," she said. "But, I promise it will be only for today and then we'll get back to normal." Polly reached over and scratched Obiwan behind the ears. "Sometimes you have to give things up to take care of the girls in your life, got it?"

Polly was thankful the veterinarian's office opened at seven. They had told her to come in any time between then and eight o'clock. She picked her phone up off the bedside table and looked at the time. 6:30. Gah! In a town the size of Bellingwood it would take exactly three minutes to get there.

Sitting on the edge of the bed to tie her shoes, she said, "I'm locking you boys in my bedroom. This is the most animal-proofed room I have, but I expect you to be good while I'm gone. Promise?" She picked up both kittens and flopped backwards onto her bed. Obiwan jumped up and sat beside her. "Normal schedules are what we appreciate, right guys? I swear I'll try to do better next time."

She closed her eyes and thought through her day. There wasn't much to do this morning. Elise Myers, her only guest didn't want anything for breakfast other than coffee and there were still bagels downstairs. The rest of the morning didn't hold anything interesting, but Lydia was picking her up after her church meeting to drive to Iowa Falls to see a bedroom set that, from its description, would be perfect in one of the guest apartments. If it was what she hoped, there would be one less room to worry about.

Polly looked at the clock one more time. 6:45. Fine. She was leaving. She and Leia would sit in the truck and wait for the office to open, but waiting here was going to make her crazy. Pulling her outerwear back on, she picked Leia up in a blanket, shut the door to the bedroom, shoved her phone in the back pocket of her jeans, picked up her keys and walked out to her truck.

It was cold enough the truck seemed to whimper in protest as she started it. Leia hadn't been out of the house since the Geise's brought her to Polly and began clawing at the blanket trying to escape. "See, I'm not so dumb," Polly whispered. "You'll be fine. Just stay where it's warm and before you know it, everything will be back to normal." They sat in the parking lot for a few minutes while the truck warmed up.

She saw lights on in Dr. Ogden's office, but the reception area was still dark, so she continued to hold tightly to her little girl. "I know you don't understand what is going on, Leia, and I'm fairly certain you won't be happy for a few days after this, but someday you will have forgotten all about it and I won't have to worry about more kittens at my house."

Marnie Evans unlocked the front door and waved for Polly to come on in as she flipped on the lights. Polly jumped out of the truck, cat package in hand, and went inside.

"I can take her from here," Marnie said.

Polly looked around. She was looking forward to talking with Mark Ogden.

"The doc isn't in yet. He won't get here this morning until about seven thirty," Marnie smiled and reached for the blanket containing Leia. "Do you want to leave the blanket for her?"

"Sure," Polly said, "When should I pick her up?"

"You could probably take her home tonight, but maybe with Obiwan and Luke in the same house, she should rest here overnight?" Marnie trapped the squirming kitten under her left arm. "If you came by after ten tomorrow, she'd be ready to go home."

"Alright," Polly said. "I'll see you then." She reached out and scratched Leia's ears and turned around to leave. Looking back, she watched Marnie walk away with her kitty and headed on out to her truck.

"Well, phooey. I had myself all worked up to see Dr. Hottie and he isn't even here," she said to herself as she pulled out of the lot and drove home. It was time to feed a couple of not-so-patient animals and get her day started.

Polly was in her office later that morning when Lydia came in, dropped into a chair and said, "Polly, I don't think I realized you were such a geek."

"What could you possibly mean?"

"I knew you liked Star Wars, but have you seen this office lately?" Lydia laughed.

"What. This?"

She looked around the office. With Henry's help, she had designed shelves spaced around the room for her Star Wars Legos. The Millennium Falcon was hanging from one corner and the Death Star from another. Crossed beneath them were two light sabers; one red and one blue. A framed cutaway poster of the

Falcon was hanging on a wall and a robot R2D2 stood in one corner. A glass-covered cabinet held action figures, some still in their packaging and others arranged independently.

"Okay, I'm a little bit of a geek," Polly said. "This was one of the things Dad could buy for me. Then, along the way, my friends discovered my collection and continued to ensure I got more pieces."

Lydia smiled. "It's too bad we didn't know about this before Christmas. But, I know now!"

"It's become kind of a big deal, I guess," Polly smiled. She stood up and walked to the cabinet. Pulling out a Luke Skywalker figurine, she rubbed her thumb across its head. "This was one of the first pieces Dad bought for me. I loved it! It wasn't until later that I figured out they were worth more if I left them in their packages."

"It's kind of hard to play with them in the packages," Lydia said.

"Uh huh. I'm not playing with those toys any longer."

"But, you like Legos?"

"I do. It's like putting puzzles together," Polly acknowledged. "Are we having lunch before we go to Iowa Falls?"

"Well," Lydia said, "Andy and Beryl are going to be here in a few minutes and I thought we'd go to Webster City for lunch."

"That sounds great!" Polly responded.

"And would you mind if we checked in on a friend of mine before leaving town?" Lydia asked.

"Sure, is there something going on?"

"I want to make sure my friend Madeline is alright," Lydia said. "I'm a little concerned about her."

"Good morning!" Beryl and Andy came in the front door and around the corner. They stood outside the door to Polly's office.

"What star system exploded in here?" Beryl asked.

Lydia turned her head to look back at her friends, "You hadn't seen this either? Our Polly is a nerd!"

"I just finished unpacking the boxes this weekend," Polly said, "and I wear the nerd badge proudly!"

Beryl walked in and looked around, "Do you dress up in cute little cinnamon roll buns and white silky robes and go hang out with other nerds?"

"I've been known to go to science fiction conventions," Polly said, "but I've never gone in costume."

"Have your little friends, Doug and Billy, seen this?" Beryl asked.

"They helped me get it all together. We had to do a little repair work on the big Lego pieces and then assemble everything else," Polly responded.

"I'll bet they are completely and totally in love with you now," sighed Andy. "You have become their reigning princess."

Polly laughed. "Enough. Let's get going. I'm starving."

Lydia asked her, "Do you have to take Obiwan out before we leave?"

"Nope, my Jedi Knights said they would take care of him this afternoon, so I'm free to go. Let me step in and tell everyone I'm out of here." Polly stuck her head in Jeff's office door and said, "I'll see you later, I'm off to check on the bedroom furniture."

"Okay!" he replied. "See ya!"

She walked across the hall to the classrooms, "Bye guys! I'm taking off for the day. Doug?" She heard a grunt. "Thanks for taking care of the dog!"

He came out from behind a spool of wire, "We got it, Polly. See ya later."

"Alright," she said as she headed for the front door, "Let's get this day moving!"

Polly got in the back seat of Lydia's Jeep with Andy. Beryl rolled her eyes and got in the passenger seat, then said, "I think we should have a new rule. Instead of the first person calling shotgun, the last person in should sit up front."

"Hey!" exclaimed Lydia. "I don't smell, I'm a nice person, I drive well. What's up with no one wanting to sit with me?"

Andy patted her shoulder, "Polly and I are just worried about Beryl's old legs. We don't want her to have to struggle in and out of the back seat."

Lydia chuckled and said to Beryl, "Back to you, missy. What'cha got next?"

"Oh yeah?" Beryl declared. "Yeah?"

She slumped in her seat. "I've got nothing right now. But, when I do get a good one, you're going to know you've been retorted. So there." She jammed her seatbelt into the lock and sat back in a huff.

Lydia drove out of the parking lot and into town. She turned left onto Monroe and Beryl cried out, "I thought we were going to lunch in Webster City. Where are you taking us?"

"I'm sorry," Lydia said, "I want to check on Madeline Black. She wasn't in church on Sunday or at the women's meeting this morning."

"Alrighty then," Beryl said. "That makes sense. I didn't want to think about you getting lost in Bellingwood. That would mean the world was ending!"

Lydia pulled up in front of a small brick home and put the car in park. "I'll leave it running. I should just be a few minutes." She got out of the car and walked up the walk to the front door. No one said anything as they watched her ring the doorbell. She turned around and looked at the three of them and shrugged her shoulders. She opened the screen door and reached down. They watched as she picked up several newspapers, obvious confusion on her face. Then Lydia flipped the lid open on the mailbox and pulled out bundled batches of mail.

Polly saw real distress on the woman's face and reached for the door handle as Lydia peered inside the front room window. Beryl reached over, turned the Jeep off and took the keys. All three women joined Lydia on the front porch.

"Do you see anything?" Polly asked.

"No, not here. I'm going to walk around back and look in her kitchen. I hope she didn't fall down and hurt herself." Lydia's voice was concerned. The four of them walked around the house on the shoveled sidewalk to the back stoop. Lydia knocked and peered in. Reaching down, she tried the door and found it unlocked.

"Alright, I'm going in. She wouldn't leave it unlocked if she was gone. Something has happened," she said.

Beryl touched Lydia's shoulder, "We're coming with you, even if we do make a strange-looking parade."

They walked in through the small back porch to the kitchen. Lydia called out, "Madeline? Are you here?" and then said, "Oh no!"

Madeline Black was motionless on the floor of the dining room behind the table. Polly realized the smell and sight of the body was affecting her stomach and ran back out the back door, followed closely by Beryl and Andy.

"Lydia! Get out of there right now!" Beryl called out.

Lydia came to the back door, tears filling her eyes. "How long do you suppose she was there? I have to call Aaron."

She started to walk back to the car and Polly stopped her. "Here, use my phone. It's already dialing him," and she handed the telephone to Lydia.

"Aaron, you aren't going to believe this, but I just walked in to Madeline Black's house and she's dead." Lydia listened for a moment, then said, "Yes, she's dead. Really dead. Can you get someone up here?" She listened for a few minutes more, "No, I don't think anything bad has happened, other than she's dead." A few more moments, "Alright, I'll call her son and we'll wait. But, I'm not going back inside that house; I'll be in the Jeep. I love you."

She handed the phone back to Polly and pulled the back door shut. "Stu is close and he'll be right over. I'm supposed to call her son. What do I say, 'Son, your mama is dead?'"

Beryl took her arm and started walking back to the Jeep. "Yes, that's exactly what you say. Then, tell him to get his butt over here and deal with it."

Lydia looked up at her friend, "Compassion is definitely your strong suit, isn't it!"

"It sure is," Beryl said. "Compassion for you. You do not need to take care of this today."

"I'm not going anywhere until it is taken care of, though," Lydia declared.

"We know that, and we're staying here with you. Right girls?" Beryl said as Polly and Andy nodded their assent. "Now let's get back in the car and warm up. My toes and nose are unhappy with me right now and I like to keep all of my body parts singing my praises."

CHAPTER THREE

"I guess I took care of that." Lydia put her phone into a drinkwell in the console beside her, and said, "He didn't sound terribly surprised or upset. I can't believe Madeline raised such a brat."

Beryl patted her forearm, "Maybe he was just shook up by the news."

"Maybe he doesn't care about his mother and that annoys me," Lydia said.

"Does that mean he's not coming over?" Polly asked from the back seat.

"No, he's too busy," Lydia responded. "But, at least he'll call his sister and tell her."

Stu Decker pulled up behind Lydia's Jeep and walked to the driver's window. She pressed the button to lower it.

"I'd like to say I'm surprised to see you here, but I'm beginning to wonder if I'll ever encounter anything interesting in this town without you all involved," he said. "Polly, these women led boring lives before you came to town."

"It's not my fault!" she protested; then said a little more quietly,

"It's not my fault. I didn't even know this woman."

Andy patted her knee, "Of course it's not your fault. I think that since you are around and injecting energy into the atmosphere here in Bellingwood, we're just that much more aware of the stories which surround our normal, everyday lives. Does that sound better?"

"It's not my fault," Polly repeated.

"I watched that movie Friday night, Polly, so I could figure out why you liked it. You and Han Solo ... troublemakers just because you're in the room. It wasn't ever his fault either, but that didn't change the fact he couldn't get to hyperspace, now did it?" Beryl said, laughing.

Stu chuckled. "I'm going inside. The funeral director will be here soon."

Lydia said, "You have to go around to the back door, the front is locked."

"Alright," he said, "Would you send Ben around when he gets here? Will her kids be coming?"

Lydia's nose crunched up in disgust, "No, not today. I'll give Ben her son's phone number and they can go from there, I suppose. Brat."

Stu continued to chuckle as he walked around the side of the house. It took less than two minutes for him to come back outside. Beryl turned her window down, "Is there a problem, Officer?"

"No, I'm fine. Everything is fine," he said. "But, I've decided to wait out here for Ben to show up. There's no reason to wait inside on a beautiful day like today."

"That's what we thought, too," she said. "This beautiful day is why we're snuggled in our toasty warm car."

Stu walked back to the Jeep and held out a piece of paper, "I think she knew she was dying and started to write a note."

Beryl took it from him and read it out loud, "Tell Laurence and Amy I love them very much. Please take care of Dean's"

"That's all there is," she said. "Dean's what?" She looked at the three others in the Jeep, "Dean's what?"

Andy shrugged and Lydia thought about it, then said, "Dean

died two years ago. He wasn't the gardener in the family, so it's not a plant. Madeline bought a new car last fall, so it's not his car. I can't imagine what it is!"

Polly spoke up from the back seat, "Did he have a pet or a boat or anything like that?"

"Not that I know of," Lydia said. "Maybe Laurence knows what she was worried about."

Beryl handed the piece of paper back to Stu, who said, "Oh, here they are!" and walked away as three people got out of a vehicle. Two of them went around to the back of the vehicle and pulled a rolling cart out, the other stopped to shake Stu's hand and talk to him. They watched him shake his head, then the four walked to the back of the house.

"Well, what now?" Beryl asked.

"We wait until poor Madeline is on her way to the funeral home, that's what now," Lydia said.

Beryl looked sideways at her friend, "I should have known. Polly, are we going to be late for the appointment in Iowa Falls?"

"I forgot!" Polly said. "Let me call. Do you still have time to run over there or should I reschedule and go by myself?"

They all looked at each other and Lydia asked, "Is anyone hungry or are your delicate constitutions upset?"

"I could eat," Beryl said.

"Me too," Andy replied.

"Polly?" Lydia asked.

"Sure. I guess I can count on my iron stomach to make its way through any catastrophe," sighed Polly.

"Then, I say we keep to our plan for the day."

Stu came around the side of the house and trotted up to the car. "Lydia," he said through Beryl's opened window, "these are Madeline's keys. Can I give them to you and ask you to meet the people Ben will have here tomorrow to clean the house? We talked to her son and he asked us to take care of it and send him a bill."

Lydia rolled her eyes. "Of course I will," she said. "See, I told you. He's a brat." She held her hand out in front of Beryl, who batted at it as Stu attempted to drop the keys in it. "Brats everywhere," Lydia muttered as she took the keys from him, then swatted Beryl in the chest!

"Assault! You saw that, didn't you, Officer?" Beryl cried out.

"I saw nothing. You women are weird," he said. "Lydia, I'll have Ben call you later to get things scheduled. I appreciate this, even if her son doesn't." He patted the door and turned to go back into the house.

"Well, I think we've done our job here for the day. Polly, can you call them and see if we can be there about an hour late?" Lydia asked.

"On it. And by the way," Polly said. "I'm not particularly fond of any job that includes discovering dead bodies. I just want that on record."

"What's this," Andy asked. "Your third now, right?"

Polly cuffed Andy's knee, "Stop it. We're not going to count. Not now, not ever!"

In order to end the conversation, she pulled up a number on her phone, punched the Send key and waited for it to connect. Lydia pulled the Jeep away from the curb, went around the block and got back to the highway.

"Do you want light sandwiches or ... " she stopped, then said, "Oops!" as Polly said hello into her phone.

Lydia turned north onto Highway 17, heading for Webster City while Polly spoke. When Polly hung up the phone, she said, "I'm not sure what to think about that."

"What do you mean?" Andy asked.

"First of all, it's fine for us to be late. But, then the woman asked me how I liked living in Iowa again and if the renovation was nearly finished at Sycamore House. She called it by name and I hadn't told her anything more than my name!" Polly said, "A neighbor of hers down the road is good friends with Helen Randall's sister's daughter." She looked up and around. "Are you kidding me?"

Then she stopped and thought. "Right. I might have been away from Iowa too long. Of course that's the way it works."

Beryl snorted with laughter. "No one out here needs to count all the way to six degrees of separation. It's probably more like three or four. Everybody knows somebody!" She craned her head around to look at Polly, who was sitting behind her. "And don't you ever forget it. If you need something in this region, all you have to do is start asking questions. Someone is going to know someone you know and will help you out just because you're connected."

Lydia said, "She's right! Last summer, Jim wanted a job at the state fairgrounds. Well, earlier in the year, Aaron and I were at a party. Jim had just announced that's what he wanted and I was telling someone and would you believe that a woman from their human resource department was the sister of the host? She gave me her number and told me to have Jim call. Before we knew it, he had a summer job. Somebody always knows somebody."

"Well, I hope I like the bedroom set. Otherwise, I'm going to feel guilty about this whole thing now that she knows about me," Polly said.

Lydia asked, "What do you want for lunch? A full meal or just a sandwich? Pizza or Chinese?"

"Sandwiches seem safe," Andy said.

"Sure!" Polly remarked as Beryl nodded in assent.

"Great!" Lydia said. "There's a cute little sandwich shop downtown. You'll love it."

After they finished lunch and had climbed back in the Jeep, Lydia said, "Polly do you have the address for the GPS?"

Polly sighed. "GPS. Just another way technology stops us from getting to know each other."

"You really don't like it, do you?" Lydia laughed.

"Nope," Polly said. "I guess I don't. The thing is, I have no reason to be so adamantly against it. It's about the only tech I despise." She opened the note program on her phone and brought up the address, then set it on the console in front of Lydia. Soon they were back on the road and heading east on Highway 20.

Lydia's GPS directed them to a home on the northwest side of town. Polly looked at the big house as they drove in the lane and laughed. "Alright," she said. "Which door do I approach this time?"

"I'm going to drive right up to the front door," Lydia responded. "I'd recommend you knock on that door. Easy enough for you, you chicken?"

She turned to Beryl beside her, "You'd think she hadn't ever lived on a farm. These houses scare her to death!"

Beryl chuckled. "Maybe we should do a scavenger hunt sometime in the country and make her knock on every door in three counties!"

Polly popped Beryl in the back of the head and opened the car door. "Just a second. I'd like all of you to see it if it's alright." She walked up to the front door and rang the doorbell.

A woman in her early sixties answered the door. Two cocker spaniels pushed forward in an attempt to see who was there.

"Get back, you beasts," The woman said. "Are you Polly?"

"I am," Polly replied.

"I'd invite you in, but the beasts are overly friendly and the furniture is already in the garage. We moved it out of the bedroom so I could start changing things around. I'll open the garage door." She smiled and walked away, leaving the main door open. The dogs continued to try to get to Polly through the screen door, even as she walked away. Lydia drove on up and turned the Jeep off as the garage door opened.

Polly walked into the garage and took a breath when she saw what was in there. Turning around to see if her friends were paying attention to the treasure in front of them, she said, "There are more pieces here than you advertised on Craigslist."

"You're right, and you don't have to take them," the woman said. "I figured it would be easier to get rid of everything if we broke it up a little."

In front of Polly was a dresser with a mirror, a chest of drawers, two bedside tables, a vanity, a secretary, two high back chairs, a luggage stool, a curio cabinet and the headboard and footboard for the bed. The pieces had been well cared for over the years and were a dark, burled walnut. She nearly wept when she saw the entirety of the collection. There was one tall piece with a door she didn't recognize and asked what it was.

"That's a shoe closet," she was told. "I don't suppose we ever used it for shoes, but it has deep shelves."

"I want everything!" she exclaimed, then turned to the woman. "I don't understand why you are letting these go!"

"My kids told me they weren't interested at all. I must not have brought 'em up right, because they seem to prefer new furniture. And, their dad and I bought both of them nice bedroom sets as wedding gifts."

"But, this is gorgeous!" Beryl said. Her fingers began tracing the knots on the headboard and soon she was stroking the wood.

"I always thought it was, too. My husband hurt his back last year, though, and we had to change beds for him. Rather than wait until we died, I figured I would see if I could find it a new home or two." She reached over and touched the dresser. "It was a wedding gift many years ago, but it would make me happy if you could enjoy it." Her smile seemed a little strained, but she smiled all the same.

Polly opened a couple of drawers in the chest. The scent of lavender greeted her nose. "I would love to put this into one of the rooms at Sycamore House. It will be my favorite room!"

The woman smiled and her eyes filled. "I'm glad you want to keep everything together. Now, there aren't any rails for the bed, but we were able to use it with our queen mattress."

"Don't worry," Polly said. "I've got just the carpenter to make sure this goes together perfectly." She pulled her checkbook out of her back pocket. "Will it be alright if it takes a day or so for me to get a truck and some guys to pick this up from you?" She wrote a number on the check and said, "Tell me if you think this is fair for the entire set?"

"That's more than I was asking. Are you sure?"

"I'm positive. I have been looking at furniture for several months and if you think it is a good number, it is fair for both of us," Polly responded.

"Thank you, and you can pick them up whenever you are able.

Adam is going to be glad I finally have a plan to get his garage back. He thought it was unfair I got my house all put back together only to disrupt his little sanctuary."

She turned to the door leading inside. "If you give me a couple of minutes, I will put the dogs into our bedroom. I'd love for you to come in and have a cup of coffee. I made sweet rolls this morning."

Polly wasn't about to make that decision on her own and turned to look back at her three traveling companions.

Beryl looked around and said, "We never turn down coffee and homemade sweet things. It will be the perfect way to close this deal!" She marched up to the door and said, "We're not afraid of a couple of dogs, now, are we, girls?"

The door led directly into the kitchen. Polly and Beryl both cleared the door so the others could join them and immediately went down on their knees to accept the onslaught of puppy dog love. Polly looked up, "It's easier if you just take the love first and they won't jump up on you as much if you get down to their level."

"Well, listen to the expert!" Beryl laughed. "But, she's right."

Andy chuckled. "Beryl, you go ahead and love the dogs all you want." She turned to the woman of the house. "I'm sorry, I didn't get your name."

"Oh!" the woman said, "I'm Vera Lucas and these are Sampson and Delilah."

Andy blinked. "Those are big names!"

"Yes, our son thought it was funny. His kids were learning about those characters in Sunday School when he got the dogs for us." Vera said. "Adam and I are pretty sure we are nothing more than fodder for his entertainment. But then, that's fair. He always made us laugh. Now, come in! Sit down! I want to hear all about this Sycamore House and what you are doing down in that little town. Did I hear you found bodies in the ceiling?"

Vera put her hands on Sampson, "Down, Sampson. Sit. Down." He wiggled a little and Beryl stood up, then he sat and waited while Vera pulled a treat out of a container on the counter. "You too, Delilah. Sit." The other dog obeyed and received her treat while Polly and Beryl walked over to the table to join Lydia and Andy.

"Can we help you?" Lydia asked.

"Sure," Vera said. She pulled mugs out of the cupboard, handing them to Lydia who had jumped up to help. They passed everything around until plates, napkins, forks, mugs, coffee and sweet rolls were laid out. "Adam is going to be sorry he missed this! When he read about the bodies in the ceiling, he remembered the whole thing. I was busy with a wild toddler. I think I missed everything that was going on in the world until our son was in Junior High. "

Polly said, "Lydia's husband," and she pointed to her friend, "is the sheriff. He took care of everything and these ladies took care of me." She continued, "and this is Beryl Watson and Andy Saner."

Vera nodded, "Nice to meet you." She turned back to Polly. "Tell me what you're doing with that old school?"

Polly described her dreams for Sycamore House as the women devoured their sweet rolls. With frosting dripping from the left side of her mouth, she said, "These are fabulous! Would you share the recipe?"

Lydia swiped at frosting on Polly's mouth with her napkin.

Polly stuck her tongue out and licked her lips clean. "Better?" she asked.

"Yes." Lydia said. "I didn't know your daddy raised you so poorly."

"I was appreciating the goodness of it, so there," and Polly stuck her tongue out at Lydia again.

Vera laughed. "It's a simple recipe. I make them all the time."

She began rattling off ingredients and Polly put her hand up. "Whoa! I don't type that fast! Just a second." After a few swipes on her phone, she said, "Okay, go."

Vera began listing the ingredients again and Polly stopped her. "Orange Zest? That's why they taste fresh! I'm sorry, go ahead."

"Orange juice, too," Vera said and continued. "You can also mix up the icing with orange juice too, but I like to use a plain icing so the flavor is more subtle."

"Thank you, so much" Polly said. "I can't wait to try these out on the guys."

Vera looked confused and Polly went on. "I still have plenty of people working at Sycamore House during the day. I'm a little concerned it might become their second home. They aren't going to know how to work anywhere else."

Polly looked around and saw that her friends were finished, "Thank you for your hospitality today. I can't wait to get your furniture into place. Do you have an email address I could send pictures when I get everything finished?" She typed Vera's email address into her phone and stood up.

"Thank you again. I will call tomorrow to let you know when we'll be back to pick everything up."

Vera walked them back out through the garage, pushing the dogs aside so everyone could escape. They waved goodbye as Lydia drove back down the lane.

"Well, that was a much better way to end this day," Beryl announced.

They all chuckled. "I think I'm finally rid of that awful smell," Andy said.

"Me too," Polly said. "If I never have to see ... or smell ... another dead body, it will be too soon."

"What did you think of the bedroom set?" she asked her friends.

Beryl turned around in her seat, "I don't know what you paid for it, but I would have called it priceless. How can you put a price on something that gorgeous ... and with so many pieces?"

Lydia nodded from the driver's seat and Andy said, "I would have had trouble giving up something like that. I'm glad Billy is staying in the house because I discovered I even had an emotional attachment to the washer and dryer his dad had picked out for me."

Beryl laughed. "Andy here is emotionally attached to anything anyone ever gives her. If we didn't keep her out of trouble, she'd become a hoarder like Lydia's new friend, Doug Leon. But I go over there often enough to show her how to toss out magazines and newspapers."

"I don't keep those things," Andy protested. "Just the sweet gifts people have given me over the years"

"And they're all neatly labeled and identified with the date and name of the gift giver, too, aren't they!" Beryl said.

"I'm not talking to you anymore," Andy grumped.

Polly laughed at them. "Speaking of organizing and labeling, Andy, would you be up to curating the pieces of history Doug Leon collected in those crates?"

"What do you mean?" Andy asked, her mood brightening.

"We're installing glass doors on all the bookcases Henry installed in the auditorium ..." Polly began, but Andy interrupted her.

"I could arrange everything according to year and decade and start building a little history about the time period and we could even collect posters. It will be wonderful! When can I begin?"

"Is that a yes?" Polly asked.

"It's a hell yes!" Andy said.

Lydia laughed. "This is exactly what she needs to keep her from getting old. Polly, you're a wonder woman!"

"I'm not old," Andy said, pouting.

"Not yet you aren't," Beryl laughed. "But the potential for elderly behavior was in your future. You needed a project."

Polly spoke up and said, "This is going to be a big project. There will be people contacting you to reclaim their lost items and if everything doesn't fit, you'll need to ensure there is a good rotation of items."

"When can I start?" Andy interrupted again.

"The glass company won't be finished until the end of next week, but I guess you could probably start arranging things tomorrow if you'd like. Maybe you can tell them where to start, and work behind them." Polly shrugged. "I'm glad to hand the entire project over to you. You can work with Henry and the glass company and make it happen!"

"Thank you, Polly," Andy gushed. "I'll be there tomorrow

morning ready to go!"

"You know," Polly said. "I'll bet Sylvie's boys would help you out after school if you'd like some extra hands. They were fascinated with those things."

"They'll be my arms and legs when they're around," Andy said. "That's a great idea."

"You know she's starting classes next week, right?" Polly asked. "The boys are going to be at Sycamore House every day anyway."

Beryl said, "I think she called us all yesterday after she saw you. Goodness, Polly, you're putting everyone to work!"

"I like giving my friends an opportunity to do what they love," Polly said. "And no, I'm not going to hire you to come in and harass the town just because that's what you love to do."

"You're mean, Polly Giller. Just mean." Beryl laughed.

CHAPTER FOUR

Cold and empty. Polly was standing in the middle guest room when she heard the main door chime and realized she didn't have a clue how she was going to fill this room, especially since she'd found the perfect pieces for the back room. She trotted out the door and down the steps, opened the door to find Andy standing there with a travel briefcase on wheels.

"You look like an Avon lady!" she laughed. "What are you hauling?"

"I have my laptop and notebooks, and labels and pencils and other office supplies. I want to make sure this is organized from the outset," Andy replied.

"Well, come on in!" Polly said and stepped back from the door. As Andy entered, Polly asked, "I didn't give you a key?"

"I guess I didn't really need one. Someone is always here when I'm here," Andy replied.

"Well, it's all digital now, here, let me email you." Polly brought up the application and emailed a key to Andy. "There, now you've got access to this main door. You can come and go any time."

"Thank you," Andy replied. "And what a great idea!"

"Yeah," Polly said. "I was getting tired of running up and down the stairs to let people in. This system is pretty handy. Now what do you need to get started?"

The two women walked into the auditorium and Polly flipped lights on.

Andy said, "I thought I'd start on the stage today. I know I was involved in identifying things, but I want to wrap my head around what we have. Can you get the database back from the Sheriff?"

"I already have it and it's in pretty good shape. There is a computer whiz in his office who assembled the entire thing, even aligning the photographs with their descriptions. They gave me a drive we can plug right into your computer."

"That will make everything easier! I will wander around a bit and try to get a visual idea of what we have and how things might fit. This afternoon, maybe Sylvie's boys and I will dig in and make a mess."

Polly smiled. "I'm glad you are ready to take this on. It makes my head hurt thinking about it."

"Then it's good you have me around," Andy laughed and reached out to hug Polly. "And it's good that I have you around. This is going to be fun." She hefted her bag up onto the front of the stage and unzipped the top, pulling out her computer.

Polly stood and watched her, then when Andy looked at her expectantly, said, "Oh, right! I'll go get that drive and be right back. There's coffee in the regular place in the kitchen and I made breakfast pizza this morning. There's still some in the first oven, staying warm. If you want hot and fresh, I'll have two more coming out in about ..." she looked at her phone ... "thirteen minutes. By then, most everyone should be here and hungry."

She bolted out of the door and jogged to her office. When she got back to the stage, Andy was drinking coffee. "No pizza?" Polly asked.

"I had breakfast before I left. Sorry. If I'd known, I would have waited."

"It's alright. You never know when I'm going to get crazy in the kitchen. The girl upstairs, Elise, says she doesn't want breakfast, but every time I make something, she eats it. I don't want the poor thing to starve while she's working on her dissertation. so I'll cook if she'll eat," Polly replied.

"Has she been down yet this morning?" Andy asked. "I'd love to meet her. Do you know what doctorate she's working toward?"

"I really don't. Something to do with math and people and ... well, I didn't pay any attention. According to my clock, though, she should be down ..." they heard footsteps on the stairs. "... now. Come on into the kitchen and I'll introduce you two."

Andy followed her and stood beside the oven as Polly pulled the breakfast pizza out. She had covered one half with bacon and the other with sausage; the eggs were golden and the cheese was toasty.

"Good morning, Elise!" Polly said as the young woman walked over to the coffeepot.

"Hi, Polly," she said. Elise Myers was the epitome of Polly's ideal bookworm geek. Pale skin with big blue eyes behind dark rimmed glasses. Her long, brown hair was pulled back into a pony tail and looked flat on one side, like she'd slept on it and hadn't looked in a mirror. She was wearing an oversized sweater hoodie and baggy sweatpants. There were silver rings on most of her fingers and this morning she had come downstairs in a pair of well-worn moccasins.

"Elise Myers, this is my friend Andy Saner."

Andy reached out to take her hand, which Elise offered up tentatively. "It's nice to meet you, Elise. How long are you staying at Sycamore House?"

"Hopefully I will be finished in another month or two. I can't believe I found a place like this to stay. I needed to be away from everything for a while so I could focus."

"Where are you going to school?" Andy asked.

"University of Chicago," she responded.

"Then, how did you find out about Sycamore House?" Andy continued. "Are you from around here?"

"No," Elise said. "I'm from Chicago, but one of my aunts is from

Clarion and she read an article about those bodies being found, then I guess she asked some questions and found out a room would be open after the first of the year. All of my family gave me money for Christmas so I could rent the room and finish my dissertation."

"That's wonderful!" Polly said. "I didn't know that. I'm glad you found me. Now, would you like some breakfast pizza, Elise?"

The girl nodded as Polly began putting pieces on a plate for her. As Polly lifted a third piece off the pan, Elise held her hand out to stop her. "That's plenty. Thank you!"

Polly moved toward the refrigerator. "Would you like some fruit or juice this morning? I have bananas, or oranges and grapefruit. And here are some clementines."

"I'd love a banana and ..." she paused. "No, that's enough, I suppose."

"Please!" Polly exclaimed. "Take whatever you like!"

"Could I take an orange with me, too?" Elise asked.

"Of course!" Polly pulled the fruit out of a basket and placed both on the plate. "Really, Elise. Any time you want anything, just come get it. Unless you're storing food up there, you don't eat enough to keep those brain cells working!"

Elise giggled shyly as she took the plate from Polly's hand. "Thank you for taking care of me. When I write, I have a habit of forgetting everything else around me. Would you do me a favor?"

"If I can," Polly said.

"If you don't see any sign of me for a while, will you knock on my door and remind me to be a human?"

Polly and Andy both laughed and Polly said, "Of course I will. But, Jeff said you flip flop hours when you're writing."

"I do, but you should at least see me down here every twenty-four hours, don't you think?" Elise's eyes were pleading for assurance.

"We'll keep an eye on you. When you get started, why don't you let us know what your schedule looks like and I'll have your back. No worries. You just do the work."

"Thank you! I know I sound like a nut, but Mom and Dad tell

me I have a tendency to forget what planet I'm on when I'm working." Elise picked up her coffee and walked out of the kitchen to the stairway.

Polly heard the front door slam open and then crashing, banging and a yelp. She and Andy both went running out and found Doug Randall, Billy Endicott and Elise Myers in a heap on the floor, surrounded by coils of electrical wire and scattered tools.

"What happened?" she asked.

Elise looked up sheepishly. "It's my fault," she said. "Are you guys okay?"

She pulled her leg out from under Billy's ankle, then stood up, reaching down to give him a hand. "I wasn't paying any attention to where I was going and when they came in the front door, I got startled, tripped him with my foot and crashed into him." She nodded to Billy first, then to Doug.

Both Doug and Billy were still in shock. Billy looked down at his pants. "I give up!" he said. "Hot coffee is not my friend in this place."

Polly couldn't help it. Laughter erupted as she reached down to give Doug a hand. When he was standing, she picked up the broken plate and began collecting the spilled food. Andy helped her, then, giggling, took everything from Polly's hands and went back to the kitchen.

"Doug Randall and Billy Endicott meet Elise Myers. She is my first guest at Sycamore House," Polly said. "Is everyone alright?"

The boys moved their shoulders around, Doug shook out his arms and Billy shook the leg which had been soaked in coffee. "We're good," Doug said. "Are you okay, Miss Myers?" he asked.

"I'm fine," she stammered. "I, I, I'm so sorry!"

"Don't worry. This isn't the first time we've fallen into the building," Billy laughed. "And it isn't the first time someone has spilled coffee on my pants. I should be used to it by now." He rolled his eyes in Polly's direction.

"Hey!" she said. "That was your fault, not mine."

Henry had come up the steps and saw the chaos in the

entryway. "Was there a party and I wasn't invited?" he asked.

Elise took one look at him and bolted up the steps.

"What did I say?" he asked.

"I think she had too many people in her face at one time," Polly said. "Don't worry, I've got it. You guys clean this up and, Oh no!" she exclaimed. "The pizza! There will be hot breakfast pizza out in a minute." She took off for the kitchen only to meet Andy who was on her way out with another plate filled with food.

"I made another plate for Elise," Andy said. "Where did she go?"

"Come on back to the kitchen," Polly replied. "I'll tell you in there." Andy followed her back into the kitchen. Polly pulled two more breakfast pizzas out of the oven and slid them onto cutting boards. She ran the pizza cutter across the pizzas, then set them on the counter.

"I think she terrified herself, so she took off upstairs. Let me get another cup of coffee and I'll take these up to her. Thank you!" she said to Andy. "I'll be right back. Help yourself."

Polly took the food and coffee and moving past the boys who were gathering their things, went upstairs. She knocked on the door to Elise's room and heard, "Just a minute."

She waited and the door opened. Elise's face was bright red as if she'd been crying.

"I brought you a plate of food," Polly said. "Are you hurt?"

"I'm fine," Elise responded. "Just terribly embarrassed. I don't do well around a lot of people and I don't do well at all around a lot of men. They terrify me. I'm sorry to be such a bother."

Polly put the food and coffee on an antique study carrel she had found. "Don't worry about those boys or Henry. They will not bother you and probably feel as badly as you do about the crash. They're all good guys and if they thought you were uncomfortable around them, would probably hide rather than let you see them."

Elise slumped down in the chair. "I'm awful with people. That's why this was the perfect place. No one knows me here and no one will try to get me to go out and do things."

"Do you want to do things or be with people?" Polly asked.

"Not really, but," Elise looked up at her. "I don't know what I want. Sometimes I want to be normal and have friends and go to the movies and hang out at bars, but then I realize that I don't want that at all. I just think I do. I'm so confused." She put her head in her hands. "I don't know. Back at the University, they ignore me and I can do my research and nobody bothers me. But, sometimes I watch everything happening around me and wonder why I don't fit in."

She shook her head, "I've always been on the outside."

"I'm sorry, Elise. If there's anything I can do, I will," Polly said.

"I don't even know why I'm telling you this. I don't usually talk about it with anyone." Her look of confusion made Polly smile. "Not even my mom. She thinks this is all a choice I've made. She loves me and has always given me space to do whatever I wanted, but she never pushed me out of the house or forced me to make friends."

Elise sighed, "Well, this isn't going to get any work done. Thank you for bringing food to me. I'm sorry I broke your plate and I'm sorry if I hurt those boys."

"The boys are pretty hardy," Polly chuckled. "And plates aren't worth worrying about. Here," Polly said and picked up a pen and a pad of paper. "This is my cell phone. You can call or text me any time you need anything if you are too freaked out to come downstairs. I'm not going to make you be friends with anyone but me. However, you are going to be friends with me. That's already established. Got it?"

Elise didn't say anything, simply looked at the paper Polly had handed to her. "Elise? Do you understand? You're my friend now. That means I'd like to see your face every once in a while. And when you're not working and need a break, you and I might hang out over in my apartment and watch a movie or television with my animals. How does that sound?"

"It sounds heavenly," Elise said. "Thank you. Can I text you any time?"

"Any time. Even if you only need me to run upstairs and bring you an apple, alright?"

Elise stood up again and seemed a little uncomfortable, but reached out to hug Polly. "Thank you," she said again. "No one has ever made me be their friend before."

"Well, I guess you've never met my friends," Polly said. "When you're ready, I've got a crazy group of them here and they'll love you!"

The girl shuddered and said, "I don't think I'm ready for that yet."

"Then, don't worry about it. Now, I'm going back downstairs to get some work done. I have to rescue my little girl kitty cat from the veterinarian in a little bit. She had surgery yesterday and I can't wait to get her back home. Leave the empty plate on the table outside your door and I'll deal with it later."

"Thank you, Polly," Elise said.

As Polly walked back downstairs, she chuckled to herself, "Lydia would be so proud of me," she murmured. "I'm turning into her clone!"

By the time she got back to the kitchen, there was quite a crowd gathered around eating breakfast and drinking coffee.

"I hope we didn't freak her out," Doug said. "But, she ran into us!"

"It's alright," Polly replied. "I think she freaked herself out. She's a lot more comfortable with books and numbers than she is with people. So, your job ..." and she looked at everyone around her, "is to avoid her when you see her. Don't try to make her talk to you. Just smile and be your nice, normal, polite selves and then move on. Alright?" She looked at them each in the eye once more to make sure they understood her. They all nodded.

Andy combined the rest of the pizza onto one pan and took the others to a sink. Soon, the kitchen was empty as everyone went to work.

Polly was putting plates into the dishwasher as Jeff walked in and said, "Is there breakfast this morning?"

"You're just in time!" Andy exclaimed and pulled a plate back out of the cupboard. She set it down in front of him.

"I swear, Polly. I've already gained 3 pounds since I started working here," he complained.

"Not my fault!" she said. "And if you want to start running Obiwan around the property every day, I'm fine with that. Otherwise," she turned and waggled her index finger at him, "choices and consequences, bud, choices and consequences."

"Whatever," he said and taking a cup of coffee with his plate, left for his office.

Polly wiped down the counter and prep area, started the dishwasher and set some napkins beside the leftover pizza, checked the coffee pot and then said to Andy, "Thank you for your help. I didn't expect that this morning."

"I suspect you didn't expect a catastrophe at the front steps either. Sometimes we have to go with the flow."

"Well, thank you anyway. I kept you away from what you were planning to do, though."

"I'll go in and get started. I can't wait to dig into that database."

"Why don't I send Doug and Billy in to set up a table for you," Polly said.

"That would make it easier," Andy said. "Thanks."

Andy went into the auditorium and Polly walked over to the classrooms to ask the boys to handle the table setup for Andy. Without any hesitation, other than to look at Jerry for permission to leave their work, they trotted over to help out. She wasn't sure what she was going to do when they were no longer around. While Jerry had them out on other jobs, they'd spent quite a bit of time at Sycamore House and were beginning to feel like family. Polly felt a little sad at the thought of these projects closing down and having everyone gone. She walked into her office and woke her computer up.

Before she could start feeling too sorry for herself, Jeff peeked around the corner. "Got a minute?" he asked.

"Sure," she said. "Come on in."

"What has you looking so sad," he asked. "Did something happen?"

"I was thinking about how much I'm going to miss having all this activity around here. These people are like my family now and pretty soon, they'll finish all of this and be gone!"

"Umm. Well. I don't know what to say about that. Nothing lasts forever?" He looked at her with his eyebrows raised.

Polly picked up a piece of paper, wadded it and threw it at him. It landed well short of its target.

"What did you want?" she asked.

"Henry has the wood ordered for the barn I've set a date. What do you think?"

"As long as the weather holds out and Sylvie thinks she can pull it off, I think it is great!" Polly replied.

"Then I'm going to start advertising and Henry is lining up workers. I'm talking to a couple of bands to see who is available that night for the dance."

"Dance? Wait. What? There's going to be a dance?" Polly cried out.

"What did you think we would do at a hoe-down?" Jeff asked.

"I thought there would be a lot of food and maybe some entertainment or something, but a dance?"

"Do you have a problem with dancing?"

"It might be the same problem you have with riding horses. I fall down!" Polly said.

"We're going to have a dance and you can either dance or hide, I don't care."

"Surely I can say no," Polly said. "I still have some rights as the boss around here, don't I?"

"Nope. You can't tell me no because you're scared of something. You can only tell me no because you think it is a bad idea."

"Then I think it's a bad idea. The owner of Sycamore House should never be seen with her bottom on the floor and her feet straight up in the air. It's embarrassing!"

Jeff didn't say another word, just rose up out of his chair and left the office.

"Hey!" she called out. "Hey!" Polly followed him into his office.

"It's not going to work," he said as he sat down at his desk. "You can't be so scared of dancing that you will stop me from

44

doing this."

"Fine," she said. "Fine. I'm going to head over to Dr. Hottie's office to pick Leia up. I'll be back after a while."

"A dance," Polly muttered as she went back to her office and grabbed the truck keys. "A dance. It's not fair."

CHAPTER FIVE

Tapping her fingers on the exam table, Polly stood in a small room waiting for Leia to be returned to her. The door opened and Mark Ogden walked in, followed by Marnie Evans, who was holding Leia on top of her blanket.

"Good morning, Polly!" he said, shaking her hand. "Everything went fine yesterday and she's ready to go home." Marnie placed the cat bundle onto the exam table and kept her hand on Leia while Mark Ogden pulled a sheet of paper out of the folder he was holding. "Here are recommendations for the next few days. I know the boys in her life are going to want to play with her. You might want to think about separating them."

He unconsciously brushed a lock of curls away from his forehead and Polly tried not to stare. She suddenly realized he was still talking to her and she hadn't heard anything, so she nodded and smiled.

"So, Marnie here will take care of setting that up, then," she heard him say and snapped back into consciousness. She was supposed to respond now and looked desperately at Marnie who shook her head and grinned.

He reached down and rubbed the top of Leia's head and said, "You did well, little Leia. We'll see you next week." He put his hand out to take Polly's again and she nodded at him as he left.

Marnie laughed out loud, "You're not the only one who has that reaction to him, but I'd have to say you have it worse than most!"

"Oh no," Polly gasped. "Was I that obvious?"

"Not to him. That man is completely oblivious. All the girls working here have a terrible crush on him. Heck, even I do and I'm happily married. It doesn't occur to him that all of our walk-in customers are female. Fortunately, he's generally out of here pretty early to work out on farms. Have you met his partner? He's not quite as adorable, but he's single too!"

"His partner? I had no idea!" Polly said.

"He came into the practice a few months ago. Doc Ogden needed someone to concentrate more on small animals so he could do what he really loves."

"What's that?" Polly asked.

"He's a horse man from way back. Those animals have his heart and soul, it seems. He likes being outside too. You know, you're one of the lucky few he decided needed his personal attention in the office."

Polly blushed. "Whatever," she said.

"No, really!" Marnie insisted. "He has cut back his small animal clientèle to a scant few. You're one of them."

Polly grinned and couldn't help it, her insides skipped up and down. But, this was crazy. She had a date with Henry on Friday and for Pete's sake, she didn't need more men complicating her life. She reached over and grabbed Leia and the blanket into her arms and went out to the front counter with Marnie following. As Marnie scooted around her to get behind the counter, she said, "Will next week work to bring her back in to remove the stitches?"

"Sure," Polly said and pulled a credit card out of her back pocket to pay her bill. "Sure, that will be fine."

"Here's a card with the date and time on it. Put it in your calendar, alright? You don't seem to be thinking on all cylinders right now," Marnie laughed and completed the transaction.

Polly shook herself and kissed the top of Leia's head. "I'm fine. Thanks and I'll see you next week."

As soon as she got into her truck, she put Leia on the seat beside her. "Did you hear that, little girl? He kept me as a client! I'm swooning a little on the inside, but maybe I should pay attention while driving us home!"

She pulled out of the parking lot and drove back to Sycamore House. Lydia's Jeep was sitting in the parking lot, and she pulled in beside it. She jumped down out of the truck, gathered Leia and the blanket into her arms and went inside to her office. Until she figured out how to keep her animals separate, the kitten might as well hang out down here. She'd bring down an extra litter box and some food and Little Girl would be fine for a while.

Polly got Leia settled in behind her desk and left her office, pulling the door shut behind her. The kitten looked up and snuggled back into the blanket, promptly falling asleep. Polly stuck her head in the classrooms and waved at Henry, who was installing bookshelves, then walked to the auditorium. She found Lydia and Andy sitting on the edge of the stage with a crate of items between them. They looked up as she approached.

"There you are," Lydia said. "How's your cat?"

"She's good. I have to keep her away from the boys, so I might have to build a nest for her in my office. What are you doing here this morning?"

"I just came from Madeline Black's house. You know I had to meet the company that would clean up the area where she died, right?"

"Sure. How was it?" Polly asked.

"I was just telling Andy. Once the body was gone, it wasn't quite as awful, but they'll be there for a while. I called her son again this morning. He's not a nice guy." She paused and thought. "And it doesn't make any sense. Madeline was such a sweetheart. I don't know what happened to him. He told me that he was talking to the funeral home and if I wanted to know more about the particulars, I could call them." She shook her head. "I wish I knew how to reach out to him, but I don't think he wants that from me."

"Did you ask about the note she was writing when she died?" Polly pulled a chair out from the table and sat down in front of the two ladies.

"I did and he didn't have any idea what she might have been talking about. I did manage to get his sister's telephone number from him, though. I'll call her this evening to ask if she'd like us to help with anything. Maybe she has more information."

"Neither of those kids stayed around here after graduation, did they?" Andy asked.

"Laurence is down in Creston and Amy lives out in the San Francisco area. Her husband works for some software company." Lydia took in a deep breath and said, "Laurence informed me that since they had both spent Christmas day with their mother, he wasn't recommending they do anything other than lock the house up and leave it until they had more time."

Polly nodded her head slowly, "So no one is going to worry about what Madeline meant in her note?"

"He's not," Lydia huffed. "I am, though. I'm not sure how, but I'm going to make sure her last request isn't tossed aside."

Polly turned around when she heard footsteps on the floor. Sylvie walked in and over to the three of them.

"Hi there!" she said. "I bought books today from Amazon. They'll be here on Friday. Did you guys know I was going to college?" She giggled and pulled another chair up.

"What a wonderful surprise!" Lydia laughed with her. "We're proud of you, Sylvie."

"Thanks. What are you doing today? I drove by and saw your cars, so I thought there might be something fun going on. I'm a free woman until the boys are done with school."

Polly checked the time on her phone. "We should go out to lunch!" She jumped up, then sat back down. "Wait. I have a cat who just came home from the doctor. I don't want to leave her in my office all alone, and I should take Obiwan out for a run before I do anything."

Lydia shook her head, "That's what happens when you get kids in your life. I like having my kids all grown up. How about you, Andy?"

Andy smiled. "It is nice to be free again. I miss seeing them every day, but I don't miss being stuck at home. Why don't we run up to the Diner and bring something back? Isn't that close enough to going out for lunch?"

The four figured out what they wanted to order and Lydia called Joe's Diner while Polly ran upstairs to get Obiwan. As she pulled the door shut to her apartment and headed back to the stairway, Elise Myers' door opened. "Polly?" she asked quietly.

"Hi, Elise. Is everything alright? I was going to take Obiwan out for a few minutes."

"Everything is fine. I was going to head downstairs and make a sandwich. Would you want to eat lunch with me?" Elise said timidly.

"Well, I have some friends here," Polly began.

"I'm sorry. I don't want to interrupt," the girl said.

"No, what I meant to say was that we were going to bring in takeout from Joe's Diner. I'd love to have you meet my friends. There are only three here today and we could bring back lunch for you, too."

"No, that's alright. I don't want to be a bother." Elise turned to head back to her room.

"Elise. Really. We'd love to have you join us. We're going to sit around a table downstairs and eat and jabber. Please join us."

"Are you sure?"

"Absolutely. Would you like a club sandwich?" Polly asked.

"If it's a diner, I'll bet they have a killer hot beef sandwich on mashed potatoes. I'd love something like that."

"I'm on it," Polly said. "When the food arrives, I'll run up and get you. You will be perfectly safe with these ladies, alright?"

"Thank you, Polly." Elise closed the door softly behind her.

"Obiwan, I believe that was a big step for her. Now I have to tell the ladies to be gentle." They walked downstairs and into the auditorium. Lydia had just hung up her phone.

"Lydia, I'm sorry. Could you place one more order? The girl who is staying upstairs is going to join us. She'd like a hot beef sandwich," Polly said.

"Sure! Just a second." Lydia redialed and ordered the sandwich, then turned back to Polly. "I haven't seen her around town or anything. It will be nice to meet her!"

"Well, she's quite shy and easily intimidated. She literally ran into Doug and Billy this morning and had everyone on the floor. When Henry arrived on the scene, it was too much and she ended up in her room in tears. So," and she looked at each of them, "go easy on her when she joins us, okay?"

They smiled, then Andy said, "At least Beryl isn't here." They all laughed with her and Polly left to take Obiwan outside. It was too cold to spend much time in the yard, but the two of them made one good lap around the building. When they arrived at the front door, Lydia was backing out of the parking lot and waved at them.

"Alright, bud. Upstairs with you. I think the boys will be here this afternoon to play, be patient," she said as they walked up the steps to her apartment. She gathered up the extra litter box, litter, food and a dish for Leia. Setting things down in the outer office downstairs, she jogged back to the kitchen to grab a dish of water and when she looked in the window to her office, saw Leia standing on her desk.

Polly opened the door, "Well, hello there! You're awake! Here, let's get things set up for you." She cuddled the kitten in her arms as she set the litter box on the floor behind a bookshelf and poured in the litter. Putting Leia down so she could smell it, Polly set out food and water. The kitten took a few drinks and sniffed at the kibble, then nudged Polly's foot.

"Are you missing your peeps, little one? It's going to be a few more days and I need to figure out what I'm going to do with you at night." Polly picked her up again and sat down at the desk with the cat on her lap. "But I won't leave you alone, I promise. I'm awfully glad you're home."

She snuggled the kitten with her left hand while using her right hand on the mouse to check email. Nothing terribly important was happening, so she closed it down and sat back in her chair. Leia crawled up onto Polly's chest, set her head on her right shoulder and began to purr.

"Well, isn't this the life," Henry said, walking into Polly's office. He sat down across from her and leaned back.

"It is pretty wonderful, isn't it?" Polly agreed.

"We're nearly finished installing bookshelves in the first two rooms and I think Jerry and the boys will be completely done with electricity tomorrow."

"It hit me how much I'm going to miss everyone when this is finished," Polly said. "I wish I could keep you all around forever." She chuckled. "I couldn't afford that, I suppose, but I'm not going to like having the place quiet."

"I'm sure you'll find a reason to keep us coming back often enough. I heard Doug and Billy talk about using the computer room for their game parties. They're pretty excited about the wiring they are putting in. You might think they were putting in their dream game room."

"They can come in and use it whenever they want. I've never known such respectful young men." She snorted. "Listen to me, 'respectful young men,' I sound like I'm sixty years old or something."

"Their mamas raised 'em right," Henry said. "And Jerry has done well with them. When they finally grow up, they'll make pretty terrific men."

Lydia walked in the front door and waved at Polly. Henry saw the box of take-out bags and said, "Hey! You didn't get lunch for me?"

"Nope," Polly responded. "It's a girls' lunch." She held up her finger. "And don't give me any trouble about it. Elise is coming down to eat with us and you made her cry this morning."

"I what?" he exclaimed. "I didn't mean to make her cry. All I did was walk in the front door."

"I know," Polly laughed. "It's alright. She's uncomfortable around people and all of a sudden I think you were one more than she could handle. So stay away, okay?"

He dropped his chin to his chest. "Fine. I'll eat my boring lunch with the rest of the guys." He stood up to leave. "You should stop in and see our progress after lunch."

"I will. Now go." She shooed him out, then put her sleeping kitty back on the blanket, shut the door and ran up the steps. A quick knock on Elise's door and the girl met her, wearing jeans and a blue top. Her feet were still in slippers, but she'd curled her hair and put mascara on.

"Do I look alright?" she asked Polly.

"You look great. So ... you're meeting Lydia, Andy and Sylvie. They're three of my best friends in the world and they are very nice and easy going. Don't worry, okay?"

"I'm fine," Elise said. "This is good. I'll be fine."

Polly led Elise to the auditorium. Andy and Sylvie had set things up and Styrofoam containers sat at places around the table. After introductions, everyone sat down and the chatter quieted as they began to eat.

Polly looked up from her pork tenderloin sandwich, "Will I ever get to the point where I have had enough of these and can order something else?"

Elise peered at Polly's plate, "I don't think I've ever tasted one."

"We have to change that! Here!" Polly sliced off a chunk of her sandwich, complete with all the toppings and, spearing it with her fork, pushed it toward the girl. "You have to try it! This is one of those things Iowa restaurants have made nearly perfect."

Elise took the piece of sandwich off Polly's fork with her hands and put it in her mouth. As soon as she began to chew, she smiled. "I like it! I'm going to have more of these."

They all chuckled and Lydia said, "Stick with us, girl. We'll show you all the joys of eating in Iowa. And there are plenty! What are you getting your Doctorate in, Elise?"

The poor girl rapidly swallowed the bite in her mouth and said, "Mathematics. You won't believe it, but I've been researching social networks. It sounds kind of funny since I don't seem to have any of my own." Her eyes drifted off for a moment and she dropped her head.

"Social Networks? Like Facebook and Linked In?" Andy asked.

"Yes, and many others. I posit that we can measure a person's friendship network and predict future relationships. That's where my research has been taking me and that's the math I've been working out," Elise responded.

"You can tell me what relationships I will have in the future?" Lydia looked astounded.

"Well, yes and no. I did some experiments on and pulled data from some of the popular social networks as relationships between friends and friends of friends were created. The numbers tell me that to some degree math can predict how you will interact and build your network of friends based on who your current friends know."

Polly shook her head. "I feel like I'm watching an old episode of NUMB3RS and Charlie Eppes is about to say, 'Imagine, if you will …'"

Elise giggled. "I'm not nearly as cute as he was, nor am I as at ease telling people what is going on up in my head. He always had great analogies for the things he was doing. I just do them."

Lydia patted her arm, "You were fine. I'm an old lady and I think I get what you're saying. And if I don't, that's alright, too."

Polly tossed a french fry across the table into Lydia's container while Elise looked on with wide eyes, "You're not old."

Lydia turned to Sylvie, "Did you hear about our dead body yesterday?" she asked.

Elise stopped with her fork poised in the air, "You found another dead body? Here at Sycamore House?"

"Oh no, dear. I went to check on an elderly friend of mine, and she had died in her house," Lydia said.

Elise put her fork back down into her Styrofoam container with her mouth wide open.

"It wasn't that bad and she's at the funeral home now, don't worry," Lydia continued.

Sylvie said, "Was that Madeline Black? I heard she died, and I should have known you were there." She shuddered. "I'm glad I wasn't. I think I'd like to keep my limit of dead bodies at zero. Have you talked to her kids?"

Lydia scowled. "I talked to her son yesterday. He wasn't at all interested in doing anything other than call in professionals. I didn't talk to Amy, though, because he said he would let her know."

"I should probably call her and find out when she's coming home," Sylvie responded. "We were pretty close friends in high school. And her brother was always kind of a jerk. For some reason, he thought he was quite a hot shot. He was a lot older than we were and out of college while we were still in high school. I think he is an engineer and works down in Creston."

"He sure does," Lydia said. "Would you really call her?"

"Of course! When she does come back to the Midwest it is always for such a short time and we rarely see each other. I should make a point of it this time," Sylvie said.

"Well, I have a little mystery maybe she could help me solve, if you wouldn't mind asking her about it," Lydia said and told Sylvie and Elise about the note that had been found on the table and the fact that Laurence Black had no intention of looking into it.

"I will call her and ask," Sylvie said. "In fact, I'll step out and do that right now." She picked up her phone and walked out of the auditorium.

"How's your kitten, Polly?" Andy asked. "Did everything go well?"

"She's great, though I'm not sure what I'm going to do with her at night. Dr. Hottie thinks I should keep her away from the boys until she heals up a little more." Polly's voice lowered into a conspiratorial whisper, "That man is gorgeous! And Marnie told me I was one of the few small animal clients he didn't turn over to his partner. What do you think about that?"

Lydia's laugh filled the auditorium. "Oh my, the single men of Bellingwood are going to enjoy having you around, Polly. The single women? They're going to hate you."

"I'm just having a good time. It's nice to have some freedom and enjoy hanging out with people. It's not like he's acted terribly interested in me, though. This morning he told me how to take care of Leia and then left. I guess I'll have to settle for enjoying my date Friday night with Henry," Polly said.

"Yeah. Like that's settling," Andy smirked.

"I know! But, tell me what I'm supposed to do with my little girl? Do I just hover over her and not let her on the floor with Luke and Obiwan?" Polly asked.

"I could help you," Elise said timidly.

"I don't want to bother you with animals. You have a lot of work ahead of you and this is the week you start flipping your schedule, isn't it?" Polly said.

"But, that would be perfect. She'd be a great companion while I was shifting my sleep hours. My cats were always up all night and slept during the day. We'd do fine. Really. I'd love to have her around for a while."

Polly looked around the table, "My life was never this easy when I lived by myself in Boston," she remarked. "Thank you, Elise. I think Leia would love having all your attention. It will only be for a week. We'll mix her back in with the boys and you can play with the kittens any time after that."

Elise smiled and picked up her food. "I'm going upstairs to finish this and get back to work. There are some things I want to research about real, live friendship networks before I start writing."

She stood up and walked to the door, then turned around. "Thank you," she said.

Polly said, "I'll bring Leia up in a little while and we'll get everything settled in your room, okay? Thank you!"

Sylvie walked back in after Elise had left and sat down, "Was everything okay with her?"

"Sure. I think she had a little inspiration," Lydia said. "What did Amy have to say?"

"She's coming into Des Moines by herself tomorrow and her family will come out for the funeral on Monday. She says she is planning to go through some of her mom's things this week. She doesn't know anything about a mystery or what her mom could possibly have meant, but was wondering if you," and she looked at Lydia, "might have time for lunch at her mother's house on Friday or Saturday."

"And," Sylvie continued, "she said to tell you that if Laurence was short with you on the phone, you shouldn't take it personally. He's annoyed because Madeline asked Amy to be the executor of the estate and he's informed her that if she is going to do it, she will do it all. He's mad at the world, not at you."

Lydia smiled. "That makes more sense, then. And I'd love to have lunch with her. Thank you, Sylvie."

CHAPTER SIX

A ha! There was the ace of diamonds! Polly was in her office Friday afternoon playing a game of Solitaire on her computer. Things had been quiet the last couple of days. Elise had taken Leia in and seemed to love having the companionship even though Polly worried a little bit about getting her kitten back. The glass company had quite a few of the bookcases covered and Andy was already filling them with items from the crates. She had set up an account with the newspaper office downtown to print signs and information placards for the displays.

Yesterday afternoon it had been cold enough that Polly met Jason and Andrew outside their school to bring them over to Sycamore House. Even though Sylvie didn't start classes until next week, she was working as many hours as possible and everyone seemed happy with the arrangement, especially Obiwan. Those boys wanted to be out as often as possible with him, so one or the other would take him out to play throughout the afternoon and early evening. Polly had made supper last night and invited Elise to come over and eat with them. She was quite comfortable with the boys, telling Polly they reminded her of her older brothers when they were kids.

Henry popped his head in the door at four thirty. "I'm taking off now. You're picking me up, right?"

She looked up and nodded at him. "Sure. I'll be there around six."

"Do you even know where I live?" he asked. "You've never been there. In fact," Henry paused and scowled at her. "You've never seen my shop!"

"You're right. I know," she responded. "But, I think I can find your house. You're over on Willow, aren't you?"

"Yes," he agreed. "But, do you know which Willow?"

"Well, it's not the one that goes past the Elevator, so I'm assuming I'll turn on Monroe and go over and find your place. The shop should be obvious, shouldn't it?" Even she knew she was sounding a little snippy.

"Yeah," he said. "I guess you can find me. I'll see you at six, then."

"Great," she said, trying to put a smile back on her face. "I'll see you then."

He left and she closed the Solitaire window. What was up with her? Then it hit her that it might have something to do with the fact that she'd made absolutely no plans for tonight and it was her responsibility to take him out on a date. She'd set herself up for failure on this one, hadn't she.

Polly quickly opened her browser and searched for theaters in Ames. It had been a long time since she'd paid any attention to what new movies were out, she was sure nothing would be familiar. She didn't even know what kind of movies Henry liked. Great date planner she was. As soon as she'd found the theaters, she looked for restaurants she could get into. It took her about 15 minutes to get her plans in place, but then she felt better. She had a plan and a general idea where to head once she got into the city.

Sylvie walked past the window to her office and waved. She poked her head in and said, "I'm here to pick the boys up. I take it they're in with Andy?"

Polly stood up and walked out with Sylvie, "I think they're

having as much fun as she is." They opened the doors to the auditorium and walked in. The boys and Andy acknowledged their presence by looking up from a crate they were digging through and went back to their work.

"What are you doing tonight, Polly?" Sylvie asked.

"I'm taking Henry out on a date. Can you imagine that?" Polly said. "I got a little pushy with him about making things equal, so it ended up being my turn. We're going to dinner and a movie. What about you?"

"Amy's in town and staying at her mother's house. I told her we would take her out to dinner at Davey's tonight." Sylvie stepped forward and spoke in a louder voice, "Boys, we have to get going."

Andy looked up, "What time is it?" she asked.

"Nearly five o'clock," Sylvie said. "And I need these boys to get dressed up for dinner, so I'm going to steal them from you."

Andy flung her hands in the air. "Five o'clock! I told Bill I'd come out tonight and babysit. I have to scoot!" She followed Jason and Andrew to the door. "These boys are a great help to me, Sylvie." She wrapped her arms around Andrew, then patted Jason on the back. "Thanks for everything boys, I'll see you next week!" She stood there beside Polly as they left.

"Did I hear you say you're taking Henry out tonight?" she asked Polly.

"I am. We're going to Ames. I should probably hurry upstairs and get ready to go. It does feel strange being in charge of this date."

"You'll be fine and you'll have fun. Now, do you mind if I leave a mess in here?" Andy asked.

"No, I don't mind at all. We'll pull these doors shut and lock them, and it will be here for you on Monday." Polly walked Andy to the front door and watched as she drove away. Jogging up the steps, she stopped at the top, hearing what sounded like crying coming from Elise Myers' room. She walked over to the door, listened for a moment and heard steady sobbing.

She knocked on the door, "Elise? Are you alright? Elise?"

"I'm fine. Just a minute." The door opened and Elise stood there in her hoodie and sweatpants, her face and eyes red, tears still on her cheeks. "I'm sorry, was I bothering you?"

"No," Polly said. "I was just a little worried about you. Is everything alright?"

"It will be," Elise said. "But, I can't talk about it now."

Her eyes filled with tears again and Polly reached out to touch her, but Elise pulled away and moved to shut the door. "I'm sorry," the girl said. "I need to get back to work."

"Alright. Let me know if you need anything. But, you should also know, I'm leaving for the evening. There's plenty of food in the refrigerator downstairs. Help yourself to anything you want."

"Thank you, Polly," Elise said as she closed the door to her room.

"Weird," Polly thought and walked across the hall to her apartment. Obiwan and Luke were curled up together on the sofa and looked up as she walked in. "Come on, Obiwan," she said. "I don't have much time and you need one last run before I leave.

He pulled himself up and stretched, then put his paws on the floor in front of the couch and stretched again. Luke seemed annoyed at being disturbed, but snuggled into the warm spot the dog had left behind.

"Come on," she said, as she pulled on her coat and gloves. "We have to hurry!"

He sat in front of her, waiting for the leash to be snapped on to his collar, then they went downstairs and outside. Polly looked up into the windows of Elise's room and saw her staring outside, as if watching for something. Who could know what news she had received? Elise caught her eye and waved, then moved away from the window and Polly continued walking with Obiwan. She didn't let him stay outside too long, knowing she needed to quickly shower and change her clothes. At least she didn't have to dress up tonight. She wasn't quite as formal as Henry when it came to dating.

The big "Sturtz Contracting and Woodworking Services" sign on the front of the building beside his house was a rather significant clue when it came to finding where Henry lived. His truck was another. Polly rolled her eyes and laughed. "It wasn't that hard to find you, ya nut," she said to herself as she opened the door of her truck. Then, she stopped in her tracks. Back or front door? Oh, to heck with it and she walked up the steps to the front door and rang the doorbell.

Henry was living in the same house his parents had owned for many years. He had told her it was also his grandparent's home, so it had been in his family a long time. It was a large, two-story home with a porch that extended across the entire front of the house. The door was in the middle and on one end a porch swing hung from the ceiling. He answered the door and invited her inside.

"I'm almost ready to go. Let me get my coat."

The front room was also the length of the house and looked as if it were two living rooms, one on either side of the front door. She could see through a very short hallway into what must be the dining room. There was an old piano on the far wall of that room and she could see a little bit of the dining room table. On the right side of the little hallway was a doorway, which she assumed led to the basement. The closet was at the end of the left living area. He pulled out a short leather jacket and shrugged into it, then zipped it shut.

Then he chuckled, "I hope you're not taking me somewhere fancy for dinner tonight. I'm probably not dressed for it."

"You look great," she laughed. And he did. Jeans suited this man. A dark blue sweater with small flecks of white covered a button down shirt and it suddenly occurred to her that all of that blue accented the color of his eyes. Huh. She noticed his eye color. That was new for her.

"Well?" he asked. "Are you finished? Am I fine?"

She snorted with laughter and blushed immediately. "Whatever!" she said and turned around to go back outside.

He pulled the door shut to the house and followed her down the steps, hurrying to open the door of the truck for her. "Don't even," he said as she tried to object.

Polly laughed and stepped up on the running board and into the truck. Henry walked around and got in on the other side, then asked. "Where are we going?"

"Hickory Park. I haven't been there in years. Is barbecue alright?"

"I can't believe you haven't been there since you got back. Of course it's alright!" He smiled at her. "Can I have ice cream, too?"

She laughed again. "If you have ice cream before we go to the movie, there won't be any room for popcorn!"

"There's always room for popcorn. And Twizzlers. I want popcorn and Twizzlers and an Icee. Well, maybe not the Icee. I'll have to see how full I am."

Polly shook her head and laughed. "Anything you want. But, if you eat so much it keeps you up all night, don't call me."

He pouted and said, "That's no fun. Usually if you pay for it, you own it."

"That's sick. I'm not owning your pain and agony, so there."

He turned in his seat, "Tell me what's up with your guest?"

"What do you mean?" Polly asked.

"I don't know. I was just making conversation. She seemed totally freaked out when I walked in the front door the other day and I haven't seen hide nor hair of her since then."

"I've never been around someone who is that afraid of people," Polly said. "She ate lunch with me, Lydia, Sylvie and Andy the other day, too, but other than that, she has kept out of sight. Now, she did say she is going to begin flipping her days and nights around, and she is taking care of Leia while little girl is recuperating from her surgery, so maybe she has turned into a night owl and we will never see her during the day."

"Don't you think that's odd?" he asked.

"I suppose from our standpoint it is," she replied. "But, I guess that if I open those rooms up to people who are trying to escape the real world and explore their creativity, I'm not necessarily going to be getting run of the mill clients."

Henry chuckled. "I guess not. How long is she staying?"

"She's paid me for two months." Henry's face showed the shock he was feeling and Polly said, "I know! But, she's the one paying for it. She told me her family came up with the money to send her here and it's not like she can leave. She doesn't even have a car."

"That gets stranger and stranger," Henry said. "Well, maybe when there's a movie made about another eccentric mathematician ... her ... they'll find gorgeous, young actors to play us."

"Okay, changing the subject," Polly began. "Are we truly going to be able to pull off a barn raising?"

"It's not going to be a problem, Polly!" Henry said, assuring her. "The lumber and all necessary supplies will be delivered on Wednesday. That will give us time to make sure everything is ready. I've already lined up twelve or fifteen guys to help and they're already talking about what fun it will be. I'm guessing there could be close to fifty men here that day. I've also contracted a crane and operator to lift the trusses for the roof. I think it will be fine."

"I'm trusting you with this, Henry. I have no idea how it is supposed to work," Polly said.

"I don't know how the event is supposed to work, but I can get the structure built. It will actually be pretty cool to see it go up in one day." He paused and said, "Unless we end up with a whole lot of people, the inside work will happen after the structure is up."

"Whew!" Polly exclaimed. "I couldn't imagine how you would do the electricity and build out the stalls on that day."

"No," he said, trying to assure her, "there will be plenty of work that happens before and afterwards, too."

Polly's phone rang. She pulled it out of the pocket of her jacket and looked at the number. She didn't recognize the area code, so answered it with, "Sycamore House, can I help you?"

"I'm looking for Linda Marberry, could you connect me to her room?" said the man's voice on the other end.

"I'm sorry," Polly said. "You must have a wrong number. There is no one by that name here."

"Linda Marberry. I'm certain she is there. She would have checked in two weeks ago."

"Again, I'm sorry," Polly replied. "I know no one by that name and we are not a hotel. No one has checked in using that name in the last two weeks."

"It is urgent that I reach her. There has been a death in the family and she must return home."

Polly took a deep breath. "I'm sorry that I can't help you. There is no one here by that name."

Henry looked at her quizzically. She shook her head and said into the phone, "Thank you for calling," and hung up.

"What was that?" he asked.

Polly was pulling into the parking lot of the restaurant, spotted a parking place and aimed her truck toward it as a small car pulled in. "Damn," she growled. "Brat."

She drove to the other end of the parking lot and pulled into another space, turned the truck off and sat in her seat. "Someone called looking for a Linda Marberry. He said she checked in two weeks ago, exactly when Elise got here. Then he said that someone in her family died. I wonder if that was why she was crying this afternoon. But, it doesn't make any sense."

"Do you mean, why she would change her name?" Henry asked.

"And why would someone call me to get to her and not call her cell phone. Someone has her number and called her today," Polly agreed.

"And why is she there without a car? How can you live in a rural community in Iowa without a car for two months?" Henry continued.

"And why is she hiding upstairs all the time and ... "Polly looked at him, stricken. "What is going on here? I thought I had a terribly shy math nerd upstairs. Do I?"

"I don't know," Henry said. "Is there something we should do about this tonight or can we have dinner?"

Polly sat back in her seat. "Oh, we're having dinner. What am I supposed to do, walk up to her room and ask if she is Linda Marberry? If she is and doesn't want me to know, she'll only lie to me. If she isn't, she'll think I'm nuts."

Henry got out of the truck and walked around to hold her door as she opened it. He held his hand out as she jumped to the ground, then said, "Got your keys?"

She patted her coat pocket and nodded in acknowledgment as he tripped the lock button on the driver's side door. He took her arm as they walked up to the front of the restaurant. After they were seated, Polly looked at the menu and remembered how intimidating it was. "I don't know what to order," she said to Henry. He laughed and shrugged and spent a few moments poring over the menu himself.

When the waiter arrived, Polly looked panicked and Henry ordered first, then both men looked at her expectantly. "Fine," she said. "Barbecue Dinner," and placed her menu in the waiter's open hand.

"What would you like for your two sides?" he asked, chuckling by this point and returned the menu to her when her face fell. He pointed at the listing of sides and waited while she glanced at it.

"Green beans and cottage cheese," she quickly said. "Am I done now?" The waiter nodded and walked away.

Henry said, "Not good under pressure?"

"Shut up," she responded. "Alright. Maybe not."

"How much longer ..." she began and her phone buzzed again. She pulled it out and looked at it. The area code was the same as the last call, but the number was different. She showed it to Henry, then answered it, "Sycamore House."

"I'm looking for Linda Marberry," a different voice announced.

"I'm sorry," Polly responded. "There is no Linda Marberry at this number."

"Look, lady. I don't know who you think you are, but you must connect me with Linda Marberry immediately."

"I'm trying to be polite about this. You must have a wrong number. Please do not call back."

The phone clicked off and Polly sat for a moment with her phone still at her ear.

"Is everything alright, Polly?" Henry asked.

"Okay, that was two phone calls and I don't like it." She looked up at him. "Henry, I'm sorry, but I don't think I can do a movie tonight. I want to go back to Sycamore House after dinner. I'm not comfortable with Elise being there alone if people are looking for her."

"Do you want to leave right now? I can ask the waiter to box up our meals and we can take them to go."

"Would you mind?" she asked. "I think I'm going to call Aaron and see what he says about this."

"I'll be right back." Henry picked up his coat and stepped out of the booth. She watched as he flagged down their waiter who nodded and went into the kitchen. Polly stood up, picked up her coat and walked over to him as the waiter returned with the ticket. Henry tried to take it, but Polly snatched it away, looked at it, then handed a credit card to the waiter who smiled at them. Henry shook his head and smiled back.

Within a few minutes, the transaction was taken care of, the food had come out of the kitchen in a bag and the two were heading back to Polly's truck.

"I'm so sorry, Henry. This isn't what I wanted for tonight," she apologized.

"Polly," he said, "please don't worry about it. We'll deal with this and then have dinner and a movie another night. It's alright."

"Do you mind if I call Aaron?" she asked.

"Give me your keys. I'll drive. You call Aaron," he responded.

She tossed him her keys and after he unlocked her door and held it for her, she pulled her seatbelt on and waited for him to get in and settled. As he pulled out of the parking lot, she dialed Aaron.

"Hello Polly. I thought you were on a date tonight with Henry. Do I need to arrest him for something?"

She laughed. "No, but I need your help again."

"What's up?"

Polly told him about the strange phone calls and her reclusive resident. "I'm worried about her, Aaron," she said finally.

"That does sound a little odd," Aaron agreed. "Why don't you text the phone numbers to me and I'll see what I can find out for you. I hate to say this again, Polly, but I still don't like the idea of you living in that big ole place alone."

"Good heavens, Aaron. Are you going to make Doug and Billy move in with me permanently?" she asked.

"Well, that would be pretty funny, but no, I suppose it makes no good sense. Send me the numbers and we'll talk tomorrow, alright?"

"Thank you, Aaron," Polly said and hung up.

Henry asked, "Are you worried something is going to happen tonight?"

"I don't know what to think. Do I wait to talk to Elise tomorrow after Aaron gets information on the phone calls or do I confront her with this tonight? Am I worried that someone is calling me to reach her and there are a lot of questions? Yes." She dropped her chin to her chest and shut her eyes.

"I hate feeling out of control," she said. "About the time things were getting normal again in my life, there's no more normal."

Henry reached across the console and took her hand. "I know. I get it. Tell me what I can do to help you out here."

"I don't think there's anything you can do," she responded. "Thanks."

They drove into Bellingwood and pulled up in front of Sycamore House. The security lights were on out front, but the only room with lights on was the room in which Elise was staying.

"Why don't I come in and we can watch a movie upstairs and have dinner?" Henry said.

"That sounds great," Polly replied. "I just don't feel comfortable being away tonight."

They left the truck parked in front of the building and went inside and up the stairs. Polly hesitated in front of Elise's room, but went on to her apartment and opened the door. Obiwan and Luke seemed glad to see her and while Henry took the food to the table, she snuggled them both, a cat in one arm and a dog's head under the other hand.

Soon he announced that dinner was served and they settled in to eat. After dinner, Polly and Henry pored over the movie guide and finally settled down to watch. Henry sat down at one end of the sofa and Polly took the other end, tucking her feet underneath her. She pulled a blanket over her and offered the other end to Henry who draped it across his lap. She snuggled into the pillow and promptly fell asleep.

A cold wet nose in the palm of Polly's hand woke her with a start. The movie playing on the television wasn't one she recognized as she peered across the room. She sat straight up and looked at the clock on her phone. It was 1:22 and Henry was asleep at the other end of the sofa.

"Henry?" she asked quietly.

His eyes popped open. "I must have fallen asleep!"

She laughed, "Well, that seems obvious. We both did."

"It's your fault, you know. You dropped off to sleep and looked so relaxed, I didn't want to disturb you and that was the last thing I remember."

"I should probably take you home. We have to get Sam and Jimmy and be in Ames by nine o'clock to pick up the rental truck."

"Alright." He sat up and stretched.

Obiwan had padded over to stand in front of the door and wagged as the two of them pulled their jackets on.

"Do you mind if he rides along?" Polly asked. "Then I can walk him one more time before I go to sleep."

"Sure!" Henry replied. "So, you didn't hear anything more from your callers."

"No, there was nothing more there. I don't want to do it, but I'm going to have to talk to Elise tomorrow. I can't imagine what she is going to say to me, though."

Polly hooked the leash on to Obiwan's collar and they went out to her truck. A light snowfall was coming down dusting the red truck and sidewalks. She could see the flakes in the light of the street lamps she had lining her driveway and began singing quietly to herself "Sleigh bells ring, are you listening, In the lane, snow is glistening, A beautiful sight, We're happy tonight. Walking in a winter wonderland."

"You're a little late with the Christmas songs, Polly," Henry remarked.

"Exactly how is that a Christmas song?" she chided. Obiwan began walking toward the side of the building and the two of them walked with him. Polly looked upstairs and noticed the lights were still on in Elise's room. She was well on her way to becoming a night owl.

She watched him process on the words of the song and then he said, "Whaddya know! It's not! I don't think I realized that."

"Once I get horses, I want to look for a sleigh," Polly said. "Wouldn't that be wonderful next winter?"

Henry cocked his head and looked at her sideways. "Sometime I need to show you my shop."

"Alright, random!" Polly laughed.

"It's not a random thought," Henry chuckled. "Though I didn't invite you to board my train of thought. I have a sleigh."

"You what?" she gasped. "You have a sleigh?"

"Dad and I found an old one several years ago and brought it back to restore it. It is still in terrible shape and you know how I hate restoration work."

"But now you will think about restoring it?"

"Maybe if I had some help," he smirked.

"I can't wait to see it!" Polly said. She moved the leash to her right hand and wrapped her arm around Henry's. "What fun we could have in the winter. We could have evening sleigh rides and come back for hot cocoa and popcorn. In December, we could project Christmas movies in the auditorium and turn Sycamore House into a Winter Wonderland!"

"You really love big experiences, don't you, Polly?"

"I guess I do and the more people who will share them with me, the better!" she laughed.

They'd walked all around the building and Obiwan headed back to the front door.

"Why don't you ride with us, Obiwan," Polly said as she guided him to the truck. Henry brushed the snow off the window, opened the door and pulled the seat forward so the dog could jump in to the back, then shut it and walked around to the driver's door, where he brushed more snow off and opened it for Polly.

"You're good at this whole chivalry thing, aren't you, Henry. You almost make it feel completely natural," she giggled.

He simply shook his head and shut the door when she got settled, then walked back to the passenger side and got in. Polly ran the windshield wipers and the snow scattered as she drove to Henry's house.

"Thanks for a nice evening," she said. "I'm sorry I fell asleep on you."

"Since I fell asleep as well, I'm pretty sure you don't need to apologize," he replied.

She pulled into his driveway and said, "Would you like me to walk you to your door?" Polly batted her eyelids at him.

"No, smart-stuff, I think I can make it on my own. Thanks for a nice evening."

"I'm sorry it didn't turn out to be quite the date we had planned, " she began.

"Don't worry about it," he waved her off. "It was nice relaxing with you and the animals." He turned around and looked at Obiwan who had his head on the console between the two of them. Henry moved to kiss her and the dog lifted up and licked him on the face.

Spluttering, Henry sat back. "Well, that's a first," he said. "Hoping to kiss a pretty girl and getting slobbered by a dog."

Polly pushed the dog back into the back seat and leaned across the console. As Henry bent over to kiss her, she quickly stuck her tongue out and licked his lips, then pulled back laughing. "Now, you've been slobbered by both of us!"

He whimpered a bit and shook his head. Turning back to Obiwan, he said, "You're a bad influence. This is the last time you ever get to participate in a date."

He opened the truck door and got out. "I'll be at your place around eight and we'll go from there, alright?"

"Sounds great! Good night!" Polly smiled as she watched him walk to his front door. He unlocked it, turned around and waved, then went inside and shut the door behind him. She backed out of his drive and headed home. "That was a nice night, Obiwan. But, I have to tell you. I like the idea that it's only you and me and the kitties at home when I get there. As much fun as I have with people during the day, I am not ready for someone to be living in my apartment with me!"

She patted the console and he made his way to the passenger seat, looking out the front window as they drove. When Polly pulled into the parking lot, she glanced up and saw Elise standing at one of the windows, leaning on the sill. She got out of the truck, holding Obiwan's leash and he ambled out behind her. When she looked up again, Elise had moved away from the window, so she and the dog went inside. Polly checked the door-locking app on her phone to ensure everything was locked down tight and as she mounted the first step, felt the phone buzz.

"Just wanted to make sure you are home and safe. Thanks for a nice evening." Henry's text made her smile.

She responded. *"We locked the place up and I'm heading upstairs. Thank you for going with the flow. See you in the morning. Good night."*

"Good night," came back and she trotted up the steps. She stood for a few moments at the top of the stairs, listening for any noises that might come from Elise's room, but gave up after a few moments and went to her own apartment. Curling up with her two furballs in bed, she fell asleep immediately.

CHAPTER SEVEN

"Lazy slug, I'm late!" Polly cried when she jumped out of bed at seven o'clock the next morning. "Obiwan, you always get me up at six. What's up with you! Get going! There's too much happening today to be lazing around. Get up!" She pulled on the sweatpants draped over the chair by the door and picked up a dirty pair of socks tucked under her jacket. Obiwan continued to lie on the bed as he watched her get dressed.

When she pulled on her jacket, he looked up expectantly. "Yes, you. With me! Now get moving. Come on!" She patted her leg as she walked out to the main room and he dashed past her to the front door. Grabbing the leash, she snapped it on him and said, "If you had given me more time this morning, I'd have been glad to let you wander, but you only have yourself to blame for a short walk." He licked her hand and she giggled. "You are never going to be mad at me are you, you sweet boy," she said, ruffling the top of his head. "Thank you for reminding me that nothing is all that important."

They took off down the steps and went outside for a quick run to the back of her property. As she jogged past the cement pad, she imagined what it would look like with a barn sitting there. A beautiful red barn with white trim and covered open areas on either side. She imagined a white fence surrounding the land and several horses in the pasture. She came up out of her reverie as they got to the creek. Polly and Obiwan skidded down the edge into the creek bed which was nearly dry because of the drought. He ran up and down among the vegetation sniffing at all the smells that had happened overnight. He crawled into one of the larger area of weeds and brush on the opposite side of the creek and all of a sudden, she felt a pull on her leash and he began howling.

Polly rushed to get to him, tearing apart the brush. He had gotten his front paw caught in a trap of some sort. She tried to figure out how to open it, but with his crying and whimpering and her own tears, she couldn't see how to make it work. Sitting down so he could put his head in her lap, she reached into her pocket, drew out her cell phone and dialed.

"Hello?" Henry answered.

"Henry, you have to help me!" she cried out.

"Polly, what's happened? Are you alright?"

"It's Obiwan. He's caught in some kind of trap and I can't get him out of it. He's hurting and I can't fix it." She knew it wasn't fair to him that she was close to sobbing.

"I'm out the door right now and getting in the truck. I'll be there in a couple of minutes."

Polly hung up and tried to look more closely at the trap. Her fingers were cold and she tried to pull the trap's stake out of the ground, but couldn't move it. Then she tried to pull it apart, but didn't have the strength.

Henry called her back. "Where are you? I'm here."

She described her location and heard the truck driving across her property. It didn't take long before she saw him come through the creek bed. He took one look at her tear streaked face and said, "You're going to have a tough time if you keep adding animals to your menagerie here and they find ways to get hurt."

"Shut up," she giggled through her tears. "Can you get him out of this?"

"I can," he said. "But I need your help. You are going to have to hold him still while I pry the thing apart, then pull his paw out quickly. There's a lot of tension on this thing."

Henry strained to pull the trap apart and when Polly felt Obiwan's paw give; she moved him quickly away and heard the trap snap shut again. Obiwan began licking his paw and looked at her, making soft sounds in his throat.

"Here, let me carry him," Henry said. "My truck is on the other side of the creek. When we get in, call Doc Ogden and tell him we're coming over."

He scooped the dog into his arms and waited while Polly got to her feet. The two of them crossed the creek and he waited as she got into the passenger side. He put the dog in her lap and shut the door. As soon as they were settled, she dialed the veterinarian's office and breathed a sigh of relief when Marnie answered.

"Marnie, Obiwan caught his paw in a trap. Can I bring him over so you guys can check him out?" she asked.

"Oh, Polly! Bring him right over. Doc's in early this morning because he's getting ready for a long day."

"Thanks, Marnie. We'll be right there." Polly hung up and said to Henry, "Doc Ogden just happens to be at the office. They're waiting for us." She put her head on top of Obiwan's, "And thank you for rescuing me. I don't think I could have pulled that open."

"If I couldn't get it open, I would have unhooked the trap from the stake," he began.

"What? I could have unhooked it?" she interrupted.

"Sure, but it would have meant leaving his paw in there longer. You did the right thing by calling me." He patted her knee and then reached up to stroke Obiwan's neck. "He wasn't in there very long. Hopefully there won't be any damage."

"How do you know about these things? You don't trap hunt too, do you?" she asked.

"No, but when I was a boy, my grandpa used to take me out with him every once in a while."

"You never cease to amaze me with the off the wall things you know. Thank you for coming over to help me." She looked down at herself. "For Pete's sake. I'm a mess! And we're going to be late to get the truck and head to Iowa Falls for the furniture!"

"Don't worry about that. Let's see what Doc Ogden says, and then if we need some extra time, I'll call Jimmy and Sam and tell them we'll be late. There isn't anything so important today that we can't run behind a bit. Okay?"

"Okay," she said as they pulled into the parking lot of the veterinarian's office. Henry jumped out and came over to her side. He opened the door and picked Obiwan up out of her lap. When they walked in the front door, Marnie was waiting for them and pointed to one of the consultation rooms. Henry carried the dog in and set him down on the table. Mark Ogden opened the door and came in. His eyes were drawn to Obiwan, who was holding his wounded paw out away from his body.

"Coyote trap?" he asked.

Polly said, "I don't know. Probably, I guess."

Henry interjected, "Yes. Coyote trap. I guess the farmer behind you has been clearing them out."

"Why haven't I seen one before?" Polly asked, watching as the doctor manipulated and pressed down on the dog's paw.

Mark looked up. "This is prime trapping season for coyotes. They have full, colorful winter coats which sell pretty well." Mark spread the hair on Obiwan's paw and peered at it closely. "It looks like you got him free quickly enough there isn't much damage at all. I'd like to x-ray the paw to make sure nothing is broken, but I think he'll be okay." He scratched behind the dog's ears, then opened the door. "Marnie? We're going to do an x-ray and then I'll clean up the paw. Can you get that ready?"

"This will take a few minutes," he said to them. "Obiwan and I will be right back." He picked the dog up and carried him out of the room.

"Do you mind calling the guys?" Polly asked Henry. "There's no way I'm going to be ready to go at eight o'clock. In fact, I hate the idea that I'm leaving him at all."

"We can do this without you or we can do it another day.

Whatever you want. We'll take care of it."

"No, I need to get these in place today. I have another guest coming to stay and I suppose it would be nice to have some furniture in that room. I also have to go to Boone tomorrow and pick out a mattress and box springs so they'll be delivered this week. And I can't send you over to that poor woman's house without me being there." She fell silent, trying to process on everything. Then, she pulled her phone out to check the time. Seven forty-five.

"Is it too early to call Sylvie?" she asked Henry.

"I don't know," he replied, "But, I'm sure she's up. What are you thinking?"

"Jason and Andrew could keep an eye on Obiwan while I'm gone and they like hanging out at my place."

"Call her. She'd want you to call." Polly hesitated with her hand over the keys of her phone while he spoke. "Make the call," he said.

She dialed.

"Good morning, Polly!" Sylvie's voice rang out. Polly couldn't help but think how happy she sounded these days.

"Hey, Sylvie. Can I borrow your boys today?"

"Really? That would be awesome! Why?"

Polly told her about the trap and Obiwan and that she needed to pick up furniture in Iowa Falls.

"Of course!" Sylvie replied. "In fact, I want to spend some time in the kitchen there today anyway. I'll bring my laptop and work while the boys are upstairs. I need to make sure everything is ready to go for next week."

"Next week?" Polly said. "What's next week?"

"The barn raising and hoe-down?" Sylvie asked. "Isn't that happening next week?"

"Oh!" Polly said. "I had no idea that I could lose my mind at the age of thirty-two. Is that next week?"

"It certainly is, girlfriend," Sylvie said.

"But, aren't you starting classes Monday? How are you going to pull this off?"

"I am taking two classes in Boone. It's not as big of a crisis as I thought. These are business and math classes. So, no big deal." Sylvie stifled a giggle. "Listen to me. No big deal. I crack myself up!"

"The doc is coming back in with Obiwan," Polly said.

"Then don't worry. I'll get the boys moving and we'll be over in a while," Sylvie said and disconnected.

"Thanks," Polly said to the empty phone as she slid it into her pocket.

"There's no break," Mark assured her. "We've cleaned up the paw and wrapped it for good measure. I gave him a shot of antibiotics as a precaution and he should be fine as long as he keeps out of those traps." He thought for a moment, and then said, "Why don't I talk to Dan Severt and see if he won't pull the traps along where your land borders the creek. There's no reason you should have to worry about Obiwan playing out there."

"Would you?" Polly asked. "I was going to have to screw up all of my courage to ask that of him. Thank you."

"No problem. It might take a few days, but he's a good guy and probably thought he was helping you out by keeping the coyotes at bay."

"I hear them howling at night," she said. "They're kind of creepy."

"Welcome back to rural Iowa," he laughed. "We'll take care of the traps and you take care of your boy here." He scratched behind the dog's ears. "Why don't you make an appointment with Marnie for early next week and let me double-check everything one more time."

"Will he be alright to walk around outside?" Polly asked.

"He'll be fine. If he limps around a little for the next couple of days, that's okay. Don't worry about him," Mark replied.

"Thank you for seeing us this morning?" she said. "I don't know what I would have done if you guys weren't around."

Mark smiled, "Are you ready for the big party next Saturday?"

"I totally forgot it was coming up! Jeff is planning the party. Sylvie Donovan is planning the food and Henry here is taking care of the barn."

"You're going to have a dance, right? We haven't had one of those around here in a long time."

Polly rolled her eyes. "Yes," she said snidely, "there will be a dance. I'm a terrible dancer. This is going to stink."

He laughed. "Well, I'm smooth. I'll take you around the dance floor and we'll look like Fred Astaire and Ginger Rogers."

Polly heard Henry chuckling in the background. "Hey!" she said. "Stop laughing."

"I have no basis for my assumption, but I had a picture of you stepping on the doc's feet while he was trying to impress the town with his dancing ability."

"Alright," she said. "I have stepped on a few feet in my time. Guys don't like to dance with me."

Mark laughed, "I'll wear my steel-toed boots."

Henry added, "Maybe we should recommend that all the men who want to dance with Polly bring their steel-toed boots."

She looked back and forth at the two of them and pointed at her dog. "You!" she said, looking at Henry. "Pick up my dog. And you!" she turned to Mark, "fall in some horse crap today, will you?"

She swung the door open and walked out into the lobby where Marnie was standing behind the desk listening to a woman with a rotund dachshund on a leash. The woman seemed to be haranguing her about something to do with food and diet and exercise. Marnie glanced at Polly and holding her finger up to the woman, said, "Call me later and we'll set up his next appointment."

Polly held the door open for Henry and waved at Marnie, giving her a smirk as she left. The dog tried to follow Polly out the door and was rudely yanked back to a sitting position. Polly shook her head as she got back into Henry's truck. He put Obiwan back on her lap and went to his side of the truck and got in.

As he turned the key in the ignition, Henry laughed out loud. "So, you don't like to dance, eh?"

"Shut up. Just shut up. I tried to threaten Jeff with his job, but he wouldn't buy it. Stop laughing and stop talking about it." She looked at him beneath raised brows. "Got it?"

"Got it," he said. "I'm going to drop you off and call the guys. I think we're still in good shape for the day. Are you going to be alright leaving Obiwan at home?"

"Sylvie's boys adore him and Jason is good with him. Since she'll be in the kitchen, it will be fine. I'll let him walk outside for a few minutes before we go in and then he should actually be good until we're back. Short answer - yes. I'm alright leaving him here without me."

"Great." He rounded the corner into her lane and pulled up in front of Sycamore House. Polly put Obiwan on the floor of the truck and opened her door, as Henry rushed around the front end. "It's never going to be easy with you, is it, Polly?"

"Easy isn't worth it," she laughed. "Always remember that."

Henry lifted the dog to the ground and watched as he tentatively put his paw down. He took a step, then another and in a moment began walking to the side of the building.

"I guess he'll be fine," Polly said. "See you in a bit?"

"I'll text you when I get here."

She walked with Obiwan to the edge of the building and then all around the building. He limped a little and seemed as happy to go in as she was. Polly unsnapped his leash when they got inside her apartment. The dog immediately went into the kitchen and sat down at his food dish.

"I guess you're fine, aren't you?" she said. "Good. A hungry dog is a healthy dog."

After feeding him, Polly headed for her bathroom, pulling her sweats off and dropping them back on the chair. She quickly showered and dressed in jeans and a sweater. She was running the blow dryer through her hair when she heard the doorbell of her apartment chime. Unplugging the dryer, Polly rushed out through the living room to the entry way door and saw the entire Donovan family standing there.

"Come in!" she said, backing into the living room. "I am so late!"

Sylvie giggled and pointed to Polly's feet. "You don't match."

Polly looked down. "Whoops!" She had on two different shoes; one black Rockport with a buckle and one plain black loafer. As she walked back into the bedroom, she said. "This wouldn't be a problem if I didn't have so many shoes!" She nudged the right loafer off with her left foot and uncovering the other Rockport, slipped into it.

The boys had taken off their coats and were sitting on the floor petting Obiwan. Little Luke was perched on the back of the sofa watching the action.

"Where's Leia?" Andrew asked.

"She's across the hall with Elise Myers. She can't play with the boys until next week because of her surgery, so she's on vacation," Polly said.

"Oh," his face fell. "She's fun with the fishing pole."

Polly looked confused. "The fishing pole?"

"You know. That thing with the long piece of material on it."

"That's a great name for it," Polly said. "Maybe while she's away, you can teach Luke to play with it. She picked him up from his perch and snuggled him, then put him on the floor next to Andrew.

"Thank you guys for doing this today! I'll settle up with you when I get back."

Sylvie tried to say something and Polly hushed her. "I appreciate you dog sitting for me like this when I need it. How does five dollars for each of you sound?"

Both boys' eyes grew wide and they looked at their mother. "Say thank you," she said.

"Thank you, Miss Polly!" both boys said together. "We'll take good care of them."

"Fine. Obiwan probably won't need to go outside until I'm back, so you all snuggle in and watch television or play games. I'll see you later."

She and Sylvie walked downstairs together and back to the kitchen.

"Polly, you don't need to pay them. They love having another place to hang out and they love your animals."

"They're doing me a favor today, so I'm paying them. That's enough of that. What are you doing today?"

"I have everything ordered. They will deliver most of the food on Wednesday. If it's alright with you, Hannah is going to be here to accept the order and check it out. When I get in that afternoon, the two of us will start putting things together. We'll both be here most of Thursday and Friday too."

"This isn't going to interfere with your classes, is it?" Polly asked.

"No. I've already got the syllabus for each class and have been reading through the textbooks. The first week isn't bad at all. And, I didn't take any extra shifts at the grocery store since I was going to be working here. Jeff said it would be okay to bring in two more people to help, so I asked Beryl if I could borrow her girls. They loved the idea of making some extra money and will be here after school on Thursday and Friday and then will help with lunch and supper on Saturday."

"That sounds great," Polly assured her. "This is your deal, you know. I'll help you do whatever you need me to do, but I totally trust you."

Sylvie shook her head. "That feels weird. I know I can do this, but I've never had anyone else believe I could."

Polly hugged her friend, "Everyone believed. You just needed to find the right place to shine."

"By the way," Polly went on, "Did you have lunch with your friend Amy yesterday?"

"I did!" Sylvie said. "It was good to see her again. We spent forever talking about our kids and everything we're doing. And Polly, you have no idea how wonderful it was to be able to tell her I was getting ready to go to Culinary School. Thank you."

"Oh stop," Polly said. "That's all you. I only gave you a forum for your food."

"Whatever. You're amazing and we all know it. And, you won't believe it, but Lydia, Beryl and Andy are meeting her at Madeline's house for lunch today. She had no idea what that note might mean and thought it would be fun to look around with Madeline's friends."

"I didn't know Beryl and Andy were friends with Madeline too. They didn't seem that way when we went over there on Tuesday."

Sylvie laughed aloud. "They're not. But, they weren't about to let Lydia have fun without them. After all the excitement with your bodies last fall, I believe they think mysteries are a hoot. If Madeline Black were buried already, she'd probably spin circles with the chaos they'll create today."

They both laughed and Polly's phone rang. It was Henry telling her he was pulling in the lane.

"I've got to go get some furniture," Polly said. "I'll be back later. Thank you for everything!"

She zipped up her jacket and ran outside to the truck. Jimmy Rio and Sam Terhune, who both worked for Henry, were already in the back seat, so she jumped in the front.

"Hi guys!" she said as she pulled her seatbelt on. "Well, how are we doing this?"

Henry said, "I thought we'd go to Ames and pick up the rental truck and pads. Jimmy or Sam will drive that and follow us to Iowa Falls. Does that sound good?"

"Sure!" Polly replied and turned around in her seat. "Are you guys comfortable back there?"

Jimmy chuckled. "This has more room than my little truck." Sam just nodded.

Polly hadn't taken much time to pay attention to Henry's truck this morning. She figured if he was proud of his Thunderbird, he was probably just as proud of his truck, so she ought to get the scoop on it.

"Tell me about your truck, Henry."

"Why?" he asked.

"Oh, nothing sinister. Please!" she laughed. "I don't know anything about trucks except mine and all I really know about that one is that my Dad loved it, he bought it in 2004, it's red and it's a Ford. Tell me what is so great about your truck. Because it feels like I need a crane to get me into the front here."

"The front here," he said, "is called a cab. This is a crew cab."

"It's a Ford?"

"Woman," Sam laughed. "You need help. See the logo? It's a Chevy. A Chevy Silverado."

Polly shook her head. "I asked for this, didn't I?"

"You're about to be schooled, Polly," Henry laughed. "Go ahead boys."

Jimmy leaned forward. "It's got a Turbo-Diesel V8 engine and 6-speed automatic transmission."

Polly turned to Henry. "That's good for the giddyup, right?"

"Right," he sighed. "Give it up boys, she doesn't actually want to know."

Sam spoke up, "How could she not want to know? What kind of girl asks and then doesn't want to know?"

Henry laughed, "The kind of girl who wants to be nice, but doesn't have any clue about trucks."

The boys sat back in their seats. Polly glanced behind her in time to see Sam roll his eyes. "Just you wait until you have girlfriends," she said. "You'll learn."

Jimmy said, "No, they'll learn what's important to us. And they'll learn to like it."

"Okay," she replied. "Good for you," and rolled her eyes dramatically so everyone could see.

They pulled into the truck rental company and everyone piled out of the truck and went inside. Soon they were back on the road, heading north on Interstate-35 to Iowa Falls. Henry pulled through the driveway and jumped out to help Jimmy, who was driving the rental truck, back up the driveway to the garage. Polly trotted up to the front door to ring the doorbell.

Vera Lucas answered the door, "Good morning!" she said. "Adam saw you coming and headed for the garage."

Polly heard the garage door go up and Vera continued, "The dogs are in the bedroom. Come on in and you can observe from the back of the garage." Then she stopped, "Unless you are going to help them move the furniture."

"I should probably help," Polly said. "And, I can make sure

they get enough padding around everything."

As she walked to the garage, she was met by Vera's husband, who stuck his hand out in greeting. She shook it and he said, "So, you're the little gal who is re-doing the old school in Bellingwood. That's a mighty big project you took on. I remember taking Vera to a dance over there years and years ago." He glanced around to see if his wife was in hearing distance. "I don't remember what was going on, but we danced a lot in those days." He put his hand on his back. "We don't do that enough these days."

"You two are invited to another dance over there next Saturday," Polly said. "We're having a barn raising all day long and a dance that night. If you don't want to dance, we're having great food."

Vera had come up behind him, "We'd love to come over! We don't get out to parties like we used to. It will be fun. And maybe you can show us where you've put our bedroom." She looked wistfully at the dresser as Jimmy & Sam carried it into the truck.

"This can't be easy, Mrs. Lucas," Polly sympathized.

"It's not easy seeing it finally leave," the woman responded. "But, it makes it a lot easier knowing that you're going to keep the set together and give it a nice home. It was good for us all these years, wasn't it, dear?" She patted her husband's forearm.

He nodded and put his hand over hers. "It was good. But, we can't use it any longer and even though we're old, that doesn't mean we can't accept change."

Vera smiled. "You're right." She turned to Polly and said, "He's always right. That's why I keep him around, isn't it Adam?"

"And here I thought it was for my brilliant mind and glorious body."

"That too."

Polly smiled and observed the two of them watching their furniture get packed away. She couldn't push past them to get into the garage, so she hoped Henry had things well in hand. Soon enough, he stepped around the truck and said, "Have we gotten everything?"

The Lucas' walked back into the garage and Polly followed

them. She looked into the truck and saw that everything was padded and strapped tightly to hold the load steady.

Adam Lucas looked into the truck and said, "It sure doesn't take up much space when it's all packed up that way. It also doesn't look like our furniture anymore, which makes it easier on the soul." He nodded and walked away to stand beside the steps leading back into the house. He put his hand on the door knob and stood watching them.

Polly turned to walk back out of the garage, when Vera said, "Wait. I want to give this to you." She pointed to an oversized box on the floor. "It's a little unwieldy, would one of you boys mind?"

Henry bent down and picked up the box, carrying it over to Polly. Vera followed him and unflapped the top. She moved aside some newsprint to reveal a large pitcher. "It's an old pitcher and wash basin," she said. "We picked it up at an antique store about fifteen years ago and it fits perfectly under the night stand. Somehow it seems to go with the set and it would be a shame to break it up now."

"Thank you!" Polly said and hugged the woman. "Thank you! That will be perfect in the room. I can't wait until you can come over and see it. Maybe next week?"

"We'll be there," assured Vera. "I'll get him out of the house somehow."

"Thank you again for everything," Polly said.

They left and headed back for Bellingwood. Henry said, "Would you mind calling Doug Randall? He and Billy are going to help us get all of this upstairs. Let them know what time we'll be back and they'll meet us there."

Polly made the call and smiled as it rang. She missed having those boys around.

"Hey Polly! Are you there yet?" Doug answered with a question.

"Nope, it will be about forty-five minutes. Can you and Billy come over to help? Henry said he talked to you about it."

"We'll be there! I heard Obiwan got caught in a trap this morning. Is he okay?"

"Wow. Nothing gets past you guys, does it!" she laughed. "He's doing fine. If you want to get there early, Sylvie's in the kitchen and Jason and Andrew are upstairs in the apartment with him. I know they'd all love to see you."

"Okay. We'll see you later." He disconnected and she giggled.

The phone buzzed in her hand. It was a text from Lydia.

"Supper tonight? Andy wants you to see her house. Bring bread. 6:30. Can you set up your big boy/little boy babysitting adventure so Sylvie can come too?"

"What's up?" Henry asked.

"Lydia is in hostess mode again. We're having dinner at Andy's."

"I told you! Never a peaceful moment."

Polly texted back. *"I'll talk to Sylvie and Doug. If everything is works out, I'm there! With bread!"*

CHAPTER EIGHT

"Even I know it's strange to see a farmer driving his planter through town in January," Polly said. She was bouncing her feet on the floor of his truck, with her hand on the door handle. They'd been driving much too slowly for her taste and traffic had been too heavy for Henry to pass the guy as they entered town.

He finally turned into her lane and Polly jumped out of the truck as soon as he parked, "I'm going upstairs to check on Obiwan and I'll send Doug and Billy down to help."

Henry nodded and went over to help Jimmy maneuver his truck to the front of the building. Polly dashed inside and up the steps to her apartment in time to see Doug and Billy coming out of her apartment.

"We heard the trucks come in so we're going downstairs. Do you want to unlock the room for us?" Billy asked.

"Sure! Thanks. I guess I was only thinking of getting to my dog. How's he doing?"

"He's doing fine. When he wants attention, he licks at his paw and looks at one of us. He's a smart dog, figuring that out so quickly," Doug laughed.

Polly walked to the back room and triggered the lock open with her phone, then went back to her apartment. When she walked in, she saw Andrew sitting on one end of the couch and Jason on the other end. Obiwan was stretched out between the two of them with his head in Andrew's lap, his left paw with its bright orange wrap hanging piteously off the side of the sofa.

"How's everything going, guys?" she asked.

"It's cool, Polly," Jason said, standing up with an empty glass and heading for the kitchen. Polly took his place on the sofa and leaned over to hug her boy. Obiwan barely moved his body, but turned his head to nuzzle hers as she relaxed on top of him.

"You poor stupid dog, you. Ya scared me to death this morning."

"I think he's going to be fine, Miss Polly," Andrew said in an attempt to reassure her.

She sat back up. "I think you're absolutely right and I can't tell you how much I appreciate you guys hanging out with him today." She reached into her pocket and pulled out her wallet, slipping out two five dollar bills. She handed one to each of the boys. "Thank you very much for taking care of my boy, guys."

"We love it!" Jason said. "You have great television up here and we can play games, too."

"How was Luke today?" she asked, spying the cat on top of the refrigerator.

"He played with me a lot!" Andrew exclaimed. "He even got the hang of the fishing pole."

"That's terrific," Polly said. She heard commotion in the hallway. "I need to make sure they know how I want the furniture arranged. I'll be back." When she opened the door, she turned around to see Jason slip back into the space she vacated and smiled.

Jimmy and Doug were carrying the dresser into the back room and Billy was carrying drawers up the steps. She could hear Henry and Sam talking at the bottom of the steps, but followed the dresser. She had a flash of insight. Each of the rooms needed a different name. This would be the Walnut Room ... that seemed appropriate. Once she figured out the decor of the middle room, she would name that and since the front room was still kind of hurried, she wanted to spend more time thinking about it. The boys put the dresser down in the middle of the room and looked at her expectantly, so, she pointed to the inside wall and they put it into place. Billy set the drawers in front of it and Polly began pushing them into their slots. Each drawer was a different size and had a specific way in which it fit. She ran her hands across the top of the dresser and smiled. She hoped people would appreciate the exquisite beauty of the set.

Henry and Sam came in with the chest of drawers and she had them place it between the tall windows at the back of the building. Walking over to touch that piece, she realized what a beautiful view any tenant would have in this room. It looked out over the wooded creek bed and in the winter without the leaves on the sycamore trees, she could easily see beyond them into Dan Severt's fields. The fullness of the leaves might make that a little more difficult throughout the rest of the year, but it was always going to be pretty.

Billy made another trip in with the two chairs and luggage stool. He set them down in front of her and took off for another load. Before too long the room was filled with furniture and everyone stood looking at her.

"What do you think, Polly?" Henry asked.

"I think you guys deserve lunch! On me!" she said.

"Well, alright, but what do you think of the placement?" he asked.

"For now, it's good. It isn't perfect yet, but almost. A few dark oriental rugs in here will work nicely. I'll ask Lydia to help me find rugs and bedding. Can you believe this?" She swirled around the middle of the room. "All of this beautiful furniture in one place."

Billy said, "Doug and I couldn't believe what we were seeing when we pulled it off the truck."

"Whoops!" Henry exclaimed. "Just a minute. I'll be right back." He left the room and took off down the steps.

"Will you let me take you uptown for lunch?" Polly asked.

"I'm in," Sam said. "How about you guys?" The others nodded in the affirmative.

Polly pulled out her phone and dialed a number. "Hey, Sylvie?" she said, when the woman answered. "I know you're downstairs, but do you and Jason and Andrew want to go to Joe's Diner with us for lunch? It's on me today."

She listened as Sylvie protested. "It will take less than an hour and then you can come back to your work and you should come up here and see this furniture!"

Sylvie agreed to come up and that the boys might want some lunch and they hung up. Billy opened the secretary and said, "Hey, look at this!"

There was an envelope with four antique skeleton keys taped to the underside of the desk top. He passed them around and using his, opened the glass fronts of the top of the secretary. Doug opened the shoe closet and Jim fit his into the curio cabinet. Sam took the last key and slid it into the lock of the top drawer of the dresser.

"That's way awesome, Polly," Billy said. "Here, you're going to want these." He drew one of the chairs up to the desk, sat down and pulled open a small door in the center of the insert. Slots on either side offered room for papers and mail and four small drawers at the bottom of the desk insert finished the look. Billy opened and closed each of them. "This is really cool! I've never seen anything like this."

Polly said, "My grandmother had an old desk like this, but it didn't have the top curio cabinet." She pulled out the far left drawer. "There were always stamps in this drawer and in the next she kept pencils and pens. The slots were always stuffed with letters and mail on this side, but on the right side, she kept some of her fancy writing paper. The other drawers had scissors and office supplies. Wow, I'd forgotten about that until you pulled this open. Think of all the letters that might have been written from this desk. I wonder what else will be written from here in the future."

Henry and Sylvie walked in together. He was carrying the box Vera Lucas had thrust at Polly before they left.

"Oh, Polly!" Sylvie exclaimed. "Oh, Polly!"

"I know! Can you believe it?" Polly gushed.

"I can't. This entire set really stayed together all these years?"

"I got it from its original owner and they never broke it up. But, can you believe it?"

Henry unpacked the box, pulling out the pitcher, then the basin. They had very simple lines and were porcelain white with gold trim around the rim of both the pitcher and basin. The black handle on the pitcher offered a striking contrast.

"Under the far bedside table," Polly said. "That's where it belongs." She picked up the pitcher and he carried the basin over to where she pointed. "Thank you," she said.

"Well, now I have a lot of work to do this week to finish this room before our next guest shows up. But, really ... are you ready for lunch?"

Sylvie and Polly went next door to get the boys. Andrew didn't want to leave Obiwan, but Polly assured him the dog would be fine for a little while.

There was plenty of room at Joe's Diner and they gathered tables to make room for all nine to eat together. Henry and Polly sat across from each other and Sylvie put the boys between Polly and herself. Doug was on the other side of Polly and Billy took an end while Sam and Jimmy sat on either side of Henry. Lucy showed up with menus and a tray filled with dripping glasses of water.

"What do you want to drink today?" she asked.

Polly looked up at her and said, "This is all on one ticket no matter what anyone," she scowled first at Henry, then Sylvie, "says."

"Got it," Lucy laughed. She took their drink orders and left them alone.

Andrew began wiggling in his chair, "What is it?" Sylvie asked him.

"Can I have a real meal or do I have to have a kid's meal?"

Andrew asked.

While Sylvie was shaking her head, Polly said, "It's up to your mom, but I vote for a real meal. What do you want?"

"I want a steak!" he announced.

"Can I have one too?" Jason asked a little timidly.

Lucy had walked up behind the boys while they were talking and delivered their colas to them. "How about a steak sandwich boys? All the flavor of a steak and it comes with french fries."

Sylvie's eyes filled with gratitude.

"Can we, mom?" Andrew asked again.

She looked at Polly, who said. "Steak sandwiches it is. And I'll have one too! Medium well, right guys?"

Jason looked at her. "I don't know."

Polly turned to Lucy. "Medium well for the boys and medium rare for me."

Henry said, "What, no tenderloin today?"

Polly laughed. "They serve one of the best, but if the boys are having steak today, I'm having steak." Then she giggled and said to Billy and Doug, "If you guys want steak, we won't call this the dinner I owe you. I promise."

Soon the table had placed their orders and Lucy went back to the kitchen.

"Sylvie, did you hear from Lydia about tonight at Andy's?" Polly asked.

"I did and I'd love to go, but ..." and she nodded at her sons.

"On it." Polly turned to Doug, "Would you guys be up for house sitting duty again tonight?"

"Well, uh ..." Doug hesitated.

"If you can't do it, I'll figure something else out," Polly said.

"No, that's not it," Billy said. "Ask her, Doug."

"We were wondering if we could bring some friends over and play games. The auditorium is done now and we can pull out the tables and set our computers up and it would be great if the boys played with us and we'd take Obiwan out and check on Luke. What do you think?"

Polly threw her head back and laughed. "Of course you can!

Sylvie, what do you think?"

Sylvie shrugged. "It's fine with me. Are you boys okay with that?"

Andrew's eyes were huge. "Really? Jase, did you hear that? We get to play games with the guys!"

Jason nodded. He reached under the table and took Polly's hand, pulling her down so he could whisper in her ear. "You're like my own fairy godmother ... if that's what boys have."

She pulled him close and hugged him, then winked over his head at his mother, who smiled.

After lunch was finished, Henry left to take Jimmy and Sam to their homes and Doug and Billy took off to gather their gear and call their friends. Sylvie went back into the kitchen and sat down at the prep table with her laptop.

Polly took the boys back upstairs to the apartment. "I'm going to take Obiwan outside for a bit. We won't be gone long. Can you keep yourselves occupied?"

"We could go with you," Jason said. Andrew slumped down in a huff. "I wanted to watch a movie. You said we could watch Iron Man."

"It will only be a few minutes," his brother replied. "Then we can watch Iron Man."

"I don't want to go outside," Andrew complained. "It's cold out there."

"Look," Polly said. "Jason, you can come with me. Get the movie started for Andrew and he can stay here. We're only going to be gone for a few minutes and your mom is right downstairs. There's no need to argue."

Andrew pulled his coat off and started to drop it on the floor. Then, he looked up at Polly and smiled, took it to the chair by the entrance and set it there. He pulled his shoes off and ran back, then dived into the sofa. Luke had been sitting on the back of the couch and dropped on top of Andrew's lap after he pulled a blanket over himself.

"He wants to play with the cat," Jason said.

"That's great. Luke needs more friends to play with, especially while Leia is gone." It occurred to Polly that she needed to stop by and talk to Elise at some point about the phone calls she had received last night. However, even with all the commotion of the day, she was certain Elise had been working diligently to flip flop her sleep schedule and hated to be the one to wake her up.

Polly snapped the leash on Obiwan and walked down the stairs with Jason. Obiwan limped a little, but seemed to be okay.

"Were you scared, Polly?" Jason asked.

"This morning when Obiwan was caught in the trap?"

"Well, yeah. Did that scare you?"

"It did. I cried and called Henry to come rescue us. I don't know what I would have done if he hadn't been around."

"You could always call us. I can't drive yet, but Mom would have come over."

"Thank you, Jason. You're right. I need to remember I have a lot of friends in Bellingwood."

"Were you scared when that man kidnapped you last year?" Jason asked again.

Obiwan had stopped to sniff at some snow on the ground, so they had stopped. "Yes, I was scared, Jason. But, I knew my friends were going to be looking for me. I also knew that I had friends in Boston where he was taking me and all I needed was one chance to get away from him. Someone would come find me and help me."

"Why did he take you back there when you wanted to stay here?" Jason asked.

They had started walking again and were making the usual loop around the building. "Well, Joey was all twisted up in his head. He loved me and thought I was in love with him. He didn't want to hear me say that I didn't love him, and ignored me. He made up a big, fantastic story in his mind about how perfect his life would be if he had me as his wife and couldn't believe that I didn't want the same thing. So, he kidnapped me and thought he could make me live the way he wanted me to live. But, we all have our own minds, don't we, Jason."

"That wasn't right what he did to you, was it?"

"No, it wasn't right and he's going to a place where they will take care of him and keep him safe and everyone else safe from him."

"Did they put him in jail?"

"It's a kind of a jail," Polly said. "But, it's more like a hospital. There's something wrong in Joey's head and they're going to try to help him get better. But, he'll be there for a long time."

"He's not coming back here to hurt you, right?"

"No, Jason. He won't come back here. I'm safe now."

"That's good. I never got a chance to talk to you after that. I wish I had been big enough to make sure you were safe."

"Jason, you take such good care of my animals and me. You're absolutely the right size. Don't ever think that you're not," she said.

"Am I big enough to keep my mom safe?" he asked quietly.

Polly stopped and Obiwan wandered off to smell another phantom scent. "Is there someone scaring your mom?" she asked.

"Not anymore. There was when we were little, but he's gone."

"You are big enough to keep your mom safe, Jason, as long as you remember that there are a lot of people who are your friends and all it takes is a phone call. You never have to do anything alone. Promise me that you'll remember that, okay?"

"I promise," he said. "Maybe I should get my own phone." His face brightened and he seemed to let go of the dark thoughts that had frightened him. "I think it would be the best present ever for my birthday this summer, don't you?"

"Maybe you should talk to your mom about it," Polly laughed.

"I have!" he said. "Maybe you could talk to her too?"

"I don't think I have much pull," Polly said, "But you keep reminding her."

They walked back inside and up the steps to the apartment where Obiwan jumped back up onto the couch after she released him from the leash.

"You guys hang out here for a while. I'm going to check on what your mom is doing in the kitchen," Polly said. "Don't forget there is juice and stuff in the fridge. Help yourselves."

She heard Andrew say, "This place is so cool!" as she walked out her front door.

Sylvie was bent over the laptop, typing away when Polly walked into the kitchen.

"Hey, Sylvie," she said. "I think your oldest might have a little crush on me."

"You're kidding, right?" Sylvie laughed. "That crush started the first time he met you. When you asked him to help with Obiwan, it was all over for him. He fell for you hook, line, and sinker. So, what are you going to do with my little boy's heart, Polly?" She snickered as she asked the question.

Polly said. "I can't imagine. I've never been crushed on by a kid. What am I supposed to do?"

"Honestly, Polly, if you treat him with respect like you always have, he'll get over it when he falls for some girl his own age. I think too many people get excited about this. It will be one of those good memories he has when he's older."

Polly interrupted, "And I'm a grandma? Sheesh. Okay. I can do that. You're sure he won't try to kiss me or anything, right?"

They both laughed. Then Polly went on. "He seemed concerned with me being scared both this morning with the dog and then he asked about when Joey took me back to Boston."

"He was upset when that happened, Polly," Sylvie said. "He was afraid Joey would hurt you."

"Jason also worries about you. He said something to me about someone scaring you when he was little."

Sylvie shook her head and settled it into her hand. "That was a long time ago. Everything is fine now. I hate that he remembers that."

"Do you want to tell me about it?" Polly asked.

"No, it's over now and I'll talk to him and make sure he's alright with everything. He shouldn't worry. I dealt with it then and it's in the past."

"Yeah," Polly said. "He thinks he needs a cell phone for his birthday. I believe he figures it might save your life ... especially if that will help him get the phone."

"He set you up to talk to me about it, too!" Sylvie laughed. "He'll turn thirteen in July. It's probably time to get one of those for him. Andrew will be ten in April. Those two boys are growing up way too fast. I don't think I'm ready for that!"

"You will be when it happens. That's what Mary always told me." Polly pointed at the laptop. "Are you ready for classes to start and can I help you with anything for the big day next week?"

"I am SO ready for classes to start. I think I'm glad that I didn't find out about it until last week. I'd be a nervous wreck. I haven't had time to think about the fact that I'm going to be sitting in classes again and that this fall, I'm going to be in a big kitchen learning how to be a chef. I can't wait," she said.

"And as for the party. I'm going to take a deep breath and dive in. I've got everything planned out for lunch and dinner. Breakfast is a little up in the air right now in my head. I just don't know how many people you're going to have eating here and I would hate to run out."

"Then, make more than you can dream. If there's too much, we'll make sure the food gets to where it can do some good. How's that?" Polly asked.

"I'll talk to Jeff and Henry and see if we can't firm up some better numbers and then, yes, that's what I'll do." Sylvie looked up and said, "Hi, Elise!"

Polly spun around. Her ghost-like tenant was up pretty early in the afternoon.

"How are you doing, Elise?" she asked.

"I'm alright. Is there still coffee around?"

Sylvie got up and grabbed a mug out of the cupboard. She filled it from the pot and handed it to Elise. "Would you like me to fill a thermos for you to take upstairs? I think there will be a bunch of people in the auditorium playing computer games tonight."

"Sure, thanks!" Elise said.

When Sylvie moved to take care of that, Polly said, "Elise, I have a strange question for you. Do you know a Linda Marberry."

At the mention of the name, Elise's eyes flew wide open and

Polly could have sworn she saw her hands begin to tremble. The girl swallowed the coffee in her mouth and worked quickly to regain her stability.

"I don't know anyone by that name. Why do you ask?"

"I got a couple of phone calls last night asking for her and since you're the only person who is here, I wondered if you might have some idea what was going on?"

"I'm sorry, I don't know." With every word out of her mouth, Elise seemed to gain a little more control of herself. Polly was sure she was lying, but didn't know how to get the truth out of her.

Sylvie handed Elise the thermos and said, "Bring it down whenever you're finished. We'll clean it up later."

"Thanks," Elise mumbled and walked out of the kitchen. Polly nodded to Sylvie that she was going with Elise and followed her out to the stairs.

"Elise, if you need help. I have a lot of friends around here."

"I'm fine," Elise said. "I need to get back to work on my dissertation. I don't know anything about a Linda Marberry or whatever her name was."

They walked up the steps together.

"Okay, then," Polly said as they got to the top in front of Elise's room. "I'm not going to be here tonight, but there will be people around. If you need anything at all, you have my phone number, right?"

"I have it. Thanks." Elise opened the door to her room and Polly went back to her apartment. It was time to start mixing the bread for dinner at Andy's. When she walked in, Andrew was sound asleep on the sofa and Obiwan practically covered the little boy's body as he lay across him. Luke was snuggled in between Obiwan's butt and Jason, who sat at the other end. She put her finger up to her mouth to keep him quiet and went in to the kitchen to start the bread.

CHAPTER NINE

One last check on the boys had Polly poking her head in the auditorium Sylvie picked her up to go to Andy's house. She stepped further in and saw that Andrew was sitting at a table with two high school boys. They were setting up a laptop for him as he watched in awe. Jason had found a seat at another table with Billy, who was pointing at something on the monitor in front of him. There were four tables of kids with their computers. On another table close to the kitchen were four open pizza boxes, several opened bags of chips and cartons of soda as well as juice boxes. That struck her as odd until she looked at the tables and saw that about half of the kids were sucking on a little straw attached to a box of juice. She shrugged her shoulders. Kids. Who knew?

Tires crunching on gravel drew her attention and Polly walked out to the parking lot and got in Sylvie's car. "I think they're going to be fine tonight," she said.

"Jason will keep an eye on Andrew, and Doug and Billy are good kids. I'm not too worried," Sylvie responded. "What bread did you make tonight? It smells amazing!"

"I've got a loaf of my oat bread and then a batch of my potato bread recipe made into rolls. Those just came out of the oven, so they're still warm."

Sylvie reached across the console to snake her hand into the basket Polly had in her lap. Polly slapped it away. "You have to wait!" she said.

"Why should I wait? You have hot rolls in that basket and I want one!"

Polly couldn't dispute the truth of either statement. She pulled the cloth back and held it open for Sylvie, who quickly grabbed a roll and took a bite before Polly changed her mind.

"Mmmmm, that's good. I don't like to make bread, so I never have this around the house. I should pay you to bake for me." Then she said, "You know, you could sell this up at the grocery store if you wanted to. They'd love to support you."

"Can you imagine me baking bread every day? I'd go out of my mind. Maybe when you get finished with school and start catering out of Sycamore House every day, we'll talk, but until then, you can ask me for a loaf when you want one, okay?"

Sylvie's mouth was full of the last of her roll as she said, "Mmmm. Uh huh."

They didn't have to drive too far to get to Andy's house; it was east of town next to the cemetery. Polly laughed when she saw that Andy's mailbox now sported a blue bird cover. The first day she met Andy, the woman had talked about putting a blue bird on a post in order to tell people where she lived. Sylvie drove up the short lane to a pretty, ranch-style home. It looked exactly like Andy. Everything was neat and even in winter, the bare bushes showed signs of being perfectly trimmed. The brick around the foundation gave way to light blue siding and the white posts at the entry way looked freshly painted. A light over the front door was on and the inside door was standing open in invitation.

Sylvie pulled a box out of her back seat and said, "I don't have quite as much to carry tonight. My goodness, that was a chore getting all my stuff into Beryl's house." They laughed at the memory as they walked up to the front door.

"Come on in!" Andy's voice rang out. Sylvie and Polly made

their way into the house and were met by Lydia who took the box from Sylvie's hands and then the basket of rolls and bag of bread from Polly.

"You can hang your coats in the closet there," she said, nodding to the doors behind the girls. "And Andy won't say anything, but she'd prefer it if you didn't wear shoes on her carpet."

The living room to their left was cozy and decorated in soft pastel colors. Lydia walked straight ahead into the dining room and Polly and Sylvie followed soon after. Polly looked down the hallway to her right and figured the bedrooms were down there. She walked into the dining room and to the left was the kitchen. She was surprised at the bright red walls between the upper and lower cupboards. Random splashes of lemon yellow coated the red walls and the floor was a vivid explosion of colorful tile in reds, yellows, blues, oranges and greens. The window over Andy's sink had no curtains and looked out at another portion of the cemetery filled with old trees. The yard was very well kept and the short wooden fence separating the two properties was painted a dark, barn red. There were two big windows in the dining room, artfully draped with yellow fabric and plants hung from hooks in two of the four corners of the room. The bar between the kitchen and dining room had already been filled with dishes, but Lydia found room to nudge Polly's basket of rolls in beside a broccoli salad.

"Is Beryl coming tonight?" Sylvie asked.

"She should be here any minute," Lydia said. "She was with us all day at Madeline Black's house and had to run home and do whatever it is she had to do."

Andy stuck her head under the hanging cupboards over the bar. "It makes me very afraid when I think of the things she might bring with her. I don't know why she was so insistent on going home."

"Maybe she's bringing the booze," Lydia smirked. "Or maybe she's going to make us paint again."

"She wouldn't dare," Andy said. "She can get away with that at her house, but not at mine. I won't have it!"

"Won't have what?" Everyone jumped when Beryl spoke up.

"Where did you come from?" Polly asked.

"I was sneaking up on y'all just to watch you jump. You did me proud."

Beryl was carrying two large shopping bags and set them down. "Don't you dare look in those while I take my coat off," she said. "I'll be right back." She stuck her head back in, "And tell Miss Prissy Pants that I took my shoes off before I walked across her pretty carpet."

"I'm going to ignore her," Andy said, "and ask what you want to drink. I have iced tea, coffee, water, and lemonade."

Carafes of cold drinks and a red thermos of coffee sat on a pretty tray with an ice bucket in the middle at the end of the peninsula.

Beryl scooted in between Lydia and Polly, who were pouring their own drinks and said, "What? No happy juice? Where's the booze?"

Andy rolled her eyes and said, "You're enough trouble without it. I want my house to still be standing after you leave tonight."

Beryl stuck her lower lip out, Lydia took the spoon she had used to stir cream into her coffee and brushed it over her friend's mouth.

"Hey! I don't like cream in my coffee," Beryl laughed.

Andy pulled a casserole dish out of the oven and placed it on the last open trivet. Five chicken breasts simmered in olive oil. Polly smelled the spice and asked, "What did you do to those?"

"It's simple. I mix a bunch of spices up with some flour, wash the chicken breasts, shake them all together in a big zipper bag and bake them."

"These smell great. What did you use?"

"It's actually a Greek seasoning. That's why we have lemon roasted potatoes to go with it," Andy said as she drew the lid off another casserole dish with a flourish. "Now, dish up your meals and let's eat. I've been slaving away all day in the kitchen and haven't eaten a thing."

Lydia snorted and Beryl said, "Weren't you with us when we

ate that delightful lunch at Madeline's house today or was that some strange doppelganger? And I don't remember ever seeing you in the kitchen."

"Fine, you harpy," laughed Andy. "I'm still starving."

They filled their plates and sat down to eat.

"I know you guys went with Polly the other day to Iowa Falls to see her new furniture, but you have got to see how it looks in place," Sylvie said. "How in the world did you get so lucky?" she asked Polly.

"Honestly, I can't believe it. I suppose the price put some people off, but there were a lot of pieces. It was a steal for what I ended up paying her. And once I drag Lydia in and out of a few stores tomorrow to get a mattress, bedding and rugs, that room is going to be exquisite." She cut a piece of chicken, then said, "and I've decided that I'm going to name the individual rooms. That back room is going to be the Walnut Room."

"Are you ready for next Saturday?" Andy asked.

"Everyone keeps asking me that question," Polly said. "Jeff, Henry and Sylvie are doing all the work. As long as they tell me we're ready, then I will be ready!" She looked at Sylvie who smiled and nodded, then back to Andy. "Are you doing alright with your project in there? I suppose that needs to be cleaned up before Saturday."

"The glass company has to finish the last three cases on the back wall and they'll be done. They said they would have that completed on Monday. Of course, I may never be finished, but I will have all of the shelves filled and identified as much as possible, then I'll move things around as time passes."

"I'm really going to owe you for that," Polly said. "I saw some of the work tonight when I went in to check on the computer party happening in there. You've done a nice job!"

"If there's ever anyone who can organize you within an inch of your life, it will be our Andy," Beryl said, patting her friend on the back. "She's the one who keeps me organized in my life. She knows where all of my paintings are, what my agent is up to, what I have to do next. I couldn't exist without her keeping an eye on me."

"Really?" Polly looked at Andy with a new sense of respect. "How do you have time to do anything for me?"

Andy laughed. "My kids thought I was going to rot away in this house when Bill died and I moved off the farm. Now, they complain that I'm never available to watch their little ones." She sighed. "I probably complain about that too, but I love doing what I do and those kids have the best mothers around. When they need me, I'm always there. Or here."

"You should see her family room downstairs. That's the only place there is chaos around here. Andy makes sure those kiddos have a fun place to visit away from their own home," Lydia said.

"Well, I love those little ones and I think that Grandma's house should be special. So, they get chaos and color and sounds and things their parents don't want to have around. It's a good deal for all of us," Andy said.

Sylvie said, "You must love them if you have chaos in your basement."

"I know that too much order isn't good for the mind. I don't want to hasten any onset of dementia, so I do my best to inject a little chaos in my life on purpose. I don't drive the same way to get places every day and I try to put my shoes and socks on differently in the morning. Sometimes it's the left foot I start with, sometimes I start with the right foot. Sometimes I put one sock and one shoe on. And I don't ..." she looked pointedly at Beryl, "I don't have a plan for what days I do different things. It occurs to me that I need to alter my pattern, so I do."

"Are you worried about dementia?" Sylvie asked.

"Both of my parents withered away from Alzheimer's. I plan to do everything possible to keep the neurons in my brain firing on all cylinders. That's all. If it comes, I'll deal with it, but until then, I'm fighting like hell to keep my brain busy."

"Enough about that," Andy said. "We have to tell you guys about our day at Madeline Black's house! I think there's a mystery to be solved."

Polly's questioning look prompted Lydia to say, "She's right.

That note from Madeline was very confusing. Amy talked to her brother and neither of them have any idea what their parents might have that was so important she wanted people to take care of it."

"We went through Madeline's desk today and didn't find anything that offered a clue. Actually, we went through a great many of her cubbyholes and nothing seemed especially interesting. Nothing in her checkbook looked off, at least according to Amy. But, then, she hasn't been around much in the last fifteen years. She admitted she wouldn't know if something was odd or not," Beryl said.

Lydia wrinkled her nose. "We have until Monday morning before dear, sweet Laurence waltzes in and puts the kibosh on any more searching. Amy's pretty sure he is going to lock up the house and sit on it forever. When Madeline wanted to move to an apartment, he didn't want to lose the house, but he didn't want to buy it from her either. She stayed to keep him happy. Amy said that he's already announced they aren't selling the house, just in case he wants to move back here when he retires."

"Doesn't she have a say in things?" Polly asked.

"Well, they haven't found the will yet either. Without a will, things will go to both kids and she will be able to wield some power, and if the will shows up, who knows what Bill and Madeline wanted to have happen."

"It isn't registered down in Boone?"

"Nope," Lydia said. "That was the first place Amy checked. She'll do some more searching on Tuesday, but isn't too hopeful. She remembers them talking about their will when she was young, because it made her mom cry to think about what might happen to the children if they died. There is one somewhere, it's just not showing up."

"We did find Bill's old uniform from when he was in the Army. He served in the Korean War, right, Lydia?" Andy asked.

"He did," she replied. "Do you remember the year all of the churches in town encouraged veterans to wear their uniforms to church for Veteran's Day? My goodness, that was a beautiful sight. Bill was still alive then. They all cleaned and pressed those uniforms and found their medals and polished their boots. I don't think there was a dry eye in town that day. Madeline was quite proud of her husband. He still fit in that uniform. Some of the guys only had their jackets, and those had to be let out. But, every former military person was honored all around town that day. We haven't done something that big in years. It might be time to stir up a few organizers again and get them planning."

"I'm surprised they didn't bury him in it," Sylvie said.

"He was cremated. Madeline always said he came into the world naked as a jaybird, and that's the way he wanted to go out of the world. They weren't supposed to do anything special, only burn his remains and then she could do whatever she wanted with them."

"Amy said Laurence had a problem with that when his dad died and has absolutely thrown a fit over the fact that his mother had already paid for a cremation. But, since that paperwork was easy to find, he had to live with it." Lydia giggled. "Live with it. Oh, I crack myself up."

Plates were empty in front of them and Andy moved to begin clearing the table. Sylvie said, "I have dessert," and walked over to get her box. She opened it and pulled out a pie carrier. Freezer packs fluttered out around the carrier and she scrambled to toss them back in the box.

She pulled the top off to reveal two pies. Polly's mouth began watering when she saw the meringue on the top pie. "Is that possibly lemon meringue?" she asked.

Sylvie smiled. "It sure is. I take it you like lemon meringue?"

"I would do about anything for a piece of that." Polly replied.

"Well, you don't have to do anything. I promise. You've done enough to make me want to give you one of these every week for a year!" Sylvie laughed.

She pulled off the divider and revealed a second pie covered with whipped cream.

"What's that one?" Beryl asked.

"Chocolate cream," Sylvie said. "I figured we could have both chocolate and fruit tonight. Andy handed her two pie servers and set a stack of plates in front of her, then took the carrier away and put it back in the box.

"Who wants what?" Sylvie asked.

"I have to have both!" Polly declared. "But, that might kill me. Can you cut small slices?"

A unanimous vote of small slices for everyone and dishes were passed around. Andy refilled the carafes and brought them to the table.

When everyone had pie in front of them, Beryl announced, "Alright. Now, it is time for my part of the evening." She began pulling out various sized boxes from the shopping bags she had brought in, stacking them in the center of the table.

"This is a wacky game of truth or dare. Each of us takes a box and opens it. There are three options. You can either answer the question on the paper, do the dare on the paper or pass it to someone else in the room. But, you have to declare which option you are taking before you open the box. If you choose to pass it, you have to announce who you are passing it to. And if someone passes you a box, you are obligated to do the truth or the dare. If you pass a box, you have to take another and do the truth or the dare. Are you ready?"

"How are you going to play? Didn't you stuff the boxes?" Lydia asked.

"No. I was honest. I took the boxes and papers over to Deena and asked her to put them together for me. I set this up weeks ago, knowing we'd get together again sometime." Beryl laughed and looked at Andy. "And you didn't think I was organized. Hah. I showed you!"

Each person took a small box and looked at Beryl for more direction.

"Okay. Fine," she said. "I'll start. I'm going to take the dare." She opened her box and read the paper, then began giggling. "I have to eat something old and yucky from your refrigerator." Beryl turned to Sylvie, "I didn't know we'd be at Andy's place. This is going to be a cinch. She's always cleaning out her fridge. There won't be anything bad in there."

"That's what you think, dear heart," Andy said. "I have just the thing." She went over to her refrigerator and pulled out a bag of moldy bread. "I was saving it for the birds outside and it got away from me. I should have tossed it out today, but now I'm glad I didn't." She opened the bag and set it in front of Beryl.

"That figures," Beryl said. "At least it wasn't congealed gravy or something." She reached in and took a slice of bread out that was covered in green mold. "I don't know if I can do this," she said.

"Eat the bread, eat the bread." They took up the chant Andy had started and Beryl shut her eyes and took a bite, swallowed it quickly and grabbed her glass of lemonade. After rinsing her mouth a couple of times, she shuddered and said, "Your turn, Polly."

"Okay," Polly said. "Truth," and she opened the box. "What was one of your most embarrassing moments in your work place?" she read out loud.

"Hmmm, I've had a lot. And you all know about Doug Randall seeing my underwear strewn down the stairway. Oh!" she said. "I know! It was at the Library. It was the fall I was taking classes toward my Master's Degree. I went to class in the evening, worked during the day and studied at night and during my breaks. I was tired all the time that semester. One day I was shelving some books and sat down on a step stool for a minute. I must have fallen asleep and when my body fully relaxed, I fell over and out into the main aisle. A young man working close by came over to help me up and I had absolutely no explanation for why I was all a jumble on the floor. I couldn't tell anyone I'd been sleeping. That was when I decided the degree could wait."

"Did you ever finish it," Sylvie asked.

"No, I haven't. Life and everything else kind of took precedence and I didn't need it for my job. It just seemed like the thing to do. Maybe someday, though."

Polly looked at Lydia and said, "It's to you."

Lydia announced that she would take truth and opened her box. "What is your guilty pleasure?" she read out loud. "I hate to admit it," she said. "It's a little twisted."

"What is it?" Polly asked.

"I take the kiddos to Chuck-E-Cheese because I love that hideous, awful pizza."

Andy grimaced and Sylvie said, "That's the worst pizza in the world! I was glad to have my boys get past that stage."

"I know!" Lydia said. "It's absolutely awful and I love it. I even love that stupid, dancing mouse. Whenever I get a craving, I offer to take my grandkids out for an evening and we drive to Des Moines. I get my awful pizza and they think Grandma is cool."

Lydia looked at Sylvie and said, "Alright, now it's your turn."

Sylvie looked at the box in her hand and said, "Dare. I'm afraid of truth tonight." She opened the box and pulled the paper out and read it, then looked up at the table. "This is weird," she said. "Okay, fine."

"What is it?" Andy asked.

"I'm not supposed to say," Sylvie replied and stood up. She walked into the kitchen and washed her hands. Then, she spun around three times and came back to the table, but before she sat down, she rubbed her sudsy hands all over Andy's face.

"What was that for?" Andy spluttered.

"It was the dare," Sylvie replied and handed Andy the slip of paper. "You happened to be sitting on my right side."

Polly's phone rang. She looked at the display and saw that it was a call from Doug.

"Just a second," she said. "I need to get this." She stepped out of the room and said, "Hello?"

"Hey, Polly," Doug said. "Everything is fine here, I think."

"What do you mean?" she asked.

"Well, a car pulled up and the girl who is staying upstairs got in it and drove away. She didn't say anything to anyone, but she brought Leia down and put her in the auditorium with us."

"What? That's weird! Did she have any bags with her?"

"I'm not sure, but I don't think so. Maybe she'll come back tonight. I didn't want to upset you, but I thought you should know since she never goes anywhere."

"Thanks Doug. We'll be back after a bit. Would you mind keeping Leia with you until I get there?"

"No problem."

"How are Jason and Andrew doing?"

"They're doing great. That Andrew is a little spitfire."

"He sure is. Okay, thanks for letting me know. I feel like I should build a room for you to live there. You keep taking care of things for me."

"You build the room. I'll move in!" Doug said brightly.

"See you in a bit," Polly said and hung up. She went back into the dining room and sat down.

"What's up?" Sylvie asked.

"I suppose it's nothing. That was Doug and he called to tell me that Elise just got in someone's car and drove away. She put Leia in the auditorium and didn't say a word. It's strange, that's all."

"Are you worried about her?" Lydia asked.

"Well, I got these calls last night for a Linda Marberry. Someone was certain she was staying with me. I insisted that I had no one there by that name, but it makes me wonder. I asked Elise about it today and she denied knowing anything about it, but now she's gone." Polly looked at the time on her phone. "It's nine o'clock. Where would she be going at this hour in Bellingwood?"

"Do you need to hurry back to Sycamore House?" Andy said.

"We should head back soon, I suppose, but you aren't going to get out of taking a turn," Polly laughed. "Will that be alright?" she asked Sylvie, who nodded her assent.

"Alright. Fine. I'm doing truth, then," Andy said and opened her box. "Describe your worst date." She looked at Beryl, "Really? That's what you want to know?"

"Excuse me," Beryl said. "I had no idea who would get that question. It could easily have been me!"

"But, you were there for my worst date."

"Oh, lordie. Yes, I was. That was a helluva night!" Beryl laughed.

"Well, tell us!" Polly insisted.

"It was my junior prom. I wasn't dating anyone and Miss Thing over here was dating some weird guy from Boone, so she asked him to find a buddy to be my date. He had a friend who agreed to go with me and we all met up for pizza the week before in Boone. First thing, he was short. Way short. I'd already bought these pretty white sandals, but I remember having to go downtown to find a pair of flats. Mom wasn't too happy about spending that money, but I didn't want to tower over him. He seemed like a nice enough guy, and I was willing to get past the height issue. I was even willing to try to ignore his lisp."

Everyone at the table was giggling by now. "What I didn't realize was that he not only couldn't dance, but he wouldn't dance. We sat at a table all night long. He didn't want to get his picture taken. He didn't want to participate in anything. He and his buddy kept going outside and all of a sudden, it must have hit Beryl too, we realized they were getting high. In fact, I think that was the last year they let people go in and out of the building at a dance. After that year, once you were out, you stayed out. But, anyway, when he came back one time, he started getting handsy with me. I was so shocked I didn't know what to do. I moved my chair away, thinking he'd get the hint. Well, he was all relaxed and happy and started draping himself over me, trying to feel me up. Finally I slapped him. He giggled. I pushed him back and he went over his chair onto the floor. He kept laughing and came back for more.

"That was it for me. I told him that I was calling my dad to come get me. He tried to kiss me goodbye. He totally didn't get it, I guess. I shoved him again and back he went into the chair and pulled down a bunch of decorations that were hanging there. One of the sponsors came over and asked if everything was okay and told us that if we didn't settle down, we'd be asked to leave. I started crying, picked up my purse, walked out of the gym and kept walking until I got to the highway. I got to a pay phone, called my dad and he came to get me.

"Yeeeeaaahhh," Beryl drew the word out. "I still feel guilty about that."

"You should!" Andy said, "I almost didn't go to my senior prom because I was so scared something awful would happen again."

"But, you were with your sweetheart that year and it all worked out fine, didn't it?" Beryl retorted.

"I suppose. It wasn't really your fault, though. You were just dating a weirdo who happened to be friends with someone who was even stranger. I should have picked up on it the night we met for pizza, but I wanted to believe the best about him."

"That'll teach ya," Beryl laughed. "Alright," she went on. "We should let these youngsters get home and get to bed."

"I'm sorry for ducking out early," Polly apologized.

"No! Don't worry about it," Andy said. "I get it. You go on and make sure everything is okay at Sycamore House and we'll see you tomorrow."

Lydia said to Polly, "I'll be over about one thirty to pick you up to go shopping, alright?"

"Sounds great," Polly said. She and Sylvie collected their things and went out to the car.

"I feel like I killed the evening," Polly said to Sylvie.

"Don't worry about it. It's time to get the boys home anyway. I want to have fun with them tomorrow before classes start on Monday. There's a water park up in Fort Dodge, and we are going to hang out in warmth and humidity for the day."

Leia scampered across the auditorium floor when she saw Polly, who knelt down and scooped her up. "Did you miss me, little girl? How are you feeling? I probably should have checked on you more often, but I didn't want to bother Elise! It's good to see you."

"Thanks for looking after her, Doug."

"No problem." He didn't look up from his monitor for a few moments, then stopped and sat back. "She was fine."

"You haven't seen Elise come back or anything, have you?" Polly asked.

"Nope. No one has been in or out since she left, except you."

"Okay. Are you guys going to be here for a while?"

"If you don't mind." He looked over and saw Sylvie talking to

Jason. "Is it time for you guys to leave?"

Jason looked down, "Yes," he pouted, "but we don't want to."

"Hey, that's cool, little dude," Billy said. "You gotta obey the mama. Trust me on that. It's painful when you don't. Isn't it guys?"

Everyone laughed and agreed. It was obvious they'd all been there at some time in their lives.

"We'll have you back another time and maybe you can stay later," Billy said to Jason. "Here, take your copy of the game. You earned it."

"Really? Thanks!" Jason said.

Andrew was yawning and had quit playing some time ago, watching what was going on around him. When Sylvie got to him, he put his hand in hers and let her lead him out.

"Thanks, guys. I'll see you later," Polly said and as she followed the Donovans out of the room, heard choruses of "Thanks" and even a few "ma'ams" in there. She knew Billy had to be chuckling.

Sylvie asked Jason to go back to the kitchen to get their coats and he walked away.

"Thanks for making it possible for them to hang out with the older kids. I think it's great for them to see decent role models doing fun stuff," Sylvie said.

"No problem. And I like having them around myself." Polly patted Andrew's back and watched as they all left. Then she ran upstairs to drop Leia in the apartment and to get Obiwan for a quick walk. After she dropped him off in the apartment, she thought about opening Elise's door, but then thought that might be out of line if she was coming back soon. It would wait another day.

CHAPTER TEN

"Find the girl more coffee," Jeff said. "It's awfully early for a nap, isn't it?" Polly picked her head up, held out an empty coffee cup and then moaned as Jeff dropped into a chair in her office.

"You're right," she said. "It's too early. But I still need a nap. Those stupid animals of mine."

He chuckled. "You're the one who thinks she needs a zoo. What's up?"

"Well, I have Leia back and she must have become used to Elise's schedule because she has been up and into everything the last few nights. Then that means Luke is up and if he's up, that means Obiwan is up. And to top it off, they're going to sleep all day today and roam all night tonight again." She rubbed her eyes with one hand while leaning on the other. "I'm too young to be this tired," she complained.

"Maybe you need an afternoon nap," Jeff snickered.

"Hey," she said. "Naps are a good thing. You know. My dad used to come in at noon every day and in the next hour, he'd have lunch and a twenty-minute nap and be ready to change the world. Now, if I could only figure out how to make short power naps work for me."

Henry passed by the window of Polly's office, waved and as he came around the corner, stuck his head in the main office and said, "You look tired, Polly. Have you been out partying?"

She turned to Jeff. "Do I look that bad?"

"Your eyes are tired." He looked her up and down. "And you don't look all put together this morning. I can't put my finger on it, but you seem to be in disarray."

Polly looked down at her clothing and chuckled. "Well, that might be because my buttons are off on my shirt." She ran her hand through her hair. "And for heaven's sake, I didn't rinse the conditioner out this morning."

"Do you need to start the morning over again?" he asked.

"I'm going to have to do something," she said. "I'm going to a funeral today and I can't look like this!"

Polly's phone rang and answered it, "Sycamore House, may I help you?"

"Polly?"

"Yes."

"Hi there! This is Marnie from Doctor Ogden's office. Mark wanted to see if you would like him to stop in the morning to check on Leia and Obiwan. He's going out for the day and figured it would be easier if he stopped by rather than you bringing both of them here."

"Really?" Polly was stunned. "That would be terrific. What time?"

"He'll be there about seven thirty, will that work?"

"Sure. If you will give me his email address, I'll send the key to the main door to him. That way he can get in and come upstairs to the apartment."

Marnie had to ask a few questions about how emailing a key worked and then gave Polly the address.

Jeff had left her office during the exchange, shaking his head. He and Henry were talking out in the hall. After Polly sent the email to Mark Ogden with a little explanation, she joined them.

Jeff said, "Henry tells me the load of lumber is coming in this afternoon for the barn. That should start raising some interest."

"Are you having trouble getting people interested in helping?" she asked.

Henry laughed. "Not at all! No one around here has ever done anything like this and they're looking forward to the experience. I think some of them want to be able to tell their kids and grandkids they helped with a barn raising. We're going to have more than enough hands on Saturday."

"Sylvie says she is getting calls from some of the women in town who want to help in the kitchen on Saturday, too. At least those who don't want to be helping with the barn. It's going to be a big day around here, Polly!" Jeff declared.

"It all feels weird," Polly said. "I'm not involved in any of this and yet it's all going on around me." She wrinkled her brow. "That happens a lot to me, doesn't it!"

"It's because you have good people helping you," Jeff assured her. "You're our creative catalyst."

She laughed. "Well, if that's the way you want to look at it, I'm glad. I'll catalyst your creativity any day."

Andy walked in and joined them. "Good morning!" she said. "What are you chattering about?"

Polly smiled, "Good morning to you! We're talking about the barn raising on Saturday. The boys here ..." she winked at them, "both think it's going to be a huge success."

Andy took Polly's arm and began walking toward the auditorium. "Lydia says Elise hasn't been back since she took off Saturday night. You've heard nothing from her?"

"No, and I don't know whether it's my business to worry," Polly said. "She paid for her room until the middle of March. I'll wait a couple more days before I open it. I need to change sheets and gather towels up and make sure there aren't any dishes in there anyway. It's strange, don't you think?"

Andy nodded in agreement.

"Speaking of strange," Polly said. "Did you guys find anything else out last night at Madeline Black's house?" Lydia had invited her to join them in their next trek through the house filled with someone else's memories, but she declined. The two of them had spent the afternoon searching for bedding for the Walnut Room and had ordered a mattress set to be delivered this week as well. Polly was thrilled with the red, wheat and brown colored comforter set they'd found. The small leafy pattern that was woven into the comforter would be a perfect complement to the beautiful view of the trees along the creek. It would all be put together in time for her new resident to arrive the next Monday.

Even though Polly wasn't sure what had happened to Elise, she looked forward to meeting new people as they came to live at Sycamore House. It was a wonderful opportunity to expose outsiders to the joys of Iowa as well as offering them a chance to hide away and focus on whatever they were creating.

"The painting didn't have anything on the outside, but when Amy took the back off, that's what they found."

"I'm sorry, what?" Polly said. She was a little embarrassed when she realized she'd missed everything Andy said.

"The horses," Andy said. "Dean loved horses. He had written a note on the back of a painting, naming each of the horses. We're not sure what it means and we couldn't find any more information."

"What do you mean?" Polly asked.

"Did you not hear anything I said?"

Polly looked sideways at her friend, "I might have been daydreaming."

Andy laughed. "Well, of course you were. I often thought my voice sent my students off into daydreams. I wanted to believe they were bored with the content and not me, but you're not helping my ego."

"No!" Polly exclaimed, and grabbed Andy's forearm. "I'm sorry. I didn't get enough sleep last night because of the animals and I'm not all here. My mind seems to be wandering all over the place."

"Well, rein it back in, girlfriend. You have a busy week ahead of you."

"I know," Polly replied. "I'm sorry. Now, what were you saying?"

"Amy remembered her parents talking about how much her father had loved horses. I guess that when he was in Korea, he ended up in a regiment who had horses they used as pack animals. They figured that since he grew up in Iowa, he had to know something about livestock, so they put him in charge of them."

"Well, that's a great memory," Polly said, "but what does that have to do with the note?"

"Probably nothing, if it comes right down to it," Andy said. "But, who knows."

"Did he have horses while Laurence and Amy were growing up?"

"No. Laurence was thrown off a horse as a kid and hurt pretty badly. Amy said he whined and cried and threw such tantrums about being around horses after that, her parents finally got rid of them. In fact, they also moved into town so he would be safe from all of the things that could happen out in the country."

Polly raised her eyebrows. "Really?"

"Those were Amy's words, not mine. I think her brother is a bit of a prig," Andy laughed. "That might have something to do with the reason she lives in California. Her parents gave in to his whining and crying and it was all she could do to leave that behind and start a new life."

"I'm surprised they had a painting of horses in the house, then," Polly said.

"Actually, there were several, but Amy said they didn't start showing up until a few years before her father died. I guess he finally realized Laurence wasn't going to be home enough to care."

They were standing in the doorway to the auditorium and Polly nodded as Sam Terhune and Jimmy Rio walked past her to the classrooms.

"Well, I had better get started if I'm going to get anything done before the funeral," Andy commented. "Are you going?"

"I thought I would," Polly said. "I feel a little connection to that poor woman since I was there when Lydia found her."

"Are you going to the luncheon too?"

Polly giggled. "I haven't been to a funeral luncheon since my Dad's. Honestly, I wouldn't miss it. My memory was that the food is amazing."

"It's at the Methodist Church," Andy chuckled. "Those ladies can certainly put together a wonderful meal. Would you like to ride over with me? I'll just need to run home and throw on something a little more sedate."

Polly grinned as she took in Andy's black slacks and blue sweater. The woman did sedate as a matter of form. "That would be great. Thanks. I'll be in the office or wandering around when you're ready to leave."

Andy went on in to the auditorium and Polly wandered back into the classroom area. Walls were up and painted, bookshelves were installed and stained. It looked as if Henry and the boys were constructing the study carrels for the computer room. She had a delivery coming in tomorrow with chairs and tables. Things were coming together.

Henry stepped out of the computer room when she walked in. "We're doing well in here. I think we'll take the time tomorrow to install the ramp out front to be ready for the weekend. I know there are going to be quite a few of the older folk in town who will want to use it."

"Thanks, Henry," she said. "You've done amazing things here."

"Polly, I think it is every carpenter's dream to restore something old and make it new again. You've just given me a chance to make that dream real."

"But, I thought you said you didn't like restoring old furniture," she taunted.

"Well, I don't. It's hard work. But, even if I don't like doing that part of it, it's a good feeling to see it come back to life."

"I get it," she said. "Still, this is amazing."

"Thanks. I've enjoyed it all." He paused, and looked up with laughter in his eyes. "Except for getting snarled at by my boss last fall."

Polly flushed red. "You aren't ever going to forget that, are you?" Henry had pushed her pretty hard about the relationship with Joey before the man had kidnapped her last fall. After spending fourteen years as an independent young woman living in Boston, having people care for her had been a new experience for Polly. What they saw as caring, she saw as control. A few well-placed words with Henry had delivered the message that he needed to give her some respect and a little space.

"I'm not likely too. In fact, I think I'd be a fool if I did. A man needs to never repeat the same mistake more than, oh, say, twice."

They both laughed at that.

"Henry?" Sam called from the other room.

"I need to get back to work," he said.

"Okay. I'll talk to you later." Polly went back into her office and sat down to check her email. She opened a message from the Sheriff's office.

> Polly, we checked those phone numbers for you. They're from Chicago. I've got the names, but I'm sure they won't mean anything to you.
>
> I also did a search for Linda Marberry and since those numbers were from the Chicago area, I specified that location. There is a Linda Marberry who lives in that same community. I've pulled her Driver's License. The picture could be of the same person, but if so, she's made a lot of changes.
>
> Have you heard anything more from her?
>
> If you'd like, I'll be at the funeral with Lydia and can show you the picture. We'll see if it's the same person.
>
> Aaron

Polly wrote back telling him that she'd heard nothing more from Elise and that yes, she'd be at the funeral.

Jeff had forwarded copy for the article going into the Bellingwood Times about the barn raising and hoe-down. The paper would be out on Friday, in time to remind everyone of the Saturday event. She scanned through it, having full confidence that he'd already proofread everything. She emailed him back and assured him that it was fine. There were a few of her favorite weekly recipe emails to peruse and a note from her accountant with an attached file.

She spent the next hour going through the files he had sent as they prepared for taxes. She'd known Ed Hodgkins since she was a kid. He'd managed her dad's accounts and had filed her taxes for her every year since she'd gotten her first job in high school at the Dairy Queen. He'd been invaluable these last years since her father had died. She couldn't have had a better advisor as she began the process of renovating Sycamore House.

When she was finished, she sent a quick reply acknowledging her approval. As she leaned back in her chair, she looked out the window to see a flatbed semi pull into the parking lot. Henry was already heading out the door, with Sam and Jimmy following close behind him. She grabbed the jacket hanging behind her office door and went outside to watch the lumber get unloaded. Before she got to the front door, Jeff caught up to her, pulling on his own coat.

"We're a couple of greenhorns, aren't we, Polly?" he chuckled.

"I know!" she acknowledged. "Other than the lumberyard, I've never seen this much all in one place. And it's mine!" Her breath caught in her throat.

"Am I crazy?" she asked.

"A little bit," he laughed. "But, I think it's a good thing." He looked her in the eye. "Surely you know Henry would have said something if he thought you were making a mistake?"

"You're right," she agreed. "I have good people around me who won't let me make a fool of myself. A lot of good people. I shouldn't worry, should I?"

"You can worry, but you shouldn't," he said.

They watched as Henry talked to the driver and point where to drop the load of lumber. It didn't take long and everything was on the ground. They watched as Henry signed the paperwork and the truck drove away.

"Well, that's your barn!" he said. "Looks pretty good!"

"I'll take your word for it," Polly laughed. "Right now it looks like a pile of wood."

"The boys and I will make sure everything is in place. We're going to get started on Wednesday, so everything is ready for the party on Saturday. It's going to be alright, Polly."

Henry took her arm as they walked back into Sycamore House. "I'm not getting cold feet, but this keeps getting bigger and bigger," Polly said.

"And you're just the girl to make it happen," Jeff said. "Confidence, girl. Confidence!"

Polly went upstairs to take another quick shower and dress for the funeral. When she got back downstairs, Andy walked out of the auditorium carrying her purse. "Are you ready to go?" Andy asked.

Polly said yes and they left, driving to Andy's home. "I won't be a minute, but come on inside." Polly followed her in and sat down on Andy's sofa. She had been right. Within eight minutes, Andy was back downstairs, dressed in a neat black skirt with a blue blouse and matching black jacket. She slipped on pumps from the front closet and pulled out a knee length coat.

"Now I'm ready to go."

"That didn't take long at all."

"I had everything set out. I just needed to put it on and brush my hair once more," Andy smiled.

Cars were flowing into the parking lot as they arrived at the church. Polly was glad to be with someone who knew everyone they met. Andy made introductions while they made their way to the church basement. They stood on the stairs going down, waiting for the line to progress and she shut her eyes. It smelled the way she remembered her own church.

There was the scent of old books and furniture coupled with the smells emanating from the kitchen. She listened as she heard a low roar of chatter. There were a few voices that carried above the others and the clattering of running feet announced an oncoming rush of children who dashed past them up the steps. One young mother followed closely behind in an attempt to corral her kids.

Andy and Polly made it to the bottom of the steps and turned into the main hall. Tables were lined up and chairs were beginning to fill with people, all laughing and talking quietly. Sylvie was standing beside a young woman with her husband and two children who all looked very uncomfortable as people greeted them.

"That's Amy," Andy said as she noticed where Polly's eyes had landed. "And over there," she pointed to a man in his mid-forties standing with a prim looking lady and two older kids, all of whom looked like they would rather be anywhere but here, "is Laurence. He looks happy, doesn't he?"

Polly couldn't help herself, she snorted. "Sorry," she said. "He looks miserable; not terribly sad, just annoyed with the whole thing."

"That's about right."

Lydia and Aaron were seated in the middle of a line of tables. Lydia looked up and waved at them, then pointed at two seats beside where they were sitting.

More people found seats at the tables and the noise level rose and fell in the room. Polly and Andy finally wound their way to the seats being held for them and sat down.

"Whew!" Polly said. "This is a lot of people. Madeline Black must have been very well known."

"She was," agreed Lydia. "Some of this crowd knew and liked her husband and then there are always a few who come out to every funeral in town, so they don't miss out on the gossip and excitement. I suspect that since she was found dead in her home and the story of the unfinished note got around, that brought out even more people."

Aaron leaned across the table and stage whispered, "And it's a Methodist funeral luncheon. Some of us come for the food."

Polly laughed as she glanced at her own plate. She'd taken only a little bit of each item that looked good, but the further she got down the line, the more food had ended up on her plate. When she got to the dessert table, she'd panicked, wanting everything from the deep, rich chocolate cake to the strawberry cobbler, pecan pie and carrot cake. She finally settled on the chocolate cake, but felt a little sad at leaving everything else.

"No guilt," Lydia said. "You can't feel guilty today."

"Alright, then" Polly announced. "No guilt," and began

sampling her food.

Women moved throughout the tables, refilling emptied glasses and gathering up plates and silverware as people finished their meals. It seemed to Polly there was an efficiency here most restaurants would envy.

Aaron pulled a piece of paper out of his jacket pocket and unfolded it in front of Polly. The woman in the picture looked nothing like Elise Myers, at least on the surface. Elise's hair was brown and long, while Linda Marberry's hair was a beautiful red and cropped quite short, framing the woman's face. Linda Marberry wasn't wearing glasses, but Polly knew that didn't count. The biggest difference was in the eyes. Linda's were bright and shining. If it was really Elise, she had done a great deal to change the structure of her eyebrows and she either wore makeup to make her eyes look deep and sunken or there was something wrong. Elise probably weighed a good thirty pounds more than the woman in the photo.

"I don't know," she said to Aaron. "I just don't know. I'm terrible at faces anyway, so I can't say for sure if they are the same person."

"Well, now you've seen this," he said. "We'll keep an eye on things to see if she comes back."

"Okay," Polly said.

They finished their meal and went upstairs. They each signed into the guest register and then found a pew where they could be seated together. A pianist was quietly playing some classical pieces and there were low murmurs in the sanctuary as people filled in the pews. Polly looked up as Sylvie touched her shoulder and they moved together so she could join them. Soon the family was escorted in and Polly recognized Pastor Boehm, who walked to the front of the sanctuary.

He knelt in prayer for a few moments at the altar while the pianist continued playing and the room became quiet. He stood, walked to the pulpit and began the service. An organist joined the pianist as the congregation sang hymns. Polly watched as Amy's shoulders shook when Pastor Boehm began speaking about the relationship Madeline had with her family, the community, the church and with God. Amy's husband put his arms around her and her youngest son leaned into her. Polly glanced at Laurence and his wife, who sat rigidly at the other end of the pew. While she felt badly for Amy's grief, it occurred to her that Laurence was the one to be pitied.

The service soon came to a close and Polly was glad to get back outside. The sanctuary had warmed up quite a bit with all the people gathered and the woman in front of her had overdone it with some flowery perfume. She'd tried not to cough and Lydia pressed a piece of gum into her hand, then patted it. Polly chuckled. It was the same move Mary, the woman who cared for her after her mother died, made when Polly began squirming in church on Sunday mornings. Anything to keep the little girl occupied.

She and Andy said goodbye to Lydia and Aaron. Sylvie had already made her way back to Amy. When they got in the car, Andy asked, "Do you mind if we run back to my house so I can change and get back to work."

Polly smiled, "That would be great. Thank you for today, Andy. I'm glad I went. This is one of the best parts of being home again. Whether it's a funeral or some other event, it is much better when you're among friends."

CHAPTER ELEVEN

Polly decided to be ready for Doctor Ogden, since he planned to be in her apartment around seven thirty. She'd gotten up at five thirty, walked the dog, taken a quick shower and then spent a great deal of time with her wardrobe and makeup for the day. She checked herself out in the mirror and thought "I'll do!" She had tried to stay subtle with her makeup, not wearing more than most days, but just enough eye liner and mascara to help her eyes look wide awake. Her hair did exactly what she'd hoped as she brushed it into place, light weight curls framing her face and nestling on her shoulders. The deep violet blue sweater was a perfect color for her and black denim jeans brushed the tops of the black ankle high boots. Yep. She'd do.

Polly put an apron on and mixed a glaze for the cinnamon apple muffins, which were cooling on the counter. The coffee was brewing and she had grabbed a couple of covered paper cups from the downstairs kitchen so he could take everything to go if he didn't have time to sit down to eat. She checked her watch and saw that it was seven twenty-five. The muffins were ready, the coffee was ready and even the animals seemed ready for company. Pulling her apron back off, she hung it on a hook in the pantry closet, smoothed her sweater and fluffed her hair one more time. Now, even she was ready.

She sat down at the dining room table to wait and caught herself tapping her foot. She stood and paced until she found herself at the sofa. She sat down beside Obiwan and rubbed his shoulders for a few moments. Next, she checked on the cats in her bedroom and found them wrestling on her bed. It had been a week since surgery and Polly hoped Leia really was fine.

She'd spent an hour last night cleaning her bedroom. Mary would have been ashamed of her. She'd once laughingly told Polly whenever she was late to breakfast that the piles of junk and clothes in Polly's room might be hiding her body. She tried, she really did. Polly blamed it on not having enough storage, but she knew better. By week's end, there were always empty drawers in her dresser. The worst thing was, the hamper was empty as well.

Things had been so busy she hadn't done laundry over the weekend. Last night her room had been horrendous. Clothes had tried to creep out into the living room, but she'd managed to wrangle and clean everything and felt pretty proud of the place. Polly checked her watch again. Seven thirty-seven. She rolled her eyes and chuckled. If a messy bedroom was a vice, punctuality was another. She tried to be patient with those who were never on time, because she knew it was an obsession of hers.

Both cats stopped wrestling and ran out into the living room, jumping up onto the back of the sofa. Luke leaped up and over Obiwan, whose ears had perked up. He jumped down and walked over to the front door, wagging his tail.

"Well," she said. "I guess you guys are my doorbell. Shall we let him in?"

Polly opened the entryway door, catching Mark in the process of raising his hand to ring the bell.

"The animals heard you coming. I didn't mean to startle you."

Obiwan sniffed at the veterinarian's boots, not letting him move without trying to smell him.

"I know, guy. Those boots see more animals than you even

know yet," he said, while kneeling down. "Let's see how you're doing."

Polly realized they weren't going to make it too far into the apartment, so she flipped on the light in the entry.

Mark peeled off the bandage and began manipulating the foot.

He looked up at her and said, "It's going to be fine. The wound is healing nicely and I don't think we need to replace this."

Polly held her hand out for the dirty bandage and he said, "Thanks. He was lucky you were right there with him. We see a few of these things happen every year about this time." Mark gave Obiwan a hug around the neck before he stood up. "I'd keep an eye on the creek for a few more days. Dan said the trapper would be checking things next weekend and would pull out the traps bordering your property."

"Thank you for taking care of that, Mark. I appreciate it." Polly crumpled the bandage in her fist and said, "Well, come all the way in, then. Would you like a muffin or some coffee?"

"Thanks! I didn't get breakfast this morning, but I have a soda in the truck. I don't drink coffee," he replied.

"What?" she laughed. "I thought everyone in this town was completely addicted to the stuff."

"I feel embarrassed some days," he said. "Wherever I go, they offer me coffee. Maybe when I grow up, I'll learn to drink it."

"Do you have a minute to sit down or do you need to check the cat and run? If you have to hurry, I could pack up a couple of muffins for you."

"I'd love to stay, but I'm expected out at Harrison's barn this morning." He walked over and scooped Leia up off the back of the sofa. She and Luke had taken positions at either end and were eyeing him warily.

Polly pulled out her collection of plastic ware, finding a square container and lid. She packed four muffins in the container, then rummaged in a cupboard, finding a small brown paper bag with handles. The muffins and some napkins went inside and she walked back into the living room.

"She's doing fine," he announced. "Let her play with the big boys now that the stitches are out."

"What?" Polly asked.

"It was easy. I just pulled them out. She's ready to go. Keep an eye on her and if anything seems abnormal, let us know, but we do these all the time."

"Thank you! I'll take care of this with Marnie, but what can I do to thank you for coming over here?" she asked him.

He paused, as if thinking. "You could make me dinner tonight and let me teach you how to dance before the big day on Saturday." A small smile quirked the corners of his lips and he put his hand out to take the bag from Polly.

Mark's other hand held the cat and he reached down to put the cat back on the sofa. Polly hadn't said a word.

"Well? Dinner? I eat anything and everything. I'm easy to cook for."

Polly looked at him and said, "Okay. What time?"

"How about six thirty. That will give me time to get the day washed off and look presentable. Can I use the key to get into the building again?"

"Sure," she said, a little dazedly, then she nodded. "That will be wonderful. But, wait. You really do know how to dance?"

"I'm a great dancer," he smirked. "I'll tell you all about it over dinner. How's that for a deal?" He began moving to the front door. "I'll see you tonight."

With his free hand, he touched her elbow. It was more intimate than she expected. Maybe it was because he took that moment to look straight into her eyes. Polly couldn't think to speak. She simply watched him walk down the steps.

Closing the door to the apartment, she made her way to the sofa and sat down, finding herself immediately surrounded by animals. "Well, guys. Now I don't know what to do. I have another date and I'm cooking." She dropped her head back and forced her body to relax, feeling the soft fur of her pets as she stroked them. She wasn't even sure which hand was on which animal.

It took a few moments for her to regain her equilibrium and

then she sat up and dislodged the cats. "It looks like I'd better figure out what I have in the refrigerator." Polly opened the refrigerator door and then the door of her small pantry beside the fridge. Standing in front of the two, she considered her options. She shut the doors and flipped open her laptop, bringing up a browser. A few clicks later and there was the recipe she wanted. Scanning the ingredients and instructions, Polly jotted down a few notes, saved the page to her notes software and then turned around and opened the pantry again. She needed to go to the grocery store, but fortunately, everything necessary was at the little store downtown. She checked her list once more, opened the refrigerator door again and looked in the freezer, then shoved the list in her back pocket.

"Alright, guys. I will see you later," she said as she walked out the door into the hall. Polly stood in front of her doorway, looking across at the door to the room Elise Myers had rented from her.

"It's alright," she said to herself, "You own the place and are expected to care for the linens and keep things clean and neat. Just go in the room."

Mustering her courage, she triggered the door lock and walked in to Elise's room. Things were pretty much the same as the last time she had been in the room, so she pulled the comforter off and began pulling the sheets back. As she tugged on the top corner of the fitted sheet, the mattress pulled up and she thought she had caught a glimpse of something dark. She lifted the mattress, then let it drop.

Great. A gun.

She picked the mattress up again and bent over to get a closer look at it. She wasn't sure why she was looking so closely at it. She laughed at herself. She wouldn't know a Glock from a ... It occurred to Polly she didn't know much about handguns. Her dad had taught her how to shoot a rifle and a shotgun, but this was a bit alien.

Polly gathered up the linens and glanced down at the desk as she walked past. She saw her name and looked more closely. Now why in the world would Elise leave a note for her inside the room? How would she know when Polly would get there?

She dropped the linens and picked up the envelope. It wasn't sealed and she pulled the card out. On it, Elise had written,

I'm sorry to duck out on you in such a hurry. I need to leave town. If anyone comes looking for me, you can tell them in all honesty that I'm gone and you don't know when I'll return.

If you don't hear from me by Valentine's Day, check your email. There will be a phone number for you to call so someone will come get my things.

Elise M.

Polly read the note again. It sounded ominous. She gathered up the linens again and went downstairs. Cutting through the kitchen, she started a load of laundry and left the rest in a large basket beside the washing machine. She programmed her phone alarm to remind her to come back to the laundry room and headed for the office. Jeff was working at his computer, so she sat down in front of him, not saying a word while he typed.

"Yes?" he said, continuing to type.

"What'cha doin'?" she asked.

He grinned and said, "Why?"

"Because I wanted to know!" she shrugged and chuckled, then put the note in front of him. "What am I supposed to do with this?" she asked.

He stopped typing and picked up the card. When he finished reading, he set it down and looked up at her. "Ummm. I don't know?"

"Exactly!" Polly exclaimed. "I don't know either. Should I worry about her? I don't know what good that would do me, but for some reason I feel a little responsible for her. I don't know who to call if something has gone wrong and I won't get a phone number unless she doesn't return."

Jeff said, "Just a second," and pulled out his own phone. He scrolled through numbers and said, "I've got a number here. Do you want me to call it?"

"What's the number?"

"When she first made the reservation, I logged the call."

"Well, yes! Do you mind?"

Jeff pressed the send button and waited. In a moment he smiled and nodded, then said, "Hello. Is Elise Myers available?"

He listened for a moment, "This is Jeff Lyndsay from Sycamore House where she has been staying while working on her Doctoral dissertation. She left us on Friday. I wanted to ensure she was alright and wondered when she might be returning."

There was another pause while he listened. "I see. Thank you very much. If she should contact you would you please tell her I called."

He set the phone down on the desk and said, "Well, I'm not sure what to make of that. A woman answered and hesitated before she told me that Elise wasn't at that number. She seemed pretty shook up that I was looking for the girl and then told me that she must have had an emergency. I'm sorry I couldn't get more information, but I don't think she would have given it to me anyway."

"Can you email that phone number to me?" Polly asked. "If I get too worried about this, I might cook some fried chicken and ask Aaron Merritt to see what he can find out." She picked the card and envelope up as she stood. "Do you need me for anything?"

He looked puzzled, "I don't think so?"

"Okay," she said. "I wanted to make sure you were doing alright with plans for Saturday. I feel like I don't have anything to do."

"Do you *want* something to do?"

"That's not it. It just feels strange."

"I promise. If I need you, I'll let you know."

"Thanks." Polly dropped the card on her desk and looked out the front window of her office. Jimmy and Sam were installing the ramp today and had gotten an early start. Henry's truck wasn't in the lot, but she saw Andy pulling in. Polly turned to head back to her desk, but stopped when she saw Lydia Merritt's familiar blue Jeep park beside Andy and both Lydia and Beryl got out. She smiled as she watched the three women greet each other with quick hugs and walk toward the building. They stopped for a moment to chat with the boys building the ramp, then waved at Polly through the inside window after they walked in through the front door. She went out to meet them.

"What are you all doing here this morning?" she asked.

"They thought I spent too much time alone so they made me come do something productive," Beryl grumped. "And at this hideous hour of the morning." She sighed an immense, dramatic sigh and with a waver in her voice, said, "No one understands the needs of a poor artist." She lifted the back of her hand to the brow of her forehead as she spoke the last two words.

"Oh, stop it," Lydia chided. "If you were still in the middle of a project, I would have left you alone, but you said you were finished with the set for the Cedar Rapids gallery." Lydia pushed her lower lip out and said, "And I missed you. So there."

Beryl's whole body laughed as she hugged her friend. "I missed you too." She looked at Polly. "What's up today?"

"I have no idea. No one tells me anything," she said.

"Well, we heard you had muffins and coffee with Dr. Hottie. Do you still have muffins upstairs?" Beryl gave Polly a little push in the shoulders.

"How in the world did you hear that?" Polly asked, then sighed, "Come on up. The apartment is very clean and there are muffins and coffee. He didn't drink any of that. He doesn't like it."

She started up the steps and Beryl said, "We stopped by his office this morning with my Miss Kitty before coming here. She's getting her teeth cleaned and it's better if she and I don't see each other for twenty-four hours when that happens."

Lydia interjected, "Marnie was on the phone with him when we got there. She thought it was cute."

Polly shook her head and opened the door to her apartment. "There is nothing secret in this town, is there!"

"Not if we can help it," Lydia said. "It keeps everyone in line. So stay in line, alright?"

Polly pried the lid off the container of muffins and set it in the middle of the dining room table. She pulled four mugs out of the cupboard and began handing them to Lydia, followed by plates and forks and napkins.

"Do I need to warm them up?" she asked.

Andy felt the bottom of the container and said, "I think they're still pretty warm. They'll be fine and they smell wonderful!"

"You had Mr. Hottie all to yourself this morning? How'd that go?" Beryl asked.

"Well ..." Polly began.

"It must have gone well; she can't even start the sentence," Beryl interrupted and put a muffin on her plate before passing the container around.

"He was only here for a few minutes to check Leia and Obiwan. He had to get to someone's farm. I asked him to stay, but he was in a hurry." Polly rushed through the information.

Lydia smiled. "Did he ask you for a date?"

"Not really," Polly said.

"What do you mean, not really?" Andy's brow wrinkled. "What is not really a date?"

"He invited himself here for dinner tonight and said he was going to teach me how to dance."

Beryl sat back in her chair, "Wow! That boy is on it! I'm impressed! What are you making for dinner?"

Polly slumped forward at the table, "Stuffed Chicken Marsala."

"Of course you are! You little wild woman. You're trying to impress him."

"Well, it's a great recipe and I already have the chicken and wine."

"I suppose you're going to make a chocolate cake and homemade ice cream, too."

"Well, maybe the chocolate cake, but I already have good ice cream in the freezer."

"You're becoming quite the celebrity with the boys around town. First it's dead bodies and now you're going to start consuming all the single young men."

"Stop it!" Polly's voice rose in pitch and decibel level and she was sure the look on her face was one of pure shock.

Lydia patted her arm. "It's alright, Polly. Beryl didn't mean anything. She's just jealous because it seems like you are taking her place as the town's most desired single woman."

"I'm not jealous at all. Those boys are much too young for me. They don't have nearly the experience I expect in a man. So, Polly, you get them all trained up and when they become a little more suave and debonair, I'll step in and take over. Will that work?"

"I'm speechless," Polly announced. "Would you like more coffee?"

The three women laughed at her. "We'll change the subject, but you must know we're all going to be here again tomorrow morning for details."

"Great," Polly lamented. "Sylvie will be here all day tomorrow as well. I might as well invite you to come to dinner tonight."

"We'd love to! Thanks!" Beryl said. "I'll bring the wine. Lydia, why don't you bring the ..."

"Hush," Lydia said. "We're changing the subject." She turned to Polly, "Don't you think Henry is going to be a little jealous when you start dating Mark Ogden?"

"Thanks for the change of subject," Polly said. "But, maybe I need to clear a few things up. First ..." and she lifted her index finger. "This is not a date. He's going to show me how to dance so I don't make a fool of myself. I also owe him dinner for coming over to check out my animals."

"No. Stop!" she said as she watched Beryl about to take a breath. "Second ..." and two fingers went up on her right hand. "Henry and I are not in a relationship ..."

Beryl muttered, "Whatever."

"I said stop," Polly said, glaring at the woman, who chose to affect a dramatic, apologetic face. "Third, if Henry is going to be jealous at this point in our ..." she paused, "non-relationship, he's going to have a tough time ahead. I don't do well with people boxing me in and there's probably no one in Bellingwood who knows that better than Henry. He and I have a great time doing things together, but remember: we're not in a relationship."

Polly flashed a look at Beryl, who held up her hands in

defense. "Fine," Beryl said, "You're not in a relationship and this is not a date." She picked up her coffee. "And this is caffeine free?"

"No, it's the real thing," Polly laughed and managed to snort at the same time.

"Do you have any more thoughts on the mystery of Madeline Black's note?" she asked.

Lydia sighed and pursed her lips. "No. Laurence has managed to swoop in and kick everyone out of the house. He says he's going to lock it up and deal with it later. Amy flies back to California today with her family. She said she would keep in touch, though. I just hope there's not someone out there who is in trouble because we don't know about them."

"Leave it to you Lydia. You have to take care of someone, even if they don't exist. Maybe the old lady was talking about her dead husband's false teeth. Did you find those in the house?" Beryl laughed.

"No false teeth," Lydia said and rolled her eyes. "My intuition is trying to tell me something, but I don't know what yet." She looked over her glasses at Beryl, "And don't you start with me."

"Wow," Beryl declared. "I come out of my studio only to be told off by my friends. It's rough out here!"

"Another muffin?" Polly asked.

"Thank you, I will," Beryl said and passed the container around again. Andy passed it on without taking another and so did Lydia. "Well, I'll be. You two must not be planning to work as hard as I am today. All of this sweet stuff will be taken care of with a few trips around that auditorium downstairs. Shall we go get busy?"

They nodded and Beryl took a napkin to wrap around her muffin. As everyone headed down the steps, Lydia held back and said to Polly, "Just be sure of what you are doing with your heart, Polly. I'd hate for you to break it, alright?"

"I'm fine, Lydia. This is not a date. He's adorable and I think I'll enjoy the evening, but that's all it is, okay?"

"Okay. Please take care of yourself."

CHAPTER TWELVE

Oven on warm – check. Table set - check. Wine - check. Dessert - check. Polly ran into the bathroom to look at her hair and makeup. She fluffed her hair at the top of her head one more time, ran her tongue across her lips to moisten them, then rubbed her palms down the sides of her pants in order to dry them off. She was not going to be nervous about this.

She had tried on three different blouses. One was a pretty color, but what in the heck had she been thinking when she bought a blouse with ruffles around the buttons. That wasn't her style at all. She stuck it in the back of her closet. The second blouse was also attractive, but the shoulders didn't fit her well. If she was going to dance with someone tonight, she wanted plenty of freedom to move around. Especially if she sent them both to the floor when she tripped him. Polly had finally settled on a hot pink blouse with a low neck and small ties bringing it together at the neck. She did a couple of squats to make sure her jeans were as comfortable as she thought they were and everything seemed fine. She lit a candle for ambience and turned out the overhead light in the bathroom.

Polly found the cats sleeping together in between the pillows at the top of her bed. Just about the time she was ready to go to bed, they found a million reasons to be up and playing, but now they were sound asleep. She was fine with that.

One more check of the time. Six twenty-five. Would he be late or early or right on time? She went out into the living room and glanced at Obiwan. They'd spent thirty minutes walking this evening while the chicken baked. He was curled into a ball at the end of the sofa, watching her with one eye as she paced around the room. Another glance at the food in the oven. Yep, it was still fine. Polly opened the fridge. Everything was still in the same place it had been when she put it there.

Then, Obiwan's ears perked up and he looked at the door.

"Thank you," she said. "You're a better alarm system than anything I could install." She forced herself to stay in the kitchen. She didn't want to startle Mark again by opening the door before he knocked. The doorbell softly chimed and she paced herself as she walked over and opened the door.

"Hi there," she said.

"Hi yourself." He handed her a bouquet of colorful daisies and a bottle of white wine, which she took from him as she stepped back to allow him to enter. Obiwan jumped off the sofa and dashed to say hello and Mark knelt down to rub his shoulders and neck.

Mark looked up at her. "He didn't let you know I was coming up the steps?"

She giggled. "He did. I didn't want to startle you again like I did this morning!"

He stood up and began to shrug out of his jacket. Polly's breath caught. The man was gorgeous. He was the type of boy she had idolized from afar in high school, knowing he would never be interested in her. He was the center for the basketball team, or the quarterback on the football team. He was comfortable with every teacher and all of the students. Elected prom king, homecoming king, winter ball king ... you name it. That was the guy standing in front of her in her apartment.

"Where can I put my coat?" he asked.

"Through there ..." she nodded toward the bedroom door. "The cats are on the bed, but there's a chair inside the door. I'll get these into a vase."

She knew it was silly, but she loved these crazy daisies. They were dyed all sorts of improbable colors and she loved nothing more than scattering vases of them around her apartment. It had been several weeks since her last splurge of color had died, and she was surprised he'd known to bring these. Maybe it was only a coincidence.

"Thank you for the flowers," she said. "These are my favorites. I love all the color!"

He smiled. "Good. They seemed like something you might enjoy. I hope you like chardonnay," he said, pointing at the wine.

"I do. I'm not a huge fan of red wine, and since we're having chicken tonight, this will be perfect." She slipped her bottle of wine back beside the refrigerator and dropped his into the bucket. It seemed like it was already a good temperature, so she grabbed a corkscrew and walked over to the table with it. "Would you like to do the honors?" she asked.

"Sure. My mama taught me a few things about wine." He took the corkscrew from her and set to work unwrapping the top.

"Are you ready to eat? I can serve any time."

"I'm here to spend an evening eating and dancing. You're in charge of the timing," he smiled and she heard a thwop as the cork pulled from the bottle.

"You pour and I'll bring out the food."

Polly transferred the Chicken Marsala and wild rice into a serving dish and placed it on the table. A few more trips and a salad, carafe of iced water and a basket of beautiful rye and white rolls were on the table. She pulled a hot baking dish of cheesy asparagus out of the oven and set it on a trivet between them, looked the table over, scrutinized it for color and decided it was fine. The salad was filled with red tomatoes and colorful peppers, carrots and shades of green. Yes, she was happy with it.

"This looks great, Polly. Do you cook like this all the time?" he asked as he held her seat for her when she was finally ready to sit down. Mark sat at the end of the table, where she had put the other place setting.

"I enjoy cooking, but I probably don't as often as I should. I'm a sucker for a frozen pizza or a bologna sandwich if I'm all by myself."

"I love bologna, tomatoes, mayonnaise and potato chips in my sandwich," he laughed.

"I do too!" she said. "My mother taught me to put potato chips in sandwiches to make them more fun. Wow, that's a memory I'd lost."

He held his glass of wine up and said, "To old and new memories. May they fill our lives with laughter."

She tilted her glass into his and said, "Cheers."

"Oh!" he said, "I should have said something when I walked in, but Obiwan distracted me. Is there any reason you have someone watching your place?"

Polly set her glass down with a thud, "What?"

"Like your guest or an employee or anything? Maybe it's nothing and they're gone by now."

"Where? What?" Polly tried to breathe. "What?"

"There was a car sitting over in the swimming pool parking lot with a couple of people sitting in it. Maybe they were trying to get their bearings, but they're not from around here."

Polly got up and started to run over to the kitchen window, then thought better of it and walked quietly. She turned the water on nonchalantly and glanced out the window across the parking lot and the road. There was a car in the lot for the swimming pool, but she didn't see any exhaust coming out of it. The evening was cold and whoever was in that car had to be freezing without the car running.

"You're sure there is someone in that car?" she asked.

Mark joined her at the window. "Pretty sure. I suppose I could have ... No, I'm sure."

"And you don't recognize the vehicle from town? It's not a couple looking for a place to go parking?"

"On a county highway? In town? Sheesh, Polly, I thought you grew up around here," he laughed.

"I didn't mean that!" she protested, then said, "Okay, I probably did mean that."

"Come on, let's eat dinner and have a nice evening. If they're still there when I leave tonight, we'll call someone to check on them. How about that?"

"You're right. It's probably nothing. And I did make dinner." She laughed and said, "Thanks for telling me so I can be aware and thanks for telling me not to worry so I can enjoy the evening."

They went back to the table and sat down to eat.

"Okay," Polly said as she poured dressing on her salad. "Tell me how in the world a veterinarian is also a dancer. Where in the world did that come from?"

"It's not that strange, is it?" he laughed.

"It's maybe a little odd," she said.

"My mom was a dancer. She loved dancing and when I was a kid, she started teaching in an Arthur Murray Dance studio in Minneapolis. Then, she and Dad decided that it would be good for them if they bought the studio. He was an accountant and managed the business while she did what she loved.

"She had five boys and we all learned how to dance and we all ended up teaching dance classes at her studio. My sister has more classical training and danced some in Chicago, but when she met her husband and decided to have children, she realized that her passion was also teaching.

"In fact, she moved to Bellingwood after I settled here and opened the studio downtown. It's nice having her around. I get to spend time with great kids and leave them with her when I go home."

"Then, what brought you to Bellingwood?" Polly asked.

"I came down to Iowa State for vet school and spent time here interning. Doc Blades was pretty close to retirement and I spent a couple of years with him after graduation. Dad helped me set up the business plan and I bought the practice. Ralph was pretty much done last spring and I think he and Freida left for Arizona in their camper in November and may never return."

"Marnie says you've brought on another vet?"

"Seth Jackson. Yeah. He interned with me and had gotten a job in Waterloo. He was tired of living in the city."

Mark laughed and said, "He's good with animals and he gets it about living in a small town. I think he grew up down in southeast Iowa somewhere. I couldn't believe he thought Waterloo was a big city, though."

Polly nodded. "At least he figured it out pretty quickly. It took me fourteen years to realize I missed the small town and rural life."

"I didn't know anything about small towns until college, but I soon realized how much I loved the quiet."

"That had to be strange for you, coming from the city."

"My family certainly enjoys living in the city. Mom loved taking us to everything she could. Dad bought two season tickets to the symphony, opera and ballet every year and she would dress one of us up and make us go with her. When Lisa showed an interest in ballet, they just bought a third ticket so she could attend everything."

Polly smiled, "That sounds nice."

"I suppose it was. But, do you know how difficult it was to be cool and want to be a basketball player when your mom was only interested in taking you to the ballet?"

"What about your Dad?"

"He was so smitten with that woman, she talked him into anything. My oldest brother, Jack, though, played football in high school and when I started playing basketball, he sat Mom down and told her that she had to start going to my games. He made sure she knew she couldn't expect us to all follow in her footsteps."

"Did you play basketball in college?"

"I sure did! In fact, I got a partial scholarship to play."

"Do any of your brothers still dance?"

"Robbie is still in Minneapolis. He likes helping Mom out at the studio, and teaches with her every week."

"Does he work for her?"

"I suppose she pays him, she always did. It was nice to make extra money, but no, he's a portrait and wedding photographer."

"What about your other brothers?"

"Jack lives in Rochester. He is in IT at the Mayo Clinics. Evan lives up in Duluth. He writes for the News Tribune and Devin, who is his twin, lives in Austin. He and his wife, Ellen, own an interior design firm."

"You all have very diverse occupations!" Polly said.

"I suppose. We were lucky. Mom and Dad told us to pursue our dreams. We watched Dad completely support Mom in hers and knew that if we went after something, it could be real."

"And you all dance," she commented.

"We all dance," he agreed.

"Does your Dad dance, too?"

"He's actually pretty good, but he and Mom have been dancing since they met. He had to have learned a few things over the years."

"Did they ever compete?"

Mark laughed out loud. "We all competed at some point. She wrangled him into a citywide ballroom dance competition one year. I'd never seen him as miserable as he was during that period of time. He kept telling her that the reason he was an accountant was so that he could sit in a room and add up small numbers, not glide across a dance floor in front of judges. He did it because he adored her, but she realized that it nearly killed him. After that, Robbie or Jack danced with her."

"You said Jack was the oldest. Where do the rest of you fall in?"

"Lisa is the baby and then the twins are two years older than she is. I'm right in the middle, Robbie is three years older than me and Jack is two years older than him."

Mark put his fork down and reached for another roll. As he tore it apart and buttered it, he said, "But, that's enough about me. I've been talking and talking. Tell me something about you that hasn't hit the Bellingwood gossip train."

Polly thought for a moment. "It's been nice talking about

someone other than myself," she said. "I like hearing your stories. But, alright. Something no one around here knows about me. Let's see."

She nodded to signify that the wine he poured into her glass was enough, and said, "Until I moved to Bellingwood, my life was pretty boring. I had thought about being a veterinarian when I was a kid. I loved horses but I didn't ever have a chance to own any. Dad was so busy with everything else on the farm, he couldn't swing it. I didn't push. One of my friends, Jan, always let me ride with her, but that was it. Of course, we had lots of animals out there. Dad didn't want them in the house, so my dogs and cats were always outside animals. I remember bringing SusieQ, our mutt, inside one night. I wanted her to sleep in my room with me. Well, the poor dog didn't know what to do in my room. She whined until Dad opened my bedroom door. He took one look at me, shook his head and let the dog back outside."

Polly picked her glass up and took a sip, "I should warn you. Wine goes straight to my head. Hopefully I've eaten enough that I won't get too loopy on you."

"As long as it relaxes you enough to dance with me, you're fine," Mark laughed. "What kind of girl were you in high school? I'll bet you had a lot of friends. Did you play in the band? Did you play any sports?"

"No!" Polly declared. "If I tell you that I can't dance, I'm being totally serious. I stink at it. Now, transfer my ineptitude for dancing to a basketball or volleyball court. Imagine the damage I could do to a team in competition." She snorted in laughter. "I didn't play any sports and we'll leave it at that. But, I was in band and I always had good grades."

She paused and said, "I did have a lot of friends. There were a bunch of us who moved in and out of different cliques. I was friends with the athletic girls. I just couldn't play with them and they knew better than to ask me. I was quite glad to sit in the bleachers and cheer for them. I dated a wrestler once and the next date was with Andy Tressler, the epitome of the chess club king. He was a little odd, so that didn't work out quite like I'd hoped.

But, yes. I suppose I had a lot of friends."

"Have you seen many of them since you moved back?"

"You know, it's weird, but I haven't. I've found most of them on Facebook, but we've all got our lives going on right now and while it's good to see that they're all happy in their lives, none of us have rushed right out to get together again. I guess maybe fifteen years puts a lot of distance between us ... more than we ever thought."

"Would you like some dessert?" she asked. "Or would you like to wait?"

Mark sat back in his chair and stretched. "Maybe we should wait, if that's alright. This was terrific and I ate too much. You're a great cook! Are you ready to do some dancing now?"

"You aren't going to let me out of this, are you?"

"I am not," he replied. "I left my speakers and iPod in the hallway. That will be a great space to practice." He stood up and swooped his hand out in invitation. "Shall we dance?"

Polly put her hand in his and stood up. Obiwan had been sleeping under the table while they ate and looked expectantly as she walked to the door. "Nope, not yet. We'll go out later, I promise. First, I have to face some torture."

Mark led her out into the hall and left the door to the apartment slightly ajar. A small portable speaker system was sitting on the floor beside her door with an iPod already docked.

"Before we do this for real, I want to teach you a few basic steps." When Polly grimaced, he said, "It won't hurt, I promise."

"I'm not worried about it hurting me," she said. "You're the one in mortal danger."

"I've been with worse; I can assure you."

"Let's do it, then, if I'm not going to be able to escape your clutches," she sighed.

He stood beside her and said, "Watch my feet and do what I do." Polly mimicked the movement of his feet as he slowly took her through the basic box-step. "Walk, side, together," he said as they moved.

"Can you do it on your own?" he asked. She tried to remember where to put her feet and quickly stumbled as her left foot caught her right heel.

"See!" she said.

"Try again. Here, do it with me," he put his arm around her back and guided her through the steps again. "Now, by yourself."

She tried it again and again until finally she felt what it was he was saying to her.

"That's it!" he proclaimed. "You've got it. Now, I'm going to turn some music on. See if you can do it in time with the rhythm of the song."

It didn't take long for Polly to trip over her feet and she cursed.

"No, don't freak out," he said. "You're doing fine." He flipped the light switch off and said, "There's enough light you won't fall down the steps, but this time shut your eyes and try again."

Polly said, "I'm putting a lot of trust in you. I don't let very many people see me this uncoordinated. I hope you know that if you tell anyone, you die."

"I'm fully confident that you could find a way to destroy me. My lips are sealed. Now shut your eyes and dance."

She closed her eyes and tried to feel the rhythm of the music, and then began to move her feet. She'd moved through several patterns of the box step when she felt him slip an arm around her waist. Her eyes flew open.

"Shut your eyes," he said and put her left hand on his shoulder, and then scooped her right hand in his hand. "Now, don't forget to breathe."

Polly tried to relax, but the next thing she knew he stopped and said, "Polly open your eyes."

"What?"

"I know you're an independent girl, but you have to let me lead when we're dancing. That's why you keep tripping the guys you're with. Feel where I want you to go. You don't have to be in control of this, let me do the guiding, alright?"

Polly felt a tear leak out of her eye. She shut her eyes quickly so he wouldn't notice, hoping the dim lighting would help.

"Are you alright?"

"Fine. Let's go again," she said. "I'll try to do better."

"Polly. You're doing fine."

"Okay," she said.

"Polly, open your eyes and look at me."

She looked up at him.

"This has you absolutely terrified, doesn't it?"

She nodded, afraid to say anything.

"You don't do things poorly, do you?"

This time she shook her head.

"Will you trust me to not let you fail at this?"

Polly shrugged her shoulders and took a deep breath.

"Alright. I'm ready to try again."

"My hand on your back and the one covering your other hand will tell you where I'm going. Trust that I can get you there too, alright?"

"I'll try."

The song had ended, so Mark waited patiently with her in his arms as the iPod advanced to the next song. He tightened his grip on her hand and she felt the strength of his muscles as he began moving her around the hallway. All of a sudden, she felt what he was telling her. She felt the movement in his muscles as he was preparing to turn her or move backwards. Before she knew it, the song was over.

He stopped, released her hand and stepped back from her. "How did that feel to you?"

"If I tell you I've never felt that free before, will you laugh at me?" she asked.

"That's perfect." Mark smiled at her and said, "Shall we try again?"

"Yes!" Polly wanted to keep dancing. No wonder people had been doing this for eons. It was wonderful!

The next song's tempo was a little faster and she managed to lose her place in the step a couple of times, but each time, Mark stepped with her and brought her back into the pattern. They danced through two more songs and he said, "Now, this time, instead of the regular four-four pattern, we're going to waltz. The step is the same, but the feel is a little different. You're going to have to trust me on this, alright?"

Polly's confidence returned. She smiled and said, "I'm ready."

Within a few measures, she stopped him, laughing. "I wasn't ready. I have no idea what I'm doing here."

"We'll try again, then." He restarted the song and took her in his arms. It was a slow waltz and gave her time to concentrate on her feet. When the next waltz began, the tempo again was quick and he said, "Don't look at your feet, look up at me, we're going to fly this time."

Polly took a deep breath and decided to let him guide her. Her feet finally seemed to understand what it took to dance and when the song was over, she said, "I feel a little like Ginger Rogers!"

"You are doing well, but I have to warn you. You're probably going to ache a little tomorrow."

"Do we have to stop now?" she asked.

"Why don't we waltz once more and then return to a normal four-four song, so you have the rhythm in your memory. Then, maybe it's time for some dessert."

He turned on the music and they danced again, winding around the large hallway. He brought her to a stop in front of the door and as he backed away, he kept her hand in his and bowed deeply.

"Thank you for the dance," he said.

Polly bent her knees in a curtsy and replied, "Thank you!"

Mark picked up the speakers and brought them into the apartment. He put it on the table beside the door, and followed her to the dining room.

"I'll gather up the dishes and you get dessert," he said and began picking up the plates and silverware.

She brought a container of ice cream out of the freezer and lifted the lid off the pound cake. "Are you ready for this?" she asked.

"After that workout, I'm ready for nearly anything. Can I help?"

"No, you're doing all the work. You can stop any time. Would you like some coffee? Oh wait," she said, "Dew?"

"I don't think so. This is going to make me sleep well tonight, caffeine would mess with that."

Polly sliced the pound cake and put it on the plate. Before scooping the ice cream, she put a small pitcher of homemade chocolate sauce in the microwave for a few seconds. When it was done, she had the ice cream on each plate. She opened a drawer and pulled out two dessert forks and set them on the plates. She fit both plates into her left hand, hooked the handle of the pitcher with her right hand and walked to the table.

"Just a second," she said and went back to the refrigerator, pulling out a dish of red raspberries in syrup. "I know they're not fresh, but I think they'll do.

Scooping raspberries over his slice of pound cake, she looked at him as if asking when to stop. He put his hand up and said, "All I can say is wow!"

She scooped raspberries onto her slice, poured a little warmed chocolate over both the ice cream and pound cake and offered him the pitcher when she was finished.

Mark took a bite and smiled. "No one has ever made a dessert like this for me. Polly, you'd make a wonderful wife."

Polly blushed, "How about I make a wonderful friend who says thank you for taking care of my animals and teaching me how to dance. Well, at least how to not make a fool of myself on the dance floor."

"That's a good start," and he winked at her.

"I don't want to frighten you, but there is going to be line-dancing and all sorts of other things happening on Saturday night. I would have liked to get you comfortable with the fox-trot, but that's a bit much for one night."

"I wouldn't have been able to absorb anything else tonight," she agreed. "But it was fun. Thank you for making it fun."

"I'll tell you what. I know that it's going to get busy around here tomorrow as everyone prepares for the big day. I could come over Thursday evening, though, and anyone who is around and wants to learn some steps, I'd be glad to help. I don't want to make a big deal out of it, but I could probably even convince Lisa to come with me. What do you think about that?"

"Would you? That would be great." Polly reached out and laid her hand on his forearm. "Thank you. It's been wonderful."

Mark glanced at the clock on the microwave. "It's nearly ten o'clock. I've got another early morning tomorrow, so I should probably go pretty soon. Can I help you with the dishes?"

Polly was shocked. "Oh, no! I'll take care of those. In fact, I probably won't even look at them again until tomorrow. I'll take Obiwan down for a walk and then put the food away and deal with the rest later."

Obiwan heard his name and looked up. When Mark and Polly began walking to the door, he stood up and followed them.

"Yes, it's your turn for a little attention," Polly said. She pulled on her coat and a scarf, then snapped his leash on his collar before putting her gloves on. Mark was ready to go and opened the door of her apartment, then followed her out into the hallway.

They walked downstairs and when he got to the door, he took her hand, "Thank you for a very nice evening, Polly. I hope we do this again soon." He opened the front door and they walked out into the cold evening.

Polly glanced across the street and saw that there was no longer a car in the lot. "I guess I didn't need to worry about anything. I wonder what they were doing."

"I don't know," he said. "I'm glad they're gone. Be careful, alright?"

"I will. Good night and thank you."

Mark took her hand again and squeezed it, then walked to his car as she started walking with Obiwan. She saw his lights come on and heard the crunch of his tires on the gravel as he backed out and drove out of the lot. She and Obiwan walked around the building and then back to the front door. She closed it behind her and switched off the downstairs lights, walking up to her apartment. When Polly finally dropped into bed, she shut her eyes, said, "Thank you for taking care of another fear in my life. I can dance," and fell asleep.

CHAPTER THIRTEEN

Laughing at his antics, Polly brought Obiwan in through the front door, stamping her feet. "You know, if Dad were still around, I wouldn't have missed the forecast of snow. What in the world happened last night, Obiwan?"

He shook himself and looked up at her with what seemed to be a smile. "Yeah. Yeah. You love playing in fresh snow. I get it. But, what in the world?"

She started up the first step, waiting for him to join her. "Are you coming?"

Obiwan sat down at the bottom of the steps and looked up at her. "What are you doing, you crazy dog?" His tail was wagging, so she didn't think anything was wrong but he wouldn't budge. Polly stepped back down on the floor and knelt down in front of him. "I'm not going back outside. It's cold and windy and it's blowing snow everywhere."

Her phone rang. She saw that it was Henry. "Good morning, Henry. It snowed!"

"Thanks for the update," he laughed. "Are you going to be alright if we don't get over to plow you out right away? I need to take care of some people first if you don't mind."

"I'm fine, except that I'm worried about Saturday. Does this create a problem?"

"The forecast calls for warm weather tomorrow, Friday and Saturday. I think we're going to be fine. Don't worry."

"If you say so, I'm not going to worry about it. Get here when you can. I'll call Andy and Sylvie and tell them to stay home until later. Thanks."

"See you after a while."

Henry hung up and Polly tried to go back up the steps. Obiwan still wouldn't budge. "What is up with you? Come on." She tugged on his leash and he finally stood up, but rather than going to the stairway, he attempted to walk back to the front door. She finally let him and went with him. He bumped his nose on the door and she said, "No! I'm not going back out there. It's cold. You've done everything you need to do and that's enough for now."

He bumped his nose against the door. The action was strange enough that Polly relented and opened the door. Pulling her scarf close to her against the wind, she followed him as he led her around the building to the door by the stage. He nosed at a something with a fine sheen of snow on top. It had to have been dropped there several minutes ago and she saw footprints leading back to the creek. Polly brushed aside snow and saw that it was a canvas messenger bag. When she pulled it open, there were two plastic covered tubs. She peered through the translucent plastic of the first tub and saw what seemed to be pictures, while the other had a piece of paper in it. Pulling the bag over her shoulder, she led Obiwan back to the front door.

This time, when they went inside, he got to the first step before she did and wagged as he waited for her to join him.

Once inside the apartment, she dropped her coat beside the door and followed him to the kitchen, setting the bag on the table as she went past it. After filling his food dish and pouring a cup of coffee, she sat down and opened it up again.

Polly pulled out the first container and opened it, then released it as if she had been bitten. Someone had taken pictures last night of her and Mark Ogden. Two were taken from her kitchen window, one was when she was standing at her sink and the next when the two of them were looking across the parking lot. There were shots of him arriving at Sycamore House and others from earlier in the day when she had been coming and going. She felt sick. What did they want?

She opened the next container and there was a folded piece of paper. She had enough presence of mind to stop herself from pulling the paper out. She'd seen enough television to know better, so she went to the kitchen and pulled two pairs of tongs out of a drawer, feeling more than a little foolish. With tongs on each corner, she unfolded the paper and read:

"Tell the bitch to go home. We know she is staying there. We're watching you."

Polly dropped the paper back into the container and stepped away from the table. She felt tears come to her eyes and she dropped her head to her chest. How could this be happening?

Then she got mad. All she wanted to do was have a nice place where people could have fun and enjoy being creative. She walked over to the sink and tossed the tongs in, then filled it with hot water. She knew it didn't make sense, but those weren't going back into the drawer after touching that damned note. She thrust her hands in the hot water pouring from the faucet and let it flow over them as the sink filled. When it covered the tongs, she shut the water off and dried her hands on a towel, then walked to the sofa and sat down, staying as far from the table as possible.

She pulled out her phone and called a very familiar number.

"Good morning, Polly. Is everything alright?" Aaron Merritt's voice came through and gave her a little comfort.

"Not really, Aaron. I think I need you again."

"Do you now! You're bringing action to Bellingwood again, aren't you Polly!" His deep laugh made her feel better.

"I keep telling you people, it's not my fault!" she laughed.

"I'm making my way through town right now. Do I need to stop by your place?" he asked.

"Could you? I have something I need you to see."

"I'll be there as soon as possible. Have you changed the key to the front door?"

"No, I haven't. You should be able to get in. I'll have coffee for you when you get here."

"I'll see you soon."

Polly still had a few muffins in the refrigerator. She put those on the countertop and then pulled two small plates down from the cupboard. She needed to make a few calls. The first call was to Jeff Lyndsay.

"Hey, Polly. It snowed!"

"You're right! It did! Are you going to stay in Ames and be safe?"

"I'll stay here until the roads clear up. But, I might bring clothes and things with me just in case I have to sleep on your couch."

"Got it. And yes, you can sleep on my couch." She laughed. "Let me know when you're going to try to get here so I can worry about you, alright?"

"See you later."

They hung up and she called Sylvie. Jason picked up the phone and said, "Hi Polly! It's a snow day! We don't have to go to school!"

She smiled. There was nothing better for a kid than a snow day. "That's great, Jason! What are you going to do?"

"Mom said we could come to Sycamore House with her and maybe we could play in the snow outside. Could we take Obiwan out with us?"

"You sure can. Could I talk to your mom, though?"

She heard a thump and assumed the phone had been dropped onto a table, then Jason's voice calling, "Mom! Polly's on the phone for you."

In a moment, Sylvie said, "Hi, Polly. It snowed. Are you worried about Saturday yet?"

"Everyone keeps telling me that it snowed," Polly giggled. "But, Henry says I don't need to worry, so I'm choosing to hold panic off until Friday night. Don't hurry over here, alright? And would you call Hannah and tell her not to try it?"

"She and I have already talked this morning. We both think the roads will be clear this afternoon. If she can get here, she will. But, no worries. I think the boys and I are going to bundle up and walk over. It's only five blocks and it will be good for us. Right boys?"

Sylvie chuckled. "They don't care what they have to do as long as they can get to you and the animals. Maybe you should put them to work shoveling off the front steps."

"Have you made breakfast for them?"

"We had some cereal. They're good to go."

"Okay. Well, don't hurry and be careful. I'd rather you stayed at home and were safe."

"I won't be safe in this apartment with two owly boys if they can't get out and expend a whole lot of energy. This is all for the better. We'll see you in a while."

"Okay!" Polly said.

She hung up the phone and quickly dialed Andy. "Good morning, Polly. Can you believe it? It snowed!"

Polly laughed out loud. "Well, if I hadn't known when I was outside with Obiwan this morning, I would definitely know by now that it snowed."

"What?" Andy laughed.

"Everyone I've been talking to this morning has told me that it snowed. It was just funny." Polly shrugged her shoulders and giggled. "I'm calling to tell you *not* to try to get here this morning."

"I'll be good," Andy said. "Lydia called and said that when the roads cleared up a little bit, she'd pick me and Beryl up and bring us over to work. I'm going to go outside and shovel my walks. My son had better show up later to plow my driveway if he knows what's good for him."

"Be careful out there, okay?" Polly said.

"I will and we'll see you later!" Andy hung up and Polly looked out to see Aaron's SUV pull into the driveway in front of her door. Obiwan's ears perked up and he looked at the front door of the apartment. This time, Polly heard Aaron's feet walking across the floor of the hallway outside her door and she opened it for him.

"I know," she said. "It snowed."

He laughed and after wiping his feet on the rug, came inside the door.

"What do you have to show me?" he asked.

"It's over here," Polly said and pointed to the table.

Aaron stood over the scattered photographs and the containers and said, "What are these, Polly?"

She told him about the car that had been parked across the street the night before and then Obiwan's strange behavior this morning.

"Aaron," she said, "whoever did this must have put it there while we were out walking and that freaks me out. I can't believe I didn't see him or hear the car drive away, but Obiwan obviously knew it."

"I know, Polly. It freaks me out a little too. You haven't seen or heard from this girl since Saturday?"

"Wait! I also got a note from her, telling me she was going to be gone for a while. I didn't find it until yesterday, but it's downstairs. When you leave, I'll walk down and give it to you."

"Did you touch this note?" Then he shook his head. "Of course you did. That's alright."

"Actually, I didn't." He looked at her in surprise.

"I watch television," she laughed, "so I used tongs to take it out of the container and unfold it."

"Where are they?"

"In the sink. I had to wash them. Do you want them?"

"No, that's fine." He snapped on a pair of gloves he pulled out of a pocket and read the note. Then, he dropped it back in the container, gathered the photographs and dropped them in the other container and placed both in the messenger bag. "I'm going to take this with me."

"I figured you would. Now, can I give you a muffin and some coffee?"

"No, that's fine. Lydia sent a thermos with me and I got my morning oatmeal before I left," he sighed. "Let's go downstairs and get that other note. I'll let you know what I find out, but there might not be any more information until later in the week. Don't worry, okay?"

"I can't help but worry, but I'll try to keep my head about me."

"I'm going to call Ken over at the police station and I'll let my guys who are driving through here know to keep an eye on Sycamore House. If we can keep them wary enough of coming close, that will help until we figure out who they are and what they want. Did you happen to see what kind of vehicle they were in?"

"No, I didn't, but Mark Ogden was the one who told me they were over there."

"Over where?"

"They were parked in the lot in front of the swimming pool."

"I'll call Mark and see if he can identify the car."

"Thanks Aaron. I appreciate it. Tell your guys there will be coffee here all day."

"I'll do that. Let's get that note and I need to head down the road."

They walked downstairs and into the office. Polly opened her desk drawer and pulled out the note she had found in Elise's room and said, "I have an envelope here, would you like me to put it in there?"

"Sure, that's fine." She did so and he slipped it into a jacket pocket. "I'll talk to you later. Now, don't worry."

"Thanks. I'll try."

Polly stood in the doorway and watched Aaron drive away, then closed the front door, locked it and went back to the main kitchen to start a pot of coffee. She wasn't sure who would show up today, but the coffee would be hot.

She went back into the hallway to head upstairs. Sylvie would be busy today getting things ready for Saturday's meals, so Polly thought she might bake cookies and bring them down, in case anyone came in and needed a little sugar. The door blew open and three bundles of coats and boots entered.

"How did you guys get here so fast?" she asked.

Andrew pulled the scarf away from his mouth and said, "Henry brought us over!"

Sylvie had unwrapped her own scarf and smiled, "He was plowing Mrs. Albert's driveway and saw us walking out of the apartment building and he gave us a ride. He said to tell you he was going to run one path through for you and then be back later."

"Drop your coats and boots here in the corner," Polly said, "and come upstairs and get warm. That was nice of him!"

Sylvie nodded. "It was. He's a keeper, Polly."

Polly smiled. "He's a good guy."

The boys had both sat down against the wall and were pulling their boots off. They left everything scattered around on the floor and started up the steps.

"Boys!" Sylvie barked and they both stopped, poised to continue moving. "Come back down and clean up your things. You know better than that."

They backed down the steps, one at a time, giggling at each other. When they hit the floor, they ran over to their things and pulled everything together in a pile.

"Better?" Jason asked.

"Not better," Sylvie said. "Here." She walked over, stood their boots up and then laid the coats on top of them. "Does that make sense?"

"Yes, mom," Jason said.

"Good, now you do it." Sylvie picked the coats up and scattered the boots, chuckling as both boys looked at her in shock.

"Why did you do that?" Andrew asked.

"I want to know that you understand what is supposed to happen. Now, straighten up your things."

Their shoulders slumped and they each picked up their boots, then came over and took their coats from her and laid them neatly on top. Sylvie hugged them both and said, "Very good. Now, ask Miss Polly if you can run upstairs and play with the animals."

Andrew took Polly's hand and said, "Would it be alright if we went upstairs to play?"

"You bet," she responded, squeezing his hand. "You know where everything is. I'll be up in a while. I'm going to make cookies in a bit and if you want to help me, you can."

The boys ran up the steps, laughing and squealing.

"You're a tough mom!" she said to Sylvie.

"I figure it is easier to be tough now than it will be when their friends are telling them what to do. It's already started and makes me so angry sometimes. I'm just glad they learned to listen to me from the very beginning." Her eyes looked a little sad. "Well, not the beginning, but at least when they were very little. I wasn't always a good mom to those boys, but I figured it out as quickly as I could."

"So," Sylvie continued, "I think I have enough in the kitchen to get started on the cupcakes. We're going to need hundreds of them, if what I'm hearing around town is any sign. This place is going to be hopping on Saturday."

They walked together back to the kitchen and Polly asked, "You don't think we need to worry about the weather?"

"No," Sylvie said. "There might be some still on the ground, but it's going to be in the forties tomorrow and Friday. That will melt most of this off. Saturday is supposed to be sunny and forty-nine degrees. It's going to be a beautiful day!"

"That's what Henry said. I suppose it will take me a few years to understand Iowa winters again," Polly lamented.

"I hear you had a date last night with the hot vet!" Sylvie said, tapping Polly lightly on the arm.

"It wasn't a date. Well, it was kind of a date. But, not really," she said.

"What was it, then?" Sylvie took her coat off and walked to the back of the kitchen. She put it on a hanger and pulled a white jacket out and slipped into it, adjusting the belt until it was snug.

"I made him dinner to thank him for coming here to check out my animals rather than making me drag them to his office." Polly giggled. "Okay, even I don't buy that. But, that's how it started. I promise!"

"How did it end?"

"He taught me how to dance in the hallway upstairs. It was wonderful."

"You're kidding me. The hot veterinarian knows how to dance? How do you keep scoring these great guys? I've lived in this town all my life and had no idea there were so many treasures."

Polly said, "I don't know. They find me. His mom was a dance teacher in Minneapolis. He learned from her and then taught dancing lessons in her studio."

"Probably to little grey-haired ladies who wanted to feel his firm arms around their old bodies."

They both shuddered. "Well, I hope they enjoyed it. I certainly did," Polly snickered.

"You said it was wonderful. You learned how to dance, then?"

"I think I did. He said he would come over tomorrow after work and teach anybody who was here some of the steps. It's a good idea, because once I'm flustered, I'll forget everything."

"I haven't been to a dance since high school. It will be fun to see it all happen."

"You think you're going to get out of it because you're in the kitchen?"

"I know I'm going to get out of it since I'll be in the kitchen. But, I'll watch and enjoy. Now, you get out of here. I'm going to start flinging flour and sugar everywhere." She fluttered her fingers in dismissal.

"I'm going, I'm going. But, I'll be back later with cookies to go with the coffee," Polly warned. "Don't make too much of a mess."

Sylvie waved her off and Polly went upstairs to her apartment.

Jason was sitting on the floor, playing tug of war with Obiwan and one of his rope toys and Andrew was on her bed with the kittens. The television was on and it looked like some type of Japanese anime.

"Everyone doing alright?" she asked.

"Great!" Andrew called from the bedroom. "I think Leia is okay, don't you?" he asked.

"Doctor Ogden says she is fine. But, you might still want to be a little careful with her," Polly said.

"I am. I promise. Luke is jumping on me, though." His laughter filled the room as he romped on the bed with the cats.

"We'll shovel your steps for you, Polly," Jason said, looking up as he held on to one end of the rope. Obiwan had planted his feet firmly and was pulling backwards. Jason stood up and dropped the toy. Obiwan scrambled, then brought it back to Jason, nudging it into his hand.

"Why don't we all go outside after I bake cookies? There's no hurry," she said.

Jason had absentmindedly taken hold of the rope toy and it was dangling from his hand as he followed her into the kitchen. Obiwan was doing everything possible to get his attention and finally yanked the toy back out of the boy's hand.

"Can I do anything to help you in here?" Jason asked.

Polly wanted to ruffle the hair on his head, but something in her told her that would kill him, so she said "What if you go play with Obiwan in the living room and talk to me while I make dough for sugar cookies. Then, I'll make chocolate chip cookies while these are in the refrigerator and you can help me drop them on cookie sheets."

Jason ran after the dog and grabbed the toy back. The two played with each other while Polly flipped through her recipe file. One of Mary's favorite sugar cookie recipes had to be ... there it was. She pulled it out and looked out the kitchen window to the lot across the street. There were no tracks and no car there now. A shudder went down her back as she realized how vulnerable she had been last night. This was Bellingwood. Things weren't supposed to be that strange in Iowa.

Shaking her head, she opened the refrigerator and pulled out a pound of butter and a container of eggs. Setting four eggs into a dish, she returned the container to the refrigerator and flipped the arm of her mixer up. Butter went into the microwave for a few seconds and then she dropped some into the mixer, creaming sugar into it. Adding the eggs and vanilla, she let it run while she sifted together the dry ingredients. After it was mixed, Polly turned it into a roll and wrapped it in plastic wrap, then placed it into the bottom of the refrigerator to chill.

Once that was finished, she rinsed everything out and began

combining ingredients for chocolate chip cookies. While the sugars and butter blended, she pulled out two large cookie sheets and set them on the counter. After she folded in the chocolate chips, she pulled the bowl off the mixer and set it between the cookie sheets.

"Guys, do you want to help me?"

Both boys came running over.

"Wash your hands and dry them really well. Then, I have gloves for you to put on!"

Polly had found small disposable gloves to fit her own hands and hoped they wouldn't be too large for the boys.

"Look!" Andrew said as he pulled his on. "I'm a doctor!" He pointed his finger at Jason's nose.

"Stop it," she laughed, "Or you'll have to start all over again."

"Why are we wearing gloves?"

"Because we're making these cookies for a lot of other people. They don't want your germy germs." She poked him in the nose.

"Scoop out this much dough and drop it on the sheet, alright?" She showed them what she wanted and they went to work. With the first batch in the oven, she put two more sheets in front of them, and they filled those as well.

Andrew looked at her with his lips pursed. "What?" she asked.

"Do we have to wait?"

"You have to wait until we're nearly done. We'll leave enough dough in the bowl for you to eat. I promise."

"I have to wait?"

Polly laughed and had no hesitation in ruffling the hair on the younger boy's head. "Fine." She grabbed two ramekins from the cupboard and scooped a teaspoon of dough into each. "Take those over to the table and I'll finish up here."

Andrew grabbed his and ran over to the table. Jason said, "Thank you" and followed a bit more sedately.

Soon, cookies were cooling in racks and Andrew was standing in front of them, looking intently at the first level of cookies. "This one looks like it is too small," he said.

"You haven't had enough?" she asked.

"But you don't want to give that one away, it's too small," he insisted.

"What if we give that one to your mom? It wouldn't be too small for her, would it?"

Andrew looked up at Polly, crushed. Then, his eyes lit up and he pointed to another cookie. "That would be a better size for her."

Polly took the first cookie off the tray and put it on a plate, then took the second cookie off as well. "I tell you what. When we take cookies downstairs, this one will be for you and that will be for your mother."

Andrew looked chagrined. "That's a good idea," he said and went back in to the living room to play with the animals. Polly chuckled. She'd have a million kids if they were as good as these two.

She took the roll of sugar cookies out of the refrigerator and sliced them, placed them on freshly cleaned cookie sheets, and sprinkled colored sugar on top of each before putting them in the oven. When the cookies came out, she began arranging things on platters to take downstairs. She covered each platter with plastic wrap and said, "Alright guys. Shall we take these to your mom and go outside to shovel?"

"Can we take Obiwan?" Jason asked.

"Not right now. You can come back up and get him in a bit, alright?"

She handed each boy a plate and they headed downstairs with their morning's work.

CHAPTER FOURTEEN

Light streaming through her windows gave Polly hope that the snow would melt away before Saturday as she leaned back in her desk chair. There was nothing she enjoyed more than having Sycamore House filled with people coming and going during the day. Everyone seemed to be in perpetual motion this morning, trying to make up for the enforced holiday yesterday's snow had granted them. By late afternoon, between the plows and the sunshine, the roads had been clear enough for travel to resume and deliveries began arriving at Sycamore House. The furniture store called to reschedule its delivery of the mattress, box springs and three lamps for some time this morning.

Lydia, Beryl and Andy had shown up around three o'clock yesterday. Andy wanted to get items from the crates either behind glass or under cover before Jeff had people in to begin decorating. Bruce and Hannah McKenzie came in not long after and, with a little negotiating, Sylvie and Hannah decided he could head home and Hannah would spend the night at Sylvie's. This was great news for Jason and Andrew, who soon discovered they would get to spend the night in Polly's apartment, since Jeff had decided that the short drive to Ames would offer him more peace and quiet.

Polly thought for a moment and pulled up the plans for Sycamore House. She needed to come up with ideas for additional rooms for overnight guests. She sent the plans to the printer and when she walked out into the main office to collect it, saw Doug and Billy walk in the front door. They waved at her and walked into the office.

"I never see one of you without the other," she laughed. "Come on in and tell me what's up!"

They followed her back into the office. "That's what our moms say, too," Doug commented.

"That's alright. You make a good team. What are you doing here today?"

"This afternoon we're going to start running electricity out to where the barn is going up. Jerry wants to bury it. I'm not looking forward to cutting into that frozen ground, but until he gets here, we're supposed to see if Henry needs us."

Billy interrupted, "Or you. You're the boss, right?"

Polly laughed. "Not in anyone's dream am I the boss."

"What are you doing with that?" Billy pointed at the layout on her desk.

"I'm trying to see what I can come up with for some additional rooms."

"In here? You've used nearly every bit of space except the hallways," Doug said. "And those make it nice."

"I know." Polly pointed at the northwest corner of the building. "I was thinking about building an addition back here, maybe even adding a garage."

Doug sat back and laughingly said, "You like having us all around so much that you're going to keep building?"

"I guess so. But last night when I didn't have the rooms upstairs finished and the only other place to put someone was on my couch, I stayed up half the night trying to figure this out. I don't even have a guest room in my apartment."

"Well, Henry is going to have to hire someone to run the rest of his business if you keep him working here all the time."

Polly was stricken, "Is he losing business because of me?"

Doug rolled his eyes, "Whatever. You're the best thing that has happened here for the local craftsman in a long time. Henry will keep up with his other customers. No worries."

Jeff Lyndsay came into the office. "Hey guys. What are you doing here today?"

"We're off for the next couple of days. We thought we'd see what you guys had going on around here. Mom told me she was coming in later to work on decorations, and then she told me to get my butt over and ask if I could help," Doug said.

"That's great!" Jeff said. "They dropped off the scissor-lift earlier this morning and I would rather not go up in that thing to hang lights in the rafters."

"Pick me!" Doug said, raising his hand. "Dibs, sucka," he said to Billy, who shook his head, laughing. The two followed Jeff out of the office.

Before he got into the hallway, he said, "I'll be right there" and turned back to Polly's office. "You're going to pay them, right?" he asked.

"Absolutely," she said, laughing. "Even if it's pizza and steak and game nights for a month."

Then he sat down across from her and said, "Would you tell me if something was wrong?"

"Sure," she said, perplexed. "What do you mean?"

"There were police and sheriff's vehicles around here all day yesterday. Does it have something to do with Elise being gone?"

"I'm sorry, Jeff. I should have talked to you about this, but with everything going on yesterday, I totally forgot. Yes, I think it does."

She took a breath and said, "I got a package yesterday with pictures of me from the night before, taken by someone parked in the lot across the road. There was also a note in there telling me to send her home and that they were watching me. I called Sheriff Merritt and I think he put everyone on high alert. The snow probably slowed down whoever it was, but if they're looking for her and don't know she's gone, who knows what they'll do next."

"Okay. I'm sorry I got you into this, then."

"What do you mean?"

"Maybe I should have asked more questions before I let her move in," he said.

"No, that's not the way we're going to do things around here," Polly announced. "We aren't going to second-guess every decision we make and we're not going to freak out when people aren't as perfect as the rest of us. You gave her a space to live in good faith. It's not your fault if she hid something from you. So stop that. We're fine."

"I know you're right, but it still feels like I could have headed this off. It's a little strange."

"Hah," she laughed. "I think strange describes who will show up next Monday. Have you seen her list of requests?"

"I saw the email come in, but haven't had time to go over it yet."

"Now, she's made it clear that money is no object, so it's not as if this is going to cost me anything, but every morning by ten o'clock, she wants me to have a fresh pad of lined paper, a new sketch pad and two sharpened pencils at her door. She has a list of foods for each day of the week that need to be available and every Sunday evening, a bag of plain M&Ms and a canister of mixed nuts with no peanuts are to be delivered to her door. She will alert us to the days she is traveling and on those days, by nine o'clock, we are to have a sack lunch prepared ... and there's a list of what is acceptable ... and delivered to the door of her room. On those days, I will be expected to launder her linens and clean her room. Otherwise, she will alert me if she needs to have them changed."

Polly thought for a moment, then said, "And we either have to provide her with six bottles of water each day or a filter system to ensure the water is clean. Is she kidding me? Does she actually believe that the water here will make her ill?"

"Well, it sounds like she knows what she wants," he laughed. "What are you going to do?"

"I've already ordered the paper and pencils and individual bags of M&Ms. That package should show up today. I'll give the food list to Sylvie and ask her to ensure things are available. Then, I also purchased two water filter pitchers. She can have one in her room and I'll keep one filled in the refrigerator downstairs."

Jeff chuckled. "It's never going to be easy, is it?"

"Honestly, I thought I'd get these wonderfully creative people who would want to bask in the glory of Sycamore House, spend time writing or drawing or painting or sculpting, and happily enjoy everything I could offer to them. So far I have a woman who seems to be hiding out from bad people in Chicago and now an obsessive who needs a full-time keeper."

"I will try to bring someone in who is a little more laid back the next time," he said. "How long are you going to keep Elise's stuff in the front room?"

"She's paid through mid-March, so I don't want to do anything right now. She said if she wasn't back by Valentine's Day, a message would come to me telling me how to contact people to get her things. I guess we wait," Polly shrugged.

Jeff glanced up, "It looks like your first delivery of the day is here."

When she turned around in her chair, she saw the furniture truck pull up in front of the steps. "Great!" she said. "This will be another task off my list."

They walked out together and when she opened the front door, Jeff turned and went into the auditorium.

Polly showed the delivery people where to put the mattress and lamps, then went downstairs to find Henry. He seemed to be all over the place this morning. The ramp out front needed a railing, he'd said something about a crane showing up for raising the barn trusses, there was a group of workmen in the classrooms, painting and finishing things and now she hoped that reminding him about installing the head and footboard for the new mattress wouldn't put him over the edge.

Henry was in the back classroom pulling tape away from the windowsill.

"How are you doing, Henry?" she asked.

"I'm doing fine. Just fine," he muttered.

"Ummm, what does that mean?"

"Damned snow storm messed up my schedule and I'm hiding in here so I can figure out how to make everything work."

"Then I shouldn't tell you that the mattress is upstairs ready to be assembled?"

"Well, you can tell me, but I don't know if I care."

"Alright, then. Should I come back later?"

"It won't help."

"What can I do to make this better for you?"

Henry balled up the tape in his hand and dropped it into an empty paint bucket, then stood up and turned around to face her. "Did you have a date with Mark Ogden the other night?"

Polly swallowed. "It wasn't a date."

"Everyone in town thinks it was a date. Mark Ogden thinks it was a date."

Polly pursed her lips and took a breath. "Do you want to do this right now and right here?" she asked.

He looked around. "You could have told me about it first."

"I guess you want to do this here," she muttered. "Exactly *what* was I supposed to tell you? No," she said. "I'll start with exactly *why* was I supposed to tell you anything? You and I have gone out on a total of two dates. Two. We work together during the day here, but I didn't know that was supposed to be some new Midwestern courting ritual, so if I missed a rule change, let me know.

"He came here Tuesday morning to check out my dog and cat so I wouldn't have to manage getting both of them to his office again. Yes, we had dinner that night. I thought it was to say thank you. Then, he offered to teach me how to dance so that I wasn't terrified to be in public at a dance in my own home this Saturday night. It was wonderful and we had a great time.

"Mark Ogden is a nice guy. He's good looking and I think he's fun. But, let's get something straight. Whether or not it was a date, I don't have to clear it with you first."

"Fine," Henry said, turning back to the blue tape on the window sill. "If that's the way you want it."

Polly shook her head. She recognized that her fury was about to take him out one more time and that wasn't what she wanted to do with him.

"Henry, is there something going on between us that I'm not understanding? Have we committed to a relationship together?"

"No, I guess not."

"What do you mean, you guess not? You can't back out of this conversation now. You started it."

He spun around again. "Maybe I had hoped we could have a relationship. I like you and I thought you liked me too."

Polly walked over to him and put her hand on his arm. "I do like you. I love doing things with you."

"Then why are you dating the vet?"

"Because as much as I love doing things with you, I'm not ready to settle down into a committed relationship with anyone. Are you telling me that if I want to date other people that will upset you?"

He flung the next ball of tape at the bucket and missed. "Damn," he said. "Of course that will upset me."

"How much will that upset you?" she asked.

"What in the hell do you mean by that?"

"Will it upset you enough that we can't ever date again? Are you laying down an ultimatum for me? Is it you or no one?"

Henry shook his head. "No, I don't suppose I mean that. It sounds stupid when you put it that way."

"I don't want you to feel stupid and I don't want you to feel like I'm screwing something up between us, but I don't think I'm ready to commit to a lifetime relationship right now. Sheesh, Henry, I'm just beginning to figure out what I want to do with my life."

"I know that." He took a deep breath. "I'm sorry. I guess I built up some expectations and then I didn't bother to tell you what they were."

Polly bent over and picked up the errant ball of tape. She tossed it back and forth before dropping it in the bucket.

"Maybe we can't date and be friends," she said. "That would be really disappointing, but it's more important for me to have you as a friend than to lose that because we dated and then screwed things up."

"Is that what you want?"

"Well, I want to be friends with you, that's for sure. I want you around and in my life for a very long time and if we can't manage this other part of the relationship, I'd rather it go away now than destroy everything later."

"I can't believe we're doing this. It feels like I'm an adolescent all over again," Henry said. "I should have quit playing these games twenty years ago." He spoke again through gritted teeth, "But that ticked me off."

"And that's why you're in here doing stupid work like pulling tape off of windowsills when you have a million other things to do?"

"I suppose it is. Good lord, woman, you make a man nuts."

"That's usually a compliment, but I think it might be an annoyance this time," she laughed.

Henry grabbed her arm. "I'm not going to like seeing you date other men. I've become ... what do they say? Smitten. I'm a little smitten with you."

"What do you want me to do about that, Henry?" she asked.

"Well, my first choice would be for you to fall into my arms and tell me that you'll do anything I'd like you to do."

"And your second choice?"

"Forgive me for being an adolescent ass and see what happens from here on."

"I like that option," Polly said. "Can we be friends?"

"We already are. I'll be fine. Now, let me round up some help and we'll deal with that bed. We're going to install the rails on the ramp this afternoon when it warms up a little more."

"Doug and Billy are here today and tomorrow. Feel free to conscript them to help with your dirty work. They're in the auditorium hanging lights for Jeff."

"He had Jimmy and Sam in there as well. I'll gather my guys and talk to you later."

They walked out into the hallway and when she went back toward the kitchen, he walked into the auditorium.

Several of the kitchen windows were open and when Polly walked into the kitchen, she could feel why. Sylvie and Hannah had been baking since six. Rows and rows of cupcakes filled every counter space, with racks stacked three and four high.

"Good morning!" she called out over the beat of the music coming from a music player sitting inside the cupboard. There were speakers throughout the building and Sylvie was able to plug her music directly into the system built into the kitchen. Sylvie picked up a remote and brought the level down as Polly asked, "How are you guys doing in here?"

"We're doing great," Hannah said. "This is fun!"

"What's all this?" Polly gestured around the room.

"We're doing cupcakes for Saturday evening. That way people can move around and not have to carry plates or forks unless they want them. We will have red velvet, chocolate, vanilla, carrot cake, lemon, strawberry, and key lime." Sylvie picked up a light green cupcake, peeled back the paper and handed it to Polly. "Here, taste this. Hannah found the recipe. It's amazing!"

Polly took the cupcake and bit into it. The tart flavor exploded in her mouth. "That's fantastic!" she said. Hannah smiled and went back to washing out a mixing bowl.

"We'll finish baking this morning and then we will frost them tomorrow. This afternoon we're going to start the soups for lunch on Saturday. I think we'll plan to call tomorrow our absolutely insane, crazy, make me nuts day."

"Can I do anything to help avoid that?" Polly asked.

"Nope. We're good and I'm exaggerating. Just keep sending the deliveries back as they come in." Sylvie smiled, "I'm having a blast and I can't wait to do this every day."

Polly smiled and wrinkled her nose, "I know. We should always have fun. But, soon you'll have your degree and nothing will hold you back."

"Thanks, Polly." Distractedly, Sylvie turned away and said, "We need to make sure to pull out butter tonight so it starts softening, Hannah. Don't let me forget."

The two began talking and Polly chuckled. She'd been forgotten so it was time to leave. She headed back to her office. The front door opened and she smiled at Jerry, her UPS driver. He had a two wheel cart filled with boxes.

"Good morning, Polly! I have more deliveries for you. Where do you want them?"

"Bring it all in here." He followed her into the office and she pointed at a corner.

"Are you guys ready for Saturday?"

"Not yet," Polly said, "but we will get there. Are you coming?"

"I told my wife I wanted to see what this was all about. Does it matter what time we show up?"

"No. We'll serve breakfast between seven and eight, but Henry says he's pounding the first nail at eight. Lunch is right at noon and we'll close work down at sunset. Dinner is at 6:30 and there will be a band and dancing until midnight."

"We'll be here in the morning. Carrie said she wanted to help build a barn with me, so it should be great fun! Heck, I think it will be fun to drive by with my kids someday and point at the barn and say I helped build that."

Polly laughed, "And then you'll have to bring them inside and let me feed them cookies and milk, okay?"

"I'll do it."

She walked back to the front door with him and held it open as he left and another food delivery came in. She smiled and pointed back to the kitchen, then shut the door and went into her office. She pulled a utility knife out of the drawer of the receptionist's desk and slit the top open on the first box. Pads of paper. Polly giggled and carried it into the conference room. The next box had four sets of queen size sheets. She hoped the largest box held the comforter and a couple of blankets. She slid the knife along the sides of the flaps, loosening the tape, then stripped it off and popped the boxes open. Yep, everything was here. She carried the blankets and sheets to the washer and dryer behind the stage and wandered through the auditorium so she wouldn't disturb Sylvie and Hannah again.

It looked as if everything was coming along. There were rows of white lights twinkling from beam to beam and the lift was parked at the back by the door. Doug and Billy, Sam and Jimmy were rolling tables out and setting them into place. Jeff had placed taped Xs on the floor where he wanted each table to be centered. Polly thought that was a little obsessive, but since he had it all in hand, she was going to leave well enough alone.

"How's it going out here?" she asked Jeff.

"As long as there is no strange catastrophe, it's going well. This afternoon will be a riot, though. You're going to want your camera."

"What do you mean?"

"Your friends are bringing thirty of their closest friends over to create decorations for the tables."

"That's great!"

"Uh huh. They decided that mason jars would be the theme of the evening. We have cases and cases of mason jars. There are green jars and clear jars, tall jars and short jars, large-mouth jars and ... Polly, I didn't know there were that many types of mason jars."

She laughed out loud. "I'm sure it's going to be beautiful!"

"It will be awesome. They're going to make candles and snow globes and vases and then I think they're planning to put wash tubs filled with ice around the drink table and put cocktails in mason jars in the tubs." He chuckled. "We have a lot of mason jars here right now. And I forgot. They're going to put a jar with a slit in the lid at each table to raise money for the food pantry."

"They're great, aren't they?" Polly laughed. "I'm glad you get to enjoy all their love, too!"

She saw Henry standing in the doorway and said, "I need to see what he wants. He's working on the bed upstairs."

"This is going to look great again, Polly," Henry said, when she approached. "We have the bed installed. When Adam Lucas attached a queen size mattress to it, he knew what he was doing. You're ready to go. But, you're going to want to unwrap the lamps and get those in place. We didn't know what you wanted to do with them."

"Thanks, Henry. I'll quit worrying about that room now. I'm getting the sheets washed and at some point, it will be ready for its first guest."

They walked into the hallway and she saw Leroy Forster and Ben Bowen coming down the steps. "What's next, boss?" Leroy asked.

"Head out to the concrete pad and start pulling things into place. Got your Carhartts?"

"Out in the truck. We'll meet you out there."

Henry stepped into the auditorium and said, "Jimmy? Sam? Time to get to work."

"We're right there, boss!" Jimmy called and finished arranging the chairs around a table, then jogged over to the door with Sam and headed outside with Henry.

Doug looked a little lost and finally said, "Jeff, where do you want us when this is done?"

"I could still use you guys for a while, if you don't mind."

"Got it. You've got us, then."

Polly smiled and went back to the office and pulled the comforter and accessories out of the box. She took them upstairs into the Walnut Room and after unpacking the lamps, assembled and arranged them. She hoped her guests enjoyed this room as much as she enjoyed putting it together.

CHAPTER FIFTEEN

Yards of muslin and balls of twine were laid out and being cut and measured. Stacks of gingham tables clothes, colorful bandannas, and small galvanized pails were being passed out to women who were carrying them to various tables in order to begin working.

Polly had stopped to talk to Lydia and Beryl on her way to the laundry room. "This is quite the production," she said. Women were wrapping silverware and unwrapping mason jars around the room, while others were assembling bandannas into some type of folded art.

"Isn't it fun?" Lydia responded. "Everyone had ideas and Jeff selected several and then brought in the supplies."

"I can't wait to see it when it's completed. Can I help with something?"

"Oh, honey. You can stay and help if you'd like. We'd love to have you hang out with us, but we have plenty of people to do the work," Lydia assured her.

"Alright, then. I'll finish up some things and check in on you all later." Polly reached out and surprised Lydia with a hug. "I didn't know you were doing all of the organizing for this. Thank you."

Lydia hugged her and patted her on the back. "This is my posse," she said, waving her hand across the room. "We could all sit around and drink tea and gossip every day, or we could find fun things to do." She nudged Polly with her elbow, "Besides, we're a lot more fun at home in the evening if we have something to talk about other than dusting and vacuuming."

Polly giggled, "I don't want to think about you all being more fun at home," she said. "I'm going to go do some laundry."

She walked through the room and the hallway to the washer and dryer. She put one load of sheets in the dryer, then opened packages and started the washing machine again. She set the alarm on her phone to remind her to return and went into the kitchen. Sylvie and Hannah had been joined by two girls who were beginning to decorate some of the cupcakes.

"Sylvie," Polly said as she neared her friend, "Do I know these girls?"

"This is Janice and Deb," Sylvie said. "They're going through the same program I am at the Culinary Institute and thought it would be fun to come work in a kitchen like this."

"Hi girls," Polly said.

Sylvie nodded her way and said, "Janice and Deb, this is Polly. She owns Sycamore House."

They smiled and nodded and went back to their work.

"Will you and Hannah stick around for Mark Ogden's dance lessons tonight?" Polly asked Sylvie.

"That's a great idea," Sylvie said. "Hey, Hannah. Can you stay for dance lessons tonight? Polly's very hot veterinarian is apparently a dance teacher, too!"

"Can Bruce come?" Hannah asked.

"That would be great," Polly laughed. "As it is, we're probably going to need to round up some more guys to balance things out."

"I'll call him to make sure, but we'll be here."

"The boys can't wait to come back after school to see everything," Sylvie said. "I'll bet Jason would learn to dance if there was a possibility of dancing with you, Polly."

Polly chuckled and sighed. "Men are the bane of my existence," she mumbled as she walked back out into the hallway.

She was upstairs later that morning pulling the comforter up over the freshly made bed, when she realized something was cooking downstairs. Her stomach rumbled as if to remind her that she hadn't fed it since much earlier when the boys were getting ready to go to school. She smoothed the top of the bed, tucked the comforter under the pillows and shams, and went out into the hallway. Sure enough, something heavenly was happening downstairs in the kitchen. Polly ran down the steps in time to see people lining up at the window of the kitchen.

Henry stopped her and said, "This was a great idea. None of us thought about what we were going to eat today."

"Yeah," Polly laughed. "But, I don't actually know what is happening here. It wasn't my idea!"

They made their way to the kitchen and Polly saw that Sylvie and Hannah were dishing something onto plates as people walked through. "What did you cook?" Polly asked as she reached Sylvie.

"I figured with everyone on site today and tomorrow, I'd make lunch. It's a Shepherd's Pie casserole today. Would you like some?"

"Ummm, yes! I can't believe you did this!" Polly said.

"It's alright, isn't it?" Sylvie sounded a little concerned. "I asked Jeff and he said yes."

"Sylvie. It's great and I'm glad you thought of doing this. Thank you."

"Whew. I couldn't see making everyone go home for lunch if they didn't want to."

"You're a natural at this, my friend. You keep coming up with great ideas and I'll keep telling you how wonderful you are. Deal?"

"Deal. There are bananas and apples on the tables in the auditorium and we made extra chocolate cupcakes for today. Make sure you get one."

Polly and Henry went into the auditorium and she felt tears in her eyes as she looked around and saw people laughing and eating together in her home. Andy waved when she saw them and pointed at the table where she was seated, so they made their way over to join her.

"How come we didn't know our Sylvie was such an amazing cook?" Andy asked.

"Probably because you and Lydia are such great cooks yourselves. You know," Polly said, "sometimes all it takes is one person to encourage a dream. Lydia is the one who did this for her."

"Don't sell yourself short, Polly," Henry interjected. "You did too."

Polly smiled and shook her head. None of this was ever supposed to have been about her. She was happy that her friends were having fun and she got to be a small part of their lives.

Lydia walked up behind them and put her hands on the backs of Henry's and Polly's chairs, bent in and said, "Word around town is that our resident hot, young veterinarian is a dance teacher and will be holding court here tonight. Who's in?"

Polly glanced at Henry's face and there was no change in his demeanor, he simply remained stoic.

"Well, since I talked him into it, I'm going to be here," she said. "Are you and Aaron coming over?"

Lydia laughed out loud and said, "That'll be the day. He was miserable when we made him dance at Marilyn's wedding. When Jill got married, he offered her two thousand dollars to elope. She made him dance and be miserable, too."

She pushed Henry's shoulder. "If I come tonight will you dance with me?"

Polly snorted with laughter and Henry broke out into an immense smile. "If you come tonight, I will be here and dance with you, Lydia. I haven't done any dancing since I was in college, but I can probably get you around the floor without dropping you on your ..." he looked at Polly, and then said as an aside, "Huh, I walked into that one with no way out. Anyway, yes Lydia, I will dance with you tonight. But, you tell Aaron he had better be here.

There might be a whole lot of men who want to dance with you."

Lydia patted his back and said, "If it would keep him off the dance floor, I think he'd be fine letting the entire cast of South Pacific dance with me."

She walked away humming "There Ain't Nothing Like a Dame" and Henry turned back to Polly. "This sounds like it might be bigger than your friend expected."

Polly punched him in the leg and said under her breath, "He's your friend too. Stop it," and then out loud, she replied, "I suppose I should text him so he's ready for a crowd. That might be a bit of a shock." She pulled out her phone and did just that. In a few moments, her phone rang.

It was Mark, who asked, "What? A crowd?"

"Well, you told me to let people know. That's what I did."

"You know more people than I expected, Polly."

"I might have had a little help from Lydia," she giggled. "But you can handle it, right?"

"Right!" He drew the word out and then said, "Okay. I gotta go. I'm calling Lisa for help. What have you done to me?"

Polly laughed at him, "The town is going to know more about you now. Be prepared!"

"Great," he said and hung up.

She looked around the table and shrugged. "He knows now!"

Sylvie had brought out two large, lined waste cans and said, "When you're finished, drop everything in here, but if you want more to eat, we have plenty."

People at the tables stopped talking and Polly began to clap for her friend. Henry picked it up and began to hoot and holler. The entire room erupted into applause and Sylvie smiled and blushed, put her hand out as if to stop them, and then backed away and ran out of the auditorium.

Lunch soon ended and everyone returned to their tasks. Sylvie found Polly and said, "People are trying to give me money to cover the cost of the food today. What am I supposed to do?"

Polly said, "Well, since they're here helping me out, I don't want them to pay for anything, but if they insist, let them know that any money which comes in between now and the end of Saturday night will be split between the Bellingwood Food Pantry and Habitat for Humanity. There are going to be mason jar banks on the tables Saturday night because you're right, people want to be able to give something. Thanks, Sylvie."

The afternoon passed quickly. Polly finished washing linens and placed the folded items into the wardrobe she had set up in a corner of the upstairs hallway beside her apartment. She decided to go ahead and remake the front room's bed, in case Elise returned, so pulled a set of sheets out and finished that task before heading back down to her office.

Polly saw Sylvie pulling her coat on as she headed for the front door and ran out to catch her. "Do you need something? I could pick it up if you need help. I know you have a million things going on back there."

"I was going to get the boys from school," Sylvie said.

"Let me get them for you, unless you need the break."

"I can use the break, but you could come with me."

Polly ran back to her office and grabbed her jacket, then joined Sylvie and they walked out to her car.

Sylvie drove up to the school and pulled in to a line of vans and cars.

"This is kind of nuts," Polly said looking at the chaos of vehicles parked everywhere around the school.

"I suppose it is, but the boys know to look for me if the weather is bad. Otherwise, they walk home."

They waited and chatted for several minutes and soon Sylvie said, "There they are and ..." she paused and watched, "now they see me. Here they come!"

The two boys ran to the car and stopped when they saw Polly in the front seat, then scrambled to get in back.

"Why are you here, Polly?" Andrew asked.

"I wanted to ride along with your mom today, is that cool?"

"Cool!" he said. "Mom, I got a hundred in spelling!" He thrust a piece of paper with a bright red 100% circled on top.

"Congratulations!" she said. "You only need two more of those and I will take you to Joe's Diner for Saturday breakfast. How was your day, Jason?"

"Fine," the older boy said.

"Just fine?" Sylvie asked as she turned around to look at him.

"It was fine," he replied.

Sylvie checked her mirrors and then eased back out into the street and drove a block to make a turn and head back to Sycamore House. "Didn't you have a geography quiz today? How did you do on it?"

"I did okay," he said.

"Did you bring it home? Can I see it?"

Jason pulled his backpack up into his lap and zipped it open. He fumbled around inside and pulled out a piece of paper. When Polly put her hand out, he gave it to her and said, "It's not a big deal."

She turned the paper over and showed it to Sylvie. The grade in the top corner of the sheet read, "100%."

Sylvie smiled and reached around to pat his knee. "I'm proud of you, Jason. That's great. It looks like all three of us will have breakfast soon."

Polly handed the quiz back to Jason and, as he shoved it down in his backpack, she said, "You've got a couple of bright boys, Sylvie."

"I'm proud of them. We keep a record of all their A's and every time someone gets ten of them, we celebrate with a Saturday morning breakfast. Andrew needs two more and Jason needs ... how many more do you need, Jason?"

"Just one," he said.

"We end up going out to breakfast every couple of weeks. They stay pretty close to each other and if they're within one, we make it happen, don't we!"

Andrew was bouncing in his seatbelt. "I like pancakes the best, but sometimes I get scrambled eggs and bacon. Have you taken Obiwan out to walk this afternoon? Can we play with the kittens?"

Polly chuckled. "I saved Obiwan's walk for you guys."

"Yeah!" he shot his hands up in the air.

Sylvie said, "We're going to be here a while tonight. Make sure you take your backpacks in and you can do your homework on Polly's dining room table."

"With the cats!" Andrew announced.

"With the cats," she agreed as she pulled into the parking lot.

Within a heartbeat of her turning off the car, both boys were out and running toward Sycamore House.

"The apartment is unlocked, boys," Polly called out. "Make sure you shut the door behind you when you leave with Obiwan."

"No problem, Polly," Jason said and followed his brother in the door.

"I love your boys, Sylvie," she said as they walked across the gravel and up the steps. "I'm going to enjoy having them around."

"I love 'em too and I'm glad they have you around. I couldn't have done this if you weren't helping me with them." Sylvie squeezed Polly's arm. "Thank you."

They approached the front door just as it crashed open and two boys and a dog flew out. Polly laughed, "It looks like everyone needed a good run this afternoon."

By five o'clock, Sycamore House was empty again. Bruce had driven over to get his wife and Polly could hear him in the hallway complaining, without much success, as Hannah reminded him they were staying for dancing lessons. Henry and Jeff came in and sat down in the chairs in her office.

"We should go get some dinner," Jeff said. "Do you want to go to Davey's?"

"Let's go!" Polly said and jumped up. She invited Bruce and Hannah, and went upstairs. Sylvie had already run up to check on the boys and their homework.

When she walked into her apartment, Andrew met her at the door with his index finger over his mouth. "Shhh," he said. "Mom fell asleep."

Polly smiled. Sylvie had curled up on the sofa and both cats were tucked in behind her knees. Polly walked over and pulled a blanket from a pile beside the couch and placed it over the sleepers, then whispered to Sylvie, "We're going to Davey's. I'm taking the boys. I'll bring you something back."

"What? What?" Sylvie's eyes opened. "Oh, I didn't mean to fall asleep. Now, what?"

"Go back to sleep," Polly said. "A bunch of us are going to Davey's. I'm going to steal your boys and bring something back for you."

Sylvie snuggled into the pillow. "Really? I'll let you and pay you back later. I haven't been this tired in years."

Polly motioned to the boys to get their coats on and they followed her out. She glanced back and Sylvie's face had already relaxed back into sleep.

"Let's go," she said as they got to the bottom of the steps and everyone left for dinner.

When they got back to Sycamore House after dinner, there were quite a few cars in the driveway and more were pulling in behind them. Henry, who had ridden with Polly and the boys to the steakhouse, said, "Looks like your friend is going to have quite the class tonight."

"You're going to be good, right?" she asked.

"Probably," he laughed. "But, I'm not making any promises."

Polly wasn't sure what that meant, but hoped for the best. They went inside and when she walked into the auditorium, there were already fifteen people moving through line dance steps in front of the stage. Mark saw them come in and whistled. Sylvie was at one end of the group and broke away.

"Thanks, Polly. I couldn't wake up when you were upstairs, I was exhausted!"

"Here's Chicken Parmesan. Amber said you order that when you're there."

"She remembered? It's my favorite. Thank you! Boys, you can stay down here and learn to dance if you want." Sylvie tucked herself in to a table by the wall and opened up the takeout container. "This smells great. I'm hungry." She looked up and said, "Shoo. You dance. I can eat by myself."

People were continuing to come in to the auditorium and before Polly knew it there were close to thirty people on the floor listening as Mark gave instructions. Several young people were at the front with him and after he counted them off to get started, he walked over to Polly and Henry.

"Lisa was still teaching, but she asked some of her older students to help me out. They thought this would be fun, so here they are. Do you remember what to do, Polly?"

"I hope so, or I will make a fool out of myself."

The song finished and he took Polly's arm and led her to the front of the group. Then he announced that they were going to work on the basic box step. He walked through the steps, and his sister's students placed themselves around the room, mimicking his movements. Polly followed along and when she looked up, saw that Lydia and Beryl had walked in and surrounded Henry. They were moving with him and she could see them all laughing.

Mark said, "Grab a partner and if you happen to be the same sex, make sure you choose which one is going to lead. Men, that should be your job and don't let her forget it." He scowled at Polly, who had the grace to blush.

He pressed play and took Polly in his arms. She was immediately transported back into the sensation she had experienced Tuesday evening. He knew how to make this easy and once she relaxed, he swept her up in the beauty of the dance. The song wound down and he asked, "How did it go?"

There were a few complaints and moans and groans, but the students moved in and began correcting things. After a few more songs, Polly had the capacity to look up and around the room. People were enjoying themselves. Then, Mark announced they were going to waltz. He set the music playing and just as he was about to move her into the middle of the crowd, a couple she didn't know bumped into them and sent her sprawling to the floor. Polly was stunned and very thankful she was wearing jeans. Henry and Beryl were nearby and he managed to stop laughing long enough to help her to her feet while Mark attempted to untangle himself from the couple.

Henry said, "How about we switch. Beryl needs a little help." He winked at Beryl and swept Polly off around the room before anyone could protest.

"You didn't send them crashing into me, did you?" Polly laughed.

"Nope, just excellent timing," he replied.

A few turns around the room and she said, "You told me you hadn't danced since college. You're very good!"

"I am, aren't I?" Henry said as he let go of her hand and spun her, then pulled her back in. "Let's say I wasn't a stupid young man and recognized that girls liked boys who could do something other than sway on the dance floor. I took a few lessons."

"Why didn't you tell me that before?"

"A man has to have a few surprises up his sleeve," Henry said. Then he said in a low whisper, "And I have more surprises than sleeves."

He tightened his arm and pulled her in close and they danced until the music stopped. Mark played two more waltzes and Henry kept a tight grip on Polly's hand. Lydia stepped in for a waltz around the room with Mark and Polly saw that Sylvie and Jason were dancing across the floor. Marnie had shown up and was doing her best to keep up with Andrew, who was concentrating on his feet. Finally, one of Lisa's students rescued her and she tapped on an older woman's shoulder to get an opportunity to dance with Jeff. Polly watched him smile at Marnie in relief and she chuckled.

Mark taught them how to do the fox trot from the basic box step and then let the students go through some beginner's line dances again. He made his way to Henry and Polly and said, "You stole my dancer from me," to Henry.

"I'm sorry," Henry laughed. "I guess I did!"

"And you're pretty good, too!"

They both laughed at that and Henry said, "Didn't expect that of an old carpenter, did you."

"I guess not. Polly, do you think you're ready for Saturday night and won't be embarrassed to dance in front of everyone?"

"It wasn't that hard once you taught me how to relax," she said. "Now I can't wait. I feel like I could go dancing every night!"

Jeff came up beside them and said, "Some of the people were talking about the days when they hosted dances here on Friday nights. Maybe we should do that every once in a while."

Polly shook her head, "It sounds like a great idea. You figure it out though. I'm too tired to think all of a sudden."

Henry looked at his watch. "It's nine thirty. You've had a long day."

"I have and I think I'm going to call it quits," Polly said. "Jeff, are you going to be here much longer?"

"Don't worry. I'll close the place down tonight."

Mark laughed. "Well, I have to be on the road by six thirty tomorrow morning, so I'm going to get going as well. I'll tell the kids you're in charge," he said to Jeff. "Start kicking 'em out whenever you want." He went back to the front and pulled one of the girls aside. She nodded and moved back into the steps. Mark picked up his coat and shrugged into it while walking toward Polly and Henry.

"I'll see you on Saturday," he said. He picked up Polly's hand and laid a kiss on its back. "Thank you for a wonderful evening." He walked out and Lydia and Beryl joined them.

"That was a helluva romantic gesture, that was," Beryl said. "What do you have to match it, old man?"

Henry laughed. "I have this!" He grabbed Polly around the waist, bent her over backwards and kissed her.

She came up sputtering and blushed as several people applauded. Sylvie and her boys approached them and Andrew said, "I thought they only did that in movies."

Sylvie laughed, "And sometimes in real life. Let's go upstairs and get your things. It's time to get home and to bed. Good night, Polly. Thanks for everything."

Polly was still flustered, but managed to wave at them as they left the auditorium. Others walked past and said goodnight.

"We'll be back in the morning, Polly. Be good tonight," Lydia said as they all walked into the hallway. She and Beryl pulled their coats on and went out into the evening.

Henry said, "I'll walk you upstairs," and followed Polly up the steps to her apartment. They said good-bye to Sylvie and the boys who passed them on their way back down. When they reached the top, Polly looked over at the front room and saw a light under the door.

"I didn't realize I turned that light on," she said. "Just a second."

They walked over and she triggered the lock and went in the room, then jumped back, bumping into Henry.

Elise was huddled in the far corner of the room, her knees up to her chest and a gun in her hand. Her hair was dirty and her eyes looked as if she hadn't slept in days.

"It's just me," Polly said. "It's Polly. What are you doing?"

CHAPTER SIXTEEN

"Stop! They might see you!" Elise's words halted Polly's entrance into the room. She lowered the gun to the floor and wrapping her arms around her knees, dropped her head and began to weep.

"Who might see me, Elise?" Polly asked, even as she knelt down on the floor. Henry stayed in the doorway and watched Polly crawl to the sobbing girl.

"What's going on?"

Elise didn't say a word, just continued to cry. When Polly touched her hand, she pulled in on herself even tighter.

"Elise, you can't stay on the floor in here. If you don't want to be seen, come with me to my apartment."

"I know I can't stay here on the floor, but I don't know how to get away from them. They're watching for me."

Polly asked, "How do you know you're being watched?"

"I saw them in Boone. They must have been here first, especially since they called you. I don't want you to have any more trouble than I've already brought."

Polly heaved a sigh and said, "I suppose I can handle a little trouble. Come with me. Let's get you to my apartment. You can take a shower and change your clothes and get some sleep. We'll figure things out. I have a lot of great friends who are experts at that." She threw a sideways glance at Henry who smiled.

Elise picked the gun back up and then handed it to Polly. "Take this, please."

Polly pulled back as if it were a snake. "I don't want that. I won't use it."

"Take it and I'll come with you to your apartment. Otherwise I'm staying here."

They were obviously not going anywhere without it, so Polly slipped her finger into the trigger guard and made her way back to the doorway where she immediately handed it to Henry. He helped her stand up and they waited as Elise crawled through the doorway. He pulled the door shut and Elise stood up, then they walked along the wall to the back by the bathrooms and across to Polly's entryway. Polly walked in and was met by a very happy dog.

"Have a seat, Elise. Can I get you something to drink? Have you eaten lately?" Polly took Elise by the arm and led her to the sofa. The girl dropped down and absentmindedly began rubbing Leia's head when the cat snuggled up to her.

"I'm so sorry. I'm so sorry. I didn't mean for anyone else to get involved. I'm so sorry," Elise kept repeating.

"Elise. Stop it," Polly said.

When there didn't seem to be any response, except repetitive stroking of the cat's head and murmuring, Polly put her hand on Elise's knee and sharply said, "Elise!"

The girl looked up and said, "I'm sorry, what?"

"Henry is going to boil water for tea and run downstairs to get leftovers from lunch today and I'm going to get you into the shower. You're going to eat and drink something and then you're going to crawl in my bed and sleep. When you wake up tomorrow morning, we're going to figure everything out."

Polly walked with Henry to the front door and stepped outside with him. "Would you call Aaron and tell him what is going on here? I think we'll be fine tonight, but I want him to know."

"Sure," Henry said. "And I'll bring up food and make tea for her, but I can't leave you two girls alone here tonight."

"We'll be fine, Henry, but I'm not asking you to leave right now anyway. Help me get her settled and then we'll talk."

"I'm calling Aaron, but you're not going to talk me out of staying here. You don't know how to use that gun and if your friend in there is afraid enough of someone to think she needs it, that worries me."

"Whatever. I'm not talking about this now. She needs to clean up and eat before we make any other decisions, now go." She pushed him a little and gave him a small smile, "And thank you."

Elise was still sitting in the same position and Polly walked back over to her. "Come on. Let's start with a shower." She held her hand out to the girl, who took it and stood up. Polly walked with her into the bathroom and turned the shower on. Elise flipped the lid down on the toilet and sat there.

Polly tested the water and said, "It seems fine. I'm going across the hall to find you some clothes ..."

"No! You can't go in that room. If they see you moving around in there, they'll know I'm here."

"Elise, don't worry. I've been in and out of that room all week long. I'll make sure that if someone outside sees anyone in there, they know it's me. Now, you get into the shower. I'll be back in a few minutes. The door to my apartment is locked and the only people who can get in tonight are me and Henry. You're safe."

Elise nodded and stood up, kicking her shoes off. She bent down to pull off her socks and then as she reached to pull her shirt over her head, Polly walked out and shut the door.

She went across the hall and walked in front of the windows, checking their latches and bending over as if picking things up. She filled a laundry basket with clothing for Elise to wear for several days, kicked the basket across the floor to the door, reached up and turned out the light. She bent over to pick the basket up and heard footsteps on the stairs.

Henry came up the last set of stairs. "I talked to Aaron. He's coming over to watch your place while I run home to take care of things so I can spend the night. He said he'd be back in the morning to talk to you and Elise, but if anything comes up to let him know."

They walked together back to the door of her apartment and Polly said, "You know, rather than feel like a helpless little girl who needs all of these men around to take care of me, I think I'm going to choose to be thankful for you guys in my life."

Henry laughed. "Well, that's a start!" He held the door open and she walked in with the basket in her arms and headed into the bedroom. She heard him opening cupboard doors and stuck her head out and said, "The teapot is in the cupboard over the stove, mugs are to the right of the sink and dishes are in the one beside that cupboard. Silverware ... oh, you've got it. Thanks."

She heard him drawing water as she shut the door.

"Elise? Are you doing alright?" Polly asked through the door. "Are you still in the shower?"

"I'm fine. I'll be out in a few minutes."

"I'm coming in to set out fresh towels. I'll lay them on the counter," Polly said. She quickly went into the bathroom and pulled one of her big sage towels out of the linen closet and put it beside the sink. Then it occurred to her Elise might need a few other things and she dug around looking for a fresh toothbrush. There were two unopened combs in her travel kit, so she pulled those out as well and set them on top of the towel.

"Elise?"

"Yes?"

"There's a basket of your clothing on the bed. When you're ready, come on out into the living room."

"Thank you, Polly."

Polly left the door open between the bathroom and bedroom. The cats scurried into the bedroom and she left them there as she pulled the door shut and walked into the living room. She dropped to the sofa, put her feet up on the coffee table and asked, "Has everyone gone home?"

"I saw Jeff's car pull out when I went down," Henry replied.

"Good. That was kind of fun tonight, wasn't it?"

"Which part?" he asked snidely.

Polly chuckled and said, "The whole thing, you nut, though that kiss was a little more than I expected."

"I told you. More surprises than I have sleeves."

He brought over a mug with steaming water and put it in her hand, then held out the basket of bags. Polly selected one, opened it and dropped it in water, dunking it in and out as she took in the aroma of Chamomile. Henry pushed her feet off the table and she giggled, then kicked her shoes off and rearranged herself, tucking them under her. When they heard the water turn off in the shower he went back into the kitchen and started the microwave.

"I didn't mean for you to do all of this," Polly said. "You've had a longer day than me."

Henry said, "Don't worry. I've got it. You sit there and relax and don't worry," he said. "I have a long memory and a lot of patience."

Polly rolled her eyes, then shut them as she held the mug to her face and allowed the steam to warm her.

The bedroom door opened and Elise walked out, dressed in sweats and a fresh t-shirt, holding a pair of thick socks in her hands. "Thank you," she said. "I feel much better."

"Sit here," Polly patted the sofa. "I think we have Henry as our waiter tonight. Sylvie made a terrific Shepherd's Pie for lunch and he's reheating some for you."

Henry walked over with another mug of hot water and placed it in front of Elise. He also put two saucers and teaspoons on the table between the girls.

"Wow," Elise said, "I have never been pampered by a man. If you don't want him, can I have him?" She bent over and slipped her socks on her feet.

Polly looked up at Henry, who simply grinned at her. "Can she have me?" he asked.

"I'm not giving away men tonight," Polly said. "Just a bed and a shower."

"I shouldn't be taking your bed from you, Polly. I can sleep on the couch."

"You look like you haven't slept in several days. It's alright, as long as you don't mind a couple of cats sharing your space."

Leia had jumped up between them and was rubbing her head against Elise's leg. Luke was perched at the far end of the sofa back licking his front paw as if nothing else was happening in the world.

"I don't mind them being in the bed," Elise said. "Leia always slept with me."

"Then, it's settled. Now, eat something."

Henry had put the plate of food on the table and Elise reached over to pick it up. He pulled his phone out of his back pocket and said, "Hello? Okay, thanks."

"I'm going to run home. Aaron is across the street in Lydia's Jeep. He'll keep an eye on things until I get back. Why don't I take Obiwan with me. Then you won't have to go out with him again tonight."

Polly unfolded her legs and got up. She pulled Obiwan's leash off the table beside the door and snapped the hook onto his collar, then handed it to Henry.

"Thank you."

Henry took her by the elbow and guided her out into the hallway, then nudged the door shut without latching it. "We're going to be a while. I told Aaron I was going to walk the perimeter while he's here to make sure you're safe. Don't go anywhere, alright?"

He kissed her on the cheek and headed down the steps. Polly followed him to the top of the second landing and watched as he put his coat on and went out the front door with her dog.

Her phone rang, "Hello?" she said.

"Hi Polly," she recognized Aaron Merritt's voice.

"Hey Aaron. You missed the dancing fun tonight."

"Actually, I don't believe I missed anything fun at all tonight."

"You're going to be okay with your gorgeous wife dancing around the floor with other men?"

He had a deep, hearty laugh. "If it means I don't have to make a fool of myself, she can dance with anyone in town. How are you doing?"

"Good, I guess. I'm not sure what to do with all of this added excitement. I thought that raising a barn was enough, but apparently I was wrong."

"Have you found anything out from your guest yet?"

"No, not yet and speaking of finding anything out, have you been able to uncover anything about that note and those pictures?"

"We're still waiting, but when I can, I'll let you know. Now, you be careful tonight, alright?"

Polly said, "Thanks Aaron. I'll see you Saturday, right?"

"I'll be there. It isn't every day something this exciting happens in Bellingwood."

Elise had found the remote and turned the television on. She looked up and asked Polly, "Is everything alright?"

"I think so," Polly replied. "Henry's walking the dog and is going to run home to get some of his things. He'll spend the night here.

"Where's he going to sleep?" Elise asked and then as soon as she thought about it, she said, "Oh, I should sleep on the couch. You two can have the bedroom."

Polly threw her hands up and said, "No, No! It's not like that. We're not like that."

"Really? Because you certainly look like you are together like that. You're awfully comfortable with each other if you aren't ... like that."

"No. And don't start putting those thoughts out there. I don't want the universe to get any crazy ideas. I'm a long ways from wanting a relationship ... like that. For now, we just enjoy spending time together."

"I'm not very good at understanding relationships, but I think Henry wants more than that," Elise said.

"He might, but if he's smart and doesn't want me to throw a hissy fit at him, he'll go slowly and there will be none of the 'like that' until much, much later."

They both giggled. Polly sat down on the other side of the two cats, who had found a soft spot in the sofa and were snuggled together beside Elise. She turned to the girl and said, "Will you tell me what is going on?"

"Can I sleep first? I'll talk to you tomorrow, I promise."

"Elise, I have to know something. Is that even your real name? Who is Linda Marberry?"

"I am," Elise said, her voice pitched low. "I am."

"Why are you here as Elise Myers?"

"Because ..." she stopped, "I don't want to talk about this right now."

"Are you running away from something? And where have you been these last few days?"

"I've done nothing wrong!" Elise declared. "But, I guess you could say I'm running away. I didn't think anyone would find me before ... I really don't want to talk about this."

"Are you really in grad school and working on your dissertation?"

Elise looked up and nodded. "Yes! I am! All of that is true. And my family did give me money so I could go somewhere and dedicate myself to finishing it. But, it isn't really true that I have an aunt who heard about Sycamore House. I made that up."

"That's a start. Now, tell me where you've been and why you looked so awful when I found you tonight? And why do you have a gun?"

The girl sighed. "The gun is what I don't want to talk about." She took a deep breath. "When you told me you had received a couple of calls about me, I knew I had to leave. I figured they would show up, discover I wasn't here any longer and go away. I called a taxi service in Boone and went down there, but then I realized I couldn't register under either of my names. I hitched a couple of rides, slept in some rest areas and a few barns and finally, when I couldn't take it anymore, I hitched a ride back here. When I saw all of the activity, I knew I could sneak in with a group of people coming in to work."

"Should I call you Elise or Linda?"

"Elise is fine. It's my first name. Linda is my middle name, but since my Mom was Elise too, I always used Linda. But, you know me by Elise, so that's alright."

"Where are you from?"

"Chicago. I promise all of that is true."

"Did something happen to you there? Is someone trying to hurt you?"

Elise's face looked so wounded, Polly wanted to hug her, but she said, "Nothing happened to me, but I think these guys want to hurt me."

"Do you know them?"

"No, I don't know them personally. I think they were hired to find me."

"What do you mean?" Polly asked. Now she had hired goons chasing her guests in Bellingwood? She was never going to live this one down. If Bellingwood had a railroad, they'd want to run her out of town on the rails. As it was, she was already getting a reputation for shady characters hanging around.

She sighed and said, "Who hired them?"

"I don't want to talk about that," Elise replied.

"Who brought you here?"

Elise shook her head. "It was just a friend. But, if they know I'm here, he's the only person who could have told them. I hope he's alright."

"Told who? Elise, who is after you? What's going on?"

"I didn't even know anyone knew I was there," she said. "I waited until everyone left before I came out."

"What are you talking about?" Polly asked.

"Polly, really. I don't want to talk about this tonight. I haven't had any sleep in days and I want to lie down in a real bed." She rubbed her eyes. "Do you have any idea what it is like for someone with my fear of the world to be stuck out there not knowing what's going to happen next? I've been sick to my stomach all week long and scared out of my mind."

Polly's heart broke. "Of course you have. I'm sorry I was pushing. Tomorrow will be fine. And Elise, one of my best friends is the Sheriff here. Will you talk to him and let him help you? He's a great guy and ..."

"No! I know you might think he's a great guy, but I can't trust anyone. I can't even believe I've told you this much." She seemed frenzied and then Polly watched her bring herself under control.

"I just need some sleep," she said. "If I can sleep through the night, I'll make better decisions tomorrow."

"Will you think about talking to my friend?" Polly asked.

"I'll think about it tomorrow. But, first I need to go to sleep." Elise stood up and began to walk to the bedroom. "I'm sorry that I've involved you in all of this. If I had anywhere else I could go, I'd have stayed away, but right now this is all I've got."

"It's alright," Polly said. "You get some sleep. I can wait until tomor ..."

Polly's front door crashed open and two men wearing black ski masks and carrying handguns rushed in. They took in the situation and while one of them grabbed Elise, the other strode over and as she rose up off the couch, thumped Polly in the back of the head and everything went black.

CHAPTER SEVENTEEN

Polly opened her eyes. She was sprawled across her coffee table. One of the mugs had been overturned. Henry hadn't returned, so she hadn't been out very long. She pushed herself up and sat back on the sofa, rubbing the back of her head, then picked up her phone and dialed.

"Aaron. Two guys just broke in and took Elise."

"What? I'll be right up. Are you okay?"

"I think so. One of them hit me over the head and I blacked out."

"Don't move. I'm calling the squad. They'll be right behind me."

"Okay. I'm not going to move. My head hurts."

From the background noise of his phone, she heard his tires spinning across her gravel as he said, "Do you hear anyone still in the building?"

"I don't know. They broke my door, Aaron."

"I'm here. I'll be right up."

"Thank you, Aaron." Polly ended the call, shut her eyes and rubbed the back of her head again. Yes. That was going to leave a mark.

Aaron rushed through the door followed closely by Henry. Polly heard sirens and wasn't any too happy to realize they were coming for her. She giggled as both men came in close.

"What are you laughing about?" Henry asked as he sat down beside her. "Are you alright?"

"I'm fine. I heard the sirens and thought about how they were coming for me and all I could think was, 'They're coming to take me away, ha ha, they're coming to take me away.'

Polly sobered, "Don't let them take me away, Henry. I have too much to do. Please?"

Aaron chuckled. "You're going to let them take a look at you and if they say you will be alright, you can sign their refusal form and stay home tonight. But, if they say anything different, I'm going to act like your father and tell you to be obedient."

Polly turned to Henry, "Don't let them take me away. I hate hospitals."

"I'm with him. Whatever he says, I say."

When Aaron left the apartment, Polly said to Henry, "They broke my door."

"I know. Are you really alright?"

"Apparently, I have to wait for someone else to tell me whether I am or not," she said and slumped back on the couch.

Aaron came in with two people. Polly recognized the girl from the night last fall when Doug had been beaten by her ex-boyfriend, Joey. "Hi there," Polly said sheepishly. "You're back."

The girl grinned and said, "Yes, I guess I am. Don't move. I need to make sure you are going to live. Sheriff Merritt says you're afraid we're going to take you away to the funny farm because you got knocked in the head," and she winked at Polly.

Henry had gotten up and walked away, giving the EMT room to look at Polly.

"Can you tell me your name?" she asked.

"Me? Didn't Aaron tell you who I was?" Polly asked.

"Yes. I'm trying to make sure you're alright. Would you answer the question?"

"Oh," Polly giggled, "I'm Polly Giller."

"Good answer. Now do you know where you are?"

"In my apartment in Sycamore House in Bellingwood, Iowa. Is that enough?"

"That's perfect. Now, do you know what time it is?"

"Ummm ... I don't think I knew what time it was before this happened. Probably around ten thirty. Is that close enough to keep me out of the hospital?"

"It's ten forty-five, but that's close enough."

"She's alright, Sheriff. We won't take her away if she doesn't want to go. But," she turned back to Polly, "are you sure? You got hit hard enough to knock you out. It wouldn't hurt for you to get checked out."

"Don't make me go. I'm fine. I answered the questions and I'll sign your paper."

The EMT turned to her partner and held her hand out. He placed a clipboard and a pen in her hand. She said, "Read through this refusal and then sign and date it here, alright?"

Polly took the clipboard and said, "So what's your name? When I meet someone like this a second time, I figure it might be the start to a pattern."

"I'm Sarah and I hope we meet under better circumstances if there's going to be any pattern."

Polly signed the paper and handed it back to Sarah, then said, "Well, I'm not going to die tonight, right?

Aaron interrupted. "Girl, you are going to be the death of me, even if it doesn't kill you. How does this keep happening to you?"

"Am I supposed to feel guilty? Because I feel lousy enough right now it would be an easy next step."

He laughed. "No, you don't need to feel guilty," then he said, "I'll be right back. It sounds like my people are showing up and I want to know what happened here tonight. He passed his wife as she walked in. They nodded and she stood beside Henry, taking his arm.

"Why are you here, Lydia?" Polly asked.

"Aaron called me. Did you think I wouldn't come over to check on you?"

"Elise didn't have a coat or shoes or anything. They just took her!" Then Polly looked around. "Where are the cats? Are they okay?"

Henry spoke up. "They're in the bedroom. Don't worry."

Polly tried to stand up and reached for the arm of the sofa. "Okay, whoa," she said. When she got her bearings, she continued. "That's a little more excitement than I want to have." She blinked her eyes and rolled her shoulders, then reached around to touch the back of her head. "Ow! He thumped me hard." She sat back on the couch and breathed.

Everyone in the room was watching her and she giggled, "I'm not dying. Sarah isn't making me go to the hospital so I'm pretty sure that's the truth. You need to get those grim looks off your faces, and besides, if I were dying, do you think that's what I'd want to stare at?

"Polly, you scared us to death." Lydia rushed over and sat beside her on the couch, putting her arm around her back.

"Again with me scaring you," Polly said. "I didn't do it on purpose. I promise!"

"I know. I know. But when Aaron called, I couldn't think of anything but getting over here."

Polly allowed herself to relax and be hugged by Lydia, who held on to her far longer than Polly expected.

"Aaron needed his vehicle tonight, so I brought it over since he was driving mine and he refused to leave you. Honey, I was worried!" Lydia pulled Polly in close again. "If you aren't going to the hospital tonight, you're coming to my house."

Polly pulled back from her. "No. I just want to stay here. They got what they came for and I can't imagine they'd come back. Please don't make me leave."

Lydia looked up. "Henry? Can you talk to her?"

He laughed. "Are you kidding me? No. I'm not walking into that minefield. I am not that stupid. However, I already have my things and will stay on her couch."

Polly looked at Lydia, asking if that was acceptable.

"Fine." Lydia said. "I don't like it, but you're an adult and I'm not your mother."

Sarah and her partner were heading to the open door in Polly's entryway.

"Thanks, guys," Polly said. "You should come back for the dance on Saturday, as guests, not to work."

Sarah smiled and said, "I just might! I hope you have a good night." She looked at Henry. "Call us or get her to Boone if anything weird happens, alright?"

He nodded and they left.

Aaron came back in, sat down on the coffee table in front of her and said, "Polly did they touch anything in here?"

"I don't know. I don't think so. One of them grabbed Elise and before I could get up, the other one crossed the room and hit me." She rubbed her head again. "I'd like to kick him in the balls, that one. Damn, that makes me mad."

Aaron chuckled. "I'm not sure if you're going to be able to, but if the opportunity arises, take it. I'd like to get into Elise's room and see if I can find something that will tell us what has happened and where they might have taken her."

Polly felt around for her phone and couldn't find it in her pocket. "Where's my phone?"

Lydia tried to rearrange some of the chaos that had happened on the coffee table. She picked up the scattered teabags, put them in the basket and handed the basket and mugs to Henry. He returned with a towel to sop up the spilled tea.

Aaron stood up from the coffee table and Lydia laughed, "There it is," she said. "Under the newspaper you were sitting on."

She handed it to Polly, who peered at it and then pressed a few keys and said, "There, I emailed you her key so you have access to that room. How did those guys get past you?"

He sat back down in front of her on the table. "I don't know. We're going to figure it out. I don't know how long we'll be here tonight, but I won't bother you again until tomorrow. Try to get some sleep."

He put his hand on Lydia's knee. "And you need to go home and let her sleep. Here are your keys," and he dropped them in her outstretched hand. "I'll be home when I can."

Lydia pulled Polly close one more time and said, "I'd much rather know you were safe in a room next to mine, but if I have to be adult about this, I will. I love you, sweet girl, so you take care of yourself tonight. Do you promise?"

"I promise," Polly said and drew her finger across her heart, "but I'm not going to say hope to die, if that's alright."

Lydia stood up and followed her husband out of the apartment, turning around at the door to wave.

"Wait, Aaron?" Polly called.

"What?" he asked.

"I talked to Elise tonight. She said those guys were hired to find her. I think something bad happened in Chicago and she saw it. Whoever did it didn't know she was there, but the friend who brought her to Bellingwood must have told them. She's been hiding out in Boone and around the area for the last week and saw those two guys down there. She recognized them."

Lydia had stopped with Aaron and when she realized that he wasn't walking out, said, "I'll see you later. I'm going home. Let me know where you are tonight, will you?"

He bent over and kissed her forehead, "Check your phone whenever you wake up, I'll text you and let you know throughout the night."

"I love you." She hugged him and waved at Polly, then went on out into the hallway.

Aaron walked back into the room and sat down in the chair. "What else can you tell me, Polly?"

Polly told him everything she could remember from her conversation with Elise.

"Most of the information she originally gave me about herself was true, I suppose. Maybe some of that can help you figure out what's going on," Polly said.

"I've got some contacts in Chicago. I'll reach out to them." He stood up, then said, "We're looking for her. Doc Ogden saw the car Tuesday night, so we know what we're looking for. You get some sleep now, alright?"

Henry walked him to the door and she watched the two men shake hands. Aaron said something quietly to Henry, who nodded and then held the door as he left.

Once the apartment was empty, Henry sat down in the chair next to the sofa. "Is it always going to be like this with you?" he asked.

Polly grinned at him, "I guess I have a few surprises up my sleeve as well!"

"I swear, mine are much more fun," he replied. "When I saw Aaron flying in your front door, I nearly had a heart attack and poor Obiwan was so upset, he practically dragged me up the stairs."

"Where is he, by the way?"

"I should probably let him out. I put him in the bedroom with the cats."

Henry opened the bedroom door and Obiwan rushed out and jumped up on the couch beside Polly. He nudged her arm with his head and when she began to pet him, he lay down with his head on her lap.

"Henry, we have to get that door fixed."

"I know." Henry sat back down. "It's fine for now. It will close enough so the cats won't escape. Don't worry, I've got it."

"I'm worried about her, Henry. Somehow I feel responsible for Elise."

"Of course you do. But Polly, tonight I'm worried about you. Can you sleep?"

"Not yet. Can we just sit here for a while?"

"Sure. Here. Scoot over and make room for me." He slipped in between her and the arm of the sofa.

Polly leaned on him and looking up, smiled and put her feet up on the table. Henry pulled the blanket from the back of the sofa over both Polly and her dog, leaned back and put his feet up beside hers. He held her tight and then listened to her breathe as she drifted off to sleep.

Obiwan woke Polly up when he jumped off the sofa and paced in the entryway.

"What is it?" she asked and checked the time on her phone. It was a little after two o'clock.

Henry pulled himself up and said, "Just a minute, I'll check." He put his hand on Obiwan's collar and pulled the door open and stepped out into the hallway. She heard voices, then he came back in and nudged the door back into place.

"Everyone has left. Aaron said he'll make sure all the doors downstairs are closed tightly and that he'll talk to you tomorrow."

"Did he say if they found anything to lead them to Elise?"

"No, he didn't say anything about that, but, he did say they found a broken lock on the kitchen door. He's fixed it for now, but I get to replace another door." He walked over and put his hand out. "Now, come on. You should get into bed. How's your head?"

"Well, the knot feels like hell, but I think I'm alright. I think I feel better." She put her hand in his and let him pull her upright. "Yep, definitely better. I'm not dizzy now."

Instead of walking toward the bedroom, she headed for the kitchen.

"What are you doing?"

"I want a drink of water." Polly giggled and kept walking. "Or are you going to stop me and make me let you pamper me."

Henry put his hands up in surrender. "I don't think I could make you do anything you didn't want to do."

She waggled her finger at him and kept walking. "Now you're learning. Do you want anything?"

"Are you going to bed?" he asked.

"In a little bit. I'm afraid I might have just had a really nice nap, though."

"Yeah. Me, too. Shall I put a movie in?"

"Sure! Do you want anything?" she asked.

"Water would be fine. How about one of those cupcakes I brought up?"

"Would you rather have milk with that?"

"That sounds great. Can I have both?"

Polly laughed, "Of course you can."

She reached to open the cupboard and moaned. "Umm,

Henry?"

"Are you alright?"

"I'm fine. But, everything in the upper part of my body hurts. I might need your help here."

He dropped what he was doing and ran into the kitchen. "Are you sure you're alright."

"Well, I might have pulled something in my shoulder," she said. "But, if I work it out, I'll be fine."

"Here, let me." He massaged her shoulder and she felt some of the muscles relax, so she rolled her neck.

"I'll get this. You go back to the couch and find a movie," he said.

She drooped her shoulders dramatically and slowly walked out of the kitchen. "I had to let you pamper me after all," she said under her breath.

"I heard that. I'm not pampering you. I'm being polite."

Polly heard him chuckling as she sat back down on the far corner of the sofa. She wrapped her feet up under her and pulled the blanket out from under Obiwan. "You have to share," she said to him. "How did you get to be such a slug of a dog?" She maneuvered the blanket to cover both of them and left some for Henry.

He handed her a glass of water. "Did you want a cupcake ... cupcake?"

She rolled her eyes at him. "No, thank you."

"Are you nauseous?" he asked.

"No, I just don't want anything. Hopefully, I'll get tired pretty soon."

"No movie?"

Polly handed him the remote control. "I don't care."

"Well then you can watch me eat my dessert. I'm sure it will be terribly exciting."

"It's not boring," she laughed. "Thanks for staying tonight. I know I make a lot of noise about being independent, but I'm glad you're here. I'm only sorry you have to sleep on my couch rather than in your own bed."

"I can sleep in my bed any time," he laughed. "How often do I get to sleep on your couch?"

"Okay," she said. "Thanks, though. I do appreciate it."

The cats had come out into the living room and were wrestling on the floor in front of the television. Henry pointed and said, "Now, there's some entertainment."

"I'm glad they have each other. Those little nocturnal brats would keep me up all night if they had their way. They get better as they get older, but sometimes it takes them an hour of play before they're ready to come back to bed."

Polly took a drink and said, "What do you think has happened to Elise?"

"I have no idea, Polly, but I'm sure Aaron has called in the troops and they're looking for her."

"I just wish I knew what was going on with her."

Henry finished his cupcake and put the paper wrapper on the plate, then set that on the table. Luke looked up at the noise and leaving Leia behind, jumped up to sniff at the remnants.

"That's chocolate," Henry said.

Polly said, "Just a second. Watch him."

Luke sniffed for a moment, then batted at the paper and backed away. He sat down and stared at it for a few seconds, then turned his back on it and jumped off the table.

"He's the funniest thing," Polly said. "He wants to know everything that is going on, but once he's figured it out, he wants nothing more to do with it."

"That's weird."

"Leia likes to taste different things, but she's really not interested in any of it. I think for the most part, it's only curiosity. Unless," Polly said, "unless it is a milk product. They both love cheese, cottage cheese, cream cheese. I have to be careful not to leave those things out. But, then, if I give them a little bit, they're satisfied and leave me alone. They're pretty good cats."

She yawned and reached down to put her glass on the table. "I suppose I should try to get some sleep. Tomorrow and Saturday are going to be long days."

"Are you sure you're doing alright?" Henry asked.

"I'm sure." Polly pushed Obiwan off the couch and he yawned and stretched. "Come on, you slug. We need to get some bedding for Henry and you're NOT taking up space out here tonight. Come on." She stood up and took his collar to move him toward the bedroom door. "I'll be right back with pillows and things. How about we leave the bathroom doors open unless we're in there - that way we'll know, okay? And the cats need to move around anyway. Is that alright?"

"Sure. That's a good idea."

She went through the living room door to the bathroom and rustled around in the linen closet, pulling out a pillow and flat sheet. Then she took them back into the living room. Henry had walked back to the kitchen with the dishes and set them on the counter beside the sink, so she dropped the pillow on a chair and shook out the sheet, draping it over the back of the sofa and tucking it in.

"I don't know how much warmth you'll need tonight. There are plenty of blankets in the pile back there," and she pointed behind the chair to a large basket filled with blankets. "Use what you want."

Henry walked back and looked at the sofa. "Thanks. I'm sure I'll be fine." He picked the pillow up and dropped it at one end, then he took her hand. "Are you going to be alright tonight?"

Polly winked at him. "Are you just trying to get in my bed?"

He dropped her hand and in shock, he said, "NO! That's not what I meant at all!"

She laughed. "I know. I was only teasing. And yes, I'm going to be fine. Good night." She began to turn away to head to the bedroom when he took her arm and stopped her.

"Good night goes something like this," he said and pulled her close for a kiss.

"Hoookay," she gasped, when they broke apart. "That's a nice twist."

Polly walked away and into the bedroom. She closed the door behind her and then shut the door to the bathroom while she changed into her pajamas. Obiwan had already jumped up into the bed and was sprawled across it. She pushed him out of the way and crawled under the covers.

She reflected on the last few kisses from Henry. Those were definite heart-melters. Polly giggled. After the night she licked his lips, he wasn't letting her get away with that again. She pulled the blankets into a cocoon around her and shivered. No one had ever made her feel as comfortable and safe as Henry did while at the same time tipping her heart off balance.

"No," she said out loud to herself. "You are not falling for someone right now. No matter how wonderful he is. A man isn't in the plan. Don't forget that."

She sighed and realized that if the heart wanted what the heart wanted, her head wasn't going to have a lot to say about it. After flipping off the light, she turned over, wrapped herself around the dog and promptly fell asleep.

.

CHAPTER EIGHTEEN

"Evil man," she thought. Polly peered through her eyelashes as her door slipped open.

"What is it?" she asked.

Henry stepped in. "I was going to take Obiwan outside before the day got started. I didn't mean to wake you, but how are you feeling?"

She turned over on her side and faced him, then rolled her neck around. "I'm doing fine, I think. What time is it?"

"It's only five thirty. Go back to sleep. Come on Obiwan." Henry patted his leg and the dog stood up, then walked across Polly to jump down to the floor.

"Erumph," she grunted. "You couldn't get on the floor and walk around, could you?"

"I'll shut the door. You take another nap, alright?"

"What are you doing up so early anyway?" she asked.

"It's when I get up. When we get back, I'll be quiet, but I might make breakfast for you. See ya later."

He walked out and shut the door. She heard him talking to Obiwan and then allowed herself to drift back to sleep.

Polly's alarm on her phone rang and she reached for it, knocking it off the bedside table. When she bent over the bed to pick it up, she moaned. "Damn. That's going to hurt today!" She rubbed the back of her head and felt the knot. "It's good my hair is covering that thing or I'd spend all day explaining it," she mumbled to herself.

Her phone told her it was six thirty and when the cats realized she was waking up, they jumped off the bed and headed to their perches on the cat tree, looking out at the moonlit sky. "One of these days, there will be daylight in the mornings again," she said. "That ought to make you kids happy." She sat up on the edge of her bed. Things were awfully quiet in the living room. Walking over to the door, she opened it and saw Henry at the dining room table with his laptop open.

"Good morning," he said. "How are you doing?"

"I have a headache and I'm a little grumpy. How are you?"

"I'm certainly doing better than that! I've had a walk, a shower and a cup of coffee. How can I help you get started?"

"Don't mind me. I'll take my grumpy self into the shower and see if that helps. Back in a bit."

She shut the door and headed for the bathroom, making sure the outer door was shut. A scalding, hot shower seemed like a good idea. While she waited for the water to warm up, she opened the cabinet and pushed things around looking for ibuprofen.

When Polly re-entered the living room, she smelled bacon. "You really are making breakfast! Thank you!"

"The coffee is already poured and breakfast will be ready soon."

"Can I do anything?"

"I think I finally found everything. You sit down and drink your coffee."

She did and took a sip of the hot coffee, "This is nice," she said. "Thank you."

"It's too bad that it took you being hit on the head for me to make you breakfast."

Polly looked up and said, "What?"

"Wait. That didn't come out right. Sorry. Strike that."

"What did you mean by that, though?"

"Nothing. I was thinking about all the mornings you made breakfast around here and I'm glad I finally got a chance to return the favor. It was nothing more than that. I'm sorry." He started laughing. "Wow, walked right up to the cliff and kept going, didn't I!"

Both cats had come out to the kitchen and were winding around his legs as he stood at the stove. "Are they going to cause me to fall on my face when I try to walk away?" he asked.

She looked over at his feet. "They might. They want their breakfast." Polly went to the cupboard where the cat food was kept. She pulled out the tub and poured it into their dishes.

"Thanks," he said.

"Did you feed Obiwan yet?"

"Look at him," Henry said. She turned and looked at Obiwan sitting under the end of the peninsula separating the kitchen from the dining room.

"You're right. He'd be a panic-stricken mess if he hadn't gotten his breakfast after his walk. Thank you."

"He's a good dog and by the way, he found where Elise was dragged across the creek. And guess what, you know that trap that he ran into down at the other end of the property?"

"Yeah?" she said.

"I wonder if the Sheriff knows that one of Elise's attackers probably ran into a trap up here. There's a mess over there and some blood. Obiwan found it this morning."

Polly looked at the microwave for the time. "It's seven o'clock. You should call him."

"Let me finish this and I will."

He brought a plate filled with bacon and toast to the table, then went back and brought a dish filled with scrambled eggs. "Now, these are my grandma's scrambled eggs. I hope you like them."

Polly murmured, "You dance, you build things, you kiss, you have a great car, and you cook? How are you not already married?"

"What did you say?" he asked.

"How are you not already married? You are perfect!"

"You just keep thinking that. And I'm not already married because sometimes a guy spends an hour with a girl and discovers she's got nothing in her brain except wedding bells and babies. That stuff bores me to death."

"I'm certainly not that girl," Polly commented.

"No, you're not and you are definitely not boring. You've brought more entertainment to Bellingwood than it has seen in years."

"I'd like to be a little more boring than that," she said.

"Do you know that there is a pool at the grain elevator on you?"

"WHAT?" she demanded.

"That upsets you?"

"What in the hell ... a pool ... about what?"

"About when you'll find the next dead body around here."

"No way," she said. "No. Way."

"Well, yes way," he laughed. "No one saw Madeline Black's death coming, but there are some gruesome ideas over there."

"Are you involved in this?"

"Not me," he laughed. "I wouldn't get involved in anything quite so ... ummm ... despicable."

"I don't believe you. What dead body do you have me finding?"

"I'm not saying. But, when I win the pool, I'll take you out to dinner."

Polly shook her head at him. "Rotten rat. You know, it's one thing to be famous for the good a person does, but to be infamous for being around dead bodies, that's not quite as much fun."

Henry picked up his phone. "I'm going to call Aaron. Just a second." He walked into the living room and then wandered into the entryway. She could hear him pushing on the door frame as he spoke.

Polly continued to eat her breakfast until he came back in and sat down. "Aaron's team didn't get that far in the dark last night. He's got a team who will be over before eight o'clock, though. This kind of changes things. If one of them is hurt, it will probably slow them down a bit."

"I hope they are found before they get too far. I'm so worried about her."

"I know you are. She's going to be fine. I'm sure of it."

They finished breakfast and he picked up the dishes to carry them into the kitchen. Polly said, "Leave the dishes. I'll clean things up tonight."

"It's alright," he said.

"No, really. I think we'd both rather get going with today and something as normal as washing dishes will be good for my evening."

"So, no big wild date tonight?"

Polly said, "I'm going to ignore that," and walked into the living room, picking up her tennis shoes before she sat down on the sofa. Henry had folded up the sheet and laid it on top of his pillow, the blankets were all folded and back in the basket and things on the coffee table were straightened up.

"You're good at this whole cleaning thing, aren't you," she laughed.

"I suppose. Mom wasn't much for a messy house and now that I own her house, I can't bring myself to let it fall apart. I have a feeling that if she thought I wasn't keeping it clean, she'd make Dad drive back to Bellingwood just to yell at me."

"Thank you for cleaning up," Polly said. "And thank you for staying last night. I'm sure I slept better knowing you were out here."

"I wouldn't have been able to leave you. You scared me to death."

She stood up again with her shoes on and tied and said, "I'm good. And thank you again." Polly stepped in close to him and reached her arms around him. He enveloped her and pulled her head against his chest. They stood there for a few moments, then she reached up for a kiss. "Thank you," she said.

Another few moments in his arms and she broke away. "I suppose we should get to work."

He stepped back. "It's going to be a busy couple of days. If you don't mind, I'm going to leave my stuff up here until later. I don't want to have to think about it today."

"No problem," she said. "Well, shall we?"

She swung the door open, touched the frame and asked, "This should be alright today, shouldn't it?"

"It will be fine for a few days. The cats will stay inside. Don't worry about it."

"Okay. You're the boss."

They went downstairs and Polly headed for her office. It was only seven thirty and Jeff hadn't yet arrived. In fact, the building was empty and things were quiet. She spun around in her chair and looked out the windows, watching as the giant orange ball in the east began rising over the community. Bruce and Hannah drove up to the entrance and Polly watched her kiss him goodbye and then get out and come in the front door. In moments, more vehicles pulled in. Jeff got out of his car and stopped to talk to Sam Terhune. They were laughing about something as they approached the front steps. Sylvie pulled in and Polly watched her open her trunk and pull bags of items out to bring inside. Jimmy Rio was right behind her and he quickly jumped out of his car to help her carry things.

Polly smiled. She had a lot of good people in her life. She turned back to her desk and was startled to see Aaron Merritt standing in her doorway.

"I didn't see you come in!" she said.

"I snuck in the back door. We've been out searching through your back yard and into the creek. Henry and Obiwan made great find. It changes how we look for these guys. We're calling the local hospitals to see if anyone came in last night with wounds from a trap. If that doesn't turn anything up, we'll call drugstores. We'll find her."

"I suppose it's too early to have heard from anyone in Chicago about what she might have seen?"

Aaron smiled, "It's a little early. As soon as I know anything, I'll find you."

"Thanks."

"How are you doing this morning?"

Polly rubbed her head. "This hurts, but I'm going to be fine."

"Lydia was still up when I got home this morning. I think she worried all night about you."

"I'm sorry. I didn't mean for that to happen."

"It's good for her. She hasn't had anyone around to worry about since Jim left for college. Every once in a while I make him come home so she can fret over him instead; but he figured me out and doesn't fall for that trick unless I beg."

Polly chuckled, "Does everyone know what happened last night?"

"What do you think?" Aaron asked. "Of course they do. I'm sure you were the topic of conversation at breakfast all over town this morning."

"Did you hear they had a pool at the grain elevator on me discovering dead bodies?"

"Henry finally spilled the beans, did he? I told him you weren't going to be happy."

"I don't even know those guys! Isn't that odd?"

"But they know you. A lot of them were here for the Christmas party, more of them will be here for the barn raising. You know their wives from the slumber party and some of their daughters and sons are going to be having wedding receptions here this spring. These guys know you and they like you, Polly. It will take you time to get to know everyone, but don't worry, one of these days you will know seventy percent of this town by name and the rest by sight."

"And then imagine what they're going to say about me!"

"Have you considered staying away from dead bodies?"

"Madeline Black is not on me. Your wife found her. I was only along for the ride."

"See, the good news is that everyone is focused on you, Lydia gets away with it. I like it that way," he laughed.

"Thanks a lot," Polly said.

"Take care of yourself today. We're going to be outside and

upstairs for a while. I'll find you when I've got more information."

Doug and Billy were standing in the outer office and Aaron said, "Looks like you have a line waiting for you. Take care." He walked out and stopped to shake hands with the boys. Polly watched him put his hand on Billy's back and nod to Polly. She shook her head and waited for them to come in.

"Hey Polly! Sheriff Merritt says we're supposed to move in with you."

"I saw your girlfriend again last night," Polly said to Doug, attempting to deflect the conversation.

"My who?" Doug asked.

"Sarah. The EMT you were flirting with last fall."

"Hey. That's not a bad idea. Why didn't I think of that?"

"Because she's eight years older than you, dude." Billy laughed and poked his friend in the arm.

"It wouldn't matter if we were meant to be together."

"If you were meant to be together, she would have fallen for you rather than strap you onto a gurney," Billy remarked.

"Okay, whatever. Polly, how are you feeling?"

"I'm fine. It's a hard head. Are you guys working today?"

"Yep, Jerry says it's an all-hands-on-deck day. But, we wanted to see if we could schedule a twenty-four hour game party next Friday and Saturday."

"Twenty-four hours?"

"The new Saturn Flight release hits on Wednesday and ..."

Polly stopped him with her hand. "I don't want to know." She opened the calendar on her computer and said, "It doesn't look like there is anything going on next weekend. The auditorium is yours."

"If we get the classrooms finished, can we use the computer room? It's perfect for gaming and we won't have to move things around."

"Sure. I don't care where you play. Alright, I've put you on the calendar. The room is yours."

"Thanks! What do we owe you?"

She pursed her lips. "Guys, you pretty much have lifetime

access whenever the room is available. Don't ask me that again, alright?"

They did some fancy handshake, high-five, fist-bump thing with each other and Billy smiled and said, "Thanks, Polly. You're awesome."

"Now, if we could move in here and out of our Mom's houses, we'd be a lot less lame," Doug said.

Polly slowly nodded, "You would be, wouldn't you!"

They left and Polly reached into a drawer and pulled the layout of the property back out. "It would be really good for them to move out of their parent's houses. It would be good for me to have a garage. It would be good for everyone if I could build more guest quarters." She opened the middle drawer of her desk and took out a pencil, then began drawing lines around the building. "Henry is going to kill me," she mused aloud.

"Why am I going to kill you?"

"People keep sneaking up on me this morning. How is that possible with all the windows in this place?"

"Why am I going to kill you? And if you weren't so intent on what you were doing ..." he bent over her desk and saw what she was doing.

"I'm not going to kill you, but aren't you ever going to be satisfied?"

"Come here," she said. "Look at this."

He pulled a chair up beside her and watched as she pointed things out on the map to him. "I don't have a garage. One of these days I'm going to own all of these things that need a garage and I don't want to be bringing them up and down from the basement."

"You're going to have a barn, Polly."

"But, I don't want to put my truck in a barn. I want to put it in a garage. And I was thinking we could build an apartment over the garage. It could be a guest house or maybe Doug and Billy could rent it."

"You really like those guys, don't you."

"I do. They're fun to have around. Like little brothers I never had. On this other side we could build a matching structure with four more guest rooms, two upstairs and then two accessible apartments downstairs. I can't believe I didn't think about that until now. There are plenty of creative people who use wheelchairs instead of legs or need to have things more easily available to them. If we build those rooms on this side, all we have to do is build a covered walkway and put in automatic doors."

"Are you ever going to be finished building here, Polly?" he asked, laughing.

"Well, I was kind of thinking about talking to you about that."

He sat back and lowered his eyelids at her, "About what?"

"What do you think about going into partnership with me and renovating some of the old buildings around town?"

"To what purpose exactly?"

"Well, we can rent them out. We could sell them. Some of them are in such bad shape that no one sees their potential."

"You've lived in this town less than a year and you've spent more time thinking about it than a lot of people who have lived here forever," he said.

"Maybe it's because everything is new to me. People around here are used to seeing those empty dilapidated buildings and forget that they don't have to be that way."

"You're probably right. Let's talk about this sometime when things aren't quite as busy."

"I'm in no hurry. Barn first, then we talk about a garage and another building. This conversation can take place in several months. I'll still be here."

"So will I," he said and pushed his chair back from the desk. "They're delivering the crane this morning, so I'm going to be outside. How are you doing?"

"I'm fine," she replied. "And of all people, will you quit asking me that?"

He started to reply, but she interrupted him, "I know you're worried. But, stop it. I'm fine."

"Okay. I'll see you at lunch. I hear Sylvie is making tacos."

Polly watched him leave and went back to her plans. She pulled paper out of a drawer and started sketching out more ideas.

People were in and out all day long and Polly was glad when she saw the day ending. She'd offered to pick up Sylvie's boys from school and gotten a harried thank you. Jason and Andrew were upstairs in her apartment after taking Obiwan outside for an hour. Aaron had stopped back to tell her they didn't have anything yet, but were still hopeful to find Elise and her captors in Iowa. The crews of decorators in the auditorium had decided to keep their plans as secret as possible, so after lunch they'd shut and locked the doors and told Polly even *she* couldn't see it until Saturday afternoon. Sylvie and Hannah had been managing an influx of women bringing pies and soup stock in for lunch as well as assembling breakfast casseroles and preparing the evening meal.

Polly had tried to stay out of everyone's way, but found herself exhausted as the building began to empty. Sylvie finally dropped into a chair in Polly's office and waved as Hannah left the building with her husband.

"I think we're ready," she said. "It's going to be a great day."

"I'm glad to hear you say that, Sylvie. I know you've never done anything like this before."

"Honestly, I haven't done it by myself, but Mom used to do meals down at the fairgrounds all the time. It's not that big of a deal if you have a plan and stay organized. Hannah is good, too. She's spent enough time working around food, she knows how to time things out and she's not afraid of hard work."

"Good. Are you going to be able to rest tonight?"

"Probably not, but that's okay. The boys and I will put a movie in and I'll fall asleep in the middle of it. Then, I'll wake up and panic and make a million notes for myself. If I get everything written down when I'm panicking, hopefully I'll be able to go back to sleep. I'm going to be here at five o'clock tomorrow morning to start cooking breakfast, though, so don't worry if you hear noises down here. Bruce and Hannah are coming by six. We'll be ready to serve at seven."

Sylvie stretched both arms out and said. "I'm glad you're doing all of this and not me. I'd never sleep fretting over it. I think we both have found good places to be. Now, I'm going to run upstairs and get my boys and get out of your hair. We'll see you tomorrow."

"Are you bringing the boys with you at five?" Polly asked.

"No, I told them they could sleep until seven. Lydia said she'd stop by for them at seven thirty and bring them over for breakfast."

"I was going to tell you that if you wanted to bring them early, they could come up to the apartment."

"Nope. You get to sleep all by yourself tonight."

Polly winked at her, "Thanks. I'll see you later!"

Sylvie left and went upstairs while Polly shut her computer down. Jeff stopped in and said, "I'll see you in the morning."

"Have a good evening!" she said. He left and the building continued to quiet down. She shut the lights off in the office and closed the door, then wandered around the empty hallway downstairs. Sylvie and the boys came down and waved as they walked outside and Polly sat down on the stairway. Her headache had returned with a vengeance. She rubbed the knot and thought it might be going down a little. Tomorrow was going to be a much better day.

Henry walked in the main front doors and saw her sitting there. "I think everything is battened down and ready to go for tomorrow." He sat beside her on the steps. "Your eyes look like you're in pain. Can I help?"

"My head really hurts. I need to get some ibuprofen."

"Why don't you go on upstairs? I'll make sure all the doors are locked and the lights are off. I'll come up and get my stuff in a few minutes."

"Thanks," she said and stood up. She put her hand out to pull him up and he let her.

"You are an independent girl, aren't you?"

"And don't you ever forget it. But, look, I'm letting you take care of me. Isn't that good?"

"Very good. Now go upstairs and I'll be there shortly."

"Pushy fellow," she said as she began walking up the steps.

Polly had taken the ibuprofen and then lay down on her bed to try to quell the pounding in her head. Henry came in and found her there and said, "I'm not going to be able to relax at my place knowing you feel like this. Do you care if I hang out in the living room and watch television?"

"I don't care. I'm going to shut my eyes for a while until the pounding goes away."

"I'll be out here if you need anything," he said.

"Thanks."

He turned the light off and closed the door most of the way. She heard his footsteps in her living room and the television turn on, but it didn't take long for her eyes to shut and the world to be gone from her consciousness.

When she woke up, it was dark out and there was light coming through the crack in the door. The cats were snuggled up with her, but Obiwan was nowhere to be found. She moved her head around and felt much better. Sitting up, she rolled her neck and shoulders and then, put her feet on the ground and stood up. Yes, she was feeling a lot better.

Opening the door to the living room, Polly found Henry asleep on the sofa with the television on. Obiwan looked up from the spot he had made behind Henry's legs, and apparently decided he was going to stay put. She quietly walked past him to the kitchen and realized he had washed the dishes and put everything away. The clock on the microwave read 7:36. She opened a cupboard door and selected a glass, then filled it from the tap. When she turned around, Henry was sitting up.

"You washed my dishes," she said.

"Good, your powers of observation are still intact," he laughed.

"Do you want some supper?"

"I could order a pizza," he offered.

"No. I think I have ingredients to make a pizza." She pulled out a pre-cooked pizza shell. "What do you like on it?"

"Anything you have. Can I help?" He had walked out to join her in the kitchen.

Polly began pulling items out of the refrigerator, and said, "Sure. Here, start slicing mushrooms and I'll chop the onions and peppers."

They had a pizza in the oven in only a few minutes.

"I didn't mean to fall asleep on you like that. My head was killing me."

"And I didn't mean to intrude on your Friday night. I couldn't leave you the way you looked."

"Well, aren't we a pair," she said.

They talked about Henry's plans for the next day while waiting for the pizza to bake. When it came out of the oven, Polly said, "How in the world could I have pulled off any of this without you, Henry, and how did I get so lucky as to land in the same town you live in?"

"You know," he said thoughtfully, "I always figure there's a grand plan in motion. Sometimes it's obvious and sometimes we can't see it happening. This time, I think it's obvious."

CHAPTER NINETEEN

Running back and forth from her bed to the front door, Obiwan finally woke Polly up.

"What is wrong with you?" she finally asked. Then she checked the time. Five fifteen. Sylvie was in the building and the poor dog didn't know what to think. "Are you really going to keep this up?"

Frustrated, she threw the blankets back and after dislodging two confused kitties, she grabbed Obiwan by the ruff of the neck and wrestled him down on the bed. "You make me nuts, you know that? I had one more hour of sleep and I'm up because of you."

He licked her on the face and she wrestled with him for a few more minutes. Both cats had leaped away, jumping to ledges on the cat tree and watching the morning's entertainment. When she stood up, he jumped to the floor and butted her in the thigh. "I know. Someone is downstairs. But, it's alright."

Obiwan sat in front of the bedroom door while she pulled clothes on to take him outside. Henry had taken him out last night before he went home. Getting thumped in the head had gotten her a day's reprieve from being out in the cold air with her dog, but she had to get back to normal today. She bundled up and snapped the leash on him and walked out into the hall. They trotted down the steps and she allowed him to take her back to the kitchen so he could check out the noise.

"Good morning," she said to Sylvie, who jumped after placing a casserole dish in one of the ovens.

"What are you doing up?" Sylvie asked.

"Jedi guard dog here heard you and wouldn't rest until he had made sure everything was safe."

Sylvie walked over and put her hand out for Obiwan to sniff. "I'm sorry. I didn't think about that," she said.

"No problem. I was at least an hour away from waking up anyway." Polly laughed, and then said, "No, don't worry about it. We're going out to get the morning started. I'll see you after a while." She heard Sylvie turn the water on and wash her hands as she walked to the front door. It made Polly giggle. Obiwan was going to have to stay out of the kitchen.

Security lights were on around the building, but Polly pulled her flashlight out. "We're not running this morning, okay? But, we'll take a long walk. They walked past the parking lot to the highway and followed that down to the end of her lot where the trees bordering the creek began. In the dark of the early morning, the piles of wood under tarps and the crane standing dormant were odd shapes in the middle of her property. She let Obiwan wander in and out of the trees, pulling him back when he tried to get too deep as they made their way around the perimeter of the grounds. Someday this area would be fenced in and a couple of her very own horses might be greeting her in the early morning. She shivered a little with excitement at the thought of it.

"What would you do with horses, Obiwan? I know the barn has six stalls, but I think I'd like to have two. I'd hate for one to get lonely." He didn't seem to be paying any attention to her, so she tightened the leash and made him wait for her to catch up. Polly knelt down and hugged him. "I got you a couple of feline companions. How do you like having them around? I think everyone should have someone warm to snuggle with. I'm glad I have you guys."

Obiwan waited patiently for Polly to stop hugging him, then rummaged through the grass at their feet. Finding nothing, he began his wandering again. He walked toward the concrete pad where all of the activity would be happening today and began nosing around the tarps.

"There's nothing there for you. Come on away from there," Polly said and pulled back on the leash. He followed her across the grass to the wooded area and they followed it around to the back of Sycamore House. She could see Sylvie moving around in the well-lit kitchen.

"I think she likes it in there, Obiwan." He looked up at her and then went back to his task. "I like it here, too. Come on, let's see if I can pick up the pace." She dropped into a slow jog and they ended up at the north end by the east-west highway. Polly slowed down and walked with him to the curving lane that led to the parking lot. "I can't wait to plant trees here this spring. Can you imagine what it will look like when they get tall and all filled out? This is going to be heavenly!"

The lane was dark and she looked up at the lamp posts, wishing she had turned them on. Now would be a good time to have Dumbledore's deluminator from the first Harry Potter book. Then it occurred to her that she should talk to Jerry Allen about those being on a circuit she could control with her cell phone. That would be close enough and a lot of fun. They'd installed smart wiring throughout the building and little by little she was bringing modules online so everything could be controlled via the internet.

As they approached the main parking lot, a truck pulled in and up to the front of Sycamore House. The door opened and a light came on and Polly realized it was Hannah McKenzie. She leaned across the seat to kiss Bruce goodbye and jumped to the ground.

"Good morning, Polly! You're up early."

"I know. It's a little too early, but Obiwan and I have had a good walk."

"How are you feeling?"

"I'm doing fine. It's still a little sore, but I think the lump is going down a bit. I'm glad he didn't clock me in the face. I'd be very angry if I had to cover up a black eye today."

Hannah laughed and held the door open for Polly and Obiwan. "I'm glad you weren't badly hurt. Can you imagine not being able to be here today?"

"No, I can't!" Polly exclaimed. "It feels like I have been getting ready for this day forever. Like it's some sort of graduation day."

"It might be! I think you're going to have a lot of people in here today. Bruce's family is coming over tonight. His brother said he might come over and see what the barn raising is all about, but I know his mom is bringing our kids for dinner."

"That's great. I can't wait to see them again. Well, I probably ought to go up and get ready. I'll see you later."

Polly went up the steps while Hannah went around to the kitchen. She pushed her apartment door open and then attempted to shove it back into place, finally getting it to fit snugly into the door frame.

Obiwan sat and waited for her to unsnap the leash, then ran for the kitchen.

"I'll never be allowed to forget your breakfast, will I, buddy?" Polly said. When she pulled his food out of the cupboard, she heard the mad dash of two cats from the bedroom into the kitchen. "Got it. I'll feed you as well."

She turned the television on in the living room and dropped into the sofa. It wasn't even six o'clock yet. If everyone was quiet, she could sneak another half hour nap in. Just to be safe, she set the alarm on her phone and placed it on the table, then pulled the blanket over her and stretched out, falling back to sleep.

Polly came up out of a dream to her phone's alarm. The cats were on the back of the sofa with their heads wrapped around each other and Obiwan had found his way into a spot at the end of the couch.

"Okay guys. Now, I have to get moving. You all stay right here and sleep, because your rough life demands so much of you." She threw the blanket off, covering Obiwan's head. He shook it off and watched as she headed for the bathroom.

"No really," she said. "Stay right there. No one move."

She stopped in the doorway to the bathroom and giggled. No one had moved.

After her shower, Polly pulled on a pair of jeans and a t-shirt, then opened a drawer and took out a Boston University sweatshirt. Grabbing her coat as she headed for the entryway, she said, "Someone will be up later to check on you. Be good."

She went out of the apartment and sniffed. Breakfast was starting to smell good.

Dawn was breaking outside and she saw a few cars coming into the parking lot. Polly dropped her coat inside her office, went back to the kitchen and said, "Can I do anything to help?"

Sylvie pulled a casserole out of the oven and shifted two others up from a lower shelf. "We're in good shape, but if you want to help dish the food up this morning, we'd love to have you in here with us."

"Sure! That would be great," Polly said. "Just tell me where to stand and what to do."

Hannah lifted a stack of plates to the counter. "We've already scored the casseroles and we'll cut them as we go. You could serve that or scoop fruit. There are cereal boxes for those who don't want casserole. Sugar and milk will be on the beverage table in the auditorium. Don't let them forget to take silverware and I think that's it!"

Henry walked up with Sam and Jimmy and a man Polly didn't recognize. "Good morning!" he said. "Are you ready to feed us yet? There are some guys wandering around outside and this is Pat McGann. He's running the crane for us today." Henry pointed at Polly and said, "Pat, this is Polly Giller. Sycamore House is her baby."

The man reached across the counter to shake her hand and said, "Nice to meet ya!" Polly smiled and waited for Sylvie to declare breakfast was ready. Sylvie handed out pairs of disposable gloves to both Hannah and Polly and said, "We're ready to go!"

Jimmy had run back outside to let people know it was time for breakfast and soon they were busy serving food. Finally, Sylvie said, "Polly, I think we're close to the end. Why don't you take a plate and eat?"

"You two are the ones who have to be on your feet all day. I'll stay here and make sure that stragglers get fed and you take a few minutes."

"We're fine," Sylvie protested.

"I'm your boss. Go eat and sit down for a few minutes."

Hannah and Sylvie glanced at each other, then both took plates and filled them. "We'll be right back and don't worry about dishes. Our lunch crew is eating breakfast and we'll clean up before we start. Promise?"

"I promise. I'm going to stand here and look pretty. Go!" Polly said.

Jeff walked up to the counter, holding his camera. He took a picture of Polly behind the counter and said, "That will be the cover for my tell-all book."

"Did you get my best side?" Polly posed with the spoon in the air and he clicked off a series of pictures.

He laughed. "You know those are going to be up on the web, don't you?"

"Great. That's exactly what I need."

Henry joined them from the auditorium and said, "You're going to have a barn by the end of the day, Polly."

"I can hardly wait!"

"If you need me," he winked, "you know where to find me." As he walked through the hall to the side doors and out to the concrete pad, men and women began making their way out of the building, pulling on work gloves and knit caps.

Jeff said, "I'll be back later. Between video and still, I have a lot of images to capture!" He followed the growing group of people outside. Polly had stripped off her gloves and was tossing them into the trash can, when Sylvie walked back in.

"One down!" she announced. "And no catastrophes."

"It's a good start to the day," Polly said. "What are your boys going to do today? Are you good with them being outside or would you like me to encourage them to stay in and upstairs?"

"They have plenty to keep them occupied inside. I told them they could go outside, but they were on the honor system. Neither of them was to try to help or get in anyone's way and if either you or I or Henry asked them to do something, even if it was to go inside, they had to obey immediately."

"Alright, well then," Polly laughed, "they can go up to the apartment as often as they'd like."

"That'd be great. I also told them they could be in the auditorium. They're supposed to check in with me every two hours starting at nine, no matter what they're doing." Sylvie giggled. "I programmed my phone's alarm to alert me, those boys don't stand a chance."

Polly said, "That's probably why people like having them around. You've taught them to respect your boundaries. Why don't I take them upstairs right now and they can leave their stuff there today."

"Thanks, Polly. I appreciate it." Sylvie had started picking up empty pans and Polly could tell she was distracted by her next tasks, so she slipped out of the kitchen and into the auditorium.

Jason and Andrew were sitting with Lydia, Beryl and Andy. Lydia jumped up when she saw Polly and rushed over to her. "How are you feeling this morning - are you alright - I didn't want to talk to you while you were busy, but I've been worried - Did Henry take care of you yesterday - Did you sleep last night - Talk to me!"

Polly's eyes expanded and she said, "Wow. You've got great breath control."

Lydia pulled her into a hug, "I'm going to hire a full time body guard for you. It's the only way I won't worry."

Polly hugged her back and they walked over to the table, "Is she this bad with her own kids?" she asked Andy and Beryl.

"Have you noticed that none of them live in Bellingwood?" Beryl asked. "Yes. She's this bad."

"I am not," Lydia protested.

"Yes you are," Andy said quietly. "We figure it's because you are pouring all your worry over Aaron into everyone else. But, we love you for it, don't we." She poked Beryl in the arm. "Don't we?"

"We love her for it and in spite of it." Beryl winked at the boys, "She's pretty lovable, though, isn't she."

Andrew giggled and Jason nodded politely.

"What are you ladies doing today? Beryl, I thought you'd be out helping them put up the barn!" Polly said.

"Twenty years ago ... hell, ten years ago I would have been. But, I have to keep these ten fingers healthy. My luck, I'd pound them into mush."

Andy said, "We're going to stay busy inside today. Us old ladies have to act our ages, so we'll wash dishes, make soup, decorate the house, and gossip."

Beryl looked at Andy over her glasses, "If you don't mind, this old lady will be gossiping first. Then, the other stuff can happen." She pushed them up on her nose and said to Polly, "Speaking of gossip, which man are you going to choose? The hot veterinarian or the hunky carpenter?"

"You're a brat, Beryl Watson and just for that, I'm not telling. I'm going to ask these two young men to come up to my apartment and play with my animals. Jason? Andrew? Why don't you grab your things and we'll head upstairs. Then, you're on your own."

The boys ran to the back of the auditorium and picked up their backpacks and coats, then waited for Polly.

"That'll teach you to gossip in front of little boys," Polly said, "I'm never telling you now." She high-fived Lydia and walked away from the table.

Once upstairs, the boys settled in on the couch with the remote and two game controllers.

"Your mom says you are on your own today. Do you have watches so you know what time to check in with her?" Polly asked.

Andrew proudly displayed a brightly colored watch and Jason said, "I made sure his watch had the right time. We'll be cool. Can we go outside later and watch them put up the barn?"

"Boys, you can go outside any time you want."

"Can we take Obiwan?" Andrew asked.

"Here's the deal. I'm going to trust you to take care of him today. If you think he wants to go outside, that's fine. Just make sure he doesn't get into anything or anyone's way. If you do that, I'll make sure there's five bucks in it for you at supper. Will that work?"

"Awesome!" Jason said. He turned to his brother, "Let's go out and see what it looks like before they get started, then we can check on it all day."

They got their coats on and headed out. Polly looked at her animals and said, "You're in good hands." She rubbed Obiwan's head, then bent over and hugged him. "Love you, bud. And you too, kitten-cats."

She walked back down the stairs and smiled at the people walking in. Some went to the kitchen, others went into the auditorium. She didn't know half of them, but everyone smiled and said, "Hello." Grabbing her coat out of her office, she went out the side doors. The outer frame was already up and a group of people were lifting the east wall into place. They had ordered the wood for the walls pre-primed, and when she saw the red color, excitement rippled through her. It was truly happening.

More people were assembling boards and she watched as Sam, Jimmy, Leroy and Ben worked with various clusters, making sure everyone had things they needed. Then, she saw one of the aprons people were wearing. Polly walked over to Henry and said, "Why don't I have one of those?"

He chuckled and pulled one out of his back pocket and held it up for her to see. "Sycamore House Barn Raising" was imprinted across the front of the apron. "These are great! Who thought of this?"

"You haven't been in the kitchen or auditorium since breakfast, have you?"

"No? Why?" she asked.

"I'll let you see it for yourself," he said. "I have to run. Talk to you later!"

She stood and watched the activity, then turned around and walked inside and headed for the kitchen. Sure enough, she found Lydia passing out denim blue BBQ aprons.

"Would you like one of these?" Lydia asked. Bright red letters spelled out the same thing on the front of these aprons.

"I must have one!" Polly said. "These are wonderful!"

Lydia slipped one over Polly's head and spun her around to tie it in back. Jeff walked out of the auditorium and raised his camera to snap a photograph.

"Were these your idea?" Polly asked.

"I'd like to take credit for it, but Henry is the one who came up with the idea that day you announced we were building a barn. It's a great idea, eh?"

"It's a fabulous idea!" She took his arm and walked away with him, "So exactly why is it that I never know about these things in advance?"

"I'm sorry." he said in dismay. "Did I screw up?"

Polly was startled. "No! Not at all. I just want to know why I'm always the last to find things out."

"Honestly? Because it's such fun to surprise you! But, I don't want to ever upset you," he said.

"I'm not upset at all, but sometimes I feel like there are a lot of surprises in my life." Polly smiled and said, "No, don't worry about it. Your surprises are good. At least they aren't gruesome or frightening."

They walked back outside and Jeff wandered around the construction site shooting pictures. Polly watched as a second wall started to go up. This was going faster than she expected. Doug and Billy joined her.

"Pretty cool, eh?" Billy said.

"It seems to be going together really fast. What are they going to do this afternoon?" she asked.

"There's plenty to do inside and out. See those guys over there?" Doug pointed to a group of men bending over something they were building. "They're getting the structures together for the stalls. They," and he pointed to another group of men, "are sorting doors and windows. Those guys with Leroy are putting together shelves and tables. There is plenty of work left to do."

Billy said, "But, I think that because there are so many people, it is all going to go very fast. Henry said that if the exterior walls go up this morning, we might even get it painted today."

Polly shook her head. "Incredible. Why don't they build barns like this anymore?"

"No one has time. You turned this into a party and because no one ever does it anymore, everyone thought it would be fun."

"It is fun."

Mark Ogden rounded the corner with another man and came over to Polly.

"Hey Polly, this is my brother-in-law, Dylan Foster. Dylan, this is Polly Giller."

"Hi Dylan," she said.

He smiled and said, "Hi."

"Looks like we got here before everything was finished," Mark said. "Come on, Dylan. Let's see what we can do to help." He led his brother-in-law to where Ben was working with a small group. Polly watched as they all shook hands and then Mark left Dylan and headed for Henry. They spoke for a few minutes and laughed, looking up at her with furtive glances.

She wondered what in the world they were talking about, but didn't have the courage to confront them, so Polly turned around and went back inside.

CHAPTER TWENTY

Chili, ham and bean, chicken noodle and vegetable beef. The outside temperature was in the mid-forties, but people came in for lunch with red cheeks and noses. Sylvie and her crew had prepared hearty soups; the smell permeated the building and drew everyone to the kitchen. There was enough help in the kitchen that Polly realized she would be in the way, so she went into the auditorium to see if she could do anything there. Many of the women who had been working on decorations were wandering through the tables refilling drinks and cracker baskets.

Hannah had four baskets filled with corn bread and warmed rolls in her arms. Polly spoke up, "Here, let me help you." She took them from Hannah and replaced rapidly emptying baskets. A few more runs to the kitchen and the frenzied rush seemed to calm down, so she stopped at Henry's table.

He was sitting with several people she didn't recognize and he took her hand and said, "Polly, I'd like you to meet some good friends of mine. This is Gary Alberts," acknowledging the man to his left. "He's a video game designer. We've been friends for years and I still don't play his games."

Gary laughed, put his hand out to shake hers and said, "Hi, Polly. This is a lot of fun. Trust Henry to get hooked up with the most exciting thing in town."

Henry punched his buddy in the arm and said, "She's a girl, not a thing." He turned to an older man on his right and said, "Have you met Fred Wayne?" Polly shook her head no and reached over to take his hand.

He clasped her hand with both of his hands and said, "Henry was in my Industrial Arts class when he was in high school. I can still outshoot him with the nail gun though, unless he nails my sleeve to the wall."

Henry laughed and said, "I only did that once ... well, maybe twice."

He began to speak and stopped when both he and Polly looked at the far entrance to the auditorium. Aaron Merritt beckoned to Polly.

"I'm sorry," she said. "I need to speak with Sheriff Merritt. Excuse me."

The men turned around and waved at the Sheriff. Henry jumped up from the table to follow her.

"I'm sorry to take you away from your lunch," Aaron said, "but I thought you might like to know that Elise has been found."

"What?" Polly asked. "Where?" Unconsciously, she took Henry's hand.

"They were at a hospital in Clinton. It seems that the idiot who got caught in the coyote trap hurt his leg pretty badly. They stopped in Marshalltown Thursday night and tried to clean it up, but in their attempts to pull the thing off him, they mangled the leg. They finally pulled into the Clinton hospital last night and rather than leave with Elise, the other bright bulb in the box stayed in town to wait for him; giving us plenty of time to track them down. Clinton police found the car at a Super 8 on Highway 30 and pulled her out early this morning."

"Is she alright?"

"She's fine."

"I'm glad. Now what?"

"These two aren't talking yet, but my buddy in Clinton says they seem to be worried about returning to Chicago, so it won't be long," Aaron said, "and Elise is on her way here."

"What? I need to get upstairs and make sure things are ready."

"She'll be here in about an hour. You have time," Aaron assured Polly.

"Why is she coming back here?"

"I don't know enough of the story. Why don't we wait for her," he said. "Now, my nose tells me there is wonderful soup and my eyes tell me Lydia is dying to know what is happening. I'm going to leave you to do whatever you have to do for Elise."

Polly chuckled as they parted, "'Fur Elise,' he said. That's funny."

She turned to Henry. "You go back in and eat with your friends. I'm going upstairs to put her clothes and things back in her room and make sure it is ready so she feels at home."

"Are you sure? You haven't eaten anything yet. You have plenty of time. It will take you less than fifteen minutes to get things ready upstairs."

"No. That's alright. I'm too nerved up to eat anything. I'll deal with it later," she said and rushed away before he could stop her.

Polly pulled the basket of Elise's clothes out of the corner of her own bedroom and went across the hall to return them to the dresser. Folding things neatly, she opened the top drawer and placed items in, then opened the second drawer. As she pushed the t-shirts in to the back of the drawer, her hand caught on something. She pulled the drawer out and bent over to look. A plastic bag was taped there. Polly pulled it out and saw that there was a newspaper article from December between the layers of plastic. She sat down at the desk and realized she had the whole story.

Elise had clipped an article about a murder that had taken place in the library on the University of Chicago campus late at night when it was probably empty. Polly was sure the poor girl had no idea it had gotten so late and was focused on her work. The victim had been the son of a prominent leader in the Chicago syndicate and his death had sent waves of violence throughout the city.

"The poor girl," Polly said out loud. "She didn't ask for this."

She set the article down on the desk and finished folding clothes and putting them back in the drawers, then looked around the room. Elise had done a pretty good job of settling into the space. Her personal things might have been scattered everywhere, but notebooks were neatly organized on the shelf and her workspace was tidy. Polly picked up one of the notebooks and rolled her eyes at the seemingly random equations filling the pages. She rolled her eyes and chuckled, slammed it shut and placed it back on the shelf. That stuff was far beyond any of the math she had taken and she didn't even know what some of the symbols meant.

The dust in the room was nonexistent. Polly muttered a thank you for radiant heat. There was no furnace blowing air into the rooms and that kept things much cleaner. She gave the room one last look and, stepping out into the hall, pulled the door closed behind her.

Polly slid down the door to the floor and sat there with her head in her hands. She felt all of her stress drain away. If this was what she had to go through with every guest who arrived at Sycamore House she was going to be a wreck in only a few months. These weren't names on a credit card receipt; they were real people living in her home. There was no way she could separate herself from their lives.

Tears leaked from the corners of her eyes. "Damn it," she whispered.

"Polly?"

She looked up and tried to nonchalantly brush away the tears.

"Polly? There you are. Is everything alright?"

Beryl sat down right beside her and slipped an arm around her shoulders.

"People get under your skin, don't they," Beryl said.

Polly couldn't help it, the tears began to flow. "This isn't even about me. I don't know why I'm crying."

"You, my dear girl, are filled with great passion for people. Look what you've done here today. You're helping us make connections with each other. You started a chain, connecting your friends and it has grown from there. One of these days, your big old auditorium isn't going to hold all the people who show up when you have an event."

"So why is there water dripping out of my eyes uncontrollably?"

Beryl laughed. "It's okay to say that you love her. Your heart exploded when you found out she was safe and coming home. All the worry you've had over her in the last few days left you and your poor heart has to recover a little bit. You love awfully easily, Polly. Not many of us have that gift.

"You know, a long time ago I heard a preacher describe the different Greek words for love. The one that fits you is phileo - brotherly love. You know, like Philadelphia, the city of brotherly love. You aren't afraid to love people and you make it easy for the rest of us to get up on that bandwagon with you. Not very many people will see it for what it is, but they sure respond to it."

Beryl stood back up and offered Polly her hand, "Come on. Let's clean those eyes up. Elise is going to be here in a little bit and you don't want to look all blotchy for whatever gorgeous law enforcement officer is with her."

Polly took the hand, stood up and hugged Beryl. "I love you. You know that, don't you?"

"I do know that. I love you too. Come on. I'll pet your kitties while you wash your face."

When Polly exited her bathroom, Beryl was back on the floor wrestling with Obiwan.

"Beryl! What are you doing?"

"Oh!" Beryl said, startled. "Am I not supposed to play with him? Is his foot okay?"

"He's fine, but what are you doing on the floor?"

"I'm obviously wrestling with your dog. And don't you dare tell me I'm too old for these shenanigans, or I'll drop you where you stand."

"I wouldn't dream of it. Wrestle away!" Polly said. "Thank you for coming up after me."

Beryl hugged Obiwan and stood up, "Let's go downstairs and watch for your friend and since Henry tattled on you to us about your not eating, I'm going to force food down your throat."

Henry was wandering around the room, talking to small clusters of people when they walked back into the auditorium. He looked up and gave them a small wave. Beryl whispered to Polly, "By the way, a second Greek word for love is eros. It means something entirely different. You need to figure that out."

Polly's face flushed red. "Stop it. You're killing me."

"I fully intend to if you don't get on board with this. And don't think I won't."

Beryl led Polly to a table and pointed at a chair beside Andy. "Sit. I'll be right back with food. Is there any soup out there you don't particularly like?"

"I can get it. I have two legs," Polly protested.

"Did I stammer? Sit. Is there any soup you don't like?"

Polly dropped her head in mock shame. "I like them all, thank you."

Andy giggled beside her. "It's easier sometimes to let her be the boss."

The auditorium emptied as people went back outside. Several stopped by and patted Polly on the back or reached to shake her hand, saying things like "This is a lot of fun, Polly" or "Thanks for putting this together!" When it had quieted down, she turned back to Andy. "I think I should make everyone wear nametags for the next year."

"You'll do fine. The young woman with red hair was Jennifer Mattingly. Her dad runs the hardware store uptown. Her mom is over there," Andy nodded at a group of women who were unfolding bandanas. "She works at the store and teaches piano lessons. The older guy with curly hair that told you he was going to have blisters is Roger Douglas. Let's see ...," Andy looked around the room. "His wife is probably in the kitchen. He's an accountant and this was probably the last weekend he'd have come out to help. When tax season starts no one ever sees his face unless they make an appointment."

Beryl had pushed a bowl of ham and bean soup in front of Polly and handed her a spoon, then set a plate with cornbread and butter down as well.

"Thank you," Polly said, batting her eyes at Beryl. "You're too good to me."

"Eat or I'll feed you myself."

Andy laughed. "I wouldn't put it past her and much as I'd like to witness the event, I think it could get messy."

She described a few more people while Polly ate and then said, "Beryl, I think it is time for us to get to work. Don't worry, Polly, you won't be alone long."

The women walked away from the table and Polly heard someone approach from behind. She turned in her chair and saw Elise, who ran across the room to her. Polly stood up and caught the girl as she leaped forward into a hug.

"I'm so glad you're alright! I've been worried sick since they took me away. I saw you go down and I didn't know what to think!" Elise exclaimed.

Polly held Elise at arm's length and looked her over. "Are you okay? Did they hurt you?"

"I'm fine. I want another shower, maybe even a bath and some clean clothes, but I'm fine."

"Have you eaten anything? We've got wonderful soup."

"Actually, no I haven't eaten anything. Carl, here, wanted to stop, but I wouldn't let him." Elise giggled, "I'll bet you are hungry, too," she said to the man beside her.

Carl looked like a wrestler, stocky and solid. He was wearing a badge that read U.S. Marshal on his belt. "I'm a little hungry," he admitted. "You don't get this physique without keeping it well supplied."

"Follow me," Polly said. "Let's get you some food and then I want to know what is going on."

She took them to the kitchen and though the women were cleaning things up, Hannah and Sylvie quickly served up a bowl of chicken noodle soup for Elise and when he nodded yes, a bowl of chili and one of vegetable beef for Marshal Carl, as Polly thought of him.

After they had taken seats at the table, Aaron Merritt joined them. He introduced himself to Elise and Carl Philips, then sat down.

"We're glad to see you are safe, Elise," Aaron said.

"I'm glad to be here. Thank you for everything," she said.

"I can't stay, Polly," she continued. "I'm here to get my notebooks and some clothes and to tell you what has happened, then we're leaving tonight."

"Where are you going?" Polly asked.

"I don't know and if I did, I probably couldn't tell you."

"What do you mean?"

"We're putting her into Witness Protection. She's already contacted her parents and when she's finished here, she'll be gone," Carl said.

"But, I thought you said you didn't see anything. You're not a threat." Polly protested.

Carl spoke up again, "Apparently, she didn't realize what she did see."

"You saw something?"

"I did. When I left, I saw two men leaving. And I also saw the car and because my mind traps numbers, I have the license plate. It's all part of their case now, so I have to go away at least until the trial."

"What are you going to do about your dissertation?"

"What better way to work in quiet than in a town where no one knows me?" Elise laughed. "I thought that was what I was going to find here, but now I'll find it somewhere else."

"Elise. I'm sorry this has happened to you. It doesn't seem fair," Polly said.

"It's alright. I've spent my entire life alone and it's better that it was me than someone else. I'll be fine. Carl says that we'll try to schedule the dissertation presentation at the same time as the trial so I have a reason to be in Chicago. After that, who knows where

I'll go or what I'll do."

Polly leaned over and hugged her. "I know you can't keep in touch, but I'm going to worry about you."

"Don't. I'm going to be fine. The best thing about meeting you has been that I have another friend in my life."

Polly shook her head. "It's still not fair."

"No worrying," Elise scolded. "Now, I'm going upstairs to take a bath and change my clothes. Then, I'm going to pack some of my things and get out of here with Carl. He promised me an adventure across the country. I think I need clean clothes for that."

She started to stand up, then said, "My parents are going to send a cousin to pack the rest of my things up and take them to their house. You'll recognize him. He looks a lot like LL Cool J. He'll have a letter for you with my signature on it."

Polly snorted with laughter. "I don't suppose Bellingwood is going to produce too many people who look like him. I suspect I won't have any trouble identifying him."

Elise giggled, "You're right. This isn't Chicago."

They finished their soup and she stood up. Carl stood as well and followed her out of the auditorium.

Aaron said to Polly, "Are you alright with this?"

"No, not really, but I don't have a choice, so I'll deal with it." She started gathering dishes and stood to take them to the kitchen. "Have you ever seen something like this before?" she asked.

Aaron picked up the baskets and followed her to the kitchen, "If I told you the truth, I might have to kill you, Polly."

"Can I get you something more, Polly? How about you, Sheriff?" one of the women asked.

"No, Jessie, we're good," he said. "Sure was wonderful, though! Thanks everyone."

Sylvie came out of the kitchen and took Polly's arm, "Two down and I'm still standing! The rest of this is going to be easy. We have everything ready to go!"

"Sylvie, you've done such an amazing job," Polly said. "You're a hit!"

"I'm having the best time. Jason and Andrew went up to your

apartment to get Obiwan. They thought he might need a trip outside. I think they want an excuse to be where the action is."

"I'm glad you're enjoying yourself and I told your boys there would be five dollars apiece for them if they watched the dog today and kept him out of the way."

"Polly, you don't have to do that."

"Don't start with me," Polly wagged her finger at Sylvie.

"Fine," Sylvie said, then she turned to head back into the kitchen. "See you later! My galley awaits!"

Aaron said, "I'm glad Elise is back and fine. I think I'll take off, but I'll see you later tonight."

"Thanks for everything Aaron. Are you planning to dance with your girl tonight?"

"Not on your life. I might have to arrest anyone who suggests that I do."

"I'll be good then."

She went back into the auditorium and joined Beryl and Lydia who were stuffing cellophane and ivory tissue paper into mason jars. "What are you doing?" she asked.

"We're making candles. Here, start stuffing."

"This seems dangerous somehow," Polly remarked.

"Nah. That Jeff thinks of everything. We have battery operated LED tea lights for these. Now get stuffing. I have to figure out a creative way to wrap bandana pieces around these," Beryl said.

Polly sat down and following Lydia's example, crumpled cellophane and tissue paper.

"Not too tightly, now," Beryl said. "It's decorative and fancy."

Polly pulled her tissue paper back apart and crumpled it back together and pushed it into the jar. "How's that?"

Beryl placed a tea light in front of her and said, "Drop 'er in and see what you think."

The candle nestled into the paper and seemed to be the effect they were going for. Polly asked, "How many of these are we making?"

"Jeff thinks we need three or four on each table so people can see. I think he's planning to make the room much too dark, but who knows!"

Tables were being rearranged and covered with blue or red gingham tablecloths. Square pieces of muslin were placed on the top and three tiered stands set into the center of each table.

"What are the stands for?" she asked Lydia.

"Sylvie has hundreds of cupcakes for tonight. Those will be arranged on the two bottom tiers. Then, someone is doing origami with bandannas and creating roses for the top tier."

"Wow. This place will look awesome!" Polly said.

Lydia nodded, "It'll be wonderful."

Jeff and three others came in carrying a large piece of wood painted to look like the front of a barn. Across the top, a sign read, "Sycamore House Barn Raising" and a white door was painted in the center. They propped it up against the back wall and left, soon to return with two split rail fence props. Those were laid on the floor and they left again only to return with two bales of hay on a cart. Polly watched in amazement as the stage was set and when she couldn't stand it any longer, got up and walked over.

"What in the world?"

"Surprise!" Jeff said, "Tell me you love it."

"I love it, but I don't know what you're doing. If it's just a decoration, it's way cool. Is that it?"

"Nope. We're going to do a kind of photo booth with it."

"I'm surprised and impressed," Polly said.

Jeff broke one of the bales open and spread hay around in front of the barn, then used the other to hold up one of the fence props. It was a little cheesy, but seemed perfect.

"Jeff, you love this, don't you!"

"I really do," he laughed. "And I keep trying to come up with ideas that you couldn't imagine. You're a challenge for me!"

She smiled and noticed that Elise was standing in the doorway watching. "Excuse me. I'll be back,"

"Go ahead," he said, nodding at her in the door. "I'm sorry about this."

"I know. It stinks."

Tears filled her eyes as she made her way to the door. Elise said, "Stop that. You can't let me leave like this. I'll feel awful."

"I'm sorry. I wish you didn't have to go at all."

"I was going to have to leave sometime. It's just earlier than we thought." Elise was beginning to choke up. She gulped and said, "It is going to be alright. Please believe me."

"I do. I just don't like it. I was looking forward to having a friend in Chicago who would take me to do crazy shopping and maybe see a show or something."

Elise reached in for a hug. "Maybe someday. Or," she said brightly, "maybe we can meet in London or Paris and you can teach me how to be normal in a big city."

"Then promise me that if you ever end up in London or Paris you will call me. Promise?"

Elise looked up at Carl, who nodded, "I promise. If that ever happens, you're my first call. Now, I have to go. Thank you for everything, Polly."

Polly hugged her one more time and watched as her new friend left.

CHAPTER TWENTY-ONE

Her heart was still a little tender, and Polly decided she didn't want to face her friends yet. She decided to check the progress on the barn and was shocked when she opened the side doors. All four walls were up and being painted. Henry had told her he would start on the roof on Monday as long as the weather was decent. She'd spent more time over the last few days checking the forecast than ever before and wondered if that was going to become a habit now that she lived in Iowa. She chuckled to herself. When she had been a kid, she accepted the weather as it came. If there was a snow day, it garnered the greatest excitement of her young life, but it never occurred to her to watch as weather approached.

Henry was framing one of the front windows and as she approached, she heard him laughing and chatting with someone inside the barn.

"This is coming along a lot faster than I expected," she said.

He stepped back and grinned. "Faster than I expected, too. We had twice as many people show up today than I had planned for and they were ready to work. I think they kept my guys busy.

What do you think?"

"I think I can't believe this. It doesn't seem real. How long are you planning to work?"

"The sun will set in a couple of hours. I want to kick everyone out of here before that happens. That will give us time to reorganize what's left and then get home and cleaned up for the evening."

He took her arm. "I saw Elise drive away. Are you alright?"

Polly nodded. "I think so. I wanted it to end differently, but she seems fine with it."

"Sometimes you have to know what the next step is in order to go forward with confidence," he said. "She found out what the next step was and took it."

"You're right," Polly said. "I need ten minutes to feel sorry for myself and be ticked off that I couldn't fix it; and then I will focus on the incredible things happening around here today!"

"Just ten minutes?" he laughed. "Good for you. Do you need company or is this something you can do on your own?"

"Oh, shut up," she shook her head and walked into the barn. Henry's friend, Gary, had been on the other side of the window and was sitting on a five-gallon bucket.

"Hey, Polly," he said as she walked past.

"Hey, yourself," she responded and continued down the developing alley in the center of the building. Outside doors for the stalls were being framed and the floor of the attic was nearly finished. When she arrived at the far end of the aisle, Henry's teacher, Fred Wayne, called her into the room where he was working.

"We're putting shelves in here and I wanted to measure your height. You're not terribly tall, are you?"

"What?" she laughed.

"How tall are you? Will I be able to hide treasures in these upper shelves or can you reach up here?" He pointed to a shelf that was well over her head.

"I'm not that tall, but I bet I can find something to step on to reach it, so don't you be hiding things up there."

"Our Henry has a thing for you. Are you girl enough to handle it?"

Polly was startled at his question and stood there dumbfounded.

"You be good to him. He had his heart broken once in a big way and I haven't seen him spend this much time courting a gal since that little witch walked out on him."

She still didn't know what to say and decided to keep quiet.

He got close to her and quietly said, "If you're going to break his heart, do it before too much time passes, alright?"

Polly nodded and backed out of the room. She left the barn and took a deep breath. How had this gotten so serious? Now she was responsible for Henry's past? She kept walking toward the creek, needing to be away from everyone long enough to breathe again. She hadn't brought her gloves or a cap outside with her, so she pulled up the collar of her jacket and jammed her hands into the pockets of the jacket, walking faster and faster until she reached the tree line. One deep breath and then another; as she began following the path along the trees back to Sycamore House. She kept her head down and tried to subdue her panic. She walked around to the far side of Sycamore House and using her phone to unlock the door, entered the storage area behind the stage. No one saw her and she rubbed her hands together to warm them as she gathered up her courage.

The auditorium had undergone a minor transformation in the short time Polly had been gone. The tables were all set. The pails had colorful bandannas tied to their handles, blue and red bandanna roses were seated at the top of the tiered stands, three mason jar candles had been placed on each table. Polly saw that there were mugs at each place setting; how Jeff had found mason jars with handles, she didn't know, but the room looked great.

Jeff, with his camera around his neck, sidled up to her. "What do you think?"

"The place looks great. I can't wait to see it with the strings of lights and candles. How's Sylvie doing in the kitchen?"

"She's sent everyone home, since they're coming back at six to finish getting ready. I believe she has gone up to your apartment to get her boys."

Polly said, "I can't believe she has this so well organized," Polly said. "I could never pull off three big meals like this in a day. I couldn't pull off one of them."

"You've put a lot of trust in her and she won't let you down."

"Thanks. Are you heading home or are you staying here until dinner?"

"I'll probably stay here. I have my things in the office."

"If you want to use one of the showers upstairs, you're welcome to hang out in my apartment until we get started."

"I'll use the shower, but don't worry about me. I have plenty to occupy myself in the office."

The auditorium began emptying as people filtered out; the women who had been working on the tables making minor adjustments to arrangements as they walked past them.

Lydia said, "I'm leaving to go home and put on my dancing shoes." She put her arm in Jeff's. "Will you dance with me tonight?"

Jeff took her hand, lifted it and twirled her around, then said, "As often as I can without having the Sheriff pull out his six-shooter, ma'am."

Lydia giggled and said, "Walk with me to the door, Polly."

Polly looked helplessly at Jeff, "It almost sounds like I'm going to be scolded for something. I'll see you in a little bit."

He smiled and waved.

"Polly, I see you smiling, but you look as if you could grind glass with those teeth. What's up with you? This is supposed to be a fun day. Are you upset about Elise or is it something else."

"It's just life, Lydia," Polly responded. "I'm fine and it has already been a great day."

"That was a not-so-neat evasion of the question, but because I need to get home, I'm letting you have it. You'd tell me if you needed to talk, right?"

"Well ..."

"Okay. I get it." Lydia gave her a quick hug. "I love you dear and I'll see you later."

Polly hugged her back and held the door open as Lydia left. Andrew and Jason ran down the stairs and pulled up short in front of Polly.

"You don't have to worry about Obiwan," Jason said. "We got back with him ten minutes ago. He should be good to go until after the party."

"Thanks, boys," Polly said. She pulled her wallet out of her jacket pocket and slipped two five dollar bills out as Sylvie joined them. "I appreciate your help with him today."

"Thank you, Miss Polly. You're the best!" came from Andrew, while Jason simply said, "Thanks."

"Thank you, Polly," Sylvie said as she patted Andrew on the head. "We'll see you later."

Polly held the door for the Donovans and then went up to her apartment. She had plenty of time before she needed to be back downstairs and what she needed right now was some hot tea and time with her animals. Obiwan followed her into the kitchen as she drew water and put it on to boil. "Sorry, bud. Nothing for you."

She watched the parking lot empty as the light of day began to fade. It had been a good day. The barn was in great shape, Sylvie was making a name for herself, Elise was safe, and people were having fun in her house. She knew it was time to shake off whatever malaise had settled in so she pulled out her basket of teas and chose an orange spice.

As the sun set, lights around Sycamore House came on. She poured hot water over the tea bag and stood for a few moments inhaling the steamy fragrance, then picked Luke up off the counter and set him back on the floor. He wound around her ankles a few times as she stood watching the last few vehicles leave.

A knock at her door startled her out of her reverie and she set the mug down. Obiwan ran to the door, wagging his tail and she attempted to walk without stepping on the cats. She pulled the door open to see Henry standing there.

"Hey, what's up?" she asked.

"Are you alright?"

"I'm fine," she said. "Did you need something?" She knew her tone was short, but facing Henry wasn't in her plans for these few moments of quiet.

A frown creased his eyebrows, "No, I guess I don't."

"Alright then, don't worry. I'm fine."

"You don't sound fine."

"Let it go, Henry. I'll see you downstairs. I need to get a shower and dressed and I assume you're wearing something other than that."

He was dressed in jeans, with a flannel shirt over a t-shirt. His jacket was well-worn, his work boots were filthy and his Chicago Cubs baseball cap had seen better days.

Henry huffed out air and said, "Something happened between the last time we talked and now and somehow you're mad at me."

"I'm not mad, Henry. Not mad at all, but we don't have time to talk about this right now."

She started to push the door shut and he put his hand on it, holding it open. He stepped forward into her space and Polly backed up.

"No. We're going to talk about it now. I'm not going to wonder what in the world I've done to set you off while you spend the evening with a couple hundred of your new friends."

Polly's eyes turned to slits. "I wasn't mad, but this could easily get me there."

"You're not going to scare me with your anger, Polly Giller. I know you well enough to know that you'll calm down once everything makes sense in your head again, so spit it out. What happened? Who said what to you?"

She turned around and stalked back into the living room, throwing her arms up in the air. "Why do I have to be responsible for your emotional health? Why do I have to worry about you falling apart if a relationship between the two of us doesn't happen? Why can't we take our time?" She spun back around on him and said, "Why does there have to be pressure? I didn't ask

254

for this. I have told you over and over that I want to go slowly, that I'm not ready for a commitment."

Henry's eyes had gotten huge and his mouth was trying to make sounds, but nothing came out. He finally choked out, "What?" then took a breath, stepped in a little closer and said, "What happened? Who said what to you? Who told you there was any pressure?"

"Look," she said. "I get it that you are some wonderful, golden boy in this community and that everyone loves you. I get it that I'm an outsider who might hurt your little heart, but don't ever forget that I had plenty of life before I got here and I can make my own damned life with or without you in it. I didn't ask to fall for you and I didn't ask you to fall for me, so if this is going to turn into a huge, big, all-community commitment, well ... you all can go to hell!"

Polly's face had gotten red in her frustration and even as she said the words, she knew that she was blowing things out of proportion. Henry listened to everything she said and led her to the sofa, pushing a little so she would sit down. He sat beside her.

"You're falling for me?" he asked.

"What? That has nothing to do with this conversation. It just fell out of my mouth," she sputtered.

"Well, I heard it and I'm going to keep holding onto that, alright?"

"Whatever," she spat and sat back, moving away from him.

"First of all, Polly, there is no pressure. Secondly, this has nothing to do with people in the community. Third,"

"Like hell it doesn't," she interrupted. "Your friend made it perfectly clear to me today that I'd better not mess with your heart."

Henry cocked his head and the left side of his mouth turned up in a grin. "Which friend is that? Because if he or she could see what happened to me here, I might be done with them as a friend."

"Your teacher. Fred whoever. He caught me at the barn and told me to break your heart fast because some witch walked out on you."

"Oh." Henry smiled. "Oh," he repeated. "Well, Fred doesn't know everything about me and he certainly doesn't need to take care of my love life." He interrupted himself and put his hands up as if in protection, "Not that I have a love life or anything. That's not what I'm saying. But he should keep his nose out of things, and you don't need to take responsibility for any broken heart I might have had in the past or might have in the future. I'm a big boy and can take care of myself."

"I'm not ready for all this stupid relationship drama, Henry."

"Then let's forego the drama and enjoy the relationship, wherever it takes us."

"That's alright with you?"

"That's fine with me."

"I don't want to feel like everyone is watching me and judging whether what I do is right or wrong or watching to see if every move I make is going to hurt you."

"Polly, you're being ridiculous. Of course everyone is watching and judging you. That's what people do, but you can't let it affect your behavior."

"I know. Most days I get it."

"Are we okay?"

She nodded. "We're okay, but we both need to hurry now. You have to go."

"I'm going, I'm going. Promise me you won't go all Polly on poor Fred tonight, alright?"

"Go all POLLY?" she asked.

"Yeah. You know. Yell at him until he wonders how long it will take for him to find his masculinity."

"Go all POLLY?" she repeated. "Get out of here and take your masculinity with you." Then her voice softened, "And thanks. I'll see you later."

Henry left and she headed for the bathroom. All of that extra time she had was now compressed and she needed to hurry. After a quick shower, Polly put on a little makeup and tied her hair into a pony tail with a red bandanna. She'd found a great red western style blouse with silver and black embroidery and rhinestones. She pulled her well-worn short black boots on under her jeans and whirled around in front of her standing mirror. Now she was ready for the evening. She pushed the phone into her back pocket and said to the animals on her bed, "Will I do?"

Obiwan was the only one paying attention. Both cats were cleaning themselves and effectively ignoring her, so she rubbed their heads, snuggled Obiwan and said, "I'm going down early. Don't want to miss my own party."

Jeff wasn't in his office, but Polly heard noise in the auditorium and saw that the band was setting up on stage. The back door was open and Jeff was watching as they worked. He saw her and strode across the floor. He looked especially nice in an ivory shirt, yoked in black with embroidered patterns sewn throughout.

"You're looking mighty good tonight," she said as he approached.

"Thank you ma'am" he said, taking a quick bow. "And you look delectable. The boys will all be panting to dance with you."

"Let's not go there," she laughed. "What's the name of the band?"

"It's a local band called Buckles and Spurs from east of Ames. I went to hear them at a country bar down there and they are great. Their cover stuff sounds fantastic and two of the guys write very well. They're ready to boot, scoot and boogie."

"I don't think those are the right words, you city boy, you," Polly laughed.

"Well, they should be. No one asked me," he replied.

"I'll be sure to call 'em up and inform them. Have you checked on Sylvie?"

"Her crew is just coming in now," he said, pointing to people walking through the hallway. "They're going to set up one line through the kitchen and a second through the new classrooms. We're putting the coats in the hallway and offices."

Three men came into the auditorium with large galvanized wash basins and began setting them out on both sides and the back of the room. Polly recognized Helen Randall, pulling a cart filled with bags of ice. She was followed by several young people who filled the basins and then began pressing more of the handled mason jars into the ice.

"What do you suppose is in the jars?" she asked Jeff.

"It is just pink lemonade or iced tea. Until we get a liquor license, I'm not walking us into any trouble."

A couple walked in with bags and stands. Jeff took Polly's arm and led her to them. "Polly, this is Chris and Debbie Johns. They own the photography studio here in town and are going to set up to shoot pictures both here at the barn," and he proudly pointed to the barn set he had created that afternoon, "and will shoot some video and stills of the evening."

"Wow. Thank you!" she said.

As they walked away, she asked, "That had to be expensive."

"Actually, I struck a deal with them. They are going to get a lot of exposure tonight, so they're kind of excited about that. Everything they shoot will be available on their website and if people want to buy prints, they handle it. They're also offering a Barn Raising discount package for studio sessions and talked to me about handing out advertisement about that with the web address." He handed her a postcard with the information on it. "I didn't think you'd have a problem with it."

"No problem," she said. "It's a great idea."

Polly walked into the kitchen and saw that Sylvie was organizing teams of young people, dressed in black pants and white shirts. "Waiters even?" she asked.

"I just want to make sure we can get things going at the beginning of the evening and then clear the tables so people have freedom to move around. They're not going to wait tables. People can feed themselves tonight."

"Awesome. Just when I think it can't get any better, you guys find a way to make me wrong. Who are these kids?"

"This is the Bellingwood 4-H team. When I contacted them, I found out they're raising money for some programs."

"You knock me out, Sylvie. That's terrific."

"Now, you get out of here. I've got to keep these people

moving!" Sylvie waved them out of the kitchen and turned around to give instructions to four kids standing beside a cart.

Polly smiled and pulled her phone out to check the time. Six thirty. It was nearly show time.

Jeff stopped her before they went back into the auditorium. "I have a huge favor to ask, Polly."

"Okay?"

"I want you to stay out of the auditorium until seven o'clock."

"Why?"

"Just stay out here and greet people as they come in. I want to see your face when you walk in that door. Promise me?"

"But, I've already seen everything," she protested.

"I know, but I want to watch you take in the whole effect. Please?"

"I'll wait," she said. "But, you're killing me here."

He gave her an evil grin, walked into the auditorium and pulled the door shut behind him. Polly went into her office and sat down at her desk. The waiting was the hardest part.

She didn't have to wait long, though, before she saw cars pull into the lot.

One of the first couples to arrive was Vera and Adam Lucas. Polly walked out to greet them and said, "I'm glad you made it! Are you ready to dance tonight?"

Adam took her hand and shook it, saying, "I don't know about that funky dancing kids do these days, but I will take any opportunity I can to hold my little lady tight."

Vera said, "Oh you, you're incorrigible."

"I have the room all set up with your furniture and it looks wonderful if you'd like to go upstairs."

"Do you have time? Surely you have things you need to do to prepare for this evening. We can come back another day," Vera said.

"No! I've been ordered to stay out of the auditorium until seven o'clock and I can't think of anything else I need to be doing right now. Come on!"

They walked in and Adam said, "You've done a lot of work on

the old school. Do you remember coming here when we were young, Vera?"

"It looks wonderful. The perfect upgrade for the old place. It sure would be nice if I could have someone move in and restore me like this!"

Polly opened the door to the Walnut Room and turned on the light.

"Adam," Vera exclaimed. "Look at this. It's perfect!" She ran her hand across the front of the secretary as she passed it and took hold of the post of the headboard. "I'm glad these pieces will stay together for another generation." Vera walked over to the window looking out toward the grove of trees. "What a peaceful, happy room. Don't you think so, dear?"

Her husband nodded as he took it all in. Polly could have sworn she saw his eyes mist, but he turned away from her. "Come on, Vera. We need to leave the girl alone so she can make her seven o'clock entrance." He held his hand out and his wife walked over and took it.

"Thank you for showing us this, Polly."

"I'm glad you like the room. We'll take good care of it."

They left, Polly turned out the light and pulled the door shut, then followed them down the steps. She still had several minutes before she was allowed in, so she wandered back to her office, saying hello to those who passed her. She sat in the outer office, bouncing her leg, biding her time. Finally she decided she'd waited long enough. She checked the time and it read 6:57. That was close enough.

CHAPTER TWENTY-TWO

"Exactly the reaction I was hoping for," Jeff said when Polly opened the doors to the auditorium and gasped. She blinked as the photographer's flash caught her off guard.

"I'm glad I was able to meet your expectations," she said. "But, oh my, this is beautiful."

As he escorted her to the front of the room she was glad for his hands on her arm, because she trying to take in the whole effect instead of paying attention to where they were walking. The main lights had been dimmed, and the room was lit with strings of white lights draped from the overhead beams in glorious, shimmering rows. Candles on each table added a golden hue to the faces of people leaning in to talk to each other. More candles glimmered in between the cupcakes on the tiered centerpieces. The three sixteen-foot lengths of tables, one on either side and at the back, were covered in muslin with white lights twinkling from underneath. Four lanterns highlighted each of those tables and more light came from the glass cases on the walls, which held items from the crates they had found in the basement last fall.

Music was coming through the sound system and the band

was wandering around the room. She watched as two of them stopped to have their pictures taken in front of the barn. The 4-H kids were scattered throughout the room and, at Jeff's nod, began inviting tables of people to move through the food lines. Jeff took Polly's arm and said, "Tonight you eat with me. No more missing meals because you're busy with people."

"Okay, boss," she said.

They walked into the hall and Polly was again thankful for the people with whom she'd surrounded herself. Sylvie had prepared a wonderful casual meal. Polly had her choice of barbecue pork or beef and giggled when it was placed in a pie tin. A scoop of baked beans with chunks of bacon, another of cheesy potatoes, and she nodded yes to the salads. When she and Jeff made their way back to a table, she found baskets filled with biscuits and sliced bread.

"I think Sylvie is going to sleep for a week after today," he laughed.

She smiled and kept eating, then looked up and around. She hadn't seen any of her friends when she came in and wondered where they were. Finally her eyes landed on a table in the middle of the room where Beryl was holding court. She was standing with her right leg up on a chair, showing off her red cowboy boots under a flared denim skirt. The skirt and bandanna around her neck were the quietest part of her outfit since the scarlet blouse she wore was covered in sequins and rhinestones. Polly watched as Lydia giggled and Aaron looked desperately uncomfortable. He was saved any more embarrassment when one of the 4-H kids stopped at their table and pointed to the food line.

The room quieted as people began to eat. Sylvie and Jeff had created a great traffic flow and everyone had been served relatively quickly. Jeff got up and asked, "Tea? Lemonade?"

"I'm fine with the water I have here," she said, pointing to the mug at her place. "Thanks."

He wove in and out of people and came back with a mug of tea, dripping from the ice in the basin.

She looked up at a touch on her back and then stood up to hug Lee Geise. "I'm so glad you guys came!"

"We couldn't get up for the barn raising, but we had to see what you were doing up here!" Lee said. "How are the kitties?"

"So you're the ones responsible for the beginnings of Polly's zoo!" Polly laughed as Mark Ogden joined them.

"They're only responsible for the cats. Those boys," she pointed at Doug Randall and Billy Endicott, "gave Obiwan to me." Then, she said to Mark, "You're the vet in town, how long do I have to wait to get a horse?"

He said, "Whenever you find one you want, I guess. That's an awfully big barn for one horse, though."

"I like to plan ahead when I can. I'm going to be here for a long time and animals seem to show up when I least expect it."

"You finish your dinner," Lee said. "We'll see you on the dance floor, right?"

"Right," Mark said for her. "She's almost a pro at it by now."

Polly pushed him away and sat back down. He bent down and said, "I'll be back in a minute with my food if you save me that seat beside you."

Before she could say anything, he was gone. "Well, that's going to be interesting," she muttered.

"What?" Jeff asked.

"Nothing. If I'm not downstairs on Monday morning, look for me at the nearest insane asylum. I'll have checked myself in."

He crossed his eyes at her and said, "I probably shouldn't ask, should I."

"No. Just watch the entertainment tonight."

A few minutes later, Mark sat down with his plate. He reached into the pail for silverware and then jumped up to get something to drink. "Do you want anything else?" he asked pointing at her water glass.

"No. I'm good," she said. Polly watched him walk away and thought to herself that it wasn't fair. He was flat out gorgeous. Working with animals all day long had done plenty for his physique. Tall and lean with strength oozing from his arms and legs and she remembered the sensation of those wiry fingers warm against her back.

"Polly. Be good."

"What?"

Jeff was watching her. "You're nearly drooling. Stop it. It's embarrassing."

"Well, dammit. He's beautiful."

Jeff watched Mark return to the table. "You're right, but still. Stop it."

"Stop what?" Mark asked.

"Nothing!" Polly snapped and stood up grabbing her water glass. "I'll be back in a minute."

She heard Mark ask Jeff what it was he had done and didn't wait to hear Jeff's response. She found one of the kids and said, "I need more water."

"Is your pitcher empty?" he asked.

"What pitcher?"

"The one at the table."

Polly looked back at the table and there, right in front of Jeff was a pitcher of water, still quite full.

She pursed her lips and said, "No, it's not empty. I'm just blind. Thanks." She decided to take the long way back to the table and walked out into the hallway. People were still going through both lines and she tucked herself into a line of people re-entering from the classroom.

As she wove through the tables, she acknowledged some of the people she knew and smiled at others. Her UPS driver was there and touched her arm, asking to introduce her to his wife. Sarah, the EMT, smiled up at her as she walked by, and little Sammy and Emma jumped out of their seats to hug her when she stopped to say hello to Bruce McKenzie and his family. She was glad to see that both of his parents were there with him.

When she sat down between Jeff and Mark, Jeff picked up the pitcher and handed it to her. "Did you find what you were looking for?"

"Yes, I did," she announced, then asked Mark, "Is your sister here tonight?"

"No. Sick kids, but she told me to ask you if you'd be interested in coming over for dinner some Sunday night. Dylan closes the restaurant at eight and then they invite friends in to create their own pizzas. It's always fun."

"What restaurant?"

"He owns Pizzazz, the pizza place downtown."

"I've ordered out from there, didn't know who that was. Sure. We should do that sometime."

"I'll tell her to call you."

Polly reached into the centerpiece and pulled out a cupcake. A small white flag on a toothpick read "Spice." Sylvie thought of everything.

Mark touched her hand and said, "Can I take you away for a minute? I want to introduce you to someone."

"Sure. Who?"

"Just come with me."

Polly followed him to a table at the far side of the room and a man stood up, his hand outstretched. She shook it and he said, "Hi Polly. I'm Dan Severt." He touched the woman who was seated with him and continued, "and this is my wife Leona. I'm awfully sorry about your dog."

"Thank you," she said.

"I've had such trouble with coyotes, I thought I could help clear some out, but I never thought to hurt anyone or their animal."

She smiled. "Thanks. I don't know if the sheriff told you, but one of those traps helped catch a couple of kidnappers this morning."

"He did tell me. I guess sometimes decisions are good and sometimes they're not. But, the trapper will be in tomorrow to pull the rest of them out of the creek area bordering your property. And I told Mark here to send me the bill for fixing up your dog."

"That wasn't necessary, but thanks," she said.

"We live down the highway in the big blue house. If you ever need anything, let us know."

"It was nice to meet both of you," Polly said and took his wife's hand. "And thanks again."

Mark nodded at him and as they walked back to the table, she noticed that band members were walking around the stage. Polly pulled her phone out to check the time: it was eight fifteen already. There was an alert that she had a text, so she opened up her messages and saw that Henry had sent a text twenty minutes ago. How had she missed that?

"Don't worry, I'm going to be late. My neighbor needed me to check her furnace. Save me food and a dance."

She felt guilty since she hadn't even noticed that he wasn't here. Polly honestly figured he was lost in the crowd somewhere, but now she felt terrible. She texted back:

"I ate all the food, now no one wants to dance with me. No worries."

She got a smiley face back from him and relaxed. Guilt assuaged.

The kids were clearing tables and checking water pitchers. They dropped extra napkins in the pails at the tables and quietly made their way back to the kitchen with no fanfare. Jeff stood up and looked around the room, then sat back down.

"Do you want to talk to the crowd or would you like me to do it?"

"I should probably say thank you for the work that has been done. We should both say something."

"Come on, then. Let's get this party rolling." He took her arm and they went to the stage. A microphone was handed down and he said, "Ladies and Gentlemen, thank you for coming out this evening!"

It took a few moments for the noise level to die down and when it did, he handed the microphone to Polly.

"I hope you've all had fun today," she started and a mild roar went through the room. "I can't begin to thank you for all of your help. I don't know what will happen next here at Sycamore House, but I look forward to it because I get to have fun with all of you. Now, I can't let any time pass before I tell you that I didn't do much except surround myself with great people. Jeff Lyndsay put everything together, Sylvie Donovan is a wizard in the kitchen and though he isn't here yet, Henry Sturtz was the one who never says no to me when I have a wild idea; he finds a way to make it happen. These are the people who made today a tremendous success."

She handed the microphone back to Jeff, who pointed out the photography opportunity at the back of the room and then said, "I have learned that you don't bring a group of people together in this state without them expecting to have someone pass the plate. We aren't asking you to pay for anything that has happened here today, but those mason jar banks on the tables are there if you'd like to fill 'em up. Everything that comes in will be split between the Bellingwood Food Pantry and our county's Habitat for Humanity. We've eaten and we've built today and it seems appropriate that we support these two groups. And now, the band Buckles and Spurs is here to play us into the night. Enjoy your evening and it's time to dance!"

The band kicked off, Jeff pulled Polly into his arms, and they started around the area they'd set aside for a dance floor.

"I would have killed you if you had done this to me without Mark's intervention," she said.

"I know," he smirked.

"What do you mean you know?"

"Who do you think asked him to figure out a way to teach you how to dance?"

"What?"

"I might have called his sister last week and found out that he was as good a dancer as anyone and I might have talked to him on Monday."

Polly punched him with her free hand. "You rat!"

"Don't call me a rat. You were so freaked out about this I had to find a way to settle you down. Look at this room. They want to see you be a part of the fun. Imagine how awful you would have felt sitting out the whole evening."

"You're still a rat."

"But you think I'm wonderful, right?"

"Sure. We'll call it that," she grumped.

"Alright. Wonderful it is," he let her hand go and pulled back from her then came back in and took her hand.

"Stop that," she said. "You're freakin' me out."

"Basic box step it is," he laughed.

The song ended and as the band picked up the next song, Mark tapped Jeff's shoulder and took Polly in his arms. More people began to join them on the floor and she saw Jeff find Lydia. He bowed to Aaron and escorted her out to join them. For the next twenty minutes, Polly found herself dancing with several others as the floor filled with dancers. Then, the band stopped and she saw Jeff pushing the dancers to the back of the floor. She was confused until she heard the lead singer shout out, 5-6-7-8 and the 4-H kids, led by Sylvie and Hannah, filed in and began to dance in unison as the music began. The room erupted in applause and before long, the floor was filled with people of all ages, mimicking the steps the kids were doing.

Her heart caught in her throat and what came out was, "Oh my."

"Do you want in on this?" a voice spoke into her ear. She turned around and Henry was standing there, dressed in all black.

"Oh my," she repeated, taking him in.

He smiled and said, "Are you ready to join them?"

"Not really, it's fun just to watch it happen. Have you eaten anything?"

"Not yet. I'm sorry about being late."

"What happened?"

"I keep telling Mrs. Naylor that she needs to get a real furnace repairman in, but I have a feeling that as long as I'm her neighbor, I will continue to be re-starting that old thing. She'd been without heat most of the day, so I took her over to my house until I got it up and running and her place started warming up again."

"You're a good guy, Henry Sturtz."

"I'm sorry I'm late, though."

"No big deal. You did miss me telling the world about how wonderful you were, but otherwise I don't think you missed much. Come on, let's find you some food."

They went into the classroom and since there was no one there, she picked up an empty pie tin and said, "Pork or Beef?" then slapped some pork on a bun and handed it to him. He scooped his own sides, then followed her back into the auditorium. She picked up an iced tea as they passed the drinks table and set it down in front of them when they got to their table, then turned her chair so she could watch the fun on the dance floor. Mark had dropped in beside Sylvie and wrapping his left arm around her waist, doubled up with her as they performed the next dance. Hannah moved into the crowd to find her husband and Polly watched him protest a little, then acquiesce and join his wife on the floor.

One more song and Sylvie pulled away and scooted her helpers out of the auditorium, leaving to another round of applause. The kids were beaming and Sylvie's face glowed. Several of the other women who chose not to dance soon followed her into the kitchen.

The band finally announced they needed to take a short break and Polly stood up, "Do you want anything more?" she asked Henry.

"No, thanks," he said.

"I'm going to check on a few people," and she headed for Beryl and Andy's table in the middle of the room.

Lydia dropped into the seat beside Aaron with a "whompf."

"That wears an old lady out. How are you doing, Beryl? I noticed that you found plenty of people who wanted to dance with you. And Andy, my friend, are you sweet on Len Specek? You two looked pretty good out there."

Andy blushed. "He's an old friend, so stop it."

"I don't know!" Beryl laughed. "You know what they say about those widows."

"No," Andy said, "Tell us what they say about widows."

Beryl looked around the table and then bowed her head. "Nothing. They say nothing about anything. Good heavens, I'm in trouble again."

"That's better," declared Andy. "We're old friends and that's all there is to it."

Aaron leaned into his wife and said in a stage whisper,

"Sounds like she's protesting a bit much."

Polly interrupted, "I'm here for a reason. Can we get a picture?" Then she said, "Wait. We need Sylvie, too! Just a minute." She looked around the table. "Don't any of you go anywhere. Got it?"

She ran into the kitchen. Sylvie was loading dishwasher racks and looked up.

"Sylvie, we need you for a picture."

"Like this? I look like hell!" Sylvie protested.

"You look great. Come on."

Sylvie sputtered and tried to push her hair back away from her face. She pulled her apron off and looked around for a place to put it. Polly took it out of her hand and said, "Go. Move it."

She pushed Sylvie into the auditorium and through the crowd back to the barn setting, beckoning to Lydia as they walked past the table. When they all arrived, there was a short wait while a young couple attempted to look at each other with adoration but couldn't get past their giggles.

The five of them finally made their way onto the set and began with a shot of all of them standing together in a row. The photographer took the shot and then said, "That's all you have for me?"

"You all make me feel like a kid again," Lydia said and she dipped Beryl. Andy looked stunned and Polly did the same to Sylvie. The picture was priceless. A few more crazy poses and Sylvie said, "I've got to get back to work."

Before she could get very far, Jeff and Henry stopped her and Jeff said, "We've done the work, we're gonna get in the shot." He and Henry each went down on a knee and patted them for the girls to be seated. Polly took Sylvie's hand and the photograph was taken.

The band had started up again and Sylvie escaped to the kitchen. Henry didn't let Polly leave the barn set until they'd taken a few shots, then Jeff insisted that he be allowed to pose with her. Doug and Billy saw what was happening and begged for a picture and the next thing Polly knew, she was posing with friends she had been meeting since moving into town.

When she was finally released, Henry said, "I don't think there is much time left and I want one dance with you tonight. I've asked for a waltz, can I have it with you?"

She winked at him and put her hand in his, "Lead on," she said.

Jeff announced that it would be the final dance. The band began a slow waltz and the floor filled up. She looked up and saw Mark find her and nod. Then he left the auditorium to return with Sylvie. Hannah was back on the floor with Bruce and when Polly found Lydia, she was stunned to see Aaron holding his wife as they danced. This was a good way to end a great day.

CHAPTER TWENTY-THREE

Reaching for the phone with her eyes still closed, Polly grabbed it to shut off the alarm. She opened them enough to dismiss the annoyance and turned over on her side where she was greeted by a quick lick on her hands. "No, don't make me," she whined. "I just want to sleep."

But, it was too late. They knew she was awake and from this point forward any hope of extra sleep was lost. She pulled the blankets up around her neck and tried to cocoon back into the bed, but her animals were smarter than that. Luke stretched, then walked up her side, settling in at her shoulder. Leia began walking back and forth across the pillow above her head, kneading her paws in Polly's hair. Obiwan stood up, wagged his tail, then lay back down in front of her face, nuzzling her with his nose. She felt guilty for making him wait, but didn't want to move away from the snuggly warm cat. The dog nuzzled her once more and Polly decided to pay attention. She dislodged Luke and threw the blankets back, covering Obiwan. He wiggled out the other side and jumped to the floor.

"You guys are mean. Why don't you ever want to sleep in with me?" The cats ignored her commentary and jumped to their ledges in the window, glancing back every once in a while to check her progress. Obiwan sat down in front of the bedroom door with expectation while Polly stretched and pulled on her clothes. "I hope you know that this is a sign of how much I love you, you dumb dog. You won't let me sleep, but I still get dressed to take you out in the cold." She snapped the leash on, stopped in the kitchen to start the coffee and then went out the back door with the dog.

The morning air was cold and she was still a bit bleary-eyed, but they walked the perimeter and were back upstairs before seven o'clock. Polly fed the animals, showered and dressed and headed downstairs. She had been so exhausted yesterday after the full day on Saturday, that she hadn't bothered with a shower. In fact, she hadn't bothered with anything, but had spent most of the day curled up on her couch with her laptop, the animals and a huge amount of recorded television. She'd taken calls all day long from her friends, but had refused any human interaction, choosing to stay inside alone instead. Henry had called to see if she wanted to do something and she'd begged off, surprised that he had any energy at all after spending the day building a barn.

Before going to her office, Polly set a platter of extra cupcakes onto the counter, leaving them covered in plastic wrap. She got things set up to feed people through the day and left a note by the coffee machine that she would have leftover soup and sandwiches ready to go at noon. Sylvie worried about all of the additional food and Polly had promised to make some calls. Lydia had told her that Rev. Boehm might have some ideas or she should start handing food out to anyone who stopped by. The phone call was first on her list this morning.

Polly rummaged around in the refrigerator and pulled out one last breakfast casserole, fully intact. Sylvie had told her that she could put it in the oven and easily re-heat it. She set the alarm on her phone and went in to her office. The kitchen and classrooms had been cleaned by Sylvie's crew before the end of the evening on Saturday, but Jeff had promised that the cleanup of the rest of the place would be great fun today, so rather than laugh at him in front of everyone, she'd simply nodded and said, "I suppose so!"

Joanna Wagner, the new guest, was arriving this afternoon and Polly hoped she was ready for her. During one afternoon Sylvie's boys were here, they'd camped out in the conference room and assembled packages of the items she had requested to be delivered to her room each day. Polly needed to run to the grocery store this morning and pick up some fruit and figured she would get a case of water to be safe.

Polly pulled up her notes program and began composing a list of things she needed to accomplish before the day was out.

She smiled at Jeff when he came in and sat down in front of her desk.

"Are you rested up from last week?" he asked.

"Just barely. It nearly killed me to get out of bed this morning."

"Me too. But, here we are. I hope you were happy with how the day went."

"Jeff, I don't know how I could have been happier. What a wonderful day."

"It was wonderful. I think we made a good impression on the community."

"I hope so. I'm going to live here for a long time," she said.

"We have people coming in to clean up the auditorium this afternoon, but I think we need to talk about bringing on a part-time custodian. You can do laundry and cleanup in the rooms, but we need more help after big events and Polly, I have eighteen emails and three voice mails requesting more information on dates for weddings, birthday parties and even a Quinceañera reception."

"That's exciting! And you're right. Let me see what I can do. I'll try to get someone hired this week. It would be good to have them on board to help us keep up."

"By the way," he said, "do you want to put some blackout dates in the calendar so I don't schedule every day?"

"What do you mean?"

"Polly, there is going to come a day when this place has a lot going on. Think about how much you needed to be alone yesterday. Could you do that with activities happening down here?"

"Jeff, I really didn't leave the apartment except to take Obiwan for a couple of walks."

"Do what you want, but I've warned you."

"Thanks. I'll think about it."

Henry, Leroy and Ben walked in. "Good morning!" Henry said. "Do I smell breakfast?"

Polly's phone chimed and she said, "I don't know how you did it, but that's perfect timing. Come on, it's ready."

She pulled the pan out of the oven and Jeff brought out plates and silverware. Jerry Allen showed up with Doug and Billy, and were soon joined by Sam Terhune and Jimmy Rio. They laughed and talked about the great day they'd had on Saturday. Temperatures were supposed to be in the mid-forties again and Henry wanted to get up on the roof and push forward. Jerry was going to install the breaker box and take electricity into the building, hooking up interior lights and power boxes. Before too long, she was going to have a barn.

Polly let them get to work and cleaned up the kitchen, then set up the buffet server for lunch. She stuck her head in Jeff's office and said, "I'm running out for a little bit, I'll be back."

He was on the phone, so he nodded and waved. Polly ran upstairs to get her coat and then headed to the grocery store uptown. It was a small store with only four aisles, but they seemed to serve the community well. She stopped at the small produce section and chose some apples, bananas and grapes. It didn't take long to wander the aisles, but Polly pushed the cart and filled it with things she needed for her own refrigerator. She stopped in front of the frozen foods and found herself drawn to a frozen pizza. It had been so long since she'd popped one of these in the oven and shared it with her friends in college. Without another thought, she whipped the freezer door open, grabbed a pizza and tossed it in the cart. She picked up some wrapped candy for the office, M&Ms for herself and headed for the checkout counter.

No one was there and she had to press the bell for service. A young woman came from the back and said, "Good morning, Polly!"

Polly smiled. This was going to be her life for a while. Everyone knew her, but it was going to take time for her to know their names. "Hi there, and I'm sorry," Polly said, "I don't know your name."

"That's alright. I'm Dana Bright. Sylvie always talks about you, so I feel like I know you." Polly put her groceries on the counter as Dana checked her out.

Henry's roofing crew had expanded and they were heading up the ladders when she arrived back at Sycamore House. She grabbed the grocery bags and went inside, finally returning to her office to make her calls.

The first was to Rev. Boehm. His secretary told her that he generally took Mondays off, but Polly told the woman what she wanted and was promised a return phone call.

She had asked Jeff for a list of people who should receive thank you notes and that was sitting on her desk. That was her next task and she figured the sooner she started, the better, but was interrupted by a woman rapping on the main door of the office.

"Good morning?" she queried.

"I'm Joanna Wagner and you have a room for me?"

Polly shouldn't have been surprised and managed to maintain a semblance of control. This poor woman was trying to remake herself into her image of a nineteen sixties artist and she'd failed miserably. In her late forties, her hair had been spikey, but was growing too long to hold its shape. She had rings filling her fingers and colorful bracelets of all widths covering her arms, under an expensive and well-tailored coat. Polly could tell she wasn't used to them, because she fiddled with them over and over. She was wearing a variegated colored skirt with a tailored blue blouse. That had to have been from her former life. Her shoes were brand new and she was wearing dark blue leg warmers. The picture in front of Polly was one of a woman desperately trying to understand a life that had previously been alien to her.

"Hi, Joanna," Polly said, as Jeff stepped out of his office. He offered to take the woman up to her room, explain the lock system to her and help her get settled. All Polly could think was that this poor woman needed a few doses of Beryl Watson before she escaped from Bellingwood. She wrote a quick note to herself; she was going to make sure that happened.

Her phone rang and she answered, "Hello?"

"Good morning, Polly. This is Del Boehm. Sue said you called about some food from Saturday night? That was quite a feast you put on."

"Hi Pastor Boehm. It was a lot of fun, but we have quite a bit of soup, barbecue and salads left over and I was wondering if you might know anyone in town who could use the food? It's all in family sized containers and I can deliver it or do anything you like to make it happen."

"Sue mentioned this to me and I called two of my cohorts and yes, we have three families among us who are in a bit of a crisis right now. This would certainly help them out. If you don't mind, I'd like to stop by in the next hour and then I'll make the deliveries. I hate to embarrass them, you know."

"That would be great. How bad are these situations?" she asked.

"One of them is pretty rough. They're close to being evicted. He got laid off and hasn't been able to find work. The other two are holding on, but just barely."

"That was another thing I wanted to talk to you about. We're looking for a part-time custodian and I don't know where to begin. I thought you might know someone who needed a job. It's not going to pay much right now, but if things keep going as I think they will, the job will grow and there is also for extra income if they want to work the events we're holding."

"You know, Polly, people around town keep talking about what you're doing here. If this is what they are experiencing, I can see why so many are big fans. I'm going to call Shawn Wesley and bring him with me. Would you mind doing the interview this morning? If they thought there was hope on the horizon, it would do wonders for them."

"Why don't you two show up around eleven and I'll have the food bagged up, then you can do what you like with it while I talk to Shawn."

"He's a little rough around the edges, Polly, and he could use a job."

"If you're putting in a good word for him, Pastor, I'll keep that in mind."

"Thank you, Polly."

She thought for a few moments and wrote a quick note to Jeff that she'd be back and left it on his desk. She ran out to her truck and drove back to the grocery store. When she got inside, Dana was finishing up with another customer.

"Did you forget something, Polly?"

"No, I need to talk to you about something."

The woman left with her groceries and Dana said, "How can I help you?"

"I need three gift cards, do you guys have something like that?"

"I don't have gift cards, but I can write out a gift certificate. Who is it for?"

Polly stopped. She didn't know any of the names except Shawn Wesley and she hadn't asked if he was the guy Pastor Boehm had talked about being laid off.

"I don't know their names. I just need to buy the gift certificates. Does it matter?"

"No, I guess it doesn't. How many do you want?"

"I need three fifty dollar certificates."

Dana looked at her and then opened up a drawer and pulled out a book. "Okay. I can do that." She filled out three certificates and said, "Do you want an envelope for these?"

"Sure, that would be great." Dana slipped each one in an envelope and handed them to Polly, who paid for the transaction.

"Thanks a lot, Dana," she said and left again. It broke her heart to think of the amount of food they'd served on Saturday when there were people in the same community who were barely getting by.

Back at Sycamore House once more, Polly went to the basement and found three boxes, then nearly tripped up the steps when one caught on the railing. She was laughing and sputtering at herself by the time she opened the door to the main hallway.

"There you are," Jeff said. "What are you doing?"

"Trying to kill myself on the basement steps. What's up?"

"Our new guest is settled in her room. She loved it and told me she would find a great many sources of creative inspiration outside her windows." He put air quotes around the last part of the sentence. "I don't think she's been doing this very long. She mentioned something about a mid-life crisis and I don't think it was hers."

"That makes some sense," Polly laughed. "Good for her, then. Did you give her the first delivery of requested items?"

"She is good to go. She appreciated the water filter pitcher in the refrigerator and the extra bottles and said she would be glad to have what we're serving the guys for lunch, but would like to take it to her room. She wants to embrace the room," he said with more air quotes.

Jeff took two of the boxes from Polly and said, "Where are we going with this?"

"To the kitchen," she said and began walking. "Pastor Boehm is stopping by to take a significant amount of our leftovers to a few families who need some extra help."

"Great!"

"I asked him if he knew someone who might work out as our custodian. He's bringing a young man with him at eleven for an interview," she dropped her box on the floor in front of the prep table. "Would you mind helping him get this stuff to his car while I do the interview?"

"Sure. He seems like a good guy. I didn't expect to see the preacher dancing on a Saturday night, but I guess anything can happen!"

Polly laughed. "He and his wife do seem awfully normal, don't they?"

They had fifteen minutes before Pastor Boehm arrived, so the two of them organized containers from the freezer and refrigerator into each of the boxes, then Polly tucked an envelope in where it wouldn't get dislodged, but could still be easily found.

"Thanks for taking care of this. I'm going to run in and print out an employment application. It shouldn't take too long and I'll get lunch going."

Pastor Boehm showed up promptly at eleven and Polly met them in the main office.

"Polly Giller, I'd like to introduce you to Shawn Wesley," he said.

"Thank you, Pastor. Jeff is in the kitchen with the boxes. Shawn, would you come into my office?"

Shawn Wesley had obviously cleaned up quickly. His longish brown hair was still damp. Polly could smell that he was a heavy smoker; his clothing was clean, but still reeked of it. He wore a flannel shirt open over a green t-shirt which was tucked into jeans with a belt cinched much tighter than it should have been and his feet were shod in well-worn cowboy boots. He strode in with an attitude of self-confidence, but Polly saw that it was nothing more than a facade.

He sat down and planted his feet in front of him. She wasn't sure if he was scared or surly, and chose to believe that he was simply nervous.

Polly pushed the application across her desk and set a pen on top of it. "Could you fill this out for me, please? I need to have some record of information before we begin."

He took the pen in hand and after glancing up at her to see if she was watching him, began filling out the various sections. Polly did her best to ignore him, paying attention to absolutely nothing on her computer screen. After a few uncomfortable moments, he set the pen down and pushed the paper back to her. He still hadn't said a word.

She looked over the paper. He'd held quite a few jobs, the last one at the chicken processing plant in Webster City. He'd been laid off from there last July and there was no record of work since then.

She was going to give him the job at this point, no matter what. He needed work, the pastor had asked her to interview him, and she couldn't help herself.

"Are you looking for other work?" she asked.

"There's not much around here to do and since I had to sell my car, I can't get out of town to apply for jobs," he responded.

"If you don't have a car, how would you get here?"

"I guess I would walk unless I can find a ride."

"How far away do you live?"

"We live up on Beech, west of the cemetery."

Polly did some quick calculations. That was a little more than a half mile away. It could be done, but she wasn't terribly confident.

"Tell me about your family," she said.

"We only have the one kid. She's in sixth grade."

"I'm willing to give you a try here, Shawn, if you want to do the job. It's not full-time yet because we don't have enough going on, but that will probably change in a few months and we'd pay you extra if you work the events that happen here."

"Okay. I'll try it."

"We have people coming in this afternoon to clean up the auditorium. If you'd like to start, I'm serving lunch at noon and you could begin at one o'clock with them. I'd show you around later on and tell you what my expectations are. Then, let's plan on four hours every day."

He fidgeted in his chair, then said. "I wasn't planning on working today. I got things going on."

"Nothing you can't change?" she asked.

"I suppose I could if you make me."

"I'm not going to make you do anything, Shawn. I'm only trying to get you started."

"What hours would you expect me here the rest of the week?"

Polly took a breath through her nose, then slowly released it. "Why don't you plan to start at ten every morning and work until two thirty. We generally have something to eat on site and you could take a half hour break at noon to eat with us."

"I wasn't planning on getting a job this week and have something going on tomorrow, too. So, I'll show up on Wednesday?"

"Alright. Come find me at ten on Wednesday and I'll show you around."

"Is there anything else?" he asked, standing up to leave her office.

"No, I guess that's all for now," she said.

He walked out into the office and around the corner, heading for the front doors. She saw him pull a smart phone out and make a call. As soon as he cleared the front door, he walked past her office window lighting a cigarette. What had she gotten into?

It hit her that she had promised lunch to the guys out on the roof, so she dashed back to the kitchen, quickly warmed up the meat, potatoes, and baked beans, and filled the buffet warmer. Whew, she'd pulled that off just in time.

CHAPTER TWENTY-FOUR

One. Two. Three. Four. Five. Six. Seven. Eight. Nine. Ten. Polly breathed as she counted off the numbers in her head. She had heard nothing from Shawn and his application was already on her desk. She'd waited long enough; she dialed his number. When she got his voice mail, she said, "Shawn, this is Polly Giller from Sycamore House. I expected you to be here this morning at ten o'clock and it is now ten forty-five. Please call me as soon as you receive this message and let me know what is going on."

It didn't take long for her anger to rise. She glanced up when she heard the front door open. That certainly wasn't Shawn Wesley. Then, she realized she was looking at Elise's LL Cool J double. She jumped out of her chair and ran out to greet him. Elise was right; he could pass for the actor any day.

"Good morning! Are you Elise's cousin?"

His voice was much deeper than she expected, "I sure am. Don Dobler is my name." He handed her a note of introduction signed by Elise.

"Let me show you to her room and then I can help you pack up her things, if you'd like."

"Don't worry. I have my boys in the truck and they're here to work. We'll get it all cleaned up and be out of your hair in no time."

She took him up to the room Elise had occupied and opened the door. He perused the room and said, "I got it."

Polly left him at the front door and from her office saw him walk back in with two men at least as big as he was. They were carrying boxes and followed him up the steps. In half an hour, he stopped in and said, "Would you mind coming back upstairs and checking the room?"

She followed him and saw that things were back to normal. He'd stripped the bed and left sheets and towels in a pile outside the room. "Can I take these somewhere for you?" Polly smiled. No one had slept in the bed since she'd re-made it last week.

"No," she said. "I've got this." The room had been completely emptied and looked a little forlorn.

"Since she left so early, I owe Elise a refund. If I write a check to her, can you make sure it gets to her?" Polly asked.

"No, Miss Giller. Elise doesn't expect anything back from you. If you ever get to Paris with her, take her out for a nice dinner." He winked at Polly.

She was a little surprised at the allusion to her last conversation with Elise, but figured she should just be quiet. "I'll do that. Thanks for doing such a nice job in here. I wish I could hire you!"

He smiled and picked up the laundry. "I bet your washing machine is downstairs, isn't it."

"No, I've got it."

"I'll carry these down and you can get it from there, deal?"

Polly nodded and followed him down the steps. When they reached the main floor, he pressed the sheets into her arms and said, "She's in a good place and is going to be fine. Don't worry about her. You might hear from her someday; she thought you were pretty special."

"Thanks Don. I appreciate it."

He left and Polly went back to drop the linens in the washing machine. She was surprised to see Sylvie pulled up to the prep table with her laptop. "What are you doing here today?"

"I don't have class today, so I thought I would hang out and get some work done. And I had a craving for pizza. The machine is mixing dough and that's what we're having for lunch. I noticed it was one of the approved meals for your guest upstairs and I figured guys always love the stuff."

"I had a craving for pizza, too!" Polly said. "But, my frozen pizza will be nothing like yours, I'm sure."

"I got a weird phone call from my friend Amy last night," Sylvie said as she followed Polly into the storage and laundry room.

"What do you mean?"

"Because her brother is such an ass, her mom's mail is being forwarded out to her in California. She got a bill from a farm up by Stanhope for feed. She asked if I would go check it out. Do you want to take a ride with me after lunch?"

"Sure. Some guy was supposed to show up at ten this morning to start a job as a custodian but apparently, he had something going on today."

"Who was that?"

"Shawn Wesley. Pastor Boehm gave me his name. In fact, he brought the guy over for the interview. Do you know him?"

"Not very well. What are you going to do?"

"I've left a message for him to call me. I'll give him the benefit of the doubt today. Who knows what might have happened, but if I don't hear from him ... well, crap. I don't want to deal with this."

"I know. Sometimes being an employer sucks."

Everyone seemed to enjoy lunch and since Polly still hadn't heard from her errant employee, she and Sylvie left for Stanhope. Sylvie had programmed the address into a handheld GPS and Polly watched it as she drove into town and then turned back west and out into the country. The directions led them to a farm and when Sylvie pulled in, Polly rolled her eyes.

"Front or back door?" she asked.

Sylvie laughed. "We'll try the front door. That back stoop looks a little iffy."

Before they got to the door, though, a man came out of a barn. "Can I help you?" he asked.

Sylvie put her hand out and said, "Hi, I'm Sylvie Donovan, a friend of Amy Hiller. She is Dean and Madeline Black's daughter. She got a bill from you yesterday and since she lives in California, asked if I could drive out here and find out what it was all about? She said it was for feed."

"I take care of her dad's horses," he said gruffly, "and I can't afford to feed them on my own. When he died, his wife didn't want to sell them, so she asked me to keep them and I agreed as long as she paid for me to feed them."

"Horses?" Sylvie looked at Polly in confusion. "Amy and Laurence don't know their parents owned horses, I can guarantee that."

She said to the man, "Can we see them?"

"They're out back here. They might not look so good, you know, winter and all."

They followed him to a gate and then behind a barn. Four black draft horses were standing there and Polly could tell immediately that these animals were in trouble. She could see their ribs and though she didn't know much about horses, she recognized that their eyes were dull and their coats weren't much better.

Sylvie stopped before she stepped in a pile of manure and said, "How long have they been like this?"

"I don't know. But, if I don't get money soon, I'm going to have to get rid of them. I can't afford to keep them."

Polly pulled Sylvie back and said, "I need to make a call."

Sylvie said, "I will get hold of Amy and deal with this immediately. Thanks for speaking with us."

The two hurried back to the car and as soon as she had pulled her door shut, Polly dialed. "Mark?"

"Hi, Polly. You sound upset. Is everything alright?"

"I don't think so. We just found out what Madeline Black wanted people to take care of. Her husband owned horses and a guy outside of Stanhope was taking care of them ... badly. Mark, these horses are in trouble. Can you get up here?"

"Calm down, Polly. Are you sure?"

"They're living in filth. Their coats aren't very pretty. They're draft horses and are way too skinny. I can see their ribs! There are patches of hair missing on one of the horse's shoulders and another was limping when he walked."

"Okay, Polly. Tell me where you are. I'm not that far from Stanhope right now. I can be there in fifteen minutes."

"Why don't we meet you at that new community center and drive you out here."

"Alright, I'm on my way."

"Did you hear that?" she asked Sylvie.

"Sometimes you know just the right person to call," Sylvie said.

"Well, speaking of the right person. I noticed the two of you dancing together several times the other night."

"He is gorgeous, isn't he? And what a dancer! But we were only dancing. The last thing I need in my life right now is a man. Good heavens, I'm finally figuring out my life. I don't need a guy messing that up."

Polly laughed. "They certainly can do that. But, he is hot."

Sylvie fanned herself. "So hot."

They pulled into a parking space and waited. Mark pulled up beside them in his truck and got out. "You two are much prettier than those stupid sheep. If you'll guide me out to this place, you don't need to worry any more. I'll take care of it from here."

He got back in his truck and followed Sylvie as she retraced her steps. They stopped in front of the driveway and Polly pointed. Mark waved them on and they went back to Sycamore House.

On the way, she called Lydia. "You aren't going to believe it, but Sylvie and I have solved your mystery!"

"What mystery?" Lydia started, then said, "You mean the note?"

"It's horses, Lydia! Four horses. Madeline had been paying a farmer to feed and care for these horses that Dean had bought."

Polly told her about Amy's request of Sylvie and the terrible shape the horses had been in.

"Mark is there now. I don't know what is going to happen next, though," Polly said.

"Polly, thank you!" Lydia said. "You kept my promise for me!"

"I just wanted you to know. I'll talk to you later."

"Thank you! I love you!"

"Love you too, Lydia."

Polly hung up as they drove into her lot and parked.

Jeff met Polly at the front door. "Your custodian showed up ten minutes ago. He's in the conference room."

"Great," she spat. "Just great."

She stalked in through the outer office, tossing her jacket on the desk and opened the door to the conference room. Shawn Wesley was sitting with his back to the door, but spun around when he heard the door open.

"Miss Giller," he said.

"Yes, Mr. Wesley," and she stood there, waiting for him to say something.

"I, uh. I didn't make it into work this morning."

"No you didn't. So, tell me. Do you want this job or not?"

"I want the job, but I had something going on this morning."

"You seem to have a lot going on. It occurs to me that for a man who has been out of work for six months, you don't seem to be in a hurry to establish a good relationship with a new employer."

"I had a good reason."

"Mr. Wesley, you didn't bother to call me and you didn't bother to return my call. You show up four hours late and you expect me to believe you had a good reason?"

"Well, I did."

"Because Pastor Boehm asked me to interview you, I will give you one last chance. If you aren't here on time tomorrow morning, I'm finished. Figure it out, Mr. Wesley."

She turned around and left the room, walked into her office and closed the door, then watched as he left the building, slouched into his coat. She was burning with fury and decided she needed to calm down before she saw anyone else.

Her phone rang and she saw that it was Mark, "Hey Mark, was I right?"

"You were absolutely right and I have a huge favor to ask of you. How's that barn coming along?"

"They're about three fourths done with the roof, why? Oh!" she said. "You want to bring those poor horses here, don't you?"

"Maybe. You're close to my office and you have plenty of space. We could get an electric fence up in a day. What do you think?"

"Mark, could these be my horses?"

"Well, there are some logistics we'd have to figure out and their rehabilitation is going to be a lot of work. Are you sure you're up for that?"

"Well, if I could get a stinkin' custodian, I'd be up for it."

"A what?"

"Never mind. Just a little problem I need manage here. You know I've never had horses before, do you think I can do this?"

"From what I've seen, Polly, you can do about anything you set your mind to. If you want four beautiful animals, they're going to be a lot of work, but that doesn't scare you, does it?"

"No, it really doesn't. You aren't going to dump them on me and leave, are you?"

He laughed out loud. "No, I will be around a lot. These are beautiful animals and I think you all will be very happy together."

Polly's stomach was turning upside down with excitement. "Who owns them and what do I have to do?"

"Don't do anything yet. I'm going back out with feed this afternoon and I've called a buddy of mine who is going to come over and string up the electric fence for you in the morning. We'll get those stalls ready tonight and then bring in hay tomorrow. Right now you're only fostering the horses until everything else settles down, okay?"

"Okay. What's my next step?"

"You might want to tell Henry what's going on. He's going to have four more warm blooded animals in his way while he finishes that barn."

"I'm going to have horses!" she shouted.

"Good. That's the attitude I was looking for. Now, go tell Henry what's coming at him and I'll see you later."

Polly pushed the phone back in her jeans and grabbed her jacket as she ran out the door of her office. She crashed through the side doors and ran for the barn. Henry was up on the roof of one of the overhangs.

"Henry, I have horses coming!"

Everyone stopped working and Henry said, "I'm sorry. What did you say?"

"I have horses coming!" She slowed down as what she said hit her. "I have horses coming," she repeated quietly.

He made his way to the ladder and came down to ground level. "You have horses, plural, coming?"

"Four of them?" she said.

"You have four horses coming. Here?"

"Yes. Here."

"When?"

"Maybe tomorrow?"

"Polly! What in the hell are you thinking?"

"I'm thinking that there are four horses in very bad shape who need out of their situation right now. Mark is going to get the stalls set up tonight and bring in someone to put in an electric fence tomorrow until we can get a real one built."

"Mark Ogden. Great. Damned veterinarian."

"Don't you start. Sylvie and I went up to Stanhope to see why Madeline Black had been paying for feed and when I saw what terrible shape these horses were in, I called him. If he's rushing to get those poor animals out of there, it has to be bad, don't you think?"

Henry shut his eyes, took a breath and in a measured tone said, "And I suppose he's going to teach you how to take care of the animals and he's promised to help you and he thinks it's great that you are so close to his office so he can ensure the horses will be taken care of."

"Well, of course! Why are you having a problem with this?"

"Because, Polly, you don't know much about horses and rather than starting with one healthy, normal horse, you are starting with four horses who are in bad enough shape that the veterinarian has to rescue them. AND, he's finally figured out a way to make sure he gets to spend a lot of time with you."

"Please don't tell me you are going to get jealous. You are here every single day and I keep coming up with more things for you to do so you don't wander off."

"At this point, I'm more worried about what he is thinking than you. He seems to be a man on a mission."

"Well, if you saw these horses, you would do everything you could to help them and why did I build this great big barn if I wasn't going to use it for something like this?"

"Why indeed," Henry responded.

"Are you going to get on board with this? Please?" she asked.

"I don't have much choice, do I?"

"You aren't going to be a creep, are you?"

Henry took her hand, "Do you want to do this? Do you really want four horses who need this much help? Tell me you aren't getting talked into something because you feel sorry for them."

"Well, I do feel sorry for them and I was going to get horses soon anyway. Why wouldn't I go where my compassion leads me? And why wouldn't I take care of these horses when I have Mark around to help me."

"Polly, this is going to be a huge amount of work!"

"I'm not afraid of that and besides, I might know of a good group of kids who are already comfortable with horses."

"What do you mean?"

"Well, when I was in high school, there were always 4-H kids who rode horses in competitions. I'll bet some of those kids would like to make some extra money."

"You are such a soft touch. Pretty soon you're going to have the entire community working here."

"Yeah. Yeah. Yeah. You know that guy I hired as custodian?"

"Shawn Wesley? I don't know him, but go on."

"Well, he didn't show up this morning, but was sitting here when I got back. I don't know what to do about this. How could Pastor Boehm not know he was a loser?"

"Did you fire him already?"

"No, I told him he had one chance left. He didn't want to work on Monday, said he had something to do. He didn't want to work yesterday, said he had something to do and now he was busy with something going on today. That's not terribly impressive, especially if he needs a job."

"Polly, if he isn't going to work out, call Pastor Boehm and tell him. And if you want to ask him for another potential employee, you can do it then."

"We'll see how tomorrow goes. I hate giving up on people, but from the first, this guy struck me wrong. I wanted to help him, but at the same time, I want someone to do the job."

"You'll figure it out; I have complete confidence in you."

"Uh huh. That's why you don't believe I can handle four Percherons."

"Draft horses? Polly, those horses are huge!"

She held her finger up to stop him. "Confidence. Remember? You believe in me."

"We have a lot of work to do today and tomorrow if you're bringing in four horses. I'd better get back to it."

"It's going to be great, Henry. I promise. You wait and see."

"I have to believe you, right?"

"You do."

"Then it's going to be great."

Polly went back in and found Jeff and Sylvie in the kitchen looking at her laptop.

"Look at my calendar Polly," and Sylvie turned the computer so Polly could see it. "We're filling up my weekends with work! I'm going to be fine after all!"

She smiled, "I knew it! You should think about catering out of here one of these days. I'll bet you could make some good money doing that as well."

"Shut up! We were just talking about how that could work," Sylvie said. "Mark called me to get Amy's phone number. He said you are going to take the horses? I said he was crazy."

Jeff dramatically fell over the counter. "Horses? You're getting horses now? I knew you might do this someday, but now?"

"Now. And don't you dare act this way."

He stood back up and laughed. "Polly, I think you're wonderful, but why didn't you become a zoologist?"

"Because I am doing this. Now, leave me alone or I'll make you ride them."

"Not happening. Not ever. I'll stay in here. You play out there. It works for me."

She laughed. "We'll see." She turned to Sylvie, "What did Mark say about Amy?"

"He's going to talk to her about transferring ownership to you. You're actually going to take this on?"

"Why is everyone surprised by this?" Polly exclaimed. "I took this building on. Why wouldn't I take in four animals that need me?"

"Because if something bad happened to the building, you'd do something else, but if one of those poor animals dies, you will be crushed!" Sylvie said.

"They're going to be fine. Mark is a great vet, right?" she prodded Sylvie.

"He's a great vet," Sylvie responded.

"He will help me do this and yes, it's going to be a lot of work, but if I wanted an easy life, I could have married Joey Delancy and lived in Boston in the lap of luxury." She shuddered at the memory of her kidnapping at his hand and said, "I'd rather work hard than be stuck in that life any day."

"What does Henry say about this?" Jeff asked.

Polly slowly turned her head and raised her eyebrows at him. "I don't think I understood that question. Surely you aren't implying that if Henry doesn't approve of my decision, I should be a good little girl and change my mind. I can't imagine that's what you were asking?"

Jeff gulped and looked at Sylvie for help. She turned her back on him and he said, "Umm, no. Just ignore the last question. I didn't ask it, you shouldn't answer it."

"So, Sylvie," Polly said, "When is your first wedding?"

"We have two in April. I'm meeting with one of the brides tomorrow and the other next Wednesday. And Jeff has booked something every Saturday in May. There's even a wedding and a class reunion on Memorial Day weekend."

"That's exciting. Well, I'm going to grab the laundry and take it upstairs, then I'm going to read everything I can about Percherons. If you need me, I'll be hiding in my office."

CHAPTER TWENTY-FIVE

New experiences didn't frighten her, but walking into the feed store with all of the guys who had chosen her name in their local dead body pool wasn't something she had hoped to do any time soon. But, no one had said a word to her.

Mark had picked her up at four o'clock and had taken her to get wood shavings and feed. She laughed when she'd gotten into his truck. "Do you live like this at home?"

"What?" he protested. "I have everything in here that I need."

"Where's your other glove?" she asked, picking up a filthy work glove that had fallen between the passenger seat and door. "Obviously you don't have too many human passengers." Before she could even get in the truck, he gathered up papers and empty containers; she recognized a bridle and halter, which he set on the floor behind her seat.

"Don't worry," she laughed. "I won't take up much room." She scooted things with her feet on the floor, so she could get in and pull the door shut.

He laughed abashedly, "Okay, so I don't ever have anyone else in my truck, but my house is perfectly clean."

Mark had introduced her to several people at the feed store, most of whom had plenty of advice and offered help if she needed it. They'd loaded the bed of his truck with bags and bags and when they got back to her barn, he showed her how to lay down bedding in the stalls. They hauled the feed into what he now called her feed room at the end of the barn and he went back to his truck to find a piece of paper and pen. What he found was the back of an instruction sheet for some medication for sheep.

He started writing out a list and said, "You need to go down to Boone tomorrow and pick these things up. Can you take care of that in the morning?"

Polly chuckled and pulled out her phone, then began entering the items into her notes program.

"Fine," he laughed.

"You know, something like this might save you a lot of hassle and mess in your truck."

"I know, I know. Marnie has been yelling at me. I keep telling her it's because she wants flashy gadgets at the office."

"Listen to her. You hired her to keep you put together, didn't you?"

"Shut up," he laughed.

Since Jason and Andrew were watching her dog, they brought him out to the barn before leaving.

"Are you really getting horses, Polly?" Jason asked.

"I am. Are you ready to learn how to help me?"

"I am! I am!" Andrew replied.

Mark ruffled the boy's hair, "You boys can help Polly a lot. That will be wonderful."

"Mom is waiting for us. Do you want us to take Obiwan back upstairs?" Jason said.

"Leave him here with me. Thank you and I'll see you tomorrow?"

"Will the horses be here tomorrow?" Andrew asked.

"They probably will."

"I can't wait!" Andrew turned around and started to run back to the parking lot, but stopped and said, "Come on, Mom's waiting!"

"I'll see you tomorrow, Polly," Jason said and handed her the leash. "Mom said the horses are sick. Will they die?"

"Not if we can help it," Mark replied. "Don't worry. You're going to watch four horses become happy and healthy again right before your eyes."

"Cool. I'll be here every day after school if you need me."

"Thanks, Jason. I'll see you tomorrow." Polly watched the boys walk away and she realized how big her family had gotten.

Mark pulled the outer doors shut on the barn and said, "Let Obiwan loose so he can get accustomed to the smells around here. He's going to have to make friends with these new additions to your life. You do know you are about to spend enormous amounts of time with these beasts."

"I know. Maybe when we get all the fencing up, I won't worry about him running out onto the highway and can let him run out here on the property, too."

"Alright. First thing. Once the horses are here, you're going to start calling this a pasture. Alright?"

She giggled. "I'll try. What did that farmer tell you about these horses?"

"He wasn't ready to talk to me at first. I think he thought I was going to have him arrested for neglect, but he got himself in a bad way with the drought last year. He didn't have the nerve to ask Madeline Black for any more money and he just kept feeding them less and less as things got more expensive. He was also spreading feed out to some of his own animals. I'm glad you guys caught this."

"Did he tell you why her husband even bought the animals?"

"Once you get these farmers talking, they don't stop, so yes, I heard some of the story."

"Dean Black worked with some of the few horses in Korea during the war and fell completely in love with the animals. I guess he had two when they were first married and had kids, but somewhere along the line when the kids were small, the boy, what was his name?"

"Laurence the twit," Polly said.

"Well, Laurence fell or got hurt and absolutely threw a tantrum every time he was around the horses. It got so bad, Madeline made her husband get rid of everything and he forgot about it. Then one day after his kids were long gone, he realized he was missing part of his soul, so he started looking for some horses and found a good deal on these Percherons.

"He was over there every day, right up until the day before he died. The farmer said Madeline couldn't bring herself to sell them until several months ago. He was hoping to have a good year and bring them back to good health. He knew what was happening, but didn't know how he could fix the problem."

"Did you talk to Amy?"

"Just for a few minutes. She was completely baffled by the fact that her mother never said a word."

They had finished up and Mark left. Polly took Obiwan back upstairs, popped some microwave popcorn and was ready to call that supper when there was a knock at her door.

Henry was there with a bag of sandwiches. "I figured you might not make supper for yourself tonight," he said.

Polly pointed to the bowl of popcorn and said, "Well, I kind of did, but thank you. Come in!"

"I'm sorry I didn't listen to you today. I jumped to a bunch of conclusions and that wasn't right."

Polly unwrapped her sandwich. He'd even made sure to put cucumbers on it. "That's okay. I know all of this came way out of the blue."

"You know I'll help you if you need it."

"I know that. But, you can't freak out if Mark is here a lot."

"Well, if I freak out, I will try not to tell you about it. How's that?"

"Better, but not perfect."

She told him some of what Mark had said about the horses and he asked, "Did you find out what their names are?"

Polly put her sandwich down and dropped her head into her hands. "What kind of moron am I? No, I didn't ask." She looked at him and rolled her eyes. "I guess I'll find out tomorrow."

She pushed the sandwich away and sat back in the couch. "Tomorrow is going to be a hell of a day. I have to train Shawn Wesley, then I have to go to Boone to get supplies for the barn, Mark has guys coming to string up a quick electrical fence, I have to talk to you about putting a real fence in, the first load of hay is coming and four horses are coming to a new home. If I think about this much longer, I'm going to totally freak out."

"Give me your phone," he said.

Polly handed him the phone and he handed it back saying, "Cute. Unlock it, please."

She giggled, unlocked the phone and handed it back. He scrolled through her calls list and pressed dial, "Jeff? Sorry to bother you buddy, but will you manage training that Shawn Wesley for Polly in the morning. We're heading down to Boone to get supplies for the horses and I want to have her out of here and back before too late in the morning."

He waited for an acknowledgment, then said, "Thanks. See you tomorrow."

Handing her back the phone, he said, "You need to remember that you hire good people and then you have to let them do the work. He's glad to do it."

Polly shoved at him with the feet she'd pulled up on the sofa. "Thank you, but I could have taken care of that call. You don't have to manage everything in my life, you know."

"I like it. It's fun."

"Well, stop having so much fun. You make me crazy."

"And not in a good way, I'm guessing. Are you done with this?" he pointed at the last half of the sandwich.

"I think so. Eat it if you want it." She reached down for the bowl of popcorn and placed it in her lap. "Do you want to watch television or something?" She had the remote in her hand and turned the power on to the system.

"Are you going to fall asleep on me if we watch a movie?" he asked.

"Maybe," laughter bubbled up from her belly. "You know your

way out of here."

"I'm not walking your dog tonight."

"If I say please?"

He tossed the empty sandwich wrapper at her and it landed in her popcorn bowl. She flung it back at him and when he ducked, the wrapper hit Leia who jumped up and ran.

"See what you did," she said.

Henry's only response was to toss a pillow, which she deflected to the floor. At that point, Luke scrambled off the back of the couch and ran for the bedroom.

"You meanie, you're upsetting my cats."

He laughed and sat back and she tossed the remote to him, set the popcorn back on the table and picked up her laptop. "I'm learning about horses. What would you like to know?"

"I have no idea," he said.

"Well, did you know that in the late eighteen hundreds, Iowa was home to one of the largest draft horse importers in the U.S.?"

"Really," he said, clearly unimpressed.

"Look," and she pointed to a horse, "they had an immense Percheron that was at the World's Fair and was a Champion Stallion."

"Wow. That's a big horse. And you're going to have four of them in your barn."

"Yes I am," she declared, "and I'm going to have the best time ever with them. You wait and see."

"You know you can't bring them up to your apartment and snuggle with them at night, don't you?"

"You're pushing it tonight, aren't you?"

Henry reached into the bag which had held the sandwiches and pulled out two chocolate chip cookies. "Will these help?"

"Gimme!" she said and reached over. He held it out of her reach and said, "What's the magic word?"

"Now?"

"No, the other magic word."

"You're going to make me say please?"

"Maybe."

Polly swung her legs off the couch and set the laptop on the table. Then she put on her best pitiful face and said, "Please sir, may I have a cookie?"

Henry brought them back in front of his body and she grabbed both of them, ran for the bedroom and shut the door. She slammed the door shut between her bedroom and bathroom and sat down on the bed. Although both cats had been sitting in their tree looking out the window, they watched as she ate one of the cookies. When she didn't hear anything and hadn't roused a response, Polly made her way to the door and peeked out a crack she opened. Henry was quietly sitting at his end of the couch eating a cookie.

"Hey!" she said, swinging the door fully open. "That's not right!"

"I'm not stupid. You have the craziest sweet tooth I've ever met. I bought extras."

She dropped back down on the couch and said, "Well, that made it less fun to hide and eat it in my room."

Henry just smirked. They'd ended up watching an old Cary Grant movie and he had left around ten o'clock. Polly was glad for the company to distract her from worrying over another new venture. But once he left and she took Obiwan for a walk around the barn and out through her pasture, her fears seemed a little overwhelming. Maybe she wasn't going to be able to do this. These were big animals and what if she couldn't get them to respect her? What if one of them couldn't be brought back to health? What if Obiwan didn't get along with them? What if her guests complained about horses? What if everybody thought she was crazy?

As she heard her mind think that last sentence, she smiled. They probably already thought she was a little nuts and so far that hadn't bothered her. She was ready to do something new, why not embrace it with everything she had.

Polly had stood for a while in the alley of the barn looking at the open stalls. Tomorrow night she would begin bringing four beautiful creatures back to health. Once that finally happened, she'd worry about what came next. She went back to her apartment and was now in bed, absolutely terrified at what tomorrow would bring.

Her alarm went off the next morning and she moaned. The night had been restless, filled with dreams she couldn't remember. Polly rolled over and sat up, dangling her feet to the floor. "Come on, Obiwan. Let's get this day started." She got dressed, ran downstairs and started the coffee maker, then decided they would take a different route this morning. She crossed the road to the wooded area separating the swimming pool from the newer neighborhood to the south. Beyond that was Bellingwood's industrial park. One of these days she needed to wander through and see what was going on in there, but for this morning, Obiwan was excited to explore new territory.

She picked up the pace and though he tried to stop and sniff every low hanging tree branch, he seemed to sense her emotions and finally just ran with her. He was panting and she was sweating when they trotted up the stairs to her apartment. Polly fed her animals and took a shower, and then since she still felt as if she had energy to burn, decided that this morning would be a good opportunity to try out a fruit coffeecake recipe. She warmed the butter and began creaming it with the sugars, while pulling out the rest of the ingredients. One look in the freezer told her it would be a strawberry kind of day.

While the cake was baking, she checked her phone and saw that there was a text from Henry. He was going to be ready to go to Boone at eight o'clock. It was seven thirty now. She texted him back: "Coffeecake in the oven. You're going to want some. Come to the kitchen when you get here."

"See. I told you. Epic sweet tooth," was his texted reply.

"Brat."

Polly took the pan downstairs and while it was cooling, set plates, napkins and forks out for those who were working today. The coffee was finished brewing. She drew off a cup and let it cool down while she cut the coffeecake and arranged the pieces on a platter. One of the edge pieces popped into her mouth. She giggled and put a full piece on a napkin and leaned on the counter. Henry walked up when she was chewing and he pointed at her mouth.

Rather than spit crumbs at him, she put a piece on a napkin and pushed it across at him, then took a drink of coffee and said, "Whatever."

"Are you ready to go?" he asked. "I need to get down and back."

"I don't know for sure why you're going with me. I could do this on my own. I'm pretty sure I can ask questions and get them to help me."

"Oh, I'm simply going for entertainment. Come on, let's get out of here."

She grabbed her coffee, pushed the last bite of cake in her mouth, and joined him. The morning sunlight hadn't pierced through the grey sky and she asked, "Are we expecting snow?"

"No. It's going to be fine. And it can't snow. Not until we're finished with the roof."

"Okay. Well, you're the boss then. Speaking of being the boss, what do you think the odds are that this Shawn Wesley will show up for work today?"

"Even money says he won't. If you were scary enough yesterday, maybe he will; if he's got something else going on, maybe he won't."

"I don't get it," Polly said. "It isn't like the work is going to kill him and why would he try to screw up his first job offer in six months?"

"People have a million reasons for the things they do. I never know what to think about them."

"You know. He's going to show up today and then he's going to be a pain in my ass over and over and over again, isn't he? He'll push me right to the edge every time and stop before he topples over it."

"Tighten the leash, Polly. Make sure he can't do that to you. He's had his one chance and he has to know that there are no others."

"Gah. That makes me sound like some kind of tyrant. Why can't people just do the right thing?"

Henry laughed at her, but when he saw the look on her face, he said, "Sorry. You were joking, right?"

"No, I wasn't. I get up in the morning knowing that I'm going to do my best for the day. Why is that so difficult?"

He patted her hand, "It's not that difficult for most, but the few who think they're entitled to an easy life make it seem like that's the way of the world. Let it go. If he works out, you've done a good thing. If he doesn't work out, it still doesn't change what you did. He has to deal with his own issues."

"Got it. Don't like it, though."

"I know. No one does. Welcome to the world of managing people. You were lucky with Jeff and Sylvie."

"And you."

"And me. You were downright blessed by me."

They laughed as he turned the corner and drove down Story Street in Boone. An hour later and Polly was sure the poor young man helping them at the Farm and Home Store would need a nap. His manager had approached and when she saw that they were buying four of most everything, began asking questions.

Polly explained about the rescue of the Percherons and the woman said, "Oh my gosh! We have some stable blankets in the back that would be the perfect size for you. We brought them in for another customer, but they ended up not wanting them. Can I give them to you and call it my good deed for the morning?"

Polly glanced at Henry, who nodded. "Thank you! That's very thoughtful." No matter how long she lived here, she was never going to be used to the easy generosity of people.

They checked out and then loaded everything into Henry's truck. When they got back to Sycamore House, Polly saw that there were already people working on the grounds around the barn.

"You know I want a really nice fence, don't you?" she said to Henry as he drove up to the barn.

"I know. This will do until the ground thaws. Then we'll build whatever you want. I promise." He laughed and said, "You are going to keep me busy for years, aren't you?"

"I hope you never get bored working here," she said. "I have more plans than you can even imagine!"

"It is never boring. Just about the time I think we're nearly finished and I'm going to have to start looking for other work, you come up with a new idea."

"I'm not keeping you from something else you should be doing, am I?"

"Doug told me you were worried about that. Maybe I'll have to expand and hire some more people. What would my Dad say about that?" He turned in his seat, "No, Polly, you're not keeping me from anything. I like that I can give my guys lots of hours and I like that I can think about bringing on more help. Don't worry."

They got out and began unloading things into the barn. Polly was pulling out the blankets when another pickup drove in, laden with square bales of hay.

Henry walked to the driver's door and said a few words, then came back in as the truck drove around to the other end of the barn.

"What was that?" Polly asked.

"He and his boys are unloading hay for you. Mark called him last night. It should be stored down there. He told me they'll be back with a large bale for you, too."

"Wow. I have absolutely no idea what I'm doing, do I?"

"Nope. You don't," he laughed, "But, I bet by this time next year, you will have not only become a pro at it, you will have found something different to scare you to death."

They finished unpacking. She wriggled up onto the tailgate of his truck so she could sit and pull labels off things and get rid of packaging. While she was working, she heard Jeff's voice calling her name from the side doors of Sycamore House.

"Hey, Jeff! You can come out; there aren't any horses in here yet."

He continued to stand in the doorway and wrapped his arms around himself like he was cold.

"You wimp! I'll be right there." She gathered up the trash and walked toward the building.

"Has he shown up yet?" she asked.

"Yes. And this is going to be interesting," Jeff responded.

"What do you mean?"

"I mean I want to fire him and he's barely gotten started."

The walked into his office and she shut the door before sitting down.

"Okay, what's going on?"

"He tried to light up a cigarette in the basement. I told him he couldn't smoke on the job; that we were a smoke-free environment and it wasn't safe around cleaning chemicals anyway. Then, when I took him upstairs to the bathrooms, I had also taken the paper and pencils to Joanna Wagner's room. She popped her head out to say thank you and I told her about the coffeecake downstairs. Then!" Jeff spread his arms out dramatically. "Then, before she can get back inside her door and shut it, he says, 'Who's the wackadoo in the green tent?'

"I pushed him into the bathroom and all he could do was ask if he had to wash this or scrub that. He told me that he didn't wash toilets, his wife did. When I asked if it was going to be a problem, he laughed and said, 'Not if you don't care what they look like.'

"Then, he went outside to have a cigarette. When he came back in, I took him into the auditorium to talk to him about the floors and the glass on the displays. I talked about the hallway floors and sweeping off the front steps. And before another ten minutes had passed, he went for another cigarette.

"Polly, this is a bad mistake." Jeff finally wound down and Polly felt herself beginning to wind up.

"I'll take care of it," she said.

"What are you going to do?"

"First, I'm calling Pastor Boehm and asking him what in the world he was thinking. Then, I'll track this jackass down and kick him off the property."

"Do you think he'll retaliate?"

"He doesn't have it in him to do anything except smoke. He's probably higher than a kite right now anyway and will forget it all happened by this afternoon."

Polly pulled the door open and went into her own office and shut the door. She dialed the church and asked for Pastor Boehm.

"Hi Polly, how are you today?" he said when he picked up the phone.

"Well, I'm sorry to say that when it comes to a new custodian, I'm not doing so well."

"Oh no, what happened?"

Polly told him about the interview on Monday and Shawn's refusal to work until Wednesday, his inability to show up until the end of the shift then and his attitude this morning. "Pastor, I can't keep him here. I'm building a family that takes care of each other and our guests. I can't have someone here who insults them and has no desire to work."

"I had no idea. His wife comes to one of our morning Bible studies and she is such a nice girl. She's been hoping to find him a job and truly speaks of him in glowing terms. I apologize and I guess I should have checked him out a little more before I brought him to you."

"No harm done. But, you should know that in about five minutes, he'll be headed out of here. I'll give him twenty bucks for the time he spent here, as awful as it was, and hopefully we'll put this behind us."

"Thanks for letting me know and I am sorry."

"If you can think of anyone else that would fit in better, let me know. I probably won't be so quick to hire them, but I would certainly interview them."

"Will do, Polly. I'll give it some thought, and thank you for the food. I got a call this morning from one of the families and she told me there was a gift certificate in there as well. That was a nice thing to do."

"You're welcome. Let me know if I can ever help again, okay?"

She pushed her phone back in her pocket and then pulled a twenty dollar bill out of her wallet. She found Shawn on the north side of the building, smoking another cigarette.

"Shawn?"

He looked up at her guiltily. "Yes, ma'am?"

"I don't think it's going to work out. Here's twenty dollars for the time you've spent here, but I can't keep you on staff."

"Did that fag tattle on me?" he asked.

Polly took a breath. "You have lost every single bit of tolerance from me. Start walking off my property. Now."

"Whatever. Bitch. I didn't want your damned job anyway. I just came to keep the old lady from whining at me." He stalked off and began walking toward town.

She watched him cross the highway and then went back inside. Jeff was standing at the stairway. "How'd that go?"

"You're a fag and I'm a bitch," she smirked.

"Well, at least we have new titles. That's one way to start the day!" he laughed.

"I'm sorry about this, Jeff. I'll be smarter next time."

"Hey, at least you handled it quickly rather than drawing it out and letting it fester until we had a real problem."

"We have a real problem. We need help here. You're getting busier and I'm getting busier and we need someone who will come in and take charge of the building and the grounds."

"It will happen, Polly. I think you need to relax. Look at me. I showed up at the last minute and then Sylvie kind of dropped out of thin air. It will happen."

She poked him in the chest, "You'd better be right, because I don't have time to scrub toilets either!"

CHAPTER TWENTY-SIX

Sylvie showed up at eleven thirty and rushed passed Polly's window to the kitchen. Polly jumped up and followed her, "What's up?"

"I'm late! I was going to have lunch ready and I'm late!"

"It's alright. Just tell me what to do and I'll help," Polly assured her.

"I got it prepared yesterday. I just need to put it in the oven."

Polly walked past her and turned the oven on while Sylvie pulled two pans out of the refrigerator. "It's okay. I can run outside and tell people to come in whenever you say."

Sylvie stopped and said, "You'd do that?"

"Of course!" Polly laughed. "We're serving them a free lunch; I think I can get some extra time for you."

"That would be great, then. These need forty-five minutes, so if they can come in fifteen or twenty minutes late, I'll be ready."

Polly said, "I'll take care of it and be right back. Don't go anywhere, alright?"

"Yeah. I'm staying right here," Sylvie said.

Polly went outside and found Henry. "Can you tell the guys

that lunch is going to be about twenty minutes late? And would you mind letting those guys know too?" she said, pointing to the team putting up the temporary fence.

"I'll take care of it. Do you have plenty of food?"

"I'm sure we do. Everyone is invited in. And if we don't, we'll make more."

He smiled at her and said, "You're happy when everyone is in your family, aren't you."

"Leave me alone," she laughed.

When she got back into the kitchen, she said to Sylvie, "What's up?"

"I had an early class and then I wanted to ask the professor some questions and before I knew it, time was running away from me. I'm so sorry."

"Sylvie!" Polly said sharply, "Stop it. You don't even have to do this for us. Please don't ever feel bad. I'm glad you are here. And next time, call or text me. I can make it easier on you."

"You're right. I'm just not used to working like this. I'll remember. So, did that guy show up to work this morning?"

"He did and he pissed Jeff off and then he made me furious. He's gone."

"Wow. I didn't know you had it in you!"

"You don't remember me ...."

"Oh, the emasculation of Henry. I heard about that." Both of them laughed at that.

"We decided to come over and see what Sylvie was cooking for lunch today," came a voice from the hallway.

Polly spun around to see Lydia, Beryl and Andy standing at the counter. "How did you guys get in here without me hearing you? Beryl, I know you walk louder than that."

Beryl held up one hand with a pair of dangling shoes. "My idea." She dropped them to the floor and slipped them back on.

"I wouldn't walk around here barefoot for much longer," Polly said. "At least not until we find someone to act as custodian."

Lydia looked at Andy, then at Polly, then she looked at Beryl and back at Polly.

"What?" Polly asked. "What are you thinking?"

"No, I think he's too old."

"Who is too old?"

"Doug Leon. He spent a lot of years in this building as custodian, but I don't think he would do the stairs very well, and I don't think he'd be any good at scrubbing things down."

"Lydia, you know I would love to help him out if I could, but I just got rid of a jerk. Pastor Boehm thought he'd work out for me and he was awful. Don't make me do that again, please?"

"You're right. It's not a good idea, but if you need someone to stand around and lean on a broom, he's your man."

"What's for lunch?" Beryl asked.

"I made a chicken noodle casserole. I wanted something warm and hearty for the guys who are outside working and at the same time make something that was on the list Polly's guest gave us," Sylvie said.

Polly heard it, but wasn't sure if she should say something. She didn't have to. Andy jumped right in, "You said 'us,' Sylvie. Did you hear that? She's a part of Sycamore House now."

Sylvie blushed. "I guess I am."

"Do you have a minute, Beryl? I'd like to ask a favor," Polly said.

"Sure, sweetheart. Anything for you."

The two walked into the auditorium and Polly said, "I think the woman who is upstairs has recently gone through a life change of some sort and she's trying desperately to be an artist. I think she's trying too hard. Everything about her tells me that at one point she lived a very formal life and now she's trying to be free." To emphasize her words, Polly put her arms out and waved them.

"Would you mind if I introduced you and then would you consider trying to connect with her and give her a little emotional guidance?"

Beryl laughed out loud. "Me give emotional guidance. Girl, you have no idea how funny that is. But, I get it and yes, if you introduce me to her, I'll step in and rock her world."

"Thank you. And I didn't bring you in here to hide anything

from the rest of them, I was just terrified Joanna ... oh, yes, it's Joanna Wagner ... might walk in while I was talking about her. This morning, the jerk I hired to be the custodian called her a wackadoo in a tent and she heard him. I don't need her thinking we're all terribly out of control with our mouths."

"No problem. I'm on it."

They walked back into the kitchen and Lydia asked, "Are you really getting those horses today?"

"I am. Late this afternoon. Are you going to be here when they arrive?"

"We might stop by. Andy and I are going over to Ames to do some baby shopping."

"You're buying babies now? Ladies, I thought we'd talked about this," Beryl interrupted. "Besides, everyone knows the best babies come from Cedar Rapids."

They ignored her and she chuckled to herself. "At least I think I'm funny."

Sylvie pulled tomatoes, cucumbers, carrots and bags of lettuce out of the refrigerator and then said, "Come in here, wash your hands and start chopping if you're going to stick around." She put two cutting boards up on the prep table and then dumped the lettuce into a couple of bowls. "We're going to have salad and warm rolls with the casserole, so get busy."

Andy and Polly began chopping and Lydia and Beryl set up the counter for serving. When Sylvie finally had everything ready, Henry peeked around the corner and said, "Are you ready for us?"

The men had begun walking through the line and into the auditorium to eat when Polly saw Joanna Wagner come around the corner from the stairs. She saw what it was that had triggered Shawn Wesley's comment. The woman was dressed in a bright green muumuu that looked awful on her. She had sprayed some type of orange coloring into her hair and had flung a hot pink scarf around her neck. She was wearing earrings that dangled below her shoulder as well as the stacks of bracelets and rings on all her fingers. She jingled as she walked and she walked as if she were in pain.

It didn't take Beryl but a moment to waltz in and say, "You must be the new artist in town. I'm Beryl Watson and I'm the old artist in town. Let's have lunch together and see what is what? I'd hate to have to run you out of town on the rails, so before I get jealous of you, I'd like to get to know you better!"

The poor woman didn't know what to say as Beryl took her arm and drew her to the counter. "You weren't planning on eating in your room today, were you?" Beryl asked, "Because I'm dying to know what you put in your hair and where you got those absolutely wild earrings!"

She put her hand down on the counter and said, "Serve us up, girls! We artists need lots of energy to bring all that creativity to the forefront, don't we, Joanna!"

Sylvie smiled and put their food on a couple of trays and Beryl, picking hers up, said, "Come on. We're going into the conference room for lunch. That's alright with you, isn't it, Polly?"

Polly nodded and Sylvie whispered, "I have a meeting with a bride at two thirty. Will Beryl be finished by then?"

Lydia laughed. "This won't take long. That poor woman is going to run for her life in about forty-five minutes. Either that or they'll be best friends and she'll spend the rest of her time here in Beryl's studio. Who wants to bet which one it will be?"

Polly said, "I'm betting on Beryl."

"So am I," Andy said.

"Me too," from Sylvie.

"Well, honestly, I think so as well. This might be good for both of them!"

They served themselves and went into the auditorium to eat.

As the afternoon passed, Polly got more and more nervous. How would these animals react to her? Was she strong enough to be in charge? Was she going to be able to bring them back to health? Were they going to be so freaked out by everything that they wouldn't respond to her? She finally went outside and walked around the barn, in and out of the stalls, touching things, making sure that it was as close to ready as a week old barn could be without enough preparation. She had no idea what to do and all she could do was pace.

Henry and his guys had finally come off the roof. At least that part was finished. They still had plenty to do over the next week and she was fine with that. At least she would have some company while she got to know the horses. Why hadn't she asked Mark what their names were yesterday and why had she been embarrassed to text him and ask?

Her mind wouldn't quit spinning and she walked outside and then back in. Henry and Sam were standing at the front door of the barn with their hands behind their backs the next time she walked out.

"What's up?" she asked. She tried to peek around and they turned so she couldn't see.

"What do you have there?"

"We made you a present. You're going to need these," Sam said, as they brought two step stools out and handed them to Polly. "We want you to be able to see them from top to bottom and right now all you can see is from middle to bottom."

"Thank you guys! See, I didn't even think about that."

"I don't think you have any more time to think," Henry said. "They're here."

She looked up and saw two trucks pulling horse trailers enter her parking lot and drive across the ground. "We're going to need to make that a circle drive," she said to Henry.

"Got it," he laughed.

Mark pulled up, opened the truck window and asked, "Are you ready?"

Polly couldn't help it. She was so excited, her eyes burned with tears. "I'm ready."

He led the first big, black horse out and said, "Polly, this is Demi. His sister is Daisy." She nodded and watched as the two horses were led into the barn. The next two horses were introduced to her as Nat and Nan. The names seemed familiar, but she couldn't make the connection with all that was swirling around in her mind. She shook it off and headed into the barn.

"Unless you have a different plan," Mark said, "They're settled in the stall that will be theirs forever. They'll soon get used to it and will automatically go home to it. Good job on getting hay and water buckets in there."

"I'm terrified out of my mind that I'm going to screw this up, Mark."

"You can't screw this up, Polly. These animals are going to take a few days to settle in. They aren't going to trust that their stomachs will be full and they probably aren't going to be used to a lot of attention, but be patient and be strong. You're in charge of them now."

He picked up one of the step stools and walked into the first stall on her right. "Here, spend a few minutes with Daisy. She's the charmer. She'll do anything you ask and be glad to do it." He set the stool down and Polly stepped up. "That's it, right there. Just scratch her a little and talk to her. Tell her that she's going to be alright and that's she's a beautiful horse. The words only mean something to you right now, but the sound of your voice will mean everything to her."

Polly leaned in and said, "Oh my goodness, you're that Daisy. Of course you are! I'm awfully glad you're here and one of these days, I'm going to come out here and read that story to you guys. You're going to be beautiful again, I promise. I can't wait to tell everyone about you."

She went from stall to stall and spoke to each of the horses, rubbing their withers and encouraging them. There wasn't a lot of response from them yet. Demi stood quietly and waited until she was finished, then went back to munching hay. Nat shied away when she opened the stall door, but Mark entered with her. She walked over, held out her hands so he could sniff her and said, "You're safe here. You'll always be safe here. I promise you that."

Polly visited Nan last and smiled from ear to ear. Dean Black had known these animals well when he named them. Nan stood tall and held her head up, then nickered at Polly. She stood her ground when Polly entered and seemed to be claiming her territory. Polly laughed and then stood face to face with the horse and said, "I know you. Your heart is golden, you just don't want the world to know it. You and I are going to be the very best of friends, I can tell right now."

She walked back out into the alley and smiled at the men who were watching her. Mark asked, "How in the world did you understand what to say to each horse?"

Polly laughed. "Because Dean and Madeline Black named their children and then these horses after characters written by one of my favorite authors. I'll bet there was a dog or two named Jo and Meg and maybe a cat named Beth. If you read the book "Little Men," you will meet Demi and Daisy, Nat and Nan. He nailed their personalities. Nan is the alpha of the group, isn't she?

"Absolutely," he said.

"And Daisy is next in the pecking order. She is sweet and wonderful, but neither of the boys mess with her. Nat is strong and will do anything you ask, but something scared him in the past and Demi is playful and ready to get in trouble at the drop of a hat. I'll bet that Daisy adores Nan and they work well together, don't they."

"Well, if you hadn't told me that you recognized the characters from the book, I'd have worried that you were psychic, but you are so close to what Mr. Benson told me about the horses, it's uncanny."

"I'm going to have to ask Amy if her mother read these books to them while they were growing up. That's the only explanation I have for all of these names." Polly said.

Henry walked over to stand beside her as she leaned over the door into Nan's stall. "See. I have every confidence in you," he said.

That made her laugh. "Uh huh. Sure you do."

Mark interrupted. "I'm going to take the trailers back and then I'll be here about six thirty to help you get them ready for the night. We'll feed them and let them get used to their new surroundings. Then, I'm coming back tomorrow morning at six thirty again. Will you be ready for me?"

Polly sighed. "I'll be ready. Obiwan and I will get up and going before that. I think I'll wait a week or so before I introduce him to these guys, but I will probably walk through here a couple of times with him. He can hang out in one of the spare stalls while we work."

"I don't think you need to worry too much about the horses," Mark said. "Mr. Benson had a few dogs on the farm and they seemed to be around them with no problem. They're used to having short horses around. Obiwan isn't too terribly excitable. He'll be fine."

"That sounds good then. I'll see you later."

When the trucks and trailers were gone, Henry said, "You're doing well with them, Polly. I'm proud of you."

"Thanks, Henry. My life has gotten pretty big in the last year, hasn't it?"

"I guess it has."

Late that night, Polly stood in the living room looking out over the little town she now called home. Obiwan was watching her from the sofa and the cats had found their perches in the bedroom. She watched as cars drove by on the highway and saw lights flicker out as businesses closed and people went to bed. She put her knee on the arm of the sofa and leaned forward. A deer was standing in her yard ready to bolt for the trees at any movement. She watched as it held perfectly still except for the twitching of its ears. Another car passed and it ran for the tree line, its white tail the last thing she saw.

This really was a big life and she'd had to move to a small town in order to find it.

THANK YOU FOR READING!

I hope you have had fun visiting Bellingwood again. The success of "All Roads Lead Home," the first book in the Bellingwood series, is encouraging and exciting. I believe it is because we all enjoy our friends, whether we live in small towns, large cities or anything in between.

Check out the Bellingwood Facebook page: https://www.facebook.com/pollygiller for news about upcoming books, conversations while I'm writing and you're reading, and a continued look at life in a small town.

The next book featuring Polly, Henry, Lydia, Sylvie, Andy and Beryl and all the rest of the friendly folk in Bellingwood will be published in July 2013. With four new horses, plans for additions to Sycamore House, and custodians who continue to bring her trouble, Polly will need her friends just as much as ever.

CPSIA information can be obtained
at www.ICGtesting.com
Printed in the USA
LVHW080941040122
707785LV00031B/724